Off

Track:

A Milford Mystery

Off Track:

A Milford Mystery

Hadley Hoover

Large Print ISBN: 978-1-312-13191-0
Printed in the United States of America.

DEDICATION

To Kendall—you keep me on track.

ACKNOWLEDGEMENTS

Thanks to:

Amber Hoover for great suggestions for names used in *Off Track*, and Margaret Miller (an author, herself) for pertinent on-site Milford information;

Margaret Aschoff and Carol Ann Wallace for good tips, listening ears, and well-timed pep talks;

Jill Hallman (ABPMR) and Jamie Denham PT for details about amputation and rehabilitation;

Russell Smith and Steve Brooks who, as career railroad engineers, *really* understand trains;

Brandon Merseal who educated me about Circle 4 and The Milford Feed Mill; and

Jack Ford, from the Utah Department of Corrections who helped me "color inside the lines" so this story didn't get messy.

These ten people provided helpful assistance and advice, and/or gave wise and accurate answers to my questions on topics within their areas of expertise. They did so even though they likely wondered or worried how I planned to use such information! Any mistakes are mine.

1

Even as I reached to scratch my foot, I knew it was futile. Right where a guy's foot ought to be, instead it was the best in rehabilitative fakery. That's my term for what's attached to the south end of my left leg; the docs euphemistically refer to it as my "assistive device." I'm an otherwise healthy fellow, just minus one flesh-and-bones foot.

When a fella with an amputation is married to a gal with clout in the medical field, *best* goes with the territory, hence my cutting-edge (telling wordage, eh?) detachable body part. While most people wake up and quickly put on shoes, I require extra time to don a foot before the second shoe. Unless they notice my slightly stilted gait, most folks never suspect I'm not like them.

Don't focus on the itching, I chided myself in a familiar mantra and lowered my high-tech appendage to the floor mat. We had been driving for hours but, thanks to Sage's lead foot on the accelerator, at least the scenery whizzed by us. *Hey: one phony foot, one lead foot . . . we're quite a team!*

Our fifteen-year-old sedan moved smoothly along Highway 21's dotted line like a zipper. *Good: think about zippers . . . What do I know about zippers? Hmmm . . . Not much!* Nonetheless, I tested the

imagery that popped to mind on my patient spouse:
"Feels like we're opening a zipper, doesn't it?"

"Huh?"

Not the hoped-for response, but that's what a
husband gets when he disrupts his wife's thoughts.
"I mean, how we follow the road's dotted line, like a
zipper's gizmo," I strived for a poetic flair: "that's
opening Utah's wonders with the wheels' rotations."

"You mean the pull-tab?" *Did she roll her eyes?*
"We'd have to be centered on the line; zippers don't
open from the side." The jauntiness of her retort
robbed it of sarcasm.

She's right; that simile needed work. Too wordy
for my style. Succinct descriptions, crisp language,
sharp analogies—those are the tools of my trade. I
earn big (by most people's standards, including my
own) bucks only because I spin baffling plots.

Anyone browsing my titles in bookstores or
airport kiosks knows I dole out words sparingly. A
person can start a Kiel Nede mystery while waiting
to board a plane, and may even finish it on the flight.
No ticket stub marking a spot, leaving the reader to
wonder on the return trip, *What was this book about,
anyway?*

Outside our car, a sensual riot ensued. Since this
was hardly our first trip to these parts, I lowered the
window expectantly and breathed in the mile-high
air; my heartbeat slowed. Traffic? *Not much.* Road
rage? *Fuggedaboutit!* This was Utah.

Always big on scenery, that day the Union's forty-fifth State was even bigger on suspense. Sage had slipped behind the wheel after we refueled in Salina. "You drove five hours; it's my turn," she insisted, but I knew more than fairness motivated her. She was antsy about what awaited us in Milford, and driving offered her a needed distraction.

Interstate 70 had taken us from Denver to I-15, which we exited in Beaver. Desert plants' aromas mingled with airborne dust—a surprisingly pleasant scent riding the stiff autumn breeze that hummed in my ears. Hawks claimed rights to road-kill along Highway 21's winding two lanes, scolding us in strident tones for interrupting their grazing while we ate up the miles.

As we climbed a grade, Sage yelped and swerved to the right. Three jackrabbits dashed before us like a furry ellipsis, somehow surviving to tell long-eared relatives about their narrow escape from Death by Volvo.

I realized what I'd been whistling only when Sage pointed to five antelope drinking from a creek bed. A scene unfurled before us—as if theatrically designed to illustrate ". . . *where the deer and the antelope play . . .*" from my interrupted song. "Who knew 'Home on the Range' was their cue to enter stage-right?" she laughed.

When I resumed fiddling in the general region of my absent foot, Sage glanced toward me, but said nothing. Three decades ago, we made vows that still hold firm. For some couples, if one spouse severed the other's foot while chopping wood during their third summer of wedded bliss, it would stamp OVER-AND-OUT to the marriage vows. For us, it fell under our *"For better or worse"* promises.

Grasping my ankle at the point where real met imitation, I shifted my attention from phantom itches to nature's painted shadows on mountainsides. Gray became blue, subtly easing back to mauve-tinted gray as clouds shifted.

Had we not been playing fast-and-loose with the speed limit, I may have grabbed my camera from the back seat, but it was out of reach. I live strictly by the "Break only one law at a time" philosophy, so I remained seated, with seatbelt securely fastened, and refrained from comments about Sage's ticket-time speed by biting my tongue.

The view reminded me of the San Francisco street artist whose hand never stilled, even as I clicked photo after photo—not of his sketch but of his face, which intrigued me even more than his rendition of sunlight on the Golden Gate Bridge.

One stony-faced mountain mirrored the craggy lines of that artist's cheeks, weather and time having carved a jutting brow and deep-set eyes into the rock. Prickly rabbit bushes completed my fantasy, sprawling like an untamed moustache above a shadowed cave-mouth.

Sage reset the cruise control and eased her sunglasses up to settle like a crown in a soft cushion of brown hair. I reached to thrust my fingers into that silky nest, cupping the curves of her head. She leaned into my hand. "I love you," we murmured in unison. Matching smiles eased across our faces. We have known each other so long that our coordinated thoughts aren't an oddity.

On high peaks marking the horizon, precariously perched rocks seemed eager to tumble in the next strong wind. If ever a State needed signs warning WATCH FOR FALLING ROCKS, Utah was it, but there were few in the more traveled parts; and even fewer in remote Beaver County.

Horses flung their manes, sniffing the air; cattle sharing far-flung fields never ceased eating. Neatly organized hay bales just beyond the animals' reach would feed them, come winter, but today the towering stacks added a golden lushness to the idyllic scene.

Phantom sensations faded. I don't blame Sage for each discomfort or inconvenience that accompanies a foot gone-missing, and she holds no grudges about our early years when my chosen career barely brought in enough moola to put raisins in our oatmeal. We thought we would never get beyond pay-as-you-go mode. But we hitched our wagon to the star named Hope shining brightly in our *"For richer or poorer"* skies and held on for the ride.

A pleasant woody aroma filtered into the car, transported on the magic carpet of elusive childhood memories . . . *Like our cedar chest we loaded with Grandma Eden's quilts.* I spotted the source of the current scent: zigzagging rows of junipers. Cedar-like perfume mingled with the scattered pines and scrubby oaks dotting the ridges.

Around a curve, a lush crop glistened, blanketing the earth like green-hued jewels. Sawed into fence posts of varying heights, a line of skinny-but-sturdy knob-crusted tree trunks attempted to halt marauding deer and antelope. Barbed wire hanging like limp ribbons in random places along the fence's line revealed the victor in that hard-fought battle.

Sage and I have known times when even our best-laid plans sagged like that wire. Then, my writing dream caught an up-draft and I bid a joyous farewell to scouting for freelance writing assignments.

Coinciding with what she called my "mood and money shift," Sage emerged from graduate school with dual Master's degrees, and then sailed through a PhD program while working at the first of several plum jobs, each more enticing and career-enhancing than the last. Life leaped and landed solidly in the *"for better"* part of those starry-eyed vows, which young Zeke and Sage Eden had made.

Ah, you caught that, hmm? You thought I penned mystery-thrillers under my real name? Nuh-uh; that's *Kiel Nede's* job.

Technically, the first name should be pronounced Key-el, since it is the tag-end of Eze*kiel*. But, at my first live interview for Book #1, the perky gal said, "So, Kyle, tell us about . . ." and I thought *Kyle, huh? Works for me,* and let it fly. Wise decision, or I'd have been correcting the pronunciation of my penname endlessly over the years.

My given name—Ezekiel Daniel Eden—weighed too much for a boy to cart around. Remember the old Spiritual about *"Ezekiel saw the wheel, way up in the middle of the air"*? Well, that made no sense to me, and Grandma Eden's bedtime Bible stories of the Old Testament's plucky Daniel and his incredible exploits *(Where was the lad's mother?)* conversely kept me awake.

Then one day a kid moved into our neighborhood who was Ted to his pals and Theodore to his parents. *Ah-ha!* Ditching Mom's chosen names for me, I switched *Ezekiel* for the less visionary Zeke and reduced *Daniel* to a simple *D*, which came without lions and fiery furnaces.

To accommodate my writing life, I then flipped the letters of my surname to become Kiel D Nede— the dude who, with each new book in print, appears on night-owl shows. But that massacre of my given name didn't cause Mom distress. Rather, it signaled a fine-tuning of what she had long considered my "little hobby" to what she instantly relabeled the "art form," which transformed me into a writer of modest renown. Mom's boundless joy and pride increased exponentially with each successive title.

Her greatest distress was my unbending rule that she is mum about her relationship to Kiel. None of that ". . . my son, the world-famous author . . ." business is allowed. Although chaffing, she honors my edict, assuming the role of Kiel Nede's greatest fan. When asked what her son Ezekiel does for a living, she remains ambiguous—"He's a freelance writer"—and changes the subject before anyone can ask further questions. With no outlet, Haze Eden has been one frustrated mother for years.

Rehabilitation left plenty of time to write—so I became adept at gait and plots as time and effort devoted to each endeavor increased. Hats-off to a talented team of physiatrists and physical therapists for my progress in gait. However, I credit Sage's miscalculation with an ax for my strides in writing. Losing a foot led to gaining a career. Go figure.

Kiel Nede is the writer, so only he uses crutches; Zeke navigates life without visible assistance. To accomplish this meant no shorts in public. My legs aren't show-stoppers, so no loss there, and hiding my prosthesis averts many stares.

Crutches proved the perfect foil to keep my two identities separate. Most people see and remember disabilities *first*, and anything else *second*. One-footed Kiel allows two-footed Zeke Eden to walk anonymously through life.

My surefootedness—whether psychological or physical—owes its existence to modern medical advances and a gifted physical therapist named Jamie who never let me quit trying. While we worked and sweated together (Guess who balked, and who gently but persistently prodded?) we created Kiel Nede's protagonist, Raven.

He absorbed all my frustration, fear, and anger emerging from my ghastly emotional chasm. *He* became the ruthless hero my readers fearfully respected—allowing me to emerge whole, despite one physical deficit. Thus, the initial entry in the Acknowledgements of my first book reads:

To Jamie Hamden PT and Raven Crowley.

I owe you both so much.

No rule against giving figments of imagination equal billing with breathing mortals, right?

We approach the point of our cross-country trip where Milford Valley spills out in understated grace. "Excited?" Reaching for Sage's hand, I closed the curtain on the past. She squeezed back and nodded briskly—a sure sign of nervous energy.

Since those dismal scant-raisins-in-our-oatmeal days, Sage has shot up the ladder of success. My chauffeur, as we approached our destination, is none other than one of two top-choice candidates for Milford Valley Community Hospital's Chief Executive Officer.

Don't be looking for the actual hospital yet. The new CEO's job is to get plans out of the Committee, off the blueprints, and literally on the ground. Definitive decisions as to who lands the job would be resolved in the days ahead.

Sage had interviewed with the Powers-That-Be several times, each meeting moving her to a higher rung. We arrived in Milford fully aware that either side could back out.

If this occurred, we would return to our home in Oklahoma to address Sage's second option, for which she had completed a final interview in Iowa prior to our trip to Utah. Iowa lacked the appeal of *coming home* for Sage but, in other respects, it was a tough call as to which alternative tempted us more.

As unobtrusively as possible, I attempted to read Sage's emotional meter. I knew how much she wanted Milford to work out. If butterflies batted against the walls of her stomach as boisterously as they did mine, we were two gastrointestinal messes.

Sage grew up here so she didn't need to look over the town, but I was along on this trip because she insisted she wouldn't take the job if I didn't think I could feel at home. I repeatedly remind her, "I can live in a box in the middle of nowhere, as long as that box offers power for my laptop and Internet access." But I appreciated the chance to look at Milford through different eyes than as a son-in-law, which had been my role for all previous visits.

As a couple, we have never lived anywhere so isolated as either the Iowa or Utah openings offered us. We have called big cities in seven States *home* while Sage gained her education and experience, building a resume packed with transferable skills.

Meanwhile I had churned out fifteen—soon to be sixteen—Kiel Nede mystery-thrillers, pretty much oblivious to my surroundings. That's how I get things done.

How could Milford be any more distracting than Boston's traffic, San Francisco's bone-chilling fog, Chicago's 24/7 din, Florida's humidity, New York's pulsing nightlife, Denver's winters that froze my nose hairs or, most recently, Oklahoma's worst storms in over ten years?

We reached the southern fringe of Milford and rolled within reading distance of a sign that hung from a railroad wigwag's pole. It had likely been there for years, but seeing it on this trip, I whooped. When Sage cocked an eyebrow, I pointed toward the rectangular warning: 5 TRACKS.

She laughed. "Won't Haze be thrilled? Her son is on-location in a railroady town!"

"I vote we keep Mom uninformed for now. She needs no such encouragement!"

Off to our left, a waterfall spilled over attractively arranged rocks into which was set another sign that welcomed us to Milford. We followed Main Street's curve and continued north.

"There!" Sage announced in a lilting voice. "The Board said the new CEO needs a temporary office and will have some say in its location. This could work. Well, at least a portion of the first floor," she added, now seeing it through my eyes rather than the rosy hue of her memory. "What do you think?" She motioned at the two-story building.

Since the waterfall's welcome sign, two blocks south, had informed me Milford was established in 1873, I was still doing the math (words, not numbers, are my forte) and thus I required a moment to refocus. Her question finally pierced my numerically induced fog.

I squinted through the windshield and read aloud from the vertical sign hanging from a brick edifice that appeared sadly neglected. "Horn Silver Hotel. Looks historical," I offered generously. *And will take a ton of elbow grease to be habitable.* "Big, too," I added in a none-too-subtle hint. "Plenty of room for you and a herd of elephants."

Offering merely a shrug in response, she stepped on the gas and continued several blocks north. *A shrug without comment? Hmm; time to dust off my fine-tuned husbandly skills.*

"That's what it is for elephants, you know: a herd. Elephants travel in herds. If the topic should happen to surface during your interview, remember: it's a mob of meerkats, and a rookery of penguins, but a pod of whales."

"I'll keep that in mind." She made a couple turns that put us parallel to the railroad tracks. A row of houses running north and south backed the tracks—many of them new dwellings, built by folks for whom there must be no finer music than the songs of passing trains. Sage drove slowly, and I thought I'd lost her again until she said, "No herds of whales, no pods of penguins. And heaven forbid if elephants want to form a rookery."

"I just want you to do well," I said solemnly. My faux earnestness visibly eased her tension. *Good job, Zeke.* I let my mind roam beyond the wide streets of Sage's hometown, knowing we would cruise before landing at the motel. For half an hour, I would only need to offer the random "I see . . ." or "Ahhh, yes . . ." during our slow-motion review of *what's-new, what's-not* in Milford.

Our many trips around the country over the years have been for my career. Sage willingly took the passenger seat, either literally or figuratively. This time, not only was the trip not about me, but I would flit around anonymously like the butterflies I hoped would soon vacate my digestive system.

Nothing's been said in the interview process about the bloke Sage married. Fine with me. Any citizens who recall June and Lefty Crowley's bragging (the word seems inappropriate, given their guarded appreciation of a son-in-law who earned a living in "such a peculiar way," as Lefty referred to my career) were either residents in retirement homes or occupied quiet graves in Milford's hilltop cemetery.

Parents. God love 'em.

Mine—Hazel and Rudy Eden—raised two boys: yours truly and my brother, Gulliver Swift Eden. I'm supposedly the more stable, while he remains the more "flexible," I believe is Mom's current term. He goes by Gull and avoids mention of his middle name, although he is one swift dude. *"Too speedy,"* some might say. *"Flighty,"* others might even deem him, especially with regard to how poorly he sticks with careers or partners.

In our family, given names surface only under duress. Mom's nickname has been Haze for years. It fits in ways she doesn't seem to realize, and is apt since her voice coats most conversations with a miasma of impenetrable chatter.

Although Dad is the sixth Rudolph in the Eden family line, Mom refused to marry "one of Santa's reindeer." Not only did the love-struck lad instantly become Rudy in order to win her hand, but Mom named her firstborn Gulliver with nary a hint of apology to our forefathers. There would be no seventh Rudolph Eden at our house.

With such evident boldness, it shouldn't have surprised me that, early in my career, Mom assumed the self-designated role of supplying me with story ideas. Her enforced silence on my true identity required some means of venting. At times, I have wondered if anonymity was truly important enough to me if putting up with Mom's gusto was the only viable alternative.

For years Mom has doggedly pursued the idea *("Here's the plan, Zeke . . .")* that I would write a mystery about a battle between expanding railroads and city planners who want track-free environs.

Despite my protests that such a story leaned more toward exposé than mystery, Mom continued to supply endless and often repetitive details of the decade-long saga unfolding in Rochester, Minnesota, which is home for her, Dad, and Gull.

It's like having a cottage industry for a mother. She reads, clips, and calls to spout verbatim what she has collected and is ready to mail. Then, several days later, she calls again to be sure I received and read each item in the stuffed envelope. And there's no fudging on whether to dump or add to the bulging file; she keeps an annotated copy. *"Compare this article to the editorial I sent you in May—you'll find the contradictions very enlightening, Zeke."*

Her persistence wasn't new, just more intense this time—probably because the Rochester railroad saga festered beneath the surface of local news, whereas other sensational stories skated through the public's awareness and disappeared, never to be seen again.

If I had written a book for every unsolicited idea Mom provided, I would be cranking out titles like popcorn. Her mind is like the popcorn machine in many high school grandstands: *"How about a story about fraud in banking?"* Pop! *"Oh! Here's an idea: bellhops hiding drugs in luggage."* Pop-pop! *"Sneaky practices in rental cars . . ."* Poppity-pop-pop-poppity-pop-pop-pop! *"Zeke, this is Mom; turn on CNN! They're talking about undercover deals in meatpacking."* Stand clear, folks—poppoppoppop!

Letters from Mom offered enough ideas to raise the metal lid on my brain's bucket and spew hot oil willy-nilly along with hot kernels. It often takes half an hour to recover from Haze's brim-full envelopes or mind-numbingly detailed phone calls.

With fifteen Kiel Nede books (tally: zero Hazel-Eden plots in evidence) and prestigious awards for eight titles, I've become the Pied Piper to a growing troop of devoted fans. But could I make them really care about a Midwestern mêlée over railroad tracks? Mom scoffed every time I expressed what she considered "such negative thinking."

Any questions or concerns while talking to Mom as to if I have the skills required to keep readers turning pages and recommending such a book to friends and relatives was like spitting in the wind.

Not to sound crass, but sales are what keeps an author's world going 'round. And I like it best when my world spins like a Tilt-a-Whirl gone wild.

A dip in the road jolted me back to Milford. We passed a fenced-and-gated brick structure that had the look of a business were it not for two bicycles, well-tended flowerbeds, a canopied swing-for-two, and dramatic lawn art, all of which gave it a private home's flair. Tab-hung curtains fluttered alluringly in tall multi-paned windows that were open to the afternoon breeze.

Across the street, an attractive basement house gave no evidence of any intent to change that status; its garden showed loving care and creativity. Milford looked homey, not like a glossy magazine feature titled "Coming Home"—it was the real deal.

The Volvo purred as we crept to the top of the curving hill where the Oak Tree Inn came into view. Papers in Sage's briefcase verified our reservation there. Even though Sage's name is on the deed to the house her parents willed their two daughters, it has been closed up for years; minimal furnishings remain. Thus, for this trip we would have pursued alternate lodging anyway had not the Hospital Planning Board offered us such.

Sage pulled into the parking lot that the Oak Tree Inn and Penny's Diner shared. Like contented cats, we pressed hands against the dusty car and stretched our muscles before entering the Diner where signs instructed us to register.

Several railroad employees were signing lodging forms and collecting take-out meals, so we used the restrooms, returning in time to see the men climb into a van ready to deliver them to waiting trains. Then it was our turn.

Sage certainly didn't require my assistance for a routine motel check-in. At my request, the clerk exchanged dollar bills for quarters. After placing our room-service dinner order, I went outside to plug coins in the newspaper stands.

Knowing how one thing leads to another, we resisted the urge to drive beyond the city limits and check over the old Crowley family homestead. The last thing we needed the night before a crucial interview was to discover that wind had blown shingles to kingdom-come, or that critters had feasted on Lefty's prized trees and bushes. Time enough for such crises after the question concerning our future was answered.

Instead we spent a pleasant and quiet evening, dining on salads and sandwiches. Next came reading the newspapers. Sage propped herself up in bed with pillows, while I occupied the easy chair.

Nearly overwhelmed by yawns, Sage eventually called it a day and climbed into a bubble-filled tub, warning me she would emerge only when she resembled a prune. I used the last of my quarters and treated my gal to a caffeine-free Diet Coke from the machine outside our room, even putting ice in the plastic cup. What a guy, huh? Then I fired up my laptop, responded to e-mails, and added a couple ideas to a computer file for my current mystery.

I keep pretty tight-lipped about my storylines. Not even Sage knows what I have chosen for any new book's plot until I present her with the draft of the first couple chapters to read.

Six months ago, when I handed her the sheaf of papers representing the beginning of my sixteenth mystery, she read the title—ON TRACK—on the top page and quickly flipped to the synopsis I always create for my editor and agent. Her hilarity allowed only sputtered exclamations until she recovered. "Oh, my Love! Haze will absolutely faint with joy!" she exclaimed and dove into the story with zest.

Yes, my Work-in-Progress is about trains, hence my earlier hoot upon seeing Milford's 5 TRACKS sign. Go ahead: call me a softie, but I buckled after one particular conversation with Mom. It wasn't so much what she said, as how she phrased it. I finally comprehended how much joy and purpose she gets from (quoting her) "working together" with me.

That was cogitating in my mind a few days later when I was chatting with a college buddy. He mentioned in that phone call how his mom doesn't even want to go out for a special lunch with him after he drives across two States to see her.

Contrast his mother with Haze who views—and purposely sets up—lunch dates with friends as prime opportunities to promote Kiel Nede, even if it slays her to refrain from The Rest of the Story. She's my personal Chamber of Commerce. Yes, she drives me crazy sometimes (okay, most of the time) but her heart's big. And I won't have her around forever.

After those two conversations, a germ (maybe even a gem) of an idea emerged. How can a son thank his mother for a lifetime of seeing him only through rosy-colored glasses? Maybe other guys' answers would be different, but mine was to write a mystery running on parallel tracks to Mom's idea.

Thus, Kiel Nede's sixteenth book is ON TRACK and the first entry in the Acknowledgements says:

> Thanks, Mom, for years of encouragement, advice, assistance and secret-keeping.

When Mom sees it, we'll have to anchor her to Planet Earth.

When I heard the tub draining, I turned off my computer. Sage's eyes glowed when I produced a bottle of scented oil from my suitcase and offered her a day's-end massage. The pillow muffled her final words: ". . . pods of whales . . ." Smiling, I kissed her cheek and turned off the light.

The up-and-coming (if the Planning Board has any sense) CEO of Milford Valley Community Hospital snuffled-and-sniffled herself into a deep slumber.

With the familiar sounds of his wife's gentle snorts and sweet sighs forming a backdrop, the author of ON TRACK stared at the motel ceiling well into the night, musing, *Is it too late to bring Milford into a nearly complete story about a Midwestern railroad debacle?*

It had been fun to weave wherever we lived at the time into each previous mystery, so if we were to move to Milford, the same should hold true. I would have a nervous editor and an agent who would fuss mightily if I pushed the publication date farther out, but hey—who's writing this book?

Reposing in the unfamiliar stillness, I thought about the little burg of Milford becoming our home for the unforeseeable future. Part of me decided *Hey, I'll just go about my business, as usual,* but I knew that was not how small towns work. Though Kiel Nede could remain anonymous, I would need to connect.

Five tracks.

I fell asleep musing about those ten lines of cold steel connected with creosoted wood becoming my ticket to acceptance in this town. This was home for the now-deceased couple who had given me the best gift of my life: the amazing woman lying beside me, her arm flung across my chest.

2

On typical mornings back home, I rise early, swing off to our kitchen on my crutches, start the coffee and, after Sage leaves in pursuit of dragons to slay, I occupy the mysterious world of my own creation. No fake foot required if Kiel Nede is in residence with no plans for visitors.

For Sage's big Interview Day, I did my best to look the part of Respectable Husband. I shaved my head slick and shiny: my Zeke-look. Before donning a carefully ironed shirt and crisp-creased slacks, I polished my shoes to a shimmer and slapped expensive and classy stuff on my sleek cheeks. I even cut a few pesky nose hairs. What is it about turning fifty that transforms a guy's nostrils and ears into disgusting little follicle factories?

I stepped away from the mirror when Sage came to recheck her makeup. What's not to love about the Eden-duo? In attire, she matched me for dignity; in overall appearance, she left me in her dust.

We circled each other, murmuring approving remarks and fussing with each other's collars, and kissed with more passion than was probably wise. We contented ourselves with holding hands as we walked across the parking lot to Penny's Diner for a breakfast we were each too nervous to taste.

"Let's review." Pushing aside a piece of whole-wheat toast, I assumed an impersonal tone to mimic the as-yet unseen interviewer: "Tell us, Doctor Eden: Why do you want this job?"

Batting her long, lovely eyelashes at me, Sage N Eden MA MA PhD simpered, "Because I just love my fellow man . . . especially this one!" She traced a tantalizing line on the back of my hand with her fingertips. Like good little soldiers, every nerve in my body snapped to attention.

A shadow fell across our table; we behaved as the server refilled our mugs with a welcomed post-meal caffeine infusion. The moment she left, however, I leaned across the table and attempted a leer. "You're hired. Okay; let's go back to our room and put the DO NOT DISTURB sign on the doorknob, and leave it there for a long time."

The diner's front door opened; the first-arriving escort for our day's activities scanned the booths. Luckily Sage's back was to the door, or he may have thought her puckered lips were aimed at him.

We engaged Eugene in idle chatter and, by nine o'clock, the other local Planning Board members had gathered. They assured us that the out-of-town Head Honchos would arrive in time for the afternoon's final interview session and dinner.

The official Town Tour began, and I was a-jitter. This was much more than a tour; this was Sage's dream. I supposed something could turn the day into a nightmare, but now was not the time to cast everything in mystery-laden hues, as was my occupational hazard.

Our group of six climbed into a van that had recently multitasked as a family vehicle. A baby's rattle peeked out from beneath the front passenger's seat, and a child's jam-outlined handprint marked the window next to me. I wondered what our driver's day must have been like, thus far. Surely, not as calm as our morning if she had to do *whatever* with a baby and a small child before devoting her day to the business at hand.

Masking tape held a list to the dashboard. Blue-crayoned letters implored someone to buy apple juice, mayonnaise, 75-watt light bulbs, and baking soda. It appeared to have been hanging there for quite some time, leaving me to ponder a dim-lit life without mayo.

Sage sat in front, and I shared the middle seat with Barney, a quiet man who fussed with the sharp creases in his tan slacks. His neck could have used a shave, although his hair was neatly trimmed. The wide-brimmed hat on his lap was obviously well-loved, but dusty—the way favorite hats get over the years, even with good care.

When I asked his line of work, he jerked as if startled to find someone so close by, and then cleared his throat several times before answering, "Farming."

A hoot of laughter from the third seat met that succinct reply. The short, stocky fellow representing Beaver County—*"Call me Peter or Pete, or even Petey, but don'cha dare call me late for dinner. Ha!"*—chortled, "It's like saying the Pacific Ocean is wet, to call Barney a farmer!"

I inferred Barney's farming operation was hugely successful, but he seemed uncomfortable as the focus of attention so I didn't pursue it. Belatedly, I noticed his farmer's tan: a telltale two-tone forehead. Were he a more garrulous fellow, I would have expected a return question about what I did for a living, but not so from Barney. Since I possess pathetically little knowledge about farming, Barney and I stared out our respective windows.

Seated behind us next to Peter, Eugene launched into a convoluted report on retiring after thirty-eight years as a railroad engineer and now devoting his "time and a fair bit of sweat to getting the hospital up and running." He called me "Zack" (correcting it each time Peter hissed, "He's *Zeke*!") and leaned forward to tap me on the shoulder throughout his discourse, presumably so I wouldn't miss a word, although he may have mistaken my comparative silence for nodding off.

Our driver, I learned (via spurts of front-seat conversation overheard above Eugene's droning) was recently divorced from a fellow striving for middle-management at Circle 4. That business is a massive hog-production operation under the umbrella of an even larger corporation, and is a primary employer in Beaver County, a definite presence that affects most humans' olfactory systems (often negatively) and the County's financial structure (definitely a positive impact).

Thankfully Sage and I had researched Circle 4 extensively because what Peggy said about her ex-'s employer was understandably tinged with animosity. She would not be an ideal FOX–network reporter since "Fair and Balanced" were missing from her comments. I gathered the rattle-tossing baby had added one-too-many stresses to an already strained relationship—that, plus too little communication, too many road trips, and too much festering anger.

Peggy hadn't used her nursing degree in five years—a time-frame matching her first child's arrival, I deduced from the jammy outline on the window. Post-divorce, she set up a home-nursing business that meshed with her children's caregiver's schedule. Life wasn't easy for Peggy, but hopefully it was better than with What's-His-Name and his lying, cheating lifestyle.

Given the disconcerting demise of much of Main Street, our tour guides worked hard to pump each viable business and organization for every drop of vitality.

We ate cookies at the spiffy Wells Fargo bank and accepted fine-tipped logo-stamped pens. I restocked my wallet at the ATM in the lobby while Sage listened to a spiel about banking in the Valley.

The nameless—at least *sign*less—grocery store on the north end of town was both quiet and spacious. A handwritten poster on the IN door announced that overripe bananas were a mere 10¢ a pound. Such a deal for anyone hankering to bake banana bread.

Clerks watched the counter while restocking shelves or sweeping. I felt silly making anyone leave a mop just to sell me a pack of gum but, since I only had the recently acquired twenties, leaving change wasn't an option, and gum was a necessity if I didn't want to offend Barney with my stale breath.

The hardware store next door had a pair of my favorite brand of work gloves on sale. A friendly young woman wearing an engagement ring and sporting a 2006 red-and-black Milford High School Cross-Country T-shirt bagged my purchase. "Yeah," she informed me, "I was a long-distance runner."

"Fastest female on two legs the Tigers have ever seen," Eugene crowed, puffing out his chest as if he had contributed to the girl's achievements. Turns out, he may have done so genetically since she called "G'bye, Grandpa" when we departed and only Eugene waved a response.

We received Circle 4 hats at their Main Street office, and Sage was delighted that the brim was substantial enough to "keep freckles at bay." This led to a conversation about preventive medicine, and several Higher-Ups bent Sage's ear while I admired photos, awards, and artwork on the walls and chatted with staff.

Before leaving, Sage accepted a small, bagged sample of hog food (*Why? Are we adopting a pig?*) that was manufactured via an intricate steam process at the Feed Mill: the towering structure just east of town. The mill was our next stop.

Wind blasting across flat open spaces dispersed most mill odors; what lingered wasn't entirely unpleasant, but I was glad for open doors. Shucks; time was running short so there would be no time to tour one of the dozens of farms comprised of multiple barns housing all those well-fed pigs.

I tried to look disappointed, but memories of collecting information for MUCKED-OUT clung like, well, *muck*. Researching the book in which a Texas Longhorn Bull figured prominently, I met a cranky rancher who gave me a horseback tour of his odorous feed lot, adding to my collection of memorable quotes: "What yer smelling, son, is one heap-o-money!" Nodding, I had employed shallow breathing techniques until I could escape.

During our instructive tour of the Milford Feed Mill, we learned that a shuttle train was headed in. "One hundred cars arrive twice a month," our guide informed us, "and deliver corn—the main ingredient necessary to nourish the million-plus pigs out on the farms southwest of town." The pellet-like feed made at the mill, he explained, "provides high nutrition, with minimal waste, since the pigs can't push aside whatever doesn't appeal to their discriminating taste buds." Smells nearly forgotten, I wondered if only I was drooling at the thought of pork roast, pork chops, bacon—the whole hog, as the saying goes.

Guess what lunch was? I was one happy camper at the barbecue set up outside the new Fire Station. All doors were wide open to western breezes as we gathered in an empty bay. We met an assortment of volunteer firefighters, just returned from an early morning training exercise.

They ceased polishing trucks and joined us for succulent pork sandwiches, potato salad, baked beans, salads that tasted like every ingredient came straight from a backyard garden, and dessert (Sage nobly selected an apple; I unabashedly picked a hefty hunk of berry pie).

While we ate, Sage asked pertinent questions in her easy-going manner and got an earful about the firefighters and EMTs' longings and expectations for the new hospital.

With the temperature doing a steady rise as the day progressed—the norm, when summer dawdles into autumn in Utah—we welcomed cold drinks in complimentary (to us) refillable KB Express mugs. This gas station, situated on a tri-angular corner lot bordering railroad property, was one of two still in action in Milford. No one seemed to object if drivers left the pumps running while they dashed to the Post Office. I mused, "In LA, the vehicle would be stolen and the credit card charged for the next fill-up!"

This place was so different than either the world I lived in or what I created for thrillers that I wondered why no one had asked to see my passport. Maybe I needed to rethink incorporating Milford into ON TRACK.

See, it's like this: People die in my books, and not peacefully in their sleep or of old age. Nuh-uh; there's murder, mayhem, madness, and nothing to calm frazzled nerves in a Kiel Nede mystery-thriller.

Remember the hero Jamie and I created? I named him Raven Crowley, which delighted my father-in-law. The only shared characteristics between the Lefty and my truly scary, razor-sharp investigator were their surnames and left-handedness.

Raven is not someone I'd care to meet outside the pages of my books. He is brutal; he slices through lies; he's merciless at the slightest hint of guilt. Upon hearing of his encounters with their contacts beyond the fence, federal penitentiary lifers promptly add his name to their banned-visitor lists. He wastes no money on deodorant and spends no time reading HOW TO WIN FRIENDS AND INFLUENCE PEOPLE so he's not invited to many social events.

If Raven agrees to meet someone, he is not hoping to share stock tips. The closest he comes to touchy-feely is checking for weapons or inflicting wounds that make meeting starved jungle animals seem preferable to coming face-to-face with The Raven.

When Raven shows up after nights of hot pursuit and days of cool calculation, the bad boys know their goose isn't only cooked, it is charred *way* beyond recognition. Raven is a criminal's worst nightmare, and he's not exactly on drinking-buddy terms with law-types, either, given his proclivity for bending rules to suit his purposes.

Trust me on this: Milford would *not* roll out the red carpet to welcome Raven Crowley to town.

I looked through the van's window and tried to imagine chalk lines outlining dead bodies, or yellow police tape marking a scene-of-the-crime. It didn't jibe. The Beaver County Sheriff's Department is The Law around here, and they appeared to be doing a fine job. Very little graffiti, minimal litter, and no over-enforcement of silly laws merely to rack-up tickets. One telling detail: not a single siren since we had arrived in town.

Several times during our tour, I noticed a white pickup truck cruising around town. The Sheriff's logo was prominently displayed on the doors, with *Deputy Ulseth* scripted on the tailgate.

When we visited Milford's Information Center, housed in an authentically repainted, retired Union Pacific caboose, I lingered on the steps to watch Deputy Ulseth. He stepped out of his truck, circled several vehicles parked haphazardly along the curb, and then strode toward a lopsided house set back from the street. I quickly assessed him as an alert, "don't-you-be-messing-with-me" fellow but, frankly, he was hardly a match for Raven Crowley.

And why should he be? Big cities needed Raven; Milford did just fine with guys like Deputy Ulseth who know the law and the citizens—and, perhaps more importantly, know which citizens might just think the laws weren't written with them in mind.

Even if there were a murder here, by the time the on-duty deputy responded (which, given the far-flung borders of their jurisdiction, could take a while) the perpetrator could be holed up in the Star Range, hoping the sheriff and his staff didn't know every deserted mine where a fugitive could hide.

Take basic traffic violations, or random breaking-and-entering. Or drug busts. Or kids showing more daring than wisdom. Or domestic disputes. Maybe a robbery or two. It was pretty much *been-there-done-that* for such bedlam in Beaver County.

As for cold-blooded murder, the likes of which require Raven's involvement? Nope; I didn't see it happening around these parts.

The sun beat down with intensity and hit us again on the rebound as it reflected off the pavement. Our party of six drove behind the gas station, parked in the lot and entered the Union Pacific Railroad depot. While Eugene joked with his former railroad cronies, I made a concerted effort (Really, I did!) to *Look-*

Friendly, Be Agreeable because I couldn't dismiss a return visit if I decided to put Milford in ON TRACK.

Fifteen minutes later, we climbed back into the van with next year's UPRR calendar and two key chains bearing the company logo. These, I tucked into the hardware store's plastic bag along with my new work gloves.

We raved suitably when observing the partially completed overpass south of Main Street's current endpoint. When finished, the bridge would mean no more unpredictable delays when trains crossed or lingered, blocking the main entrance to town.

Given Mom's propensity to load my filing cabinet with horror stories of railroad accidents, I paid close attention to this part of the tour, privately marveling at how this isolated town in a county which had not a single traffic signal within its borders could build an overpass that effectively addressed traffic snags— while bigger, far more affluent cities balked at the thought, let alone the expense of such.

At the high school, we stuck our noses into classrooms, shook hands with maintenance staff, and accepted a second calendar—this one with citizens' birthdays and anniversaries filling the squares. This small-town feature intrigued me and I discovered Sage and I could blow out candles with a half-dozen celebrants when our respective August and March birthdays arrived, though we were the sole occupants of the square for our May anniversary.

At the school office, The Question, which had been thus far avoided, finally surfaced: "What type of work do *you* do, Mister Eden?" The woman behind the counter repositioned her eyeglasses from their dangling position on a chain around her neck to her nose as if they would allow her to zero in on the truth, should I be inclined to fib.

"Please call me Zeke," I insisted, doling out the practiced smile that emerges at booksignings. Having heard the question, my male van mates got interested in the answer; they inched nearer. "I'm a freelance writer." I hoped it sounded like a reputable career to this group. The last thing I wanted was to appear to be a lazy bum who mooched off his hard-working wife.

As I expected, the others lost interest and drifted away. I've learned that tossing out "freelance writer" either empties a room or kills a conversation, causing eyes to glaze over. It worked again.

"That's great! Ever done any teaching?" A name plate informed me that my persistent questioner was the office manager. "A few students are clamoring for an honors class in writing."

"Interesting," my favorite hedge-word lingered before I added, "but our future is a bit uncertain . . ."

Ms Office Manager was undeterred. Her smile was both sheepish and engaging as she leaned on the counter. "Whoops! Well, if things work out and you move here, please contact me." She scrawled her name—*Sally Grower* (I'm a master at upside-down reading)—and added a phone number on the back of an excused-absence form. She ripped the page off the tablet and slid the paper towards me.

I didn't argue—not with Sally. Friendliness aside, she was Raven Crowley's equivalent to rule-dodging Milford students.

In the school gymnasium, we watched a lanky lad make several free throws; the sound ricocheted off the walls like bullets. No one seemed concerned that it was just one lone kid on the court; maybe he needed practice, although he didn't miss a basket while we watched. Maybe he was a trouble maker, banished from class to serve out his sentence. If so, I doubted the discharging teacher intended for him to have fun shooting baskets.

The boy sure didn't look like trouble to me, but what do I know about kids? He could be arrested tonight as the prime suspect in a rampage of slashed tires and broken windshields. He could be leading a gang of rowdies who routinely open gates which allow livestock to wander hither-and-yon. His aura of nonchalance could be as fake as my left foot.

It was a good thing our tour moved along or I would have had the oblivious kid involved in crimes serious enough to make the mob tremble by the time I finished creating his slate of offenses. It's the curse of being a writer. Don't think you have much of a life? Hang around me and I'll create a dandy one for you, but consider yourself warned: The results could severely diminish your social life.

We followed our noses to where a bevy of chattering girls tended the production of popcorn for the afternoon pep-fest (or whatever the current generation calls such events). No evident crime here. The girls could have passed for a Lawrence Welk trio, except for free-flowing hair, casual attire, and far more realistic smiles. Fluffy white kernels spilled from the swinging bucket with enough force to hold the metal cover open.

We walked away nibbling hot buttered popcorn from paper cups with two more of our five senses engaged to draw us to Milford. Sage shot me a quizzical glance in response to the grin that had taken up residence on my face when I first smelled popcorn.

"Tell you later," I murmured near her ear. It was neither the time nor place to explain my earlier Mom-and-popcorn analogy.

The remaining members of the Planning Board announced their arrival via a call to Peggy's cell phone. The shift from touring to serious discussions in an upstairs meeting room in Milford's City Offices left me free to wander unattended.

After refusing a ride back to the motel and assuring all concerned that I would meet them for dinner, I strolled back to Main Street. There, I continued my search for a sense of what it would be like for Kiel Nede and his nasty pal, Raven Crowley, to live in small-town USA.

Coming to the unoccupied Horn Silver Hotel, I pulled out my cell phone, dialed the number on the FOR SALE sign, and left a message regarding my interest in details and my number where the faceless voice could reach me "within one business day."

A few passersby gawked as I examined Sage's potential office. They may have wondered if a long-empty building was about to have a new owner. However, their thoughts more likely ran along the lines of *"What a fool, latching on to that money-hog!"* than the more genial *"Lucky dude to land such a bargain!"*

As I casually observed the intermittent traffic, an intriguing fact dawned on me: *The secret to fitting into Milford is to drive a pickup.* For half a block, I adopted the swagger befitting the owner of a trusty-dusty truck. I hooked my thumbs in my belt loops and decided Sage could keep the Volvo with its 225,000 miles, but I needed a truck. *And maybe a cowboy hat. Pointy-toed boots, too.*

I frowned. Did a fake foot mean I couldn't enjoy the whole cowboy look? *Good question for my Mayo Clinic doc the next time we talk.* Or for Jamie; I owed my favorite physical therapist a call.

Since I had grabbed my KB Express mug from Peggy's van, I bought a refill before meandering towards the bench I had noticed near the waterfall.

From the curious looks I garnered, I inferred that just because a bench was provided didn't mean folks actually *sat* on it. Settling in to observe random vehicles; I watched a train roll in and stop traffic for a few minutes and, with a whistle-blast, roll out.

I eyed a rickety old man navigate an even ricketier wheelbarrow along the street. Itching to know more, I followed him a couple blocks until I felt foolish and veered off. Wouldn't *that* be a swell claim to fame, to be the known as the guy who added stalking to Milford's short list of crimes?

After an uneventful stroll through the cemetery (a perfect place to collect character names; I filled three pages in my pocket notebook), then wound my way to the Union Pacific's Veteran's Memorial Park. Walking slowly, I read every plaque.

Next, I spent at least an hour at the public library, shamelessly eavesdropping on chatter between the friendly librarian and all who entered. After using the restroom, I roamed—shamelessly snooping on activities of those who lingered.

Some were on-site only to use the computers; keyboards clattered as they checked e-mail and surfed the Internet; some made photocopies or sent faxes, doling out payment—coin-by-coin—at the desk. Some even checked out books. The stack on the RETURN BOOKS HERE side of the desk was impressive, so I knew that Milford wasn't without readers—just few in evidence during my visit.

Selecting a chair near the circular staircase that led to the lower-level children's area (which I investigated), I selected a random book to read. It didn't grab my attention, so I returned it to the shelf and sauntered along the wall-hung shelves where I could cast a practiced eye at the N's. I noted with pleasure that a discerning soul had either purchased or donated Kiel Nede mysteries with abandon.

The librarian, who was shelving L-author fiction, asked, "Are you a mystery reader?" She beamed when assured that, indeed, I was. "Have you ever read Kiel Nede's books?" She reached in front of me to tap the spines bearing titles I knew intimately.

I inhaled sharply. *How does she know?*

Oblivious to my unease, she gushed, "We're eager for Nede's next one" while placing a slick-covered book from her cart across the tops of others on an overcrowded shelf of M-authors. "Can't come soon enough for me or his other Milford fans," she added with a fervor usually associated with chocolate-lovers or soap-opera devotees. I liked this lady.

Leaving the library, I walked the length of town on residential streets—up one, back another—and mentally filed details that could appear in a book. My stomach growled; I checked the time and hurried to rejoin the others for Chinese food at The Station.

The restaurant's name hinted at its past railroad association. A sign in the window indicated yet another business was for sale—although someone in our group knew that the current proprietors would keep cooking until it sold.

"If you want to own a restaurant, this could be it," Barney suggested, eyeing me with bland interest as he extended his first friendly overture. Like many others before him, he probably figured anyone who called himself *a writer* needed a real job.

I dodged the suggestion with a laugh and waved the extensive laminated menu. "I would only need a postcard to list the things I know how to cook!" It was a lie, although surely a forgivable one, given the circumstances.

Time spent waiting for our entrées provided a rare opportunity for me to see Sage in action. I was impressed, proud, and wanted to punch one stuffed shirt who asked if her "predominantly large-city experiences" wouldn't "pose difficulty" for her in relating to small-town blue-collar citizens.

In a stroke of genius and indisputable evidence as to why she is at her current professional level, Sage fingered her sky-blue blouse's collar. Her laughter was a gentle creek flowing over his sharp-edged gibes. "Gerald, blue is my favorite color, especially for collars! My Mom's best friend, right here in Milford, made this blouse for me ten years ago. Quality shows, and true quality lasts. And I found *this* evidence of quality in Milford, not a big city."

Sage knows blue-collar very well. Her dad, Lefty Crowley, was a mineral-miner who liked it better underground than above where people expected him to converse.

When his last mining job tapped out, Lefty turned to carpentry, letting his tools' voices block potential exchanges with gabby passersby as he constructed garages for neighbors, or added rooms for growing families, or fixed up ramshackle Horn Silver Miners' cottages for young couples' first homes. Somewhere along the way he added welding to his list of skills, perhaps amused by the knowledge that there's nothing like a flame to keep people at even greater distances.

June Crowley worked for years as a cook at the elementary school and came home every day and kept on cooking—toting pans of *this* and kettles of *that* and steaming jars of *"just something you might enjoy"* to friends, neighbors, shut-ins, or grieving acquaintances on a regular basis, brushing aside their sincere thanks with, "It's what I do; no big deal."

But it was a big deal for the recipients because June Crowley never met a recipe she couldn't improve, and rarely planted a seed in her garden that didn't flourish. To receive a dish of *whatever* from June's kitchen was to taste heaven on a fork.

June lifted her two daughters' first names from nature's palate, adding their conception months for their middle names. From childhood to adulthood, the girls bemoaned this tad-too-personal detail that June loved to share. It was this sort of "diarrhea of the mouth," to quote Sage's sister, that drove both girls crazy during their adolescence, and likely was behind Heather September and Sage November's firm decisions to remain child-free.

Despite mourning that June's cooking gene failed to enter the bloodline, both women remain hopeful any weird family traits ended with their parents' generation. That point is debatable with regards to Heather who works ghastly hours in a Las Vegas casino.

For all her careening off the beaten track in both vocations and avocations (note: we opt not to inquire into her vague references to questionable ventures), Heather, astonishingly enough, doubts Sage's sanity "to even consider moving back to Milford." When we called Heather to tell her about that possibility, she told us flat-out that if we want to see her, we come to Vegas, because "Vegas doesn't look back."

Both Lefty and June are now gone and, with their passing, the world has lost some of its luster— admittedly that's the biased perspective of someone who didn't have to live with them.

A side-benefit of moving to Milford? No family issues—not so, if Sage's career option was in Rochester, Minnesota, where the Eden tribe, (sans Zeke and Sage Eden) had settled. Milford was looking better all the time. *Don't worry*, I reassured myself, *I can find a way to deal with Raven.*

3

Two calendar pages had flipped since Sage whizzed us into Milford for our late September's scout-it-out trip. After the Chinese dinner, we spent another night at the Oak Tree Inn, and the next day Sage blissfully accepted the proffered CEO position.

We devoted several days to checking over Sage's house and to making myriad lists. We were relieved to realize an electrician's visit, new carpeting, a good cleaning, touchup paint, a heap of yard work, and several trips to the dump would take care of anything needing attention. We could live there, no problem.

Sage's proposal of the Horn Silver Hotel for her potential office was handed over to the Committee for consideration and the ultimate decision, but I dropped sufficient promises of financial assistance to propel them toward our desired end result. They voted affirmatively in time for us to hire a horde of workers before leaving town. Thanks to Kiel Nede's escalated career, Zeke Eden's financial resources would keep the new CEO of the Milford Valley Community Hospital very happy.

Back in Oklahoma, Sage turned in her resignation at the now-solvent hospital she had guided out of bankruptcy. The Board of Directors had known the day would come, but nonetheless mourned their loss with a fervor that unnerved my usually unflappable wife.

We put our home on the market, gulped (and cheered) when it sold at the first Open House, and arranged for our possessions to be hauled cross-country. Sage's last month at work was a whirlwind of meetings and farewell dinners. For my part, frantic packing and fixing my long-time editor and friend John Winthrop's masterful *Whoops!* catches in ON TRACK kept me off the streets.

John made one suggestion that would take a bit of time to rewrite, but it was a sound one. As his eagle eye noticed, I had repeated myself in a detail vital to the plot. It would not do to have characters in both ON TRACK and PENALTY BOX coming up with similar routes to nefarious ends even though a dozen years separated their publication dates.

Chalking up the oversight on my part to a crazy lifestyle and upended schedule, I broke my usual paperless-office policy and printed a hard copy of ON TRACK. Vowing to keep better records to avoid a repeat of the problem ever again, I began the arduous task of highlighting each word, phrase, paragraph, or subtle hint that required a rewrite.

I should have been ready to send the final version to John, but the tornadic activity that surrounded the whole Iowa-versus-Utah decision-making process created a situation of sensory overload. Thus, I decided to wait until the dust settled and I could think more clearly in our new locale to complete the fixes. Substituting a new, if minor, plot variation and not leaving crumbs behind from the old version was not something I dared rush through.

I had put myself on vacation: a benefit of being my own boss, although Maggie (my agent; John's wife) likes to pretend she owns the title. Welcoming the chance to head to northern California, we soaked up the rugged coastline's standard fare of comfort for our frayed souls and returned to Milford in time for Sage's mid-November starting date.

Moving and getting Sage settled into her new job not only diverted me briefly from ON TRACK, it completely purged my mind of all things dark and covert. Why couldn't something also divert Haze Eden's one-track mind? The only change Mom made was to print a batch of labels for our new Utah address. All-too-soon (to my way of thinking), thickly-stuffed envelopes postmarked Rochester MN 55902 deluged our Milford Post Office box.

With ON TRACK so near its advertised publication date, during our vacation I decided firmly it was long past the point where I could logically insert Milford into the storyline. It was enough work fixing the problems; I would save Milford for a future book's setting.

Upon our return to Utah from California, we had made a crucial purchase in Saint George: a white 4x4 pickup truck. I knew it would be trusty, but I didn't expect that it would get dusty quite so soon. The gravel road between town and our property took care of that, and I soon fit right in.

What a bonus to have a home to call our own when we arrived. Who knew, fifteen years ago, the effort we put into moving Lefty and June *and* their quaint house out to forty acres just beyond Milford would provide us with a home when we needed one? The profits from my seventh book easily paid for the remodeling then, creating a more gracious home for their retirement years without destroying memories. Now, the place was our abode.

By the third week of November, we had resumed what qualified as a normal schedule—I manned the home front and clicked computer keys, and Sage moved proverbial mountains. Then my cell rang.

It was Gull.

Have I dropped enough hints to explain why that simple, three-word declarative sentence deserves its own paragraph? If so, it is evident why, when seeing his name on the screen, I let the phone ring twice before answering with forced joviality, "Gull!"

"Hey, Zekey-boy! Utah's gorgeous!"

I sagged like a bag of wet cement in a puddle. "I assume that's your personal and up-to-the-minute insight, not based on something you're viewing on the Discovery Channel."

A breezy chuckle filled my ear. "Ya got that right! Just detoured through a funky pit-stop called

Minersville, but I'm back on the road and passed a sign that says your village is a mere thirteen miles ahead. Beam me in, Scotty!"

I pounded a fist against my forehead before answering in what I hoped was a calmer voice than what bawled in my head. "Not the easiest thing to do. Let's see; you can't miss the Union Pacific depot after you cross the tracks. I'll meet you by their parking lot. If you arrive before I do, grab something to drink at the gas station next door and hang tight."

We disconnected, and I allowed myself the luxury of one long wailed and echoing "Nooooo!" Since I had been writing so irregularly of late, I had pulled out the one-and-only hard copy of the original version of ON TRACK the night before. In addition to finalizing John's suggested changes, I desperately needed to track plot progression and character development one last time and guarantee that other clues weren't too blatant or misplaced.

ON TRACK was now completed. A computer draft was ready to e-mail to my antsy editor, but I wanted time to make a final scan to find remaining flubs before wasting John's time.

My relationship with the Winthrop's editor-and-agent team was one of hard-earned respect, built upon years of collaboration. It gradually developed into genuine friendships, though we rarely talked face-to-face. Such was life in the computer era.

My office looked like an explosion in a print shop: a flurry of papers, many marked with codes in highlighting colors. Post-It flags festooned margins; a few paragraphs were X'd out; arrows and proofing symbols abounded. Added to the chaos, my latest purview had matched text to the Haze Eden Private Collection of newspaper articles—some clipped to manuscript pages, others taped to the wall closest to related chapter-stacks, and even more dumped into the overflowing wastebasket.

"And this is where Gull will sleep?" I moaned.

I had five minutes to transform Office to Guest Room. No time for *"Why-oh-why?"* sobs. Hustling, I hummed the tune to *"It's me, it's me, oh Lord, standing in the need of prayer,"* which had been Grandma Eden's musical supplication when Gull and I acted up.

In what should win the Blue Ribbon for Fastest Clean-Up in Mankind's History, I stacked papers and clippings—maintaining chapter order, at least— and stuffed the whole mess into the plastic tub in which the now obsolete manuscript had resided since I first printed it. Shredding would come later.

I shoved the tub beneath my desk, only to spot several articles still tacked to the bulletin board; I hauled the tub out again. As long as Gull was on-site, the work was on-hold; from years of similar impromptu visits, I knew nothing would get done while he was around.

"He's your brother; be glad he cares enough to drive twenty-plus hours to see you," I reprimanded myself as I reached for crutches and headed off to don my fake foot.

"Sorry about this," I apologized to a tender spot on the blunt end of my leg. I had promised myself a day without attachment to allow the skin breathing time. "Blame it on a brother who thinks waiting for an invitation to visit is too much trouble," I groused as I tucked shirt into pants, once again humming, *"It's me, it's me, oh Lord . . ."* I grabbed keys off the dresser and snagged a hat off the coat rack on my way out the door.

Driving to town, I left succinct messages on Sage's office and cell phones: "Gull's in town."

Even before I swung into the UPRR parking lot, I spotted Gull, leaning against his Jeep, sipping a Coke—not a care in the world, not a wrinkle on his face, not a hair out of place, *new* still shimmering on every piece of his attire. As usual at first glance, it crossed my mind, *It's easy for someone like me who rarely feels put together to despise Gull.*

We engaged in the back-slapping hugs that mark our reunions, but Gull withdrew first and walked around my pickup, gaping exaggeratedly, repeating "Radical, bro!" regarding such an out-of-character vehicular purchase.

Meanwhile I did my best to keep from hollering, *How's this for a radical idea? Ask us, sometime—*

like maybe before you pack, huh, Gull?—if it's a good time to visit, instead of giving these ridiculous ten-minute warnings! I felt even less hospitable than usual, something which corresponded only to my aborted project since Gull was merely being his predictable self.

"Hey, so where's that stuffed-shirt Volvo?" he taunted, completing his third trip around the truck. If challenged, he would insist it merely was friendly teasing.

Yeah, sure. I forced a tolerant smile. We've had this Volvo-versus-Jeep debate/discussion so often since we locked into our preferred vehicles long ago, it felt like we were rattling memorized lines from a script. But the curtain had closed on that long-running play, thanks to the keys jingling in my pocket. "The sedan is Sage's car now. There's no public transportation here so we made adjustments."

He smirked. "*Riiight*, bro! And you're lovin' the pickup, ain'tcha?" He punched my arm. "Okay, let's put these fancy new wheels in motion for a tour of your new town." He was already opening the passenger door.

Crawling in behind the steering wheel, I sighed and allowed myself a mean-spirited thought: *Bet he gets a ticket for parking in a posted No-Trespassing zone!* I never should have mentioned the UP lot; the street would have been fine. I could suggest moving the Jeep. *But* . . .

With Gull gabbing nonstop while I wallowed in a gray funk, we drove the length of Main Street. I turned around at the entrance to the small airport where the most activity was high on a pole where a windsock whipped in the stiff breeze.

Coming back south, we were approaching the Chevron corner when Gull interrupted his subjective monologue on small towns versus big cities and yelled out the window, "Hey-there, Sage!"

The look on her face when she spun around from talking to a Suit-Type outside the Horn Silver Hotel told me she hadn't gotten either phone message. She waved at Gull, but looked at me and I read heartfelt compassion in her gaze. Sage knew what my goals were for the next few days and was also very aware what Gull-in-my-truck did to those plans.

A final remark and firm handshake ended her conversation. She walked briskly toward where I had pulled in behind her dismissed companion's official-looking car parked along the curb.

"Hi, Gull!" Sage welcomed my brother far more graciously than I had. "I wondered when we'd see you again—and here you are."

I declare, the woman is a pro at say-nothing remarks. This one topped her classic line: "Now *that's* a baby!" which surfaces when she's expected to admire a red and squalling newborn.

"Hey, you guys move, of course I'm gonna come see your new digs!"

Of course. Why hadn't Sage and I expected this visit? Whenever, wherever we moved, Gull had come. Why should Utah be any different?

They idly discussed the merits of driving versus flying, and then Sage glanced at her watch and said with a regret that seemed genuine even to my practiced eye, "Gosh, look at the time! I'll see you handsome fellas later. Right now, I need to get back to the people I left making dangerous decisions in my office. Can't trust them alone for too long!" After squeezing Gull's forearm, she blew me a kiss.

"Sage is a fine woman," Gull said. The words were couched in longing for the same for himself, not lust for what was mine. He genuinely loves his sister-in-law and has always tread carefully to treat her—and our marriage—with respect, despite how frequently his lifestyle veered into murky waters.

"No argument from me." I drove the short distance to where we had left Gull's Jeep. No ticket was in sight; the guy lives a charmed life. "Follow me home, okay?" Spending those few moments with Sage had centered me, leaving me feeling more kindly toward my brother.

"You call that a tour, Zeke? We never left Main Street!"

"Another day. You need to see where we live." Never having visited Lefty and June, Gull had no idea where we moved the Crowley's house. I grudgingly admitted, *I'm excited to show him!*

I kept watching the rearview mirror as our parade of two approached the property Sage and I jokingly had named Sunny Acres fifteen years ago. What was jest became reality when Lefty endorsed our whimsy by handcrafting a sign with those two words in foot-high letters. He and I hung it on a chain strung between poles on either side of the entrance.

In my rearview mirror, I saw Gull's jaw drop. His head swiveled as he tried to absorb everything. I knew the feeling. Utah is chockfull of *Wow*, and Beaver County holds up its end of the spontaneous exclamation magnificently.

When we reached our driveway, he jammed on the brakes under the Sunny Acres sign and signaled me with a horn toot. I stuck my head out my window and called back an innocent, "Yeah?"

"You live here for-real . . . I mean, literally *here*?"

"Yup, for-real and literally!" A grin stretched my cheeks too wide to restrain my belly laugh. I stepped out of my truck and walked back to him.

He whistled under his breath as he spun around, arms flung open in an encompassing expression of wonder. "It's kinda a whole lotta nothing going on, but it sure looks great." He draped an arm around my shoulders. "This place is a winner."

"We like it," I said as modestly as possible.

Seeing a rabbit whip across the driveway, Gull tossed back his head and sang, "Oh, give me a *hoooooome* . . . where the buffalo *rooooooam*!"

I knew the feeling; hadn't been that long since I had sung the same tune coming along Highway 21. "No buffalo, but antelope could show up eventually. C'mon, there's much more to see." I drove off in the pickup and he followed.

Opening the front door, I bowed my only sibling into the house with a dramatic hand-sweep. Gull ran dry on superlatives by the time we reached my office. It had been a kitchen in one of the originally separate houses which Lefty had joined together; the plumbing easily adapted into a private three-quarter bath. "This is your room, Gull—a bit more cramped than in other places we've lived, but hey!"

Cupboards rescued from both mining-era kitchens served as bookcases, some with the original doors removed altogether, and others with glass door replacements installed. These protected, while still allowing an unobstructed view of my prized collection of old books with their fragile bindings.

Gull said reverently, "It's the first place you've lived where your musty ol' books look at home."

I nodded, dumbfounded by how Gull had picked up on something I had not yet identified.

He strolled around, taking advantage of a brother's right to snoop while I doffed my prosthesis, reverting to crutches before continuing the tour.

The former kitchen's counter now held my office machines. Where the cook stove and icebox had once stood, an antique armoire hid essential supplies.

Remaining wall space accommodated the daybed below an adjustable wall-hung reading lamp.

As befit the source of my livelihood and the focus of my abilities, a teacher's desk purchased years ago at a country-school auction occupied the center of the room. Some writers sentimentally keep an old typewriter or other such talisman; I love the oak desk, ink-stain blotches and all.

"Except for hiring an electrician to add an outlet beneath the desk and beef up the lighting," I told Gull, "only paint, carpet, and cupboard-tweaking were needed to make the room serviceable."

Gull had heard the history of the house when the remodeling was underway, but it wasn't our house, and that was long ago. He wanted to hear it again; I obliged. "Both houses rolled off railroad flatbeds from Frisco. We can drive up to see that ghost town tomorrow. For Sage's growing-up years, their home occupied two cramped lots in Milford."

Pointing out what remained of Lefty's bridge between the two buildings—essentially a hallway to blur the division—I continued, "Sage's dad had originally built an oblong connecting room and done enough revamping to bring everything up to code without diminishing the old-time look."

I explained, "When constructing the current foundation fifteen years ago, we modified the footprint to change Lefty's link into an open and wider passage replacing his enclosed hallway."

Motioning with my crutch, I said, "You can see where the builders removed the roof from the transformed space, leaving this window-walled rectangular central arboretum open to the sky."

Within it, several trees and bushes sent roots deep into the soil. All this was visible from kitchen, dining and living rooms on one side and our long narrow library, my office and the master bedroom on the opposite side. The pantry/laundry sat at one end, with the entryway and guest bathroom at the other.

"Now it's your place," Gull summed up, gazing out bedroom windows facing the Mineral Mountains. Amazingly, given our uneasy history of one ne'er-do-well brother and one seemingly with a Midas' touch, I didn't note jealousy in his comment—only recognition of a job well done and rewarding results.

Back in the living room, he asked a pointed question so I gave him the highlights of how, at our insistence, June and Lefty deeded the house to both daughters. Even though Sage and I could have claimed full ownership due to our considerable investment in the relocation and remodeling, we didn't want to cause trouble between sisters.

"I doubt we needed to worry," I ended, grinning wryly, "since Heather accepted Sage's offer to buy out her share with a shout of joy heard round the world!"

"How is ol' Heather?" Gull entwined his fingers behind his head and dropped his feet—left, *plop*, right, *plop*—on the coffee table. Gull and Heather met at our wedding and developed a description-defying relationship over the years.

To me, the word *volatile* is defined as being on the same city block with Gull and Heather. Holidays and crossover visits to our house could change quickly from fête to tumult. Each time, I marveled everyone survived.

After a particularly tension-fraught weekend when we lived in Chicago, Sage commented as we waved goodbye at O'Hare, "Wouldn't you think, just once, our siblings could be predictable?" The only thing predictable about either Gull or Heather is that they'll be unpredictable. That visit, they had been in Best Buddy mode—almost as unnerving as those times when they circled each other like animals in the wild, eager to pounce and devour.

I marshaled my thoughts back to Gull's unnerving query. "We haven't seen Heather lately. She says we have to visit her in Las Vegas because she has no intention of coming to Milford."

"Bet if ya let her know I'm here, she'd change her mind," Gull scoffed; his puckish grin worried me.

"You *want* her to come? You two behave like chiefs of warring tribes waiting for the slightest infraction of unspoken rules."

No; not both of them at the same time again! I frantically petitioned the God of Abraham, Isaac and Jacob.

Neither Sage nor I subscribe to the dominant local religion or any of its feisty side-kicks, but that doesn't negate my belief in a Supreme Being Who takes pity on my helpless estate. I had a Grandma Eden who read the fear of God into me via bedtime and rainy- or sick-day Bible stories—some resulting in nail-biting fear, some producing the reverent standing-in-awe version of fear.

Gull shrugged. "Heather's the closest thing to an in-law I'll ever have, so I figure—" He left whatever he figured hanging, allowing me to fill in the blank (not something I cared to do).

I released a silent *"Thank you"* heavenward for such a speedy response to my selfish prayer.

"How many more thrillers are rattling around your head?" Gull switched topics with his usual disregard for segues. Like a fish to a baited hook, I latched on to the new line, thrilled to dodge a potential Heather-Gull reunion. Our conversation roamed widely until eventually we paused for lunch.

Putting Gull in charge of cheese and salami for sandwiches, I admitted privately that I enjoy talking to him—he is stimulating in ways that no one else is. *Of course, so is a whirlwind*, I thought wryly as I sliced tomatoes, sweet onions, and dill pickles.

"How's the writing going? Did the move put you off schedule?" he asked, spreading mayonnaise on four slices of my homemade bread. I noticed he sneaked the crust for himself, buttering it and stuffing the whole thing into his mouth to prevent the need to share.

We grew up competing for just about everything; old habits die hard. Bread-making is another way I surpass his skills, thus another topic to avoid.

"Somewhat," I responded, corralling my thoughts; my mind roams wildly whenever I talk with Gull. "Writing's a fairly portable career. I'm so glad we didn't have to live in someone else's pocket. That's what living in Milford would've felt like to me; it would have dried up my creative juices, big-time. Out here on The Bench—by the way, that's what this part of Milford Valley is called—life is better than fine; it's the antithesis of stifling."

We both glanced at the crutches leaning against the wall; Gull knew it takes me a while after every move to feel comfortable letting people know about my one-footed situation. Sometimes we have even moved again before anyone found out. I tell myself my reticence is because of Sage's role in the whole deal and my desire to protect her; she says I hide behind that excuse. Wouldn't psychiatrists have a field day with me?

"Yeah, that, too," I admitted in a cryptic response to his unspoken query. "Lots of privacy out here for one-footed guys and writers. Speaking of work, what are you doing these days?" Hey, I can leap topics as well as the next guy, even Gull Eden: the undisputed World-Champion Subject-Jumper.

He didn't meet my eye. "Same-old, same-old." This told me nothing, and everything. Keeping track of Gull's changing jobs is like chasing a hat blown off in the wind. He smoothly switched to asking, "How many of these desolate acres did you say you own?" It was a shift I allowed him without rebuke.

It does no good to try to pin him down if he wants to be evasive, so why try? We're two of a kind that way: me about my amputated foot, him about his oft-aborted work endeavors.

Despite his "desolate acres" comment, Gull fell in love with our hunk of the globe, as I knew he would. Never one to ignore free labor, I drafted him to help me reattach loose barbed wire along a stretch of fence posts. We worked together like buddies.

"You've got it made here, Zeke," Gull said as we unloaded our tools from the pickup into the detached garage/workshop. "Privacy, wide-open view of two mountain ranges, wildlife leaping around . . ."

"All that, and a home that brings history to life every day—not just Sage's family history, but that of bygone years which few who remain can recall." I poured two glasses of ice water and we got comfortable on the shaded north-side patio.

As Gull and I talked, Sage figured heavily in our conversation. I haven't mentioned much about Sage, other than to brag about her. She is a source of wonderment to me. She knows how to divide her life into compartments that never bleed into each other.

When she's at work, she would look at anyone who asked her about the finer points of cross-stitch as if they had dropped from outer space. Yet, at home, she cross-stitches with the zeal of someone who could care less about the inner workings of an office—just hand her the azure thread, please . . . not that one, the *azure*. Nearly everyone we know owns a Sage-Eden–cross-stitched something or other.

I once suggested that she could win Blue Ribbons at the County Fair—and she did: two first-place awards in Oklahoma for the pillow and wall hanging that I entered on the sly. After she recovered from the shock, the ribbons soon flanked her diplomas. I love how they give her office visitors something to ponder about the steely-willed, shrewd crusader eyeing them across her desk.

When she's deep into her work-persona, Sage scares even me sometimes. I am a veritable fount of sympathy for those on the opposite side of an issue that Sage believes in. She can be like a dog chewing a rawhide bone when she's defending a cause. And not afraid to bare her teeth, even at those holding the pen that writes her paycheck.

Dinner preparations were underway when Sage came home in the middle of my explanation to Gull about her Milford job. "Here she is now—pump her for the rest of the details, but not yet," I warned, catching a hint of exhaustion around Sage's eyes. "Give her time to change clothes."

She approached me for a lingering kiss and seemed to inhale energy from me. She drew back, at arm's length, and smiled dreamily, leaning in for a quick repeat. I watched her glide through the north hallway that leads past the library to our bedroom. Turning back, I caught a look on Gull's face—for the second time that day—which seemed wistful, maybe lonely.

That surprised me. *Lonely? Gull? Nah.* When I glanced at him a moment later, happy-go-lucky Gull was back. *Nothing lonely about Gull; he lives in the moment where no longings are allowed.*

"Wow; Sage puts in long days." Gull scooped up a fistful of peanuts and tossed them one-by-one into his mouth. "It's exhausting to have to look good and be smarter than the next guy." He spoke from a base of personal experience; Gull worships looking good, and pursues being smarter with a vengeance, but still fails.

I've always sensed that when things fell apart for Gull, he ran—and those times frequently coincided with visits to us. I wondered if this trip was truly in honor of our move or as a result of his need to escape creditors, people asking too many questions, or yet another love gone wrong. I didn't ask.

"Get Sage home and give her time to don shorts, sandals and a casual top," I told Gull, "and no shadow remains of the tailored, high-heeled woman in the boardroom making radical decisions and reining-in overspending. Those abilities shot her to the top of the headhunters' list of applicants for CEO of Milford Valley Community Hospital—known as MVCH around these parts."

Sage joined us, looking as relaxed as I had predicted. "Hey, no talking 'bout my baby, the much-anticipated MVCH! Don't you know those four letters are supposed to stay at the office?"

Gull offered Sage the jar of peanuts. "Yes, yes, *yes* . . . well, make that no-no-*no*! Let's hear every detail of your incredibly boring day, mah-dahling. Yes! Every mind-numbing, multi-syllabic word of your conversation with that snooty dude from whom your dashing brother-in-law rescued you."

Pouring nuts into her hand, she ate several. "Highly classified!" Wagging a salty finger, she said, "Such is life at still-only-on-paper MVCH. Other applications of the acronym have sprouted; I heard a new one today: Many Views, Complicated Harmony. It's the least incendiary to date!"

Gull tossed out some dandy additions—not all repeatable to the general public—to her lexicon. I loved hearing them laugh together.

"We had a good day," I told Sage when we were alone in our bedroom, "even though he wreaked havoc with my schedule." Gull had provided man-on-the-street perspectives about Rochester's railroad scandal. He expressed passionate sentiments about it—something I found at odds with his usual lack of concern for civic issues. Usually whatever doesn't affect Gull doesn't interest Gull.

Another surprise of the visit was Gull's curiosity about my writing—especially when I divulged the topic of my Work-in-Progress. Maybe it was because he owns a building providing lease income from three tenants—none of whom are happy with the proximity to the tracks. Their rent is often Gull's only income since his personal suite in the building is frequently missing evidence of monetary gains. Sadly, his business ventures repeatedly resemble box canyons: they're fine going in, but lead nowhere.

Over the years, I have downplayed my own accomplishments when talking with Gull, not wanting the contrast between us to be so evident, so painful. Mom does not show such restraint.

Gull, to put it bluntly, is not a success story. He could be, he should be. He's bright, he's personable, and we share a gene pool, sired by a father who held a rough job working on Lake Superior's docks for forty years without complaining about anything except Duluth's biting winter winds. Rudy Eden doesn't cotton to blame-dodgers, shirkers or quitters; his elder son has proven to be a huge disappointment to him on all three counts.

Gull's creativity abounds, and he has the right amount of brazenness to bring outrageous ideas to fruition. But he lacks what Mom calls "holding power." She is right, of course, but I wish she could see how all her bragging about me is like a sledge hammer pounding Gull into sullenness. But then, he could change that; he's a big boy.

It was a relatively short visit with Gull. Sage's summation fit: "Gull lands, Gull lifts-off. Zoom!" He spent two nights with us, dubbing my office "The perfect guest room, even with no closet, just hooks on the wall and a suitcase rack."

The morning Gull left Utah, I opened the tub and resumed my efforts to act like a serious writer. By mid-afternoon, ON TRACK was ready to move via the wonders of cyberspace into John's in-box. My crutches barely skimmed the floor as I swung out to the kitchen to season pork loin for a celebratory dinner.

4

We settled into life in Milford like ducks to water, though the cliché hardly fit. The closest thing to a puddle was in our birdbath—and that existed only because a drip-system kept it filled. But we felt at home. Not a packing box remained, every book was in place in the library, and our wall-art was hung.

I missed having a coffee shop where I could retreat to contemplate Raven's next escapade, but I compensated by ordering a fancier coffee maker than had ever graced our kitchen. One difference was no tip jar; okay with me.

The first floor of the Horn Silver Hotel did take a heap of work to get it habitable, but it soon looked good and worked fine. Sage settled into her new quarters faster than if we had waited for Committees to act and the budget allow it to happen. Once we got the go-ahead, we had hit the deck running. My accountant dubbed my financial outlay as "a charitable gift to a nonprofit organization." Plus, we gave the local economy a boost with all the hiring and overtime paid to get things done quickly.

Something Sage called my "dual-identity crisis" had given me jitters since we had arrived in Milford. If I were as popular as others of my ilk (we conjurers of tales intended to mystify and intrigue our readers), details behind the *Will the Real Kiel Nede Please Stand Up?* situation would be public knowledge. As Zeke Eden, I have enjoyed a life of anonymity, living in places where one barely knows neighbors' names, let alone their careers.

The transformation from Zeke to Kiel begins with the wig (designed for Kiel Nede's first public appearance) fashioned from my own Sixties' era shoulder-length mane. Secure it with my trademark beret, and voilà! It's an instant disguise, if combined with wire-rimmed clear-lens eyeglasses and a growth of shaggy beard, which my face willingly produces unless scraped severely each morning. This simple camouflage lets *Zeke* fade into *Kiel* for every public appearance or photo-shoot.

All that subterfuge may be unnecessary due to Kiel Nede's unique characteristics of crutches and footless left leg—and his vagueness about the reason. The predominant assumption is a war injury; I neither agree nor disagree but merely stare into space, which stifles even the most persistent prober. I did serve; but waited until I got home to get wounded—and then not at an enemy's hand. I mean no disrespect to our armed forces, many of whom devour Raven Crowley's escapades with personal comprehension of dreadful things.

My alter-ego began to unravel publicly during our first few weeks in Milford. It happened around Thanksgiving, just after Gull's impromptu visit, when I received a certified letter from my publisher addressed to Kiel Nede (heads should roll for that faux pas) at our post office box number. Turned out, the on-duty Ms Postal Clerk was a reader. Turned out, fifteen author photos couldn't fool her. Either she doesn't watch late-night TV, or she was too polite or stunned to voice questions about Crutches versus Foot.

As I stood there in my fully-Zeke look, she tapped the pseudonym on the label. "That's you?" Forget the United States Postal System; this woman should work for the FBI.

Her two words were an instantly numbing shot of Novocain to my brain. I could barely nod.

"I love his . . . your," she corrected in a whisper, "books! I own them all." She caught her breath. If she played it true to star-struck fan form, next she would thrust something into my hands for an autograph. What would she choose? A registered mail form? A discarded receipt?

I paused for two ragged breaths (mine) but she didn't follow the expected pattern. *Amazing.* "Do you mind keeping this quiet?" I tapped the label in a coded entreaty.

Her eyes widened. "Sure."

Relief surged. Maybe I'm naïve, but if she blabs personal data, she's out of a job, right? Turning to leave, I bumped into someone who wasn't a postal employee. Next in the short line was a silver-haired snoop who must have recognized a potential for gossip and peered around my shoulder to read the label. Unaware of her deviousness, I apologized for stepping on her toes and went on my way, thinking only of Kiel Nede's narrow escape from exposure.

Apparently The Snoop was a mobile soul. Word spread like measles. When Sage returned home, she dropped her briefcase along with this bombshell: "I hear Kiel Nede lives in Milford . . ."

I wished I could recall just which old lady did the unthinkable so I could stuff a sock in her mouth, belatedly, yes, but justifiable. Instead, I clenched my fists and pounded my desk. Sage had spent the day inside her office, yet she'd heard. All it took was a run next door to buy a soda at the Chevron where the clerk doled out my secrets along with Sage's coins.

The years of my professional career stand like a row of dominoes lined up in sharp angles, intricate curves, and dramatic swirls. All is well . . . *well*, that is, provided no one jars the table. But there is a quirk in everyone (even the most noble; they just hide it better) that makes all of us itch to jiggle the table just so we can watch the precariously arranged dominoes fall with such precision.

That night, Sage and I hardly tasted my claim-to-fame burgers. Likely little would develop and what did wouldn't match my fears, but still . . .

According to Sage's reasoning, "Milford is so far off the beaten track" that our thinking anyone here knew anyone who cared about my true identity was silly. "Rumors flash and fizzle in small towns," she assured me. "Next month, it will be 'Kiel *Who*?' and you can resume your hidey-hole existence." With minimal small-town personal experience, I could only hope she was right.

The line of dominoes, once bumped, went down quickly. I waited for repercussions from the world beyond Milford, but none came. It was eerily quiet.

Meanwhile, I constructed Milfordian responses to queries from mythical strangers: *"Do I know Kiel Nede? Sure do! See the place out yonder on The Bench? It's where Zeke Eden—that's Kiel Nede's real name,"* they'd add confidentially, *"yup, that's where he lives."* The blabbermouths might even offer to lead the way, since finding the right roads or turns could be tricky for reporters more accustomed to well-marked interchanges.

We reached Christmas without issues, partially because I didn't overreact, thanks to my wife's astuteness. Occasionally, someone waited while I paid for Sage's office bouquet (purchased weekly by Yours Truly from Dolly's Country Floral & Gifts) or dawdled in a grocery store aisle to ask, "Written anything lately?"

It showed they don't consider writing to be *real work*. I write every day, folks. It's my livelihood, not a whim. I bet no one asks professional truck drivers, "Hey, have ya driven anywhere lately?"

It was hard on my ego to admit that few Beaver County residents cared that an author lived within spitting distance. Since my presence didn't offer jobs to anyone and there was no storefront with my name emblazoned on it, I remained of little interest. Someone with star-status in movies or the music charts? Now, they would be worthy of gossip. Not a writer.

I haven't revealed much about ON TRACK. I loosely based the plot on the story Mom had been hounding me to write—that's right: the railroady one. I consider it *loosely based* in that I changed enough so neither side should feel inclined to sue me, however it seemed a pity to waste the details that have unraveled as the years progressed. An index card tacked to the bulletin board behind my desk summed up the book's underlying premise as: The Railroad versus The Rest of the World.

In the real-world account, The Rest of the World includes a world-renowned medical center with well-earned medical expertise, undisputed political clout, and understated finesse. Debates over public safety, legalities, and THE RIGHT THING TO DO are heated. That's using the kindest phraseology. Less polite terms would require a host of symbols borrowed from cartoons to show up in print: #$@&^*>|%. Even they don't do justice to describing the frenzy.

On one side of the dispute is a railroad wishing to increase revenue and diminish losses by sending increased traffic directly through a busy city. Opposite, is the vastly successful, heavily endowed medical center which sees no reason such expanded activity couldn't take place anywhere else (provided it is far away) and continues to do everything within its considerable power to block the railroad's goals.

Nipping at the heels of every issue we find The Bulldog: a woman of questionable mental stability who spouts quotable quips at every turn. The fact she is both physically well-endowed (and intent on showcasing her most enticing assets) and financially capable of maintaining *A Presence* assures her of countless interviews—with photos always including waist-up shots.

According to Dad's disgusted reports, she cries gasping tears over whatever her latest dispute is. No one can stifle her, he says; she is her side's worst foe and the opposition's most mockable nemesis.

The railroad is run-owned-dominated (you name it, she does it) by the woman everyone loves to hate. The only person John Q Public hated more than The Bulldog was her husband who died of natural causes. Some insisted the ice water coursing through his veins caused circulatory problems.

When Howard Woolden's obituary appeared, one brave soul dared to suggest via a Letter to the Editor that perhaps medical help had been delayed when Howie's identity became known to the dispatcher. That set off a tumult of responses!

The Bulldog's actual name was Honey Odessa Woolden-Landis. The initials spawned such a fitting nickname how could I not adapt it to The Howler in ON TRACK? She rose to power at her husband's demise. To many folks, this proved there is no such thing as a situation that can't get any worse.

Granted, the heart of a city may not be the best place to put some of the world's best physicians and surgeons who regularly treat extremely ill and often famous patients from around the world. But it's too late to argue that point. Over a century of occupying key downtown blocks qualifies as squatter's rights.

Yet, for the railroad to take on Medicine-with-a-Capital-M and argue bottom-line versus human life, turning a deaf ear to rational arguments? Idiotic, or so it seems to those (myself included) who are far removed from the fray. But many close at hand feel similarly, if call-ins to local radio talk-shows or Letters to the Editor, or even Gull's in-person reports (substantiated by Mom's persistent mailings and Dad's grumbles) accurately indicate public opinion.

Overpasses would help, but who should build them seems an insurmountable dilemma, especially when Medicine doesn't want overpasses because of the potential chaos that accompanies derailments, explosions, and other calamities.

On the other side, Railroad claims such structures are an unnecessary expense and time-consuming option. The issues add contestable layers to the escalating discussions which have become a perfect example of an Irresistible Force meeting an Immovable Object.

There you have it: a quick-and-dirty summation of what launched ON TRACK. Big question: Where does Raven Crowley come in? As readers of every Kiel Nede book know, Raven only shows up when there's been a murder. In ON TRACK, the corpse is none other than The Howler. A nervy idea, given the thin line between actual and fanciful characters, but it sure was fun to write. Finding The Howler and her killer (who could be any number of folks—red herrings abounded) was Raven's job.

How to bring where I live into what I write? I knew it required more rewriting than I had patience or desire to do. So, thinking to get a sense of place from unsuspecting informants, so to speak, I merged Milford into my career in an unprecedented manner: I pulled out the high school office manager's note in late December and gave Sally Grower a call.

But before we get into that, there's something I should mention about Sage and me. It doesn't prompt high opinions of us, so I'll breeze through it and there will be no questions, okay?

Here it is: Neither Sage nor I feel comfortable around kids. Even more so than our *"cute, but we don't want to own one"* opinion of small children, teenagers make us downright edgy. Luckily we identified these feelings early on and have no children of our own. No nieces or nephews either, since Gull claims "no offspring I'm aware of . . ." and Heather makes concerted efforts to ensure no one will ever call her "Mommy."

Over the years, we have had friends who spawned children, but the little critters never hung around us of their own volition. The best we could do for entertainment if they visited us was to turn on the TV. See what I mean? We'd be lousy parents.

Here on The Bench, our neighbors predominantly have either fur or feathers but, in previous locales, no neighborhood youngsters called out cheery greetings when we stepped into view. There must have been a secret sign—sort of the opposite of a Hobo's mark signaling *Food here!*—because even Scouts rarely attempted to sell us cookies or candy. Not even our paper-deliverers gave a rip about us, other than writing nice thank-you notes (tinted with Motherly dictation) in response to our Christmas tips.

It's not just that we're not fond of children; the feeling is apparently mutual. We live a child-free existence, and we like it. That's why calling Sally Grower was about as aberrant behavior as if one-footed Kiel Nede decided to take up soccer.

Two hours later, I was reintroduced to the high school principal (who fit the "pal" model from grade school's spelling lessons: my-pal-the-princi*pal*, not princi*ple*). Our chat ended with a handshake and me signing on to teach an Honors Writing Course to a maximum of four (start small; then if you fail, fewer know about it) students to be recommended by their English teachers, past and present. My confession of fleeing a teaching career after an appalling student teaching experience (in which I admit, I more often felt depressed than impressive) didn't faze the principal.

Afterwards, I sat in the pickup through the entire track of Bob Dylan's "Simple Twist of Fate" on a radio station out of Cedar City through which I muttered, "What have I done?" so frequently that it merged into an odd descant to the song. I even stepped out of the truck once, thinking to return to my-pal-the-principal and plead temporary insanity. But I didn't. I am still alive, and now consider four very decent teenagers as friends. Go figure.

My long-delayed teaching career began the last period of the day on the Tuesday after Christmas break. The four sophomores knew the *Zeke-is-Kiel–Eden-is-Nede* bit and seemed excited (as much as the unspoken teenage code allowed) about spending an hour with a card-carrying adult on subsequent Tuesdays and Thursdays.

In the first class, I realized I had met these kids already. Cale Ulseth was the boy shooting baskets in the gym during our exploratory visit to Milford. And the three girls—Mathia Meland, Jacey Belk, and Fable Hursh—were the corn-poppers. All had been dismissed from English class because, being miles ahead of their classmates, they had no need for the make-up quiz the others required.

Our first class period was a get-acquainted time. Not sure about the kids, but I learned much more than facts.

Fable—she, of the freckled nose and winsome smile—writes for the school newspaper, consistently gets A's in English, and won Beaver County Writing Contest grade-level awards for three of the past four years. She "adores!" her name and thinks it is "awesome!" that her parents gave their children such literary names. Seven-year-old Ulysses may not feel the same passion about his handle; he prefers Uly. (I, who should be Ezekiel, understand.) Uly is the bane of Fable's existence, and she actually knew the definition of *bane*. Fable's parents are Laynie, who travels great distances to put in long hours at one of the Circle 4 multiple farms, and Waylen, a tow-truck driver who works out of a garage in Minersville.

In Jacey, I sensed a depth of emotional maturity born of sorrow. A coal-haired girl, she works at the grocery store and, I learned from Mathia's teasing, Jacey takes books to sporting events because she wants to be with friends, but sees no point in the games. Her parents are divorced. I inferred that she prefers solitary activities (for instance, biking the strenuous distance to Frisco) which coincide with the isolation she, an only child, feels in living with her dad. Abbott Belk drives a truck for a company nicknamed The GASP—as in: *Gravel And Sand Pit.* (Apparently, in the teen-world, saying the name requires actual gasping, since all four of them did so.) Tabitha Crouse, divorced twice since Life with Abbott, lives in Salt Lake City. Jacey isn't crazy about the current live-in boyfriend.

Mathia is the girl we all remember from high school who is truly unaware of the effect her drop-dead–gorgeous blonde looks have on swooning guys and semi-jealous girls. Her mom, Darcia, works as a Certified Nursing Assistant at the former hospital, which is now the nursing home. Dad (Dale) is a top-notch mechanic by trade and an expert welder by hobby—both skills keeping him in high regard around Milford and in his daughter's eyes. Lithe Mathia is a cheerleader (no surprise) for some sports and a participant in others. Coaches must vie for her since she exudes winner's confidence. Dale attends every event featuring his kids, which number three due to younger boy-girl twins.

Then came Cale. "Spell it with a 'C' because I'm not kale, the vegetable. But I *will* grow on you!" The girls groaned; he grinned broadly.

Tall and lanky, Cale's muscles are the result of hard work, not sports. Seeing him in the gym had convinced me he was an athlete (when I wasn't casting him in a life of crime), but Cale has no time for what he labels "a lazy way to get exercise!" His self-motivation was evident in the list of jobs he rattled off: haying, shoveling manure, dog-walking, window-washing, mowing lawns, currying horses, barn-painting. He admitted the reason he enrolled in the Honors Writing Course is because he refuses to let English beat him; it is not his favorite subject.

Cale's dad, Rosco, is the Deputy Ulseth I spotted on our exploratory tour. He is often on-loan to other counties because of his extensive K-9 training and his partner: a German Shepherd named Nimrod. Cale's mom, Valarie, is a beautician with a shop in their home. She also does Color Analysis classes for extra income. The girls have all had their "colors done," they informed me.

Obviously, I'm deficient in many aspects of teenage femininity, so I mentally filed this odd (and apparently of female importance) color-business tidbit to ask Sage what on earth it entailed.

At the end of the introductions, I flipped into teacher mode. During my explanation of how I can only teach what I know and what I know is mystery-thrillers, Fable waved her hand wildly.

That greatly amused me, although I maintained proper teacher demeanor. At what point do we stop raising our hands to get attention? Imagine adults at lunch; one fellow is chatting about his latest deal, and then hands begin to fly, signaling that others want to speak.

"Yes, Fable?"

"We've all read your books; I mean Kiel Nede's books," she amended, giggling. She glanced around the group and received affirming nods.

"Raven is wicked-spooky—I love it!" Jacey blurted fervently. The other heads bobbed again.

"Hmm; that's, well, it's a surprise. I didn't realize teens read my books."

Cale interrupted my thoughts: "Mister Eden—"

I pantomimed a traffic-stopping cop. "You likely aren't allowed to call teachers by first names, but let's break the rule for this class." They exchanged startled glances. "Hearing 'Mister Eden' makes me look around for my dad, so please call me Zeke—" Seeing their deer-in-the-headlights stares, I slammed on my verbal brakes.

"We could call you Mister E," Mathia suggested after an awkward moment, and erupted from her seat as if fueled by her laughter. Using a white-board marker, she wrote Mister E = Mystery = Myster-E on the board, followed by a series of exclamation points that grew until the last one was a foot high.

It occurred to me that the last time I had laughed with anyone who was these kids' age, I *was* their age. In the end, we agreed: I'm Myster-E.

Fable posed a question that flipped the class from what I had planned (plots, characters, and structuring mysteries, with related assignments) to an amazingly better idea: "Myster-E, why can't we use one of your books like a textbook? We can each create our own

Raven—well, not exactly like him, but you know what I mean. Then you could teach us how to make the story scary and believable. Stuff like that."

"Yeah!" Cale chimed in. "You can tell us to write a certain scene, and we can compare how we wrote it with what you did in your book."

"Duh! We already know how he wrote it," Mathia scoffed. "We've read the books!"

If Fable's question set the proposed curriculum on its nose, my instantaneous response to Jacey's jeering remark spun me one-hundred-and-eighty degrees and left me dizzy: "Not if we used my current book—the one coming out next. Only three people have read it: my wife, my editor, and my agent."

Eight bright eyes formed full-moon circles; four jaws dropped open. Cale's Adam's apple bobbed. "What's it called?" he asked.

"ON TRACK." I watched a frown crease his face. "Something wrong, Cale?" He shifted nervously in his seat, not speaking. "Go ahead, tell me," I urged.

"Um, well, ON TRACK . . . uh, doesn't sound very mysterious. But, hey, OFF TRACK does."

Someone squeaked, *Yikes!* It sizzled.

After gulping, "I'm real sorry," Cale backpedaled: "Mom says, 'Think before you speak,' but I didn't. You know what you're doing, Myster-E. I mean, you wrote sixteen books. All I do is required assignments." Words tumbled faster than the speed limit: "I don't even know what your book is about—ON TRACK is probably a great title. Forget what I said." His face matched Utah's red rocks.

"No, please; I want all of you to speak up. Argue with me and each other; toss ideas around. You have every right to express opinions," I insisted.

Chairs creaked; feet shuffled, the air crackled like a tight spring ready to fly loose—but the kids said nothing.

As for me, I felt like Raven had thrown me against a brick wall after chasing me down potholed alleys. My heart thudded. Cale Ulseth—a lad who merely endured English class—was absolutely right about something that had blown right past me. It took a minute before I could breathe normally.

"Cale, that was insightful; inspired, actually. OFF TRACK is a much better title. My editor still has the manuscript, so the timing is perfect."

Perfect? John would undoubtedly require CPR. But, like Scarlett O'Hara, I would worry about that another time. Maggie, would first explode, then recover, and finally calm her husband. As my agent, she'd be scrambling to change my website, reissue pre-publicity blurbs, and reprint the glossy *Coming Next!* fliers. She would— Well, I preferred not to think what else she'd do . . . to me. I pasted on a crooked smile.

Four audible sighs of relief. You've heard about early bonding in relationships? Well, I don't know about the kids, but I felt like we had crossed a raging river, helped each other from one moss-slick rock to the next and somehow all survived. I felt alive.

"Where were we? Ah, yes: You'll read chapters of OFF TRACK." I emphasized the new title with a wink at Cale; he managed a shy smile, his face slowly returning to normal hues. "Good idea, but it requires signing nondisclosure forms," I joshed, glibly making it up as I went along, even as I moaned inwardly: *What am I doing?* That was rapidly becoming my life's creed. "That means none of you can breathe a word about what you read."

Four solemn, bobbing nods. I doubted anything minors signed would hold up in court, but it was good to stress the importance of confidentiality, even if copyright infringement this close to publication was unlikely. Besides, they were kids—what were they gonna do, head to Vegas to pawn my book? *"Pssst! Trade ya this manuscript for a six-pack . . ."*

Before leaving home, I had set my phone's alarm to alert me when five minutes of class remained. When it vibrated against my hip, I thought fast and came up with a new project to replace the original plans that had evaporated along with the discarded title and lesson plans.

"Thursday, I'll bring the first chapter. I expect you to guard your copies carefully. Meanwhile, your assignment is to write one page about a murderer hiding a corpse in Milford. Write what you know, and you know Milford, so make it believable, okay? Don't worry about the *Who, What, When, Why* or *How*—just jump in and write the *Where*."

Their puzzled looks reminded me they still didn't know what ON TRACK (make that: *OFF* TRACK; this switch will take mental gyrations on my part) was about. I gave them a two-minute overview.

When I finished, Cale whistled, Jacey perked up, Fable sighed dramatically, and Mathia shivered.

And I smiled broadly—a toothy grin, actually. *How about that? First reviews are in—and all are two-thumbs up!*

As they collected their backpacks, Fable said with a glint in her eyes, "So, Myster-E, if we write such good stuff that you decide to use it in a book someday, do we get a percentage of your royalties?"

I liked this girl's spunk. "Afraid not, but would you settle for your names on the Acknowledgements page in OFF TRACK?"

Four voices exploded in unison, "Yeah!"

"Okay, that's the way it goes in your contracts: no money, just recognition."

They all mouthed the same word: *"Contract!"*

I probably should have told them I was kidding—about the contracts, not the recognition. But I let it go. Why deflate their excitement, right?

Cale high-fived me on his way out the door.

I drove home in a daze, wondering how I would explain the past hour to Sage.

5

"I do *not* believe my ears, Zeke! Sixteen times you've said, 'Every story starts with the title, John,' and now you're saying you want to *change* the title? Are you drunk? Sick? Being held against your will? What's going on out there?" Clicks and whooshes accompanied John Lawrence Winthrop of JLW Literary Services lighting another cigarette on the Kansas City end of our conversation. "Did moving to Utah flip a switch in your brain?"

As I talked to my editor, I was out on the pergola, staring across five railroad tracks in the distance, and trying to decide where Milford High School was on the town's visual grid. "Listen, John," I hoped my tone sounded like I was both rational and in control, "you have to admit OFF TRACK is a much better title than ON TRACK. We both missed—"

He cut in, "I give my stable of writers advice on content, format, structure—and not much on any of those for you, Zeke; you're my winning horse, my star player. But I never give you advice on titles. We agreed on that, way back with Book Number One."

"I know; I respect you for honoring my weirdities. But I want to— No, make that I need to change the title this time."

If secondhand smoke were transmittable by phone, I would have cancer of my left ear due to the multiple times John has exhaled into his mouthpiece during our discussions about my books. Now, he did it again—a long, spurt of smoky breathing.

"I'm not arguing, just bewildered. No, I'm full-blown shocked. But, o-*kaaay* . . . OFF TRACK it is. Anything else?" His tone implied he expected me to propose something more radical like bumping-off the cold-blooded killer Raven or (even worse) enrolling him in anger management classes.

"Yeah; one more thing, but I'll e-mail it to you. I want to add a paragraph to the Acknowledgements so I can properly thank four kids."

The sky was clear, so the thunder I heard had to be John's feet rocketing off his desk and hitting the floor. A muffled curse; I assumed the trajectory had caught his coffee cup. He dropped the phone; I flinched.

"Now look what you made me do, dang it; that was a new tablet!" Sloppy mopping sounds joined his wordless mutterings. Forget about *bewildered,* and disregard *shocked*—John had landed smack-dab in *crabby*. "Kids?" he barked into the phone. "You don't like kids, Zeke!"

"I like *these* kids." I debated mentioning how a visit to Utah could help him decompress or aid in coping with his frustrations, but decided the timing wasn't the best. Not with a coffee-soaked tablet that probably contained vital information in his illegible scrawl that was now bleeding through the pages.

He puffed like a steam engine while I checked for smoke coming out of my phone's tiny holes. "Are you sure you're okay, Zeke?" His voice seemed as distant as the final car of the train leaving Milford, three miles away.

Putting the phone back to my ear, I heard pouring sounds and waited for the first sip from a replenished cup to work its calming magic on my long-distance friend. "Never better," I assured him.

"Shall I tell Maggie, or will you? She's not in at the moment, or I'd patch you through."

My stomach did a little lurch that left me queasy. *Ho-boy; that's right: there's still Maggie . . .* "Uh, I'll call her—or wait, I'll send an e-mail first."

What relief to hear a chuckle. "Good plan." We both knew Maggie accepts radical changes like what I was delivering with even less aplomb than he does.

After a bit of idle chatter with the intent (on my part) of proving just how very fine I was, I hurried inside to e-mail Maggie. She'd roll with the punches eventually, but this way I would be spared her screeching and the inevitable lecture if I dropped such discombobulating news on her via a phone call.

Message completed, I fired off the promised paragraph to John, with instructions to add it directly below my tribute to Mom on the Acknowledgements page:

Special thanks to four amazing young writers: Cale Ulseth, Fable Hursh, Jacey Belk, and Mathia Meland. Your good ideas stimulated me, your courage to speak up changed me, and your friendships enriched me. I look forward to seeing your names on author lines in the future.

Though I had yet to read anything the class written, projecting their success was neither foolhardy nor premature. When I got done with them, they would be on their way to becoming good writers.

And when they got done with Myster-E? Well, I would be a far better person. I felt it in my bones—call it a phantom sensation of a positive kind.

John wasn't alone in his astonishment. When I told Sage that evening about the most recent change, her voice shot up an octave in the breathing pattern required for three words: "You did *what*?"

Apparently I had launched a new hobby: baffling people from Kansas City to all points west.

"I changed the title from ON TRACK to OFF TRACK. It's a done deal. I called John, and already e-mailed Maggie."

"And John said . . . what?" Sage asked cautiously, cringing in sympathy for me. She knows John.

I shrugged. "The predictable: Am I ill or hitting the booze? Have I been abducted, or conked on the head? Yada yada yada."

"Zeke!" Sage waved the dish towel, swatting my words like pesky flies. Tossing the towel on the counter, she shook her head like those bobble-dogs people put in their cars' back windows. "You *never* change a book title. And *you* pick the titles. So that's two big—no, two huge . . . no, make that two *major* changes you made in the space of what—an hour spent with four kids? John's right to wonder; I do, too! *Are* you thinking clearly?"

I sidestepped her kid-comment. "I believe OFF TRACK is a better title. So do you, right? Admit it."

"I'm not denying that, in fact," she paused, "I like it; I really do. But, please, *please* think about this. Remember ranting and raving about titles? I sure do—all sixteen times. The only thing that comes close switching a title is if you changed Raven's name. And I don't see that happening."

I laughed. "The only thing close would be to kill him off, or turn him into a sensitive guy!"

"Glad we agree: doesn't happen. As for Maggie? Whoo*ee*, Zeke; that's gonna be one ear-blistering conversation!"

She expelled a long breath . . . *one-thousand-one, one-thousand-two* . . . and cocked an eyebrow.

"You're not backing down. You're sticking with the new title. Wow; these must be some special kids. Wow," she repeated as she took silverware from the dishwasher to the table, oblivious to the drips marking her path.

"They are. Four bright, funny, gutsy kids. Oh, speaking of changing names, I'm now Myster-E, that's *capital*-M-Y-S-T-E-R-hyphen-capital-E."

Sage's confusion was priceless. I used the pen and notepad we keep by the kitchen phone and reproduced Mathia's white-board rendition of how Mister E = Mystery = Myster-E. Grinning, I turned the tablet around for Sage's review.

She read the notation twice, stared at me, and finally hooted. "This explains bright and funny. So, tell me about gutsy—the 'Let's change the name of the book' part of the story so I'll understand how four teenagers managed to derail Kiel Nede's train."

Cale, Jacey, Fable and Mathia joined us in spirit for supper. Sage was intrigued, both by my reports on the individuals and by the abrupt evolution of my long-held opinions.

When I told her about Fable's idea that evolved into the kids' reading the yet-unpublished book, she pursed her lips, then arched an eyebrow, and nodded slowly. "What a good, albeit, off-the-charts idea," she exclaimed with a smile that authenticated my bizarre behavior.

When I explained my hastily revamped first assignment, she begged, "Do I get to read what your class turns in? Huh, can I, teacher, can I? Please-pretty-please?" She batted her eyelashes coyly.

"Of course." I succumbed, helpless against her flirting, but relieved to have my best friend on-board in such a wild and crazy venture. "It won't be like Kiel Nede's stuff. Well, I hope it's not that good!"

She nudged me with a mauve-tipped toe. "Hmm; modesty just doesn't sit well with you, Honey-bun, does it?" she teased.

We spent an enjoyable evening, admiring the sunset and wondering what the future would bring, now that there was what I described to Sage as "a major crack in the walls around Jericho." It was an allusion to yet another of Grandma Eden's Bible stories, although my current application changed the ancient walled city into the fortress of my long-guarded opinions and practices, which now exhibited definite signs of caving.

When I brought home the first assignments, Sage and I eagerly read and exchanged papers. She loved them all and wanted to give every one of them an A.

I was caught between needing to correct grammar, punctuation and spelling and wanting to praise the teens' creative thinking, self-expression without self-doubt, and fledgling abilities to put themselves into the frightening world of a criminal's mind.

Sage won; well-done first assignments deserved only positive feedback.

It appeared there were at least four good places to dump a body in our high desert valley. Yessireebob, it was a good thing Raven wouldn't be coming here. Murder in Milford had the potential to be quite messy.

6

I soon discovered that I looked forward to Tuesdays and Thursdays—days which previously had passed essentially unnoticed on my calendar. The solitary life of a writer has few appointments that require knowing the date, let alone the day.

But, as the snow began to melt, I continued to appreciate the pattern of two days each week when I had a schedule from which I dared not deviate. When school bells clanged, teachers (even we of the one-course variety) had better be in our places.

My four Honors Writing Course students wasted little time on chitchat or even teasing. It was so invigorating to work with such intelligent, motivated and interesting individuals that I often forgot they were young. Too young for sufficient life-defining experiences, oh-so-adolescent for jaded emotions . . . and much-too-youthful to be emerging into the unprecedented role of friends with me, ancient species that I am.

It troubled me to discover how easily pubescent souls could adopt a criminal mindset; maybe I should have next term's class write children's books—the kind where animals talk and everything turns out peachy-keen in the end. No mangled young consciences, no dead bodies in the stories, and no hoping (on my part) that parents wouldn't report me for corrupting the Youth of America.

Sage had the nifty idea to invite the four students' families to Sunny Acres for a picnic. I admitted this would be a way to showcase me to the parents as a wonderful person with no evil intents. I mentioned the idea in class at the beginning of April when the weather had turned nice enough so the mere thought of eating outdoors wasn't numbing.

"Everyone? Even the little kids?" Mathia asked excitedly.

"Sure thing. I feel like I know your families after all our conversations, so they should get acquainted with me, too." Since our class met the last hour of the day, any of them who didn't have sports or work often lingered to talk after the dismissal bell. Thus, I got to know them on a personal level—and was amazed at the depth of feelings and emotions that surrounded their perceptions of family issues.

I understood Cale's protectiveness of his six-year-old sister, Suvie; in some ways, I feel the same about Gull, even as the younger brother. I learned more about Mathia's ten-year-old twin siblings, Kash and Kasey, who accompanied her almost everywhere, even when she didn't need to be so accommodating. This perplexed Fable who begrudged every hour she was in charge of Uly because it prevented her from getting lost in the world of words—both reading and writing. "It's always Trouble-with-a-capital-T, just like in 'Music Man,' with Uly," Fable bemoaned one day after her brother had changed the color of a wall in his bedroom before she thought to check on him. Surreptitiously, I scribbled a reminder to myself: *Lock paint cans in the workshop before the picnic!*

I worried about Jacey whenever we discussed families. She usually alternated between disengaged and bitter, but when we talked about the picnic, she sounded wistful. "Maybe Mom will drive down. I don't think Dad would care if she's there, as long as she doesn't bring The Sleazeball." There was a new live-in boyfriend, just since January. According to Jacey, he was "the worst one ever."

"My dad will bring his dog," Cale warned. "They're partners, so Nimrod goes where Dad goes."

"All are welcome; we won't count legs on our guests," I assured him. "I'll even burn a burger or two especially for Nimrod."

They promised to report at the next class on who could come. We moved on to the day's assignment. Previously, I had distributed sections of the Haze Eden Collection of Articles for their review. That day, we resumed a prior discussion on the role of research in mystery writing: when to stick to facts, when to tweak them to fit the story, and when to totally recreate details.

We were getting close to the point where murder enters OFF TRACK's storyline. Reading the Rochester Post Bulletin articles had made the kids even more curious about that city, wondering how a body could be hidden so well in a place without mountains, and with a dense population. I provided a detailed city map, which they studied with great interest.

"I know your stuff's fiction, Myster-E," Jacey said, "but how can you fool people who know the setting into believing it could happen?"

That day the class had a visitor: Gull.

He had appeared the day before so I dragged him to school with me. Not dragged—it required only a casual invitation, which he accepted eagerly. I suggested that maybe he change his T-shirt, but he opted to zip his vest high enough so only an animal's furry head was visible and only he and I were aware of the squirrel's sage advice to *"Guard Your Nuts."* It was such atypical Gull attire (to purchase, let alone wear) I had to ponder what trouble brought him to Utah—and prompted him to adopt suggestive humor in lieu of his usual aiming-for-suave deportment.

Gull was actually the class' second guest. After spending a pleasant on-the-job afternoon with Rosco Ulseth, I'd invited Cale's dad to join us a couple weeks earlier. The deputy had been well received when he presented investigative techniques, protocol for arrests, and other topics he and I had discussed during the ride-along.

Rosco was intrigued by the kids' ideas for Murder in Milford. "Vivid imaginations," he told me after class, allowing a wry grin to slice his usually emotionless face. "Glad I know they're good kids or I'd add them to our 'Keep Watch' list!" He agreed all four had followed my instructions perfectly: to write what they knew best.

As educational as his talk had been, Rosco had spoken *to* the kids, not joined *in* their discussion. Gull, however, listened intently and dove into dialoguing with them. Unconsciously mimicking them, he raised his hand to signal a question. "Yes, Gull?" I barely restrained a guffaw.

"Uh, do you have to stick to the facts? I mean, I thought that was what makes it fiction, the not-being-factual aspect."

Cale beat me to the answer: "Sticking to the facts when you can makes the times you tweak facts more believable."

Good-golly, Miss Molly; the kid's been listening!

Gull saw nothing odd about such wisdom coming from a fifteen-year-old. He nodded thoughtfully. On our way home, he asked if he could read the day's assignments. I let him, and the result was that our supper discussion about the Rochester scandal and OFF TRACK became a three-cornered scuffle of opinions.

Sage had long-since moved past the shock of letting the kids read my as-yet-unpublished work. Gull was miffed that "four strangers who aren't even old enough to drive, let alone be literary critics!" had been granted a privilege never extended to him. In a perverse way, it pleased me that he cared, even if his caring took the shape of jealousy of four teenagers.

The kids loved Gull; everyone does. Gull is one interesting guy with a devil-may-care attitude that ramps up the voltage of any situation. He lives large and loves life and skirts trouble with a skill that makes the concept of holding a greased pig come alive. Hard to resist? Yup; especially if you're a kid or maybe a woman. He is just so dang enticing.

Once again, Gull's visit was an in-without-notice, out-without-warning event for no evident purpose beyond his miffed retort: "Since when does a guy need a reason to come see his family?" This time we had managed more of a tour. Gull was interested in everything from plentiful rainbow-hued rocks to the State's special salt that shows up on many home and restaurant tables in Utah and beyond.

Variety runs rampant in Milford Valley. There are mines to visit, ghost towns to explore, ruins to photograph, mountains to hike, desert areas where treasures lurk beneath the sagebrush, and silent hawks swooping for prey. Gull wanted to see and do it all.

We packed lunches, hooked water bottles to our belts and set out for adventure, though the rabbits we shot at may have defined our activity differently.

"Never thought I'd see you holding a .22! First was your pickup—*that* was a shocker. Then, you're hanging with kids and loving it; and now you have a gun. What's next, huh, Zeke? Tattoos? Piercings in embarrassing places?"

"Wait and see!" It was rather fun being the less conventional brother; I was beginning to see why a predictable, sedate life didn't interest Gull.

Our wanderings led us to one of the area's two gravel pits—the one which locals call The GASP where Jacey's dad, Abbott Belk, worked. He was there, picking up another load. He seemed pleased at our interest and was happy to explain the intricacies of transforming a mighty mountain into stones that could prevent driveways from disintegrating and keep road beds stable.

Overpowering the visual and audible scene was gargantuan equipment that effortlessly filled railroad cars moving slowly along a stub off the main line. On our way to the gravel pit, Gull and I had been stalled waiting for a forty-car train loaded with gray-white rocks to pass by, so we were curious about its destination.

"Don't know 'bout that one, but this load," Abbott shouted above the roar of tumbling rocks, "is goin' north, maybe up to Oregon, to make railroad beds. You ever see rock piles by train tracks? Trains also dumps rails an' ties so a crew can build new sections or repair tracks. There's always sumpthin' to fix with a railroad."

"So, these cars could end up almost anywhere," Gull said in an awed tone. "And it all starts here in—no offense intended—a hole-in-the-wall place like this and goes on day-after-day, year-after-year?"

Abbott grinned. "Yup; Utah supplies lotsa rocks for lotsa places. We pretty much keep stuff running 'round the clock." Overhead lights on massive poles verified his claim. "Well, 'cept for holidays—even us rockers like a day off, now and then!"

After waving goodbye to Abbott when a fellow signaled that his truck was ready to roll, we lingered a few minutes to watch several more top-loading railroad cars being filled. The noise was deafening, the dust pervasive.

"How'd you like to be the fellow who invented that?" Gull yelled, pointing to the machine funneling rocks into three mounds per car. "He must be rich!"

Every aspect of the process was fascinating—from the engine's precise pace, pulling ahead when one car was full and bringing the next car into position, to all the moving parts that sent rivers of rock roaring along conveyor belts and down shoots like water rushing through a canyon.

His question was rhetorical, but I still responded on our walk back to the truck. "He's not in the poor house, but the cost per unit must be astronomical. There can't be a big market for such machinery."

Sage had yet to meet the four kids for anything beyond introductions at ballgames or at the gas stations where every Milfordian eventually showed up to buy fuel or snacks. She had talked a bit more frequently with Jacey at the grocery store than with the other three, so she was very interested in Gull's take on what she teasingly called "Zeke's new little family."

Gull faked heavy breathing in describing Mathia: "She's in *luv* with the one guy on the planet who doesn't give a hoot. If Cale only knew!" Shaking his head, he said pensively, "Ain't that how it goes? We humans always want what we can't have . . ."

Reluctantly, I excused myself. I had to work on lesson plans, plus grade the day's assignments. Gull asked if he could help. I couldn't decide if spending time with such focused kids had unearthed a latent interest in writing, or if he was finally seeing something of importance in the work I do. Whatever his reason, I told him he first had to read the chapters from the kids' initial assignment on Murder in Milford so he could map how their skills had improved since the class began.

I dug out file copies for him. While he read, I planned the coming week's schedule. We had fun discussing the day's assignments when he finished them.

Gull enjoyed Cale's descriptions best, while I lauded Mathia's ability to set moods with few words. We both liked Jacey's creative plot. We laughed at Fable's melodramatic language, although Gull felt she showed a flair the others lacked. In the end, we each wrote our assessments of the day's projects and agreed to award one A, two A minuses, and a B. I knew that grade wouldn't surprise Mathia; she had moaned, "If only I'd had even one more day to work on it, it'd be so much better!"

Not fully, but I was almost brushing the edge of sad when Gull left the next day. "Never would have dreamed," I told Sage before falling asleep that night, "that we'd move to Utah, and I'd get a real brother out of the deal."

"What a good State slogan! It's been 'Virginia Is for Lovers,' for a while, so why not adopt 'Utah Is for Brothers'?"

"Knowing now how good it feels to talk to him about what I do, I'll have to try harder to get him to talk more about whatever it is *he* does. I try, but he always clams up. Maybe he doesn't share my warm fuzzy feelings."

"That's just Gull being Gull, Zeke. If he doesn't want to talk, there's no getting him to open up."

"I know, but I need to keep trying . . . or maybe ask better questions. What guy doesn't want to talk about his work?"

"Gulliver Swift Eden: that's *one* such guy!" Sage quipped, rolling out of range of my playful swat.

"Maybe I should pay him a visit, you know—just drop in, like he does on us. Yeah, show up where he works. At least we know that doesn't change; not as long as he owns the building. It's only what happens inside his suite that fluctuates."

"Good thinking. And you know what might not make Gull feel so much like he's the target? At the picnic, let's ask the parents' permission for you to fly the four kids to Rochester for a first-hand view of OFF TRACK'S setting. Everyone could stay with Haze and Rudy and you can use our zillion frequent-flier miles. How's that for a swell plan?"

A bee sting could not have shot me upright in bed any faster. "Are you daft?"

She laughed. "Hey, you're the one who signed on to teach an Honors Writing Course to teenagers— now, *that's* daft! Give 'em a real writer's adventure. After all, that's what you always call research."

"Their parents would never let them fly into the wild blue yonder with me." I flopped back on my pillow, heart pounding erratically. *Could this idea work? Bigger question: Is it possible what I feel rumbling around inside me is excitement?*

"Don't forget: you're married to the soon-to-be-visible hospital's CEO—that should buy you some credibility!" She tickled me; I stopped her by lacing our fingers together.

"Can we at least wait until the end of the picnic to bring up the proposal, Sage? You know, so you have the opportunity to decide, after you've met everyone, if you still think it's such a hot idea?"

"Sure," she chirped in the breezy tone that meant she had won and we both knew it. Somehow, we drifted off to sleep.

I don't know about Sage, but I hosted weird dreams all night. Some were even nightmares that jerked me awake several times and left me sweating.

Since moving to Utah, I had done so many things contrary to my nature that flying to Minnesota with four teenagers seemed like a mere blip on the screen. Now, even thinking that blip-business was scary.

Was Zeke Eden fading . . . and Kiel Nede—who blithely makes up stuff—coming alive?

7

The day we had picked for the barbecue offered a slate of ideal weather. Allowing jet streams to form pearly strands in a sapphire sky, the clouds draped themselves like silken scarves around the necks of mountain peaks. Too many days like that and word would get out; then, just watch: Utah would be packed with transplants from smoggy States.

Offering sufficient breeze to keep bugs off our food and the grill's smoke away from the pergola, Utah turned off its usual four o'clock gales which regularly set our circular clothesline to spinning like a tornado funnel. No wonder Gull kept coming to visit. April in Minnesota was still boots, shovels, slip-slide driving, and startling wind-chill factors.

Only Jacey's mom was absent. Four little kids played with Frisbees Sage bought especially for them. The teens nonchalantly checked out the property, but loitered close enough to track adult conversations. I soon deduced that the parents knew each other from church, but living in Milford for a lifetime could also accomplish that. They looked nervous as they tried to get a bead on Sage and me.

Tending the grill, I traded seasoning tips with Cale's dad; he marinates, I prefer rubs. I thanked Rosco, again, for the privilege of my ride-along with him and for his visit to class. He countered with, "Hardly a payback for what you've done for Cale. He loves your class, and that's a first for any class with 'English' in its title."

I felt too pleased to protest, but shrugged with what hopefully resembled modesty.

Jacey's dad and I discussed getting rock for the driveway and he told me to call him when I'm ready to place an order. When we walked out front so he could see what I needed, I glanced at the vehicles parked there and experienced a moment's panic. *Gull, again?* Whew; not Gull's black Jeep, but a navy-blue one Abbott was pleased to show off. For him, my initial panic passed as interest.

Abbott Belk reminded me of my father. Rudy Eden did manual labor his whole life—and without apology. He admired people who weren't afraid to get dirty and who took care of their families with the work of their hands, finding self-worth in a job well done. Dad would rank Abbott high among the "good guys," regardless of whatever had prompted Tabitha to yearn for something else with someone else.

Waylen, Fable's dad, talked trucks with me. He offered to show me a thing or two to keep my pickup running smoothly. Sounded good, so we tentatively agreed I would swing by his house the following Wednesday evening. "Wear something you don't mind getting dirty," he warned. "We'll be crawling under the truck, and it ain't pretty."

Mathia's dad was interested in the welding job on the pergola. "Somebody sure knew what he was doing here." Dale fingered an intricate twist to one of eight braces supporting the slat-board top.

"That'd be Lefty Crowley: Sage's dad."

Dale nodded. "Rumor has it, he was self-taught."

"Pretty much. Even with all the welding he did, he considered it just a hobby. If you're interested, there's some welding stuff out in Lefty's workshop I'd love to unload on someone who knows how to use it—and that sure isn't me! We can take a look later." My offer tweaked Dale's interest.

Meanwhile, Sage mingled with the mothers and got them and the teens laughing about something in our garden. "You'd better not be poking fun at my scarecrow!" I called. They laughed even harder.

Cale eventually sauntered over to the grill where the men hovered. I decided our burgers were ready and rechecked the brats and hotdogs keeping warm under foil. I handed Cale the striker and told him to ring the triangle we kept above the grill. The signal put Nimrod on full alert, but he soon returned to sniffing around the garden fence where rabbits and coyotes had left many reminders of their existence— probably as enticing to him as the aromas emanating from my efforts over charcoal and wood chips were to our two-legged guests.

When Sage heard the triangle's chime, she called out, "Let's eat!" The little kids came running and cheering from beyond the garden shed. Their moms corralled them long enough to wash hands at the garden spigot, drying them on towels pinned to the clothesline for that very purpose.

In preparing for our event, Sage had clustered chairs and side-tables around the grassy area for all but the youngest. These four lively guests she put at the card table set up on the pergola. There was an overall atmosphere of camaraderie. Everyone helped themselves to meat and buns, condiments, chips, and salads from the platters and bowls lined up on two varnished wire spool tables.

At one point, when Mathia took it upon herself to deliver iced tea and lemonade refills, Sage laughed. "Hey, Zeke! We should get ourselves one of these critters called teenagers; I could get used to this life of leisure!" She assumed the dramatic pose of a silent-movie heroine, her fork taking the place of a long-stemmed rose between her teeth. All laughed; they clearly adored her.

When Fable chased fly-away paper napkins and plates and put the litter in the covered garbage can, Sage told the three moms in mock seriousness, "I want to adopt all your daughters."

Laynie laughed, "Some days, I'd take your offer!"

Dusk crept in. We were all satiated with a good picnic that ended with apple pie which, I say humbly, turned out perfectly. When I came back from returning the ice cream to the freezer, Sage threw me A Look that said *Show time!* Nodding, I paused, waiting for my heart to cease its erratic beat.

She stood and whistled through her teeth—a skill I doubt many CEOs possess or exhibit publicly, but that's my gal: down to earth and Lefty's daughter to her core. The sound reeled the teens in from where they, their younger siblings, and the off-duty Nimrod were chasing lizards. When Sage had everyone's attention, she directed her first words to the parents: "Since you won't give us your kids—"

"Hold on, there! Says who?" Dale teased.

"Shush, you!" Darcia swatted her husband's arm.

Grinning broadly, Sage continued. "We have an alternate proposition to disrupt your families. As you know, Zeke teaches the Honors Writing Course, and one thing they're studying is the importance of research. Right, kids?"

The teens nodded, curiosity obviously mounting.

"Zeke's current book is set in Rochester, so that's where the research is based. We all know Minnesota is a long drive from Utah, but it's a relatively short flight. We propose a field trip to Rochester. We'll pay all expenses—well, not actually *pay*, since we have sufficient frequent-flier miles to get everyone there and back. And Zeke's parents have room for all. Rudy and Haze are lovely people. I called them today, so I'm not speaking out of turn—they are thrilled to think they could have four teenagers in their home for a long weekend."

Fable flew out of her chair and did a little dance of joy, spinning while she squealed, "A plane! I can't believe I'll finally get to fly some place!"

Sage grinned. "So, that's one entry for the 'Yea' column! Do I hear any 'Nay' votes?"

Dale was the first parent to recover. "I think I speak for Darcia and Mathia when I ask, isn't this a bit much for a teacher, and not even a full-time teacher? I mean, why are you willing to do such an amazing thing for our kids?"

Sage bowed toward me. "Take it away, Zeke!"

I shifted in my lawn chair. "Well, I think your children . . ." I swept my eyes around the circle of seven parents, "all of them," I included even the gap-toothed youngsters in my smile, "are some of the greatest kids I'll ever meet."

Rosco flung his hands in the air. "There you have it. Sage says Zeke's parents are 'thrilled' to house four teenagers for a weekend? Combined with this proposal, it proves insanity is hereditary!"

There was laughter all around. Sage laughed the hardest, but I was a close second.

Suvie piped up, "If I went along, I could keep Cale out of trouble—and for-sure tell Mom and Dad all the bad stuff he did when we got home!"

"You little brat!" Cale bellowed. Again, laughter erupted as the big brother chased his little sister around the garden, easily catching her, only to dump her unceremoniously into their father's lap. Rosco held the struggling body tightly and nuzzled his daughter into submission to staying put.

"Sorry, Suvie—and Uly, Kash and Kasey, too, but this offer is only for the big kids." Four predictable pint-sized groans and a pout or two followed.

I returned to my topic: "Wonderful personalities aside, parents, your teenagers are good writers. As they mature, they could succeed in any career that involves writing."

Someone whispered something, which may have been "Wow."

I continued: "Sage is right: The focus of this trip would be research, and I'd expect spectacular work from them when we're back. We'll pack a lot into four days. We'd leave on a Thursday evening and return the following Tuesday, so it would mean missing Friday and Monday in their other classes."

In the stunned stillness that came as realization that all I proposed could really happen, I mused on what the outdoor equivalent might be to the saying *"You could hear a pin drop."* Maybe *"You could hear a rabbit's nose twitch"* could work?

Sage intercepted the hush following my semi-passionate speech: "Take time to think it over—"

Valarie cut her off, but not rudely, "Cale will never speak to us again if we refuse your offer." The other parents nodded. The girls leaped up, colliding in a group hug and bouncing so much I wondered how they could escape bruising. Cale pumped my hand so vigorously I switched to worrying about if my shoulder socket could survive.

The rest of the evening was a blur. Conversations mingled and twisted and recycled the same topics repeatedly: "I can't believe this!" "When do we go?" "What should we pack?" and "Wait 'til we tell all our friends!"

In the space of two hours, our relationship with a sampling of the community underwent an amazing transformation. Four guys viewed me as a new, if unusual, friend—perhaps in over my head on this venture. Three women considered Sage the luckiest woman on earth to be married to such a wonderful guy. The teens nominated me for Teacher of the Year. The only people in the group not enamored with the whole idea were the little kids who sulked because they don't get to go.

Not bad results for one picnic, hmm?

In our bedtime conversation, my gal amazed me again with everything she either learned or deduced during what I'd viewed it as a picnic with a tacked-on surprise. Forget Guys-are-from-Mars; I must be from Neptune.

"Fable's parents," Sage said, "are thrilled with the Honors Writing Course because their otherwise-bored daughter's fervor has spilled into other classes. *But*," she warned, "Fable is self-conscious about being chubby. Her nails are much-tended because she considers them her only redeeming feature. So, *never* tease Fable if she brings manicure supplies to class, or takes a moment for a quick repair."

Upon hearing it could crush Fable if she felt I didn't admire her nails, my masculine response to this flood of bewildering feminine information was, "No problem; I can do the admire-thing."

"Next: Jacey," Sage continued in our shadowy bedroom. Pulling her close, I savored the mix of grill smoke and hair gel that would disappear in her morning shower. "Jacey thinks she's too tall; so she slouches. And she chews her fingernails; did you see how she keeps her hands hidden, if possible? And she's in love with you. To her; you're much more mature than boys her age."

"Cale's pretty mature," I protested, purposely sliding right past the alarming suggestion I might be the object of an adolescent girl's infatuation. I could understand Fable lusting after Gull. *But me?* Surreptitiously patting the tire with which middle-age gifted me, I chided myself, *Walking to the refrigerator does not constitute exercise!*—but then scoffed, *Just because Sage suggests that Jacey thinks I'm hot stuff doesn't make it so!*

"Cale has eyes only for moody little Jacey, which is totally bizarre, and Mathia's in love with Cale— which Jacey knows, so she won't give Cale any leeway. She doesn't want to hurt her friend."

"Whoa! How'd you get all this inside-scoop info? Good grief, now I'll never view them the same way.

I should borrow the FIRE-DANGER sign on the road to Cedar City and add a panel that reads HORMONE LEVELS ARE EXTREMELY HIGH TODAY!"

"Oh, it will all change," Sage informed me airily. "In fact, it could shift dramatically before you see them again. I'm just reporting on what was going on tonight." She patted my arm. "Don't worry, Zeke; it's a girl-thing to be able to figure it out."

I groused, "And here I thought I was the one who understands plots!"

"Your reputation still holds," she assured me. Our evening ended with a kiss that led to things that prevented thinking about anything but the woman who has lit my fire for over three decades.

We could have used a warning sign of our own that night. Gotta love it when adult hormones and testosterone heat up.

The number of travelers to Rochester increased by one and it was a good addition. The parents elected Abbott Belk to accompany us. The families chipped in on his fare, but I said Abbott wouldn't require a motel room. Haze would deem such a thing downright inhospitable and blame me for it.

I appreciated the underlying reason for Abbott's presence. None of the parents really know me, so sending one of the seven to help chaperone made them feel safer about sending their offspring on such an odd adventure.

I was grateful for the adult company. Abbott and I sat two rows ahead of the kids. Since the picnic, I had collected on his offer. As the plane left earth, we talked about the recently delivered load of gravel. "It's doing its job," I told him.

"Looked thin; might wanna dump a second load. All part of a day's work, so no extra money in my pocket, but could spare ya some heartaches. Spring in Utah gets sloppy; our mud's bad stuff. A good rock-job'll save yer keister *and* yer wallet."

Mud and crutches are a nasty combination, so I was quick to say, "I'm very interested. Let's set up something when we get back home."

We continued randomly commenting on this-and-that, each sensing we had a long trip ahead. Since our connection points were scant—Jacey, gravel, and driveways—it seemed wise to dole our words out more slowly, like a baited fishing line on a lazy day.

Abbott grew restless after the drink cart passed our row. Soda in hand, he cleared his throat and said in a low voice intended only for my ears, "Uh, Zeke, there's something 'bout me I don't guess ya know."

He paused so long, I felt something was required. "Oh? What's that?"

"I, uh, served time; two years in the brig up at Draper. Auto theft. While I was in, Tabby left me an' dumped Jacey on my folks."

He nodded as if I'd said something (which, due to my shock, hadn't happened). Exhaling audibly, he continued: "Took over a year after I got out b'fore Social Services finally let me keep her."

The din in my head and tremor roiling through my bones left me feeling like a railcar taking on a load of rock. *Kaboom!* Sifting rapidly through the rubble for an appropriate response, I latched on to, "Those Social Service people are smart folks to see that Jacey obviously loves and trusts you."

It could have been gibberish for all Abbott heard; now that he had opened the hatch, words spilled: "When I got out, the only place that'd hire me was The GASP. Weird, cuz Buddy Crouse who owned it then—he sold it later an' moved to Idaho—was who Tabby left me for. But me an' him, we go way back, an' he stuck by me when push came to shove. Tabby didn't last with Buddy, either." He gripped his plastic cup so hard it cracked. That detail, and his tight jaw were the only signs of emotion.

It was the longest and certainly most personal conversation I'd had with him, even though we often sat by each other at high school events featuring Jacey, or shared a booth for coffee at the Diner if we'd landed there at the same time, by chance.

"I wasn't sure if anyone told ya. Don't seem right not to come clean, what with this trip." Abbott tilted his head back and tapped an ice cube from the cup into his mouth. "Sorry I didn't tell ya sooner so ya could change your mind 'bout me comin' along. Your folks might not like an ex-con in their house."

Ice rattled around in our mouths before I said evenly, "Hadn't heard. Thanks for being up-front, but knowing doesn't change my opinion of you. You do a fine job—raising Jacey, working hard. Can't be easy, being a single father."

Then, I shared my first impression of him, of how my dad would rank him high. "It's up to you, of course," I ended my monologue, "but I see no reason to tell my family anything. Just enjoy the weekend."

Minnesota's eye-popping seasonal greenness was astounding to kids more accustomed to Utah's array of browns, but something else made an even greater impression. In a lifetime of trying, I've discovered no way to prepare the uninitiated for Haze Eden.

We weren't even through security before I heard: "There he is!" Each time she meets my plane, I'm nervous until we get past the split second when she could ditch our longstanding deal and chirp, "It's my world-famous son: Kiel Nede!" *Safe again; whew.*

No surprise: Gull stood behind Mom and Dad. The kids greeted my brother like a long-lost friend, his being the only familiar face in an unfamiliar place. He rolled out the charm like a proverbial red carpet. Even Abbott relaxed enough to joke a bit.

Not content to merely meet us at the airport, Mom had rented a limousine. Herding us toward it, she confided to me, "I pumped my friends who have teenage grandchildren for details on how to get the weekend off to a good start." The teens' glee was contagious and boundless, expressed in giddiness alternating with weak attempts to take it all in stride while maintaining a modicum of dignity.

Giddy prevailed.

On our drive in to Rochester, Abbott mentioned staying at a hotel. Mom pinned him with a *Wash-your-mouth-out!* look. If she'd had a bar of soap in her purse, Abbott would have been spouting bubbles. "Told ya so!" I murmured. He grinned.

Around Mom's table where we enjoyed our choice of banana splits or root beer floats, I sprung my first big surprise—the one especially for Mom. At my insistence, she finally quit scurrying around the kitchen and joined us at the table. Only then did I reach under my chair and pull out a giftwrapped package. Mom played her part according to tradition, arching her eyebrows expectantly.

"The best way to find out what's inside is to open it," I said, following the script we had developed over fifteen similar occasions. "Have at it!"

True to form, Mom ran her finger under each tab of tape, murmuring *"Oooh"* and *"Ahhh"* and taking excruciating care to preserve ribbon and wrappings. The ritual required three layers of tissue paper, which Gull suggested long ago in hopes Mom would eventually say *"Phooey!"* and join the royal ranks of package-rippers.

It never happened. Not once, in sixteen books.

While her family was accustomed to the theatrical routine of giving Haze a gift, the four kids were not. They were ready to explode.

With wrappings finally folded and set aside, Mom held her personal copy of OFF TRACK. She fingered the lettering and stunning gray-scale full-size photo of railroad tracks. Mouthing the title, she exclaimed, "Oh, Zeke!" Her eyes glistened with tears as they darted between my face and the book cover. "You wrote the railroady story!" As she clutched her prize, I swear we could have read by the glow on her face.

Around the table, voices soared:

"Wahoo! It's published!" from Mathia.

"How could you keep this a secret?" from Jacey.

"Wow, great cover!" from Cale.

"This was in your suitcase, Myster-E, and you didn't drop a hint?" in Fable's most dramatic voice.

If they thought Mom's way of opening a gift was agonizing, our guests were in for more torment. They had no idea she would drag out progressing from examining the book jacket to reading the blurbs on the inside flaps, then slowly turning pages until she finally reached the Acknowledgements.

As Mom read the words I had penned about her, she gasped and wiped her eyes with the closest thing at hand: the tablecloth. "Oh for pity sake, look what I did!" she sputtered around a spate of hiccups.

Laughter followed hugs. "Now you see why we came to Rochester, Mom. Earlier clues would've spoiled my surprise. The Honors Writing Course used OFF TRACK as a textbook, and they're here to explore how research forms a story's skeleton."

"And here I thought you came to see me!" Mom fussed, but the pout couldn't survive her delight.

All those bulging envelopes? Every fact-laden article? Each prolonged phone call? All worth it to see Haze Eden so happy. If only Sage could see. *Wait!* I pulled out my cell, snapped a photo and sent it to Sage's phone. Being there, the *now* way.

With Mom still on Cloud Nine, I slipped into my bedroom to do two things: call Maggie to set wheels in motion, and retrieve four copies of the book. The presentation was met by a choir of exultations around the table: "Dad!" Jacey squealed. "My name's in here!" An artist's rendering of the look on Abbott's face at seeing his daughter immortalized in print could have been titled "Paternal Pride."

Friday, Gull chauffeured my prescribed tour of OFF TRACK's important scenes. His business van usually sported magnetic door signs advertising his current efforts; as we climbed in, I noted bare doors. As is typical in *Don't-Ask-Don't-Tell* situations, he knew *I* knew what missing signs meant. Bad scene.

No wonder Gull was thrilled to see us. With so much constant and varied activity, Dad would likely keep the lid on his usual tirades.

We spent the majority of our time at Quarry Hill Park since it featured so strongly in OFF TRACK. The limestone quarry's caves had been important in the history of the Rochester State Hospital—the facility for the "criminally insane" that once stood on the site of the current Federal Medical Center. (Yes, it's unkind to label residents with mental issues, but I'm quoting. Today, similarly afflicted patients are often self-medicated and function well in any community). We followed the railroad tracks that run between FMC and the park.

"It must be hard to be a prisoner there," Fable sighed. A ballgame was in progress on the expanse of grass behind the electrified razor-wire fences in beds of glass shards. "Those guys probably wish they could hop a ride on every train that goes by."

Abbott's face was a mask, though it softened when Jacey sidled up and sneaked her hand into his for a quick squeeze. That was all it took; he left his dark past and rejoined us in Quarry Hill Park. He dropped a kiss on her head before kneeling to tighten a shoelace that didn't need it. When he rose, he joked, "I should get shoes with Velcro so I don't wear out the knees on my pants!" and the moment passed, although he blinked fast several times.

"Now I can see why the tracks made such a good red herring in OFF TRACK," Cale said thoughtfully. "Especially since they come so close to the prison."

We left the tracks and walked along a shaded path into the actual park. Abbott fell in beside Cale and asked, "What's a 'red herring'?"

Flanked by Abbott and Gull, Cale held his own as he launched into an explanation that ended with a summary of the kids' own ideas for disposing of bodies in Milford. The girls commented, throughout. Abbott listened incredulously, if nervously. I knew how he felt: astounded and frightened to see what could spring from fertile, youthful minds.

We halted outside the caves that had, long ago, served as cold storage for produce and smoked meats to feed the State Hospital's fifteen-hundred patients during its heyday. I explained how, after the facility closed, the caves remained open to explore until vandals destroyed that pleasure. The only effective recourse was to block entrances with steel doors.

"If local readers know the entrances are boarded and locked," Mathia mused, "will they buy it, that Raven could find the body in the caves?"

"Yeah, the pipes on top of the caves are too small for a body to fit through," Fable added, then snapped her fingers. "Oh! *That's* the fiction part; huh?"

"Exactly! Raven assumes the killer didn't chop up the body. I tweaked facts and made the air vents large enough for the murderer's dirty deed. Remember the disclaimer at the front of most fiction—the part about 'Any resemblance to such-and-such is coincidental'? Novelists can adjust facts to accommodate a story, but journalists better not!"

Jacey had been quiet for much of the tour, but once she let loose, her words tumbled freely. "So many trees make this part of town seem isolated, but neighborhoods are close-by; we saw them when we were driving here. Myster-E said the Nature Center gets lots of visitors, and kids must hang out here, like how we go to Star Range or The Minerals to fool around, right? So, why would a murderer take a chance somebody wouldn't catch him dumping the body? Hey! If nobody can drive this far into the park, how'd the killer get the body back here?"

I wished Sage were here to see how brilliantly her idea for this trip shone. Plot development unraveled for my young friends. They knew how OFF TRACK ended, but they had new insights into all the loose ends an author must tie together.

Deciding to let them debate the fine points among themselves, I motioned for Gull and Abbott to follow me. We walked ahead of the chattering foursome and made our way past the ball diamonds to the parking lot where we had left Gull's van.

Saturday morning, we seven (Gull, by now, was a permanent member of our little group) embarked on a scavenger hunt I'd prepared. The clues were lifted directly from OFF TRACK; all answers could be found within a ten-block radius of the sprawling medical center that forms the heart of downtown Rochester.

Gull took Cale, Mathia, and Abbott under his wing and they set off, all determined to finish first. I shepherded the equally motivated and very-human

Jacey and Fable in a search for evidence that guided the strictly fictional Raven Crowley to his prey.

The two teams explored alleys, which had featured ominously in the chase scene, and counted the steps between the various buildings to determine the accuracy of witnesses' reports to the police. They then listened from a bridge over the Zumbro River for sounds, which The Howler had heard in the hours before her death.

All loved that activity. Cale pronounced research, "Almost as much fun as target shooting!" as he mimed a one-eyed stare along a rifle's barrel.

Haze had packed bag lunches, which we ate in a Silver Lake picnic shelter. The girls fed bread crusts to the Canadian Geese that make the park their home, but Cale eyed them with a hunter's yearning. "Don't even think about it," Gull cautioned with a hearty laugh. "Those geese are protected by law around here! All twenty-plus thousand of 'em!"

That set the kids off on creating a goofy mystery they named "Who Killed Goober, the Goose?" It was silly fun; even Gull and Abbott contributed.

The plot involved goose-poop footprints leading to the culprit: a howling dog (Fable's idea; she loved merging *Bulldog* with *Howler*) living beneath the picturesque stone bridge near our table. As our party spun their lurid yarn, a wedding party was videoing memories on that arching edifice. Surely, our antics added an odd dimension to their joy. Our topic of murder was definitely in sharp contrast to promises of wedded bliss.

Saturday afternoon was devoted to my second surprise. I was nervous about the opening scene, but Maggie had burned the midnight oil to make it happen so I followed through.

When Zeke Eden disappeared into the bedroom and Kiel Nede came out, a hush descended on the living room. I had packed everything required for the transformation except crutches, a set of which Mom kept on hand for my visits home.

Although the kids knew Zeke was Kiel, we had not discussed what was now obvious—the visible, shocking aspect of my dual identity: the absent foot.

Fable recovered first. "Hey, Kiel Nede! Lookin' good, dude," she drawled. "Where ya headed?"

What a cool kid. I followed her lead and kept it casual: "Oh, just to an interview down at the KROC radio station. If anyone's interested, you're welcome to come along," I added nonchalantly.

You'd have thought all four were sitting on whoopee cushions. "Sorry to startle you with this," I raised a crutch, "and this." I thrust out my footless leg. "Seeing photos on book jackets isn't quite the same as in-your-face reality, I know."

"No sweat, Myster-E," Cale said. "There's gobs of stuff you don't know about us."

I felt humbled, looking into such accepting faces. "Right; we'll talk more later. For now, I'd like it if you remembered that, when I put this mop on my head and leave a fake foot under the bed, I'm Kiel Nede. Not Zeke Eden, not Myster-E. Mom has kept the secret for years, so can you all do the same?"

All five nodded. If anyone respected secrets, it was Abbott.

"Now, here's what will happen today . . ."

Two hours later, four kids and one father-in-tow were still speechless, having witnessed my interview with genial Stacey who had "devoured" Maggie's overnighted copy of OFF TRACK. She introduced the kids as my "collaborators." They shot their names into the microphone so quickly, I'm sure listeners had no idea what they said.

With the twinkle in her eye giving her voice a lilt, Stacey asked Abbott, "So, Mister Belk, are you another of Kiel's partners in crime?"

Abbott turned a pasty shade of pale; his eyebrows trapped sweat dripping from his brow. "No, Ma'am; I drive a sand-and-gravel truck back in Milford."

Taking pity on his nervousness, Stacey winked to set him at ease. It didn't work. Pro that she was, she continued the interview without a gap in the flow.

Sunday, I awakened before the others and didn't shave. I left a note, and walked to the nearby Kwik Trip where I bought four copies of the Post Bulletin.

I returned home to find Mom (no surprise) in the kitchen, with pans sizzling, the oven belching its heat into the room, and *Ah-yes: coffee!*

"Thank God, you're back. We haven't had even a moment alone," Mom fussed as she cracked eggs into a bowl. "You need to talk to your brother."

"Gull?" My hand jerked; coffee sloshed in the pot.

"You have another brother?" she said peevishly. Something was seriously awry if Mom was snippy with a houseful of guests and her world-famous son within hugging distance. "Of course I mean Gull."

"Mom, we've done little *but* talk for two days!"

"He's being secretive, and not just about, *you know*: his usual problems. He has a lady-friend, and won't bring her over to meet your father and me."

"Maybe he's not ready. Could be, they're not at the Meet-the-Relatives point yet."

Hands on her hips, Mom swung around. Her eyes narrowed to mere slits. *Not a good thing.* "Talk. To. Him."

Uh-oh. One-word sentences: also not good.

She whisked batter into a frenzied froth. Her "I'm worried" rose above the rattle of metal against ceramic. "Something's not right, but don't tell Gull I said so or he'll clam up."

"I'll try." I knew the only way she'd let me near the coffee pot for a refill was if I agreed, but I had no intention of interfering in my brother's love life.

After breakfast and Abbott's assurance I wouldn't be in trouble with parents if the kids skipped church "just this once," I handed each teen a newspaper. My instructions were precise: "Find articles about whomever and whatever would be affected adversely or positively by The Howler's death."

Haze provided markers, scissors, and tape; they set about their task eagerly. Of course, the comics offered some diversion, but hey, it was Sunday.

They produced remarkably thoughtful work. We followed that assignment with a lively discussion about their revamped perceptions of the role of research in writing even a mystery-thriller.

Then it was time for my third surprise. Maggie had earned her wages and sixteen peach-colored roses. The color was her favorite, and the number in keeping with my tradition of adding one more rose to the FTD bouquet for each new book.

I had insisted that no clues could reach Mom's ears until after I had presented Haze's copy of OFF TRACK—which, to my agent's dismay, had happened barely days earlier. Only then could Maggie begin arranging my media blitz, including the KROC interview and the posters she shipped overnight. The woman is nothing short of a miracle worker.

I suspect that Maggie lobbed boycott warnings alternating with "Keep-this-between-you-me-and-the-gatepost, but here's the scoop . . ." to make it all work. Whatever her secret method was, she had blanketed (some would say *swamped*) the region with news that Kiel Nede and his new book were in town. And she did it all within my stringent restrictions.

Thus, after lunch, we headed to Apache Mall for a booksigning. Dad's job was to park Mom in the bookstore's café and keep her busy drinking fancy coffees at a table that allowed her full view of the happenings, but *away*, so she couldn't blurt anything inappropriate. As always, Dad deserved hazard pay.

Cale and Abbott were quiet, yet intrigued by the event and the store itself. The three girls giggled a lot, shushed each other, and tried to maintain an acceptable level of poise as they hovered.

With crutches tucked beneath my chair, frowsy hair anchored by my trademark beret, eyeglasses planted on my nose, and footless leg in evidence, I was in a familiar groove, signing books like crazy, chatting with fans, and keeping the line moving.

Talk around the supper table was devoted to booksigning stories. The kids had overheard plenty of conversations from people standing in line, many of which made them dissolve in laughter as they repeated the fabrications of Kiel Nede's avid readers.

Fable burbled, "One lady insisted you dated her in college! She said she 'couldn't wait' to hug you, so her face turned bright red when you only shook her hand! After that, she had to do some fast-talking to the guy she'd lied to about your so-called romance!"

"Yeah," Cale added, "She told him you'd taken their breakup 'real hard' and were still hurting over it, but 'she knew' seeing her today comforted you!"

Mom's eyes narrowed and she snorted something about Sage being the only love of my life "*ever*."

I nudged Dad. "See why guarding-Haze duty is important? Imagine the brouhaha if Mom had gotten her hands on that woman!"

Monday morning was devoted to a visit to the Rochester Public Library. Abbott and Gull dropped us off at the front door, and then left for the Jeep dealership. Knowing how important appearances and associations with *Class* are to Gull, it was odd how well my brother and Abbott clicked. Maybe it was the Jeep connection. Whatever the reason, I was grateful because it meant Abbott had a good time.

I mentioned the phenomenon on the phone to Sage. She said, "Abbott has no pretense about him, and Gull has enough for both of them. They can be themselves without competing. Based on Abbott's disclosure to you on the plane, we know he's a graduate of the School of Hard Knocks. Gull's a lifelong student of the same institution."

I had called ahead to the library so the teens had a designated librarian ready to answer questions and assist in their research. Frank put them at ease and the kids were soon following leads like bloodhounds.

That done, we headed home for lunch before driving to the theater for a matinee movie with rounds of popcorn, candy, and sodas. How the kids could be hungry after devouring Mom's chicken-and-dumplings was beyond me. I called Sage from the lobby to say, "If you ever hanker to start a family, one of us will need to find a second job."

Then, it ended with reluctant goodbyes. Cale flung his arms around Mom and lifted her off her feet as he gushed, "Thanks for all the great grub!" Fable's tears glistened, Jacey sniffled, and Mathia's chin quivered during the girls' touching farewells.

Haze showed no such restraint: She sobbed, kissed, and fussed over everyone. Abbott's awkward gratitude so moved Mom she wanted to adopt him.

Having drafted Dad as her pack animal, Mom stood in the driveway and doled out shoeboxes to all six travelers as we got into the van. "They won't feed you *a thing* on the plane, so it's just a little something to tide you over." Each box had to weigh five pounds, fully ninety percent of which was love.

As he backed out of the driveway, Gull said, "Mom would make a dandy grandma, huh?" We'd seen a version of Haze Eden no one had met before. Nor would that startling rendition of our mother likely surface again since, thus far, her two sons had proven uncooperative in the grandchild-producing department.

The day after the kids returned to school, the principal called to inform me he had a waiting list of nineteen for the next Honors Writing Course, one of whom was a sixth grader. Haze's four-course meals and bottomless cookie jar guaranteed the weekend's success, but research is an enticing enterprise.

8

An uncommonly gentle breeze wafted through the window I had opened to counter the woodstove's belching heat. Even if the calendar said it should be spring, I liked to make a fire on cool mornings. But, as the sun moved across the sky, I usually regretted it. Sage muttered, "This is worse than hot flashes!" and opened more windows in all four directions, desperate to catch any air movement.

A cross-draft lifted a paper off my lap and carried it to the floor. I made no attempt to grab it midflight. Head back, I emitted a guttural sound that brought Sage scurrying to the arched doorway between living room and kitchen. This being a weekend without planned guests, she was designated cook and I was bottle-washer.

"You okay, Zeke?" She cocked her head slightly to the left in what I refer to as her Alert-Bunny Mode when she expects to *sense* more than she *hears*. Her eyes narrowed. All the better to see my anticipated deception.

"Never finer," I hedged, but a gulp negated my mild protest. "Hunky-dory. It's, uh—" Words failed me: a scary thought since they are the bones of my profession. I gripped the envelope that had held yet another of Mom's Rochester Post Bulletin articles.

However, the photo accompanying the piece was of far greater importance. Why? Because Mom had written nothing on it. No stars, no arrows, nothing.

Bearing Mom's return-address label, the envelope arrived with overnight postage paid (which for remote areas means fast, just not always that fast) and addressed to Ezekiel Eden. Being aware of the contents, that's who I wished I only were. But it was years too late to deny I am also Kiel Nede: a made-up man with a make-believe life, complete with a name that followed no ancestral line.

So tightly had I clenched the enclosed paper, my fingernail had slashed a slit in the lead paragraph's phrase: *"best-selling author . . ."* It was an eerie premonition of a reputation ruined: my alter-ego.

"Ah, Haze strikes again!" Sage's chuckle lassoed my nomadic thoughts. "With her recent success at piloting a Kiel Nede plot into the hangar, I bet her nose is pointed at the wide-open skies again, right?" She leaned against the doorframe.

That gracefully arched bare foot with sexy red toenails . . . resting on her opposite smooth-and-shapely ankle . . . My, how the mind can wander . . .

"What's her new plot proposal?" Sage asked.

Can they rescind badges if a Boy Scout lies? If so, mine are history. I skipped over the meat of Mom's latest news and offered the throw-away fat: "No plot suggestions, but Gull and his new lady-friend are giving Mom conniption fits. She wanted me to grill him when I was there because—to quote her—'He's being secretive.' I ignored her. Gull's romances are his business."

Nodding agreement, Sage returned to the kitchen, calling back, "Before she starts planning a wedding, somebody better warn that gal it won't last."

Images of ankle-bones connecting to hip-bones didn't stand a chance against Trepidation's icy fist that had a firm grip on my guts. Trembling, I stretched to retrieve the wayward clipping.

Gull was always on to something new, be it feminine or financial. Needing time to process the fearsome things bumping loudly in my mental dark night, I snapped the article briskly to flatten the creases and stared at the grainy expanse of a four-by-six photo. It depicted what must be Gull's latest misadventures. I longed to see anything but what it revealed.

Failing that, I stuffed the paper back into the envelope. Drawn to the kitchen by Sage's sudden wordless wails of frustration, I opted for a carefree attitude to hide my despair and hopefully ease Sage's irritation with all things kitcheny.

"Smells good!" I said brightly. "What is it?"

"Supper," Sage answered sharply.

What is it about me that makes women in kitchens crabby? First, Mom; now Sage. It's a characteristic I really should abandon. Living in a world devoid of women who love me was a bleak prospect.

"Ah, yes: it's evening, and it's food. Silly me!" If ever a conversation qualified as inane, it was this absurd babble. If not the inevitable end of the career I knew and loved, then whatever else lay ahead for me was a serious detour with multiple potholes.

"If it had a name, I'd be happy to tell you. As it is, I'm trying desperately hard to transform leftovers from your last grilling extravaganza so my world-famous husband will be amazed."

Abruptly, like the sun bursting through clouds, Sage's whatever-caused-it spat with our evening's menu evaporated. She swayed toward me, her lips puckered in anticipation of a lusty kiss. If my wife's trim ankles and sexy kisses couldn't pull me out of a funk, there was little hope. Another kiss and I was doing much, much better.

Supper was so good we wished it could somehow be duplicated, although the specific amount of leftovers was unlikely to occur again, and the exact proportions of added *whatevers* were lost. When she cooked, Sage always flung caution to the winds, relegating precision to her high-powered career.

Our conversation flitted through topics until she said, "Enough chatting. You are so far removed from this room and me, you might as well be out there climbing Frisco Peak! It can't be Gull's love life; he acquires and discards women like sweaty socks until it barely registers on our distress meter. So, what gives?"

I wasn't completely ready to 'fess-up, so I fudged a little. "Oh, I'm just worried I didn't do enough research before deciding OFF TRACK was ready."

"What? You did *fabulous* research, interviewing all the guys at the depot, and scouring the Internet. And Haze's input verged on overwhelming. We've had this talk before, Zeke, like when you protested you didn't know squat about gourmet cooking before you wrote STIR CRAZY. Remember? And when you insisted you knew zip about the life of a drummer before you killed that poor kid in STICK-UP."

Even a hovering bad mood couldn't stifle my amusement over that comment. Sage always falls in love with a character, and the drumming-fool victim in Book #8 resonated with her. "Point taken."

Sage knows when to stop rubbing it in about being right. She headed for the freezer, found what she wanted, and grabbed spoons from the silverware drawer on her return to the table. Like a picture of innocence, she smiled sweetly and put a pint of Ben & Jerry's Cherry Garcia ice cream (always my Waterloo) between us. When we reached the bottom of our shared dessert, Sage gave me her Alert-Bunny look again. I grimaced.

She ducked close to my face, wearing the little mocking pout she uses only when I'm in my lowest moods. "Okay, Sweet-ums, what's the real problem tonight? If you can't tell a hospital CEO all your troubles, who can you tell?"

"Maybe a wife who is so perceptive, it's spooky?"

Her chocolate-and-cherry–scented breath wafted by my nostrils when she leaned closer. "That'd be me, right?" she cooed.

"Come here, you temptress!" One long, loud and lusty kiss later, I caressed her hair until I could breathe normally. "Wait here." I left the kitchen and retrieved the article that had iced my blood.

She read; I loaded the dishwasher. "Uh-oh; is Gull the 'unidentified man' in the photo?"

"I suspect so, and presume Mom does, too."

"Interesting. *Hmm.* Isn't it assuming a lot to infer that just because Gull stands behind someone in an airport line he automatically becomes her 'traveling companion'?"

"It's a stretch, but do you recognize the woman?"

"I do: it's The Bulldog." She contorted her lips. "Okay; time to take stock. We're in shock and can safely assume Haze is, too. Case in point: Have we ever received a letter from her without comments running all over the margins?"

"Bingo. You noticed. I should've talked to Gull when she asked. Not that he'd have told me anything, being the great conversational escape-artist, but I would've— What am I saying? I never suspected my brother would, if we're to believe Mom's implication, 'take up' with The Bulldog."

Sage inhaled briskly, exhaling slowly in a tuneless but audible whistle. She thrust her fingers through her hair, leaving a mess behind. "Look at it piece-by-piece. Fact: Ms Honey Odessa Woolden-Landis stands innocently at a ticket counter in an airport."

"Nothing about her is innocent," I groused.

Sage hushed me with *A Look*. "An ordinary activity for anyone else . . . newsworthy for *her*. An enterprising photographer snaps a shot and dangles scuttlebutt in front of your least-favorite reporter: Leif Schwartz. He writes an article, which lands in the Post Bulletin, and elsewhere. With me so far?"

My growl was a poor imitation of a bulldog.

"Fact: Standing behind Odessa is a man who, yes, looks an awful lot like Gull. His mother thinks so, his brother suspects so, even his sister-in-law doesn't dispute that it *could* be him. But what if it isn't? Everyone has a double, they say, and Rochester isn't some Podunk town; it has an international airport. The world can come right to Rochester's doorstep!"

Warming to argument and strategy, I interjected, "Fact: All sorts of people from all over *do* converge on Rochester."

"Isn't it possible Gull's double could be one of Mayo Clinic's zillion patients arriving or departing daily? Or, the man pictured is a hot-shot computer nerd flying home after solving some major problem at IBM? Or, he's returning home after breeding his prize-winning dog?" A giggle. "Get it? Bulldog!"

I did grin, but my enthusiasm was cooling rapidly. "The odds are huge for any of those to be true, especially since Gull lives there. If the picture were taken at LAX, then I'd agree our thinking *'It must be Gull's double because he's in Minnesota, not Los Angeles'* makes sense. Complications arise because Mom knows Gull has a lady-friend. If that person is The Bulldog, well, Gull would never bring her home to meet the folks. Can you imagine that fiasco?"

"He's brazen, but he's no fool," Sage agreed.

Nausea swamped me. "Unless," I qualified, "his love-interest really *is* The Bulldog. In which case, here's the final fact: Gull is a world-class idiot."

"Ah, but we're forgetting something. For the past thirty years, I've stood behind all sizes and shapes of guys in airport ticket lines. *Not once* have I been in a relationship with them, unless it was you, my sweet worrier." She blew me an air-kiss. "Why should we make Gull and Honey an item just because a camera lens caught them sharing the same four-foot slab of airport carpeting?"

"Let me play the devil's advocate for a moment, okay? Mom assumes they are an item, otherwise, why send me a comment-free clipping? She has reason to think the worst. By sending it, sans any notations, she is reminding me she asked me to check on Gull, and knows I didn't. This mailing is to motivate me to do so. Pronto."

"Will you?"

Groaning, I dropped my head into my hands. "I don't know; maybe, maybe not. Let's take a drive."

The suggestion met with instant approval; we both think better with fresh air whisking cobwebs away.

Keeping the truck at a snail's pace, we eventually calmed after three trips along the road circling our property's fence line. I finally halted and pointed the pickup's hood toward the Mineral range.

We tilted our seats back to three-quarter reclining positions, reached for each other's hands, and let the sunset's reflection off the opposite horizon's rocky ridges entertain us. "Better than a drive-in movie," murmured Sage. "Name it 'Sunset in the Eastern Skies' and it'll top the charts."

By the time we returned to the garage, I had dismissed all thoughts of Gull and decided to see where acting on my earlier musings about Sage's shapely ankles could take me.

It was a good place.

July's heat inched into early-morning cracks. Our bed sheets had lost their coolness during our behind-closed-doors rendezvous. During intervening hours of blissful sleep, the linens had transformed from bedding into tangled messes trapping our legs.

The phone's irritating buzz interrupted a pleasant dream. I growled something that barely qualified as a greeting, only to hear, "Hey, bro!"

Arrgghh! The voice was too perky for my foggy brain to handle. "Gull?" Each syllable of the past evening's conversation about Mom's latest mailing whistled like a stiff wind through my brain. What on earth could I say to him?

Should I reprimand him for letting a photographer with more nerve than sense catch him standing by Honey Odessa Woolden-Landis at the airport?

Should I try to knock sense into him about time to shape up and fly right, enough with the irresponsible lifestyle . . . oh, and, by the way, who's your new lady-friend, and no dodging the answer this time?

"Where are you?" is what the bold and in-your-face guy that I am settled on.

Beside me, Sage stretched. We rose up on elbows and both looked at the clock. *5:15?* She groaned.

Gull gushed, "Las Vegas: what a great town! No one sleeps!"

"Apparently," I said sarcastically. A sigh closed my eyes like a shade-pull. "To what do I owe this phone call, and at such an ungodly hour?" I dropped back to my pillow, tilting the phone for Sage's benefit as she nestled in to listen, too.

"I need Heather's phone number. She's unlisted."

"For good reason," I wanted to retort, but bit my tongue. *"That way, she never gets phone calls from you—"* Wait; we're unlisted, but it hadn't helped. Gull always found us. "Why do you need it?"

"I'm here, she's somewhere in razzle-dazzle Viva Las Vegas! Hey, Heather and I are buddies. Come on, bro, all I'm asking for is her number. If she doesn't want to see me, all she has to do is say so.

You won't get in trouble; she gave it to me once, but I don't have it with me."

He had a point. "Why Vegas? Why now?"

"Like the commercials say: 'Hey, Baby, Vegas is calling!' I answered the call an' here I am. I figured a place where fireworks happen all year oughta do the official Fourth big-time. So, ya got Heather's number handy?"

There are brother-combinations in the world, even in Utah, in which this conversation would not take place. Brothers at home on the farm, going to bed with the sun, rising with the chickens. Or going to the family store every morning and flipping the little sign from CLOSED to OPEN. Lucky dudes.

I muffled a moan. "Hang on." Sage flopped a hand around on her nightstand to retrieve her Palm Pilot. While she read the number, I parroted it to Gull . . . each reluctantly shared digit, one-by-one.

"Wait a sec." I heard him ask someone close by for a replacement pen. I knew—absolutely *knew*—he was writing the number on his palm: the kind with skin, not a screen.

"Okay; run that by me again," he said.

Sage repeated the numbers and, with exaggerated patience, I complied.

"Super; thanks."

"Hold on!" Even though my heartbeat was twice a healthy rate, I still had to know: "Uh, Gull, are you in Vegas alone?"

"Sure, except for about a million other people. Ha! I tell ya, this place is hopping! Why?"

"You flew to Vegas by yourself, just to be there?"

"Yeah; you should drive down! We could do a Vegas Fourth of July together."

There's a super idea—not! "No, we're planning to take it easy," I said vaguely. "Sage has kept pretty busy lately so we're not doing anything more exciting than grill steaks, sit on our deck, and watch the fireworks from home."

"*Booooring*! You guys need to live a little. Well, I'd better try to catch Heather before I hit the slots and get lucky. Thanks."

"Wait! Should we expect a visit from you?"

"Nope; not this time, sorry, bro." *Click.* Dead air. One minute, Vegas was calling; the next, Vegas hung up.

Tossing the phone aside, I mused, *What's the famous motto?* before muttering without explanation: "What happens in Vegas, stays in Vegas." *Please, God: let it be true.* I wanted no more Associated Press pictures of my brother doing anything.

Sage reached for the alarm just as it began its 5:30 blare, slapping it silent. "*That* was an interesting beginning to our day," she said with mild irony.

I stared at the ceiling and processed the blur of information. "Sage, let's run away. Not to Vegas, not to any place where the Fourth is a big deal. Just away. To a place where nobody knows our names."

"Like an *un*-Cheers sort of place?"

"Precisely. Anywhere we're not likely to hear about Gull and anybody, or Gull doing anything."

"I'll pack a lunch; you pack suitcases," Sage said wryly as she swung out of bed to begin a day that, Sunday or not, had no room for worries about our siblings—just concerns about cost over-runs, unions, and such. The Edens would not be running away.

Belatedly changing my office calendar from June to July, I began the new month by fleshing out the storyline for Book #17. Murder would come to Milford via a mining story. As for a two-word title? I weighed possibilities, but nothing was firm.

When Sage returned home that afternoon, she replaced her usual greeting with, "Okay, I can't stand it. Unless you heard more from Gull today, I'm going to call Heather and see what's up with those two."

But Heather wasn't answering her cell. For that matter, neither was Gull. I know that for a fact; I had tried.

It took all evening to reach Heather. When Sage finally did, Heather wasn't perturbed that we had given her number to Gull. She was more upset about Sage "checking up" on her. "I'm a big girl, Sage. If Gull and I want to have a relationship, it's up to us. We're all grown up now, you know."

"Are you? Having a relationship, I mean?" Sage dared to ask, blazing right past her sister's rebuke with a disregard that left me chomping nervously on the last ice cube from my sweaty glass.

Amazingly, Heather let down her guard. "Gull is, well, it wasn't as much fun as you'd think it'd be to have wild-and-crazy Gull pop into view. But we ate some great food, drank some fabulous drinks, and then he said goodbye and *poof*, he was gone."

"Really? Well, that's Gull living up to his middle name, once again," Sage said vaguely.

"Huh? Oh, got it: Swift!" She laughed. "Hey, thanks for worrying, but I can take care of myself, even with someone like Gull."

"I know," Sage said soothingly.

I hoped so. The whole episode made me jumpy.

The next day I drove Sage to Cedar City's airport where she boarded a plane for a sure-to-be-tense meeting in Salt Lake City. From the care she gave to packing, I knew what her time would be like: bleak enough to require her favorite suit, the lucky blouse, the good-luck necklace, and shoes worn the day she had landed her first high-powered job and now kept in reserve for head-butting sessions.

Sage would return noon-ish on Tuesday, the third. Until then, the biggest things on my agenda were making red-potato salad for our quiet celebration of our country's birthday, and deciding what to name Book #17. Considering the naming upheaval over ON TRACK becoming OFF TRACK, I was surprisingly ambivalent about titles this time around.

Walking through the surreally quiet and decidedly elegant Cedar City airport, I got an idea that had zilch to do with book titles. It required visiting Cedar City Public Library before going home to lonely rooms and an even lonelier bed.

I was glad to dawdle in Cedar City for a while. Logging on to a public-use computer at the library, I soon had two phone numbers at my disposal and went outside to make the calls from a shaded bench.

The first number that I dialed flipped over to an impersonal message-taking company and I declined to leave either a name or phone number so Leif Schwartz could return my call "at his earliest convenience."

The next call went to Greene Phillips: the guy holding the camera for that unsettling photograph. He didn't act surprised to get a call about his picture. "In fact . . ." he imbued the words and subsequent pause with such unwarranted mystique I wanted to slap him, "that shot sure ruffled a few feathers!"

This had to be Greene's first brush with fame; his photo reached AP–attention *only* because of Leif's connections. But I decided to let someone else do the honors of whacking him down to size.

Finally, I halted Greene's monologue on his sudden fame and anticipated fortune with a question that caught him off-guard. I had no interest in speculating on who the man in the photo was, nor was I eager to suggest (which, I inferred from his veiled remarks, those feather-ruffled birds were chirping about) that, in future photo-ops, he aim for more than Odessa's bountiful cleavage. Nor did I yearn to talk cameras, lens, or resolution.

What I wanted to know was simple: "Tell me, Greene: Where was Ms Woolden-Landis headed?"

That jolted him off-script. "Chicago, I suppose, since she was at American Airlines." A brief pause, then he regained his condescending attitude: "Other choice is Northwest Airlines to the Twin Cities."

Being well acquainted with the Rochester airport, I knew all that, so I interrupted with, "Did she have a connecting flight out of Chicago?"

"Huh? Uh, I'm not sure." He sounded less cocky, but it didn't last long. "Does it make a difference?" he asked petulantly.

"Maybe." *Don't try to out-mystique me, kid,* my tone said. I knew he was frantically trying to figure out what major chunk of The Rest of the Story he'd missed. He didn't ask the question that had to be looming in his brain: *Is there photo-potential?*

"Details, Greene, details. They make or break you, every time. Have a good day."

I disconnected, never having identified myself by either my real or penname. Greene Phillips was as green as his name not to have realized the *Identify-your-source* detail was vital in any conversation.

9

"Think of it as advertising," Sage proposed. She held Mom's second unnerving mailing, which had been at the Post Office upon my return from the airport the day before. I had practically memorized the contents. "Especially if the public sees the tie-in. Remember what you always claim, 'Even *bad* publicity is publicity.' I predict zooming sales!"

With Sage's briefcase and carry-on bag lodged in the seat behind us, we breezed along Highway 130, having just crested the summit between Cedar City and Minersville. That was usually important since it meant we had cell-phone coverage again. But, with my gal beside me after a two-day separation, the last thing on my mind was using the phone.

"I predict a witch-hunt for Kiel Nede: the author who knows too much," I said glumly. "That kind of publicity I can do without, thank you. You see what the article says: 'Similarities between events and the thinly disguised story by Kiel Nede are too close to ignore.' That pesky reporter never tried to ignore anything; right now he's probably scouring OFF TRACK for more clues."

"Always nice to gain a new reader," Sage quipped, adding, "Sorry," when I frowned. "Not a joking matter." She read the lengthy clipping aloud while I played with dash buttons: fan, radio, volume control, temperature. My mind moved faster than her voice, creating a cacophonic mess in my head.

Our short-lived respite from Haze-Eden mailings had ended with two unusually flat envelopes of news that set off mental warning flares like the ones truckers put out when they break down. First, the suggestive black-and-white shot of Gull and Honey; second, the accusative article Sage held.

What I longed to know was, who suggested a tie-in between these facts and my fiction? And when did *fact* become so loosely defined? What happened to investigation preceding assumption?

Sage shifted toward me. "In OFF TRACK, you killed a fictional Howler character. According to this article, the flesh-and-blood Bulldog is missing and foul play is suspected. But this does *not* mean Kiel Nede wrote the murderer's guidebook! Don't follow Leif Schwartz's weird assumptions like a lemming leaping into the sea. You know the truth!"

"I have a real bad feeling about this." I caught my reflection in the rearview mirror. I looked like a guy who had seen a lot of battles with few survivors. *War is hell*, my visage said.

"Let's not borrow trouble, okay?" Sage insisted, refolding the article and replacing it in the envelope. "It's a given that Haze will keep us in the loop. The photographer—Phillip Greene or Greene Phillips or *whatever*—said not-so-sweet Honey bought a ticket to Chicago. Could be, she's shopping, not missing at all. Everyone's been so doggone eager to be rid of The Bulldog, they jumped to conclusions."

"And Gull just happened to stand behind her? Also buying a ticket to Chicago? No big leap there."

"True, but thanks to his crack-of-dawn phone call, we know *he* had a connecting flight to Las Vegas."

Shaking my head, I countered her logic: "But we don't know why he decided to fly, not drive."

"After driving all those lonely, empty miles to see us as often as he has, I guess I'd start flying, too."

I felt downright grumpy and it didn't help to be required by law to slow down in Minersville where townsfolk actually kept livestock in fenced-in yards. God forbid we'd hit a four-legged milk machine.

In my ill-tempered mood, I went even slower than obligated, daring a cow to lumber into our path. I welcomed a quarrel with a testy herdsman who'd blame me for maiming the inevitably pricey animal. I envisioned dollar signs followed by big numbers.

"People fly all the time," Sage said calmly, ending my imagined human-bovine confrontation. She dropped kisses on my right hand's knuckles. "Hey, good news! The Muckity-Mucks think I'm doing such a swell job; they ordered me to take a few days off, starting with the Fourth. I'll still go in to work for a couple hours, holiday or not, but how 'bout if we just lollygag our way through the rest of the weekend?" She waggled her eyebrows in synchrony.

I truly was delighted to think I'd have Sage all to myself. It just didn't sound like it from my growled "Sure." Thankfully, she's not the type to return in-kind what she gets from her sullen and testy guy. Sweetness lingered after her final knuckle-kiss.

Reaching into the back seat to unzip her bag, she brought out the pillow-front she was cross-stitching in desert hues. It would someday grace our sofa, but I could tell it had entertained her on both flights, based on the progress she had made.

Not for the first time, I wondered if I should take up needlework. *Cheaper than therapy, and with visible results, every time.*

Back home, Sage opted for a bubble bath and I drifted toward my office, jumpy as a windy-day kite. Even the New Yorker's back-page cartoons in need of captions couldn't distract me.

I knew I was guilty of borrowing trouble, but that didn't stop me from logging on to the Rochester Post Bulletin website for the scoop on The Bulldog's purported disappearance.

First-hand knowledge did nothing to settle my nerves. I spun my desk chair around and chewed my lower lip. My eyes settled on the brass plate affixed to the frame on the cheap corkboard which I kept as a sentimental carryover from early-writer days.

The plaque spelled out EZEKIEL EDEN. It was a gift from Mother Muse to celebrate my first bestseller.

In her Hazy-ness Mom had missed that *Kiel Nede* was the critics' choice.

Tacked beneath the nameplate were eight index cards labeled with the familiar headings crucial to each of my novels: TITLE. SETTING. CHARACTERS. CRIME/MYSTERY. TENSION/PLOT. TWISTS, TURNS, & THEORIES. INVESTIGATION. ENDING. Eight vital steps to move a story from brainstorm to book. In the beginning stages of each new thriller, I added cards to the columns as ideas bubbled to the surface.

Did I now need to add a ninth card labeled POTENTIAL PROBLEMS WITH WRITING A STORY BASED ON ANYTHING HAZE SENDS for future books? The entries expanding on such a heading could list all sorts of things: *death-of-a-dream . . . lawsuits . . . prison terms . . . enemies . . .* They'd only be the beginning.

Sage appeared in the office doorway. Her reading glasses did double-duty as a headband, but left a few strands of still-damp hair poking out in odd places. She looked lovely. Predictably, my gaze dropped to ankle-bones connecting to hip-bones . . . *Dang it, where's my legendary concentration?*

"Oh-oh; still stewing over the missing Bulldog and possible connections to OFF TRACK, hmm?" She cocked her head and teased, "Is Kiel Nede gonna hop a train, vowing never to write another word?"

"Not many other ways out of Milford for those seeking fast getaways without tread marks leaving clues," I griped, but immediately repented. "Just let me sit here being morose and rattled, and out-of-sorts for a little longer. Then, I'll snap out of it. Scout's honor."

I whipped off the proper salute. She winked.

As I watched her retreating backside (a sight that usually drew me like a moth to a light) a blip of chatter about Book #4 with Jay Leno on The Tonight Show sprang to mind. He'd asked me what inspired Raven's entanglements. Good question, but not one I felt comfortable discussing in front of cameras. The truth was taboo for public knowledge: nearly three decades of fabulous love-making with my wife. I'm a private guy about such matters.

In this life, we should expect toil and trouble. But the Powers-That-Be often bless us with—I flinched, as if hearing Grandma Eden's rebuke: *"Ezekiel!"* and quickly amended my thoughts—okay: *God* blesses us with gifts beyond anything we deserve. Sage was the best of God's multiple gifts to me. I didn't deserve even her presence in my life, let alone the added bonus of our knock-your-socks-off private escapades between our bed sheets. Trust me: I'm a one-footed guy with miniscule physical appeal.

Sage alone had the ability to shake me loose when life bogged me down. Only she had the wherewithal to rekindle flames when creativity's coals went cold. She empowered me to delve into Raven's dark side and crime's harsh realities and somehow emerge unstained. All that from a woman's love. *Whew.*

It required a few deep breaths before I could focus again. Several tasks required my undivided attention before decadence in the bedroom was allowed. However, I knew that particular brand of decadence would cure what ailed me much faster than staring at the computer screen with its blinking cursor.

I encapsulated the messy situation and my vague fears in an e-mail to John. I knew better than to think it would be any easier to play catch-up if the proverbial (*Yes, Grandma Eden, I'll watch my language*) stinky-stuff ever hit the fan. Six attempts ended up in the computer's trash before I condensed my sorry state of affairs to three bullets:

- Succumbing to Haze's behests, I wrote a thriller based on the much publicized conflict in Rochester MN involving a railroad and a famous medical facility. In OFF TRACK, the corpse is the railroad's most vocal advocate
- Following publication, the real-life woman (represented by my fictional corpse) disappears. Local reporter sees OFF TRACK's plot as possible solution to alleged crime
- If corpse is found and manner of death resembles my plot, it could get messy; attachment establishes how I view the links between facts (the Rochester news story) and fiction (OFF TRACK)

All that remained was to write the promised account. How hard could it be? It was just words, and words are my buddies.

I walked to the bookshelf where my collection of Kiel Nede books resided at eye level. Fifteen in-print books meant I have fired off over two million words. Doesn't seem humanly possible. And, more astonishing, people like Milford's librarian clamor for more. I ran the pad of my thumb along the row of spines as if playing a fifteen-stringed instrument. Never before had they sung such a dirge-like song.

To my knowledge, no one in the real world ever died in precisely the manner in which my fictional bad guys accomplish their heinous deeds. I always figure the least I can do in writing a mystery is be creative, thus, I studiously avoid lifting my *Who-Did-What-to-Whom-and-How* ideas from the news. Fifteen times, Lady Luck smiled on that decision. But this time did Meddling Mom divert Lady Luck?

I've from known from Book #1 that only the foolhardy base a book on current events. So why did I turn my back on first instincts? Would Lady Luck turn fickle? Like my fictional victims, I recognized that what gnawed at my innards was fear.

Suddenly, I felt a need to wander where the wind could sort out messy thoughts. Sage looked up from her needlework when I entered her line of vision. "Wanna take a walk with Haze Eden's soon-to-be-infamous son?" She was on her feet in an instant.

We had learned our lessons about pesky ground squirrels and their toe-catching holes. A lingering memory of a snarling badger intent on intimidation prompted Sage to grab the sturdy walking stick we kept in case such a confrontation reoccurred.

As we moved clockwise around the perimeter of our property, the imprints my crutches left in the sunbaked sandy soil closely resembled the entrances to the dozens of small-animal burrows we passed.

Following the narrow dirt road running parallel to the fence line, I commented on the hardy weeds cropping up between the faint tire marks. They'd soon be high enough to catch on the underside of my truck. Knowing there's nothing like physical labor to dismiss troubles, I vowed aloud, "I'll give those weeds the ol' heave-ho real soon."

Directly west of the house, we came to an unsightly pile of concrete slabs of varying sizes. Wind had half-buried some with sand, others jutted at dangerous angles that could send an unsuspecting nighttime jogger sprawling.

"This must be where cement goes to die!" Sage laughed. "If I thought there was a chance we'd have success, I'd say we should bury it all." Her voice's familiar lilt led to our scoffing in unison: "How hard can it be?" and "How long can it take?" and "How much can it cost?" The unvoiced answers should be, *"Dreadfully hard,"* and *"Forever-and-a-day,"* and *"Three times more money than brains."*

This time, we skipped the traditional responses. "Have you forgotten our fish pond disaster in Denver, Sage? All those dying fish? The struggling plant life? Mucky water? Any of that ring a bell?"

She shrugged. "That was different; we were so young and naïve then! But *this* we could transform, put it to use somehow, give it more of a Japanese-garden look than the dump it resembles now."

"Must I remind you, this is Utah? We live in a high mountain desert, not exactly a garden spot!"

The railroad tracks between the edge of Milford and the properties bordering our forty-acre stretch diverted us with a restful panorama. One train was beginning its journey north to Salt Lake City and all points east. We noted the final cars of another train on its way to Las Vegas and, eventually, the coast.

Las Vegas. I banished it from my thoughts.

The northbound train required five engines to move the numerous double-stacked containers along the straightaway. The engineer signaled his approach to the only crossing within our sight. The whistle's sound floated over the open spaces, losing its capacity to startle by the time it reached our ears.

"Nice, isn't it?" Sage murmured, nestling against my shoulder as we relaxed on the bench we had positioned precisely where it gave us the best western view. "Whenever I hear a train whistle, it's like that Roto-Rooter ad claims: our nasty troubles go down the drain."

Make that, down the track," I amended, but my nod bumped her head in harmony with her intent. We loved the train. Before Amtrak dropped its line across southwestern Utah, we often rode the rails (legitimately) to visit Sage's hometown and parents. "Whadda think?" I said. "Are we due for an Amtrak trip?" Hearing the whistle from the freight train going places in the night left me antsy to be aboard.

"You *did* write Haze's 'railroady mystery,' so a whistle-stop booksigning tour seems appropriate." She squeezed my arm excitedly. "I see it now: Kiel Nede and his happy wife take up residence in the Club Car each evening, where he reads from his latest. Grown men shiver and stylish women bite their fingernails when Raven enters the story."

I smiled; Sage loves booksignings, making every effort to attend at least one per title, although doing so was often inconvenient for her at work. I knew her mind was now interweaving a book event with a train trip: a win-win situation for both of us.

Her whimsy amused me, even though I worried. *Would posters say 'Meet the Author!' or 'Hanging at Noon!'?* When I voiced that dismal question, she tweaked my nose and kissed me soundly. I reacted, but hardly with vigor.

"Don't be a Gloomy Gus! Time to get you home, Stud-muffin." Waggling her eyebrows like a lusty Groucho Marx, she traced a path with a tantalizingly light touch from my elbows to my fingertips. Then, she moonwalked away. The unvoiced implications of her suggestion seemed a better way to welcome The Fourth than being an out-of-season Scrooge.

You likely don't have a clue as to what I really look like, so you'll just have to believe me when I reveal only that this decidedly *un*-studly worrywart of a mystery writer slipped between cool sheets with the breathtakingly beautiful CEO of MVCH, humbly and blissfully aware he is the luckiest man on Planet Earth—even if niggling thoughts about lawyers lingered.

But some things take precedence. That's the way to keep a marriage humming.

10

Sage slept like someone who (quoting her on past occasions of such bliss) "touched stars and lived to tell about it." I lay beside her, savoring the shifting light patterns of one day becoming the next, and entertained lofty thoughts about my sexual prowess. I deemed such vanity allowable since I knew, once again, my gal had enjoyed poetic flights midst celestial spheres.

I had dodged a few shooting stars myself during our wild journey, leaving me weak-kneed—a tricky condition for someone minus a foot. Hopping from bed to window, I leaned against the sill and stared at the moon. Birds' night-songs and a distant coyote's mournful wails serenaded me with discordant tunes and a total disregard for matched rhythms.

The sky was luminous, dotted by a million points of light. Until we moved to Utah, I had never seen the Milky Way. That night, it seemed close enough to touch and come away with cream on my fingertips. But maybe I was still floating.

I glanced at the bed; Sage was out cold, her smile a sliver-moon like what prompts parents to tell their kids, *"Look for the swinging Man in the Moon!"*

Swinging myself though our library with only the muffled sounds of rubber-tipped crutches on carpet marking my passage, I approached my office. Soon, I was hunkered in like a hibernating bear, completely unconcerned about the world beyond my cave.

I worked through most of the remaining night hours, fueled by my wife's feminine charms and empowered by her never-wavering confidence that I would emerge unscathed. As Sage slept, I wrote in a frenzy that made me glad Spellcheck functioned well because accuracy fled the premises while I pursued Proof of Innocence.

My mission in the early hours of the Fourth was to compile the complete history of how I came to write OFF TRACK. Mentally, I titled it "A Personal Declaration of Independence from Threats." *A pre-emptive defense, of sorts,* I told myself.

It utilized a simple format of two columns. One, I headed FACTS and the other, FICTION. I had kept Haze's newspaper clippings filed chronologically, with all key points highlighted upon receipt. This made it easy, under FACTS, to carefully enumerate sequential details of the Rochester railroad scandal, reaching far back into the earliest years as I alternately typed and flipped through the piles.

Finishing that twelve-page report, I opened the OFF TRACK document. Using the computer's Find function enabled me to fill the FICTION column with details of how each FACT-column entry either had been used factually or altered. Many points from FACTS had no counterpart in FICTION, and vice versa.

Maybe burning the midnight oil was a waste of electricity and sleep, but the final product let me breathe easier as I could see how far I had strayed from the actual story behind The Railroad versus The Rest of The World.

It was likely premature to say "Hurray!" but I did so, feeling relieved and reprieved. There would be no hanging-at-noon: I was innocent of all but writing "another bloody good story," which I said aloud, echoing a British reviewer who had employed that phrase at least a half-dozen times on my behalf.

John would groan when he logged on after the holiday and got my cyber-missive. 'Sorry, John," I said, attaching the file of my night's work to the earlier draft e-mail with its three bullets. Morning was peeking through night's clouds when I clicked Send, and returned to bed.

Easing in next to the unmoving, faintly-smiling Sage, I burrowed under the light blanket and drifted in-and-out of a delayed and restless sleep.

I awakened several hours later only because Sage showered me with kisses. Just before I thought I would explode, she touched my lips in a tantalizing kiss that mined our souls. I wondered idly if my readers had any idea how very spicy a life Kiel Nede led. *Raven needs a woman*, I mused, *but that's never gonna happen.*

"How long did you work last night?" Sage murmured, her breath tickling my ear.

"Oh, a couple hours," I fibbed shamelessly, "and then I came back to bed and—"

". . . worked in your head," she finished, grinning. She stretched before padding into the bathroom to get ready for work. Yes, it was a holiday, but she claims to find an island of sanity in a deserted office on a day when much of the outside world assumes no one is on the premises.

Sage would work a few hours before I joined her for the much-anticipated Milford Fourth of July Parade that would march right past the Horn Silver Hotel. We would watch the parade together, and I'd return home while she finished her tasks.

I don't know how Sage survives. She rejuvenates herself with just one day considered truly *off*. Part of the secret was that, whenever possible, we protected weekends like Fort Knox. We took drives, heading off with cameras and picnic lunches, but often were home in time to eat at our favorite place: our back yard, balcony or patio, depending on where we lived.

After Sage left for work, I made plans she would love. I loaded two chairs into the pickup and then began to assemble a picnic lunch. The refrigerator yielded ham and cheese, crusty rolls, assorted crudités, red potato salad that looked worthy of its own website, and plump peanut butter cookies.

I moved two steaks from freezer to refrigerator to thaw. I planned to grill our supper, so I checked a favorite cookbook's index to find a remembered recipe for baked apples with a nutty center, which gave me two reasons to heat the oven for the cheesy biscuits that go so well with a simple tossed salad.

Leaving sun-tea brewing atop a garden post, I headed to town. Sage and I joined those already seated in lawn chairs outside the chiropractor's office on Main Street's shady side. Soon, Scouts and Veterans carrying flags, three gleaming fire trucks, appropriately costumed horseback riders, more ATVs than we could count, a dozen cheerleaders hanging off pickups' tailgates, and candy-tossing adults on several floats all rolled, pranced or marched along the street. Children leaped into the fray to grab candy, which they dumped into bags only when their bulging cheeks got too full for more.

I had rarely felt as American as I did sitting on Milford's Main Street on the Fourth of July.

When an ancient, well-buffed ambulance sounded its wheezing siren to end the parade, I kissed Sage goodbye, tossed our chairs back into the truck, and drove away over asphalt that was now a-glitter with candy trampled by horses' hooves, human feet, and multiple wheels. It would require a high-powered dousing to clean Main Street of its sugary high.

By the time Sage returned home, I had enjoyed a thirty-minute power nap and researched several interesting ways to dispose of a villain in Book #17. I felt quite pleased with myself for putting senseless worries about OFF TRACK aside.

Sage cheered my plans for the rest of our day's agenda. After she changed into jeans and what she calls her "snake-stompin' boots," we were off.

I had selected Newhouse—a ghost town—for our rendezvous with nature, but warned her: "Just b'cuz it's within spittin' distance of the Horn Silver mine does *not* mean you're allowed to think about work in the similarly named building!" Along the way, we plugged quarters into the newspaper stands outside Penny's Diner and continued west.

We soon unloaded our chairs for the second time that day, explored a bit, and positioned ourselves with the peak to our right as we dug into lunch and newspapers with a miner's zeal.

The only human sounds were news snippets we read aloud, or our laughter as we recalled a girl's indignation at losing her sucker to a dog during the parade, or random talk about upcoming plans. That, and my snores as I succumbed to the results of being (if you believe Sage) "a duffer too old to stay up much of the night and expect to function the next day" made it a fine time.

Since we'd been out of cell range, we weren't surprised to have both phones beep as we reached town mid-afternoon. It was scared-sounding Mom with the same message repeated almost verbatim:

> "I don't know how you get Rochester news on your computers, but *do it* after you get this message, and call me ASAP."

I breezed through Milford without thought of speed limits or concern for signs about Children at Play.

Arriving home, our disbelief soon became gut-roiling apprehension as we logged on to Rochester's top-of-the-hour newscast that buffered in with skips-and-jumps on the computer screen.

"This is bad." I ran my hand over my stubbled head. *Time for a shave,* I thought, only to chastise myself: *Hardly the time to worry about bristles.*

I fidgeted; a long-forgotten cup of coffee tottered, tilting before I could grab it. Liquid splattered, thankfully only across the papers scattered across my desk, missing the computer altogether. I dabbed at the mess with what was closest at hand, which was papers. Not a successful strategy. Sage didn't even snort at my efforts. We were both too staggered by what was rolling off the reporter's tongue:

> "A break in the case that has stymied southern Minnesota law officials for the past few days comes from avid mystery lovers. The Police Tip-Line has been deluged by calls from readers of OFF TRACK, which is the latest hit by author Kiel Nede. This mystery/thriller offers what officials consider too many clues that are eerily consistent with the recent disappearance and presumed death of a Rochester woman, Ms Honey Odessa Woolden-Landis.

"The latest information indicates a more first-hand than fictional knowledge of both the case and its potential outcome. Local law enforcement officials have expressed interest in talking to Kiel Nede. One informed source indicates that efforts to reach Mister Nede through his agent are in progress.

"Nede named his fictional victim Betty Ullallee Daugherty—the initial letters and sounds of which alert readers see easily adapting to B-ull-dog.

"Throughout the local railroad fracas, Ms Woolden-Landis' moniker has been 'The Bulldog.' Nede boldly opted to name his character 'The Howler.' This choice requires even less sleuthing to see links to the initials for Ms Woolden-Landis' full and literal name, and has officials interested in the manner of death and discovery Mister Nede employed in OFF TRACK.

"Officials around the country are taking a closer look at unsolved murders which may follow storylines in previous books that Nede set in their locales."

Three decades' accomplishments and struggles whooshed away in one fell swoop. *Fell swoop.* Interesting phrase; the first documented use was in

MACBETH and meant *suddenly*. I shook my head, disgusted. Sage claims I evoke trivia at inappropriate times—like now, with my world imploding.

Inhaling sharply, I determined to apply wisdom and clear-headed thinking to the matter at hand. It's what Raven did when a devilish situation reached the make-or-break point: Divide and conquer. Divide the mess into components, conquer the foes.

Divide the Mess. Workable chunks. First, why did I believe Minnesota reporters could brandish swords capable of wielding a death blow to a Utah resident's career?

On the screen, the news moved quickly along to other stories. I exited the TV station's website and clicked over to the Post Bulletin's on-line presence. Sure enough, their story ranked high on the early edition. Numbly I turned on the printer and sent the grim news skipping from screen to paper.

Grabbing the first page as the printer released it, I read the headline. Emitting an anguished moan, I pinged my middle finger off my thumb, striking the paper and denting a bold assertion: "Mystery Writer Gave Too Many Clues—Traps Himself." *Good luck proving it,* I scoffed, punctuating the dark sentiment with a disdainful snort and another finger-ping against the paper.

With Sage reading Page 2 over my shoulder, I forced myself to think logically. *Inhale, exhale; relax each muscle.* Okay; fact: I write mystery-thrillers, not true crime. Next fact: it's fiction, folks! I glanced at the byline to isolate the next fact, quite sure whose feeble hand held the weapon with which he intended to bring me to my knees.

That's when I noticed ASSOCIATED PRESS.

The two words made Leif Schwartz' name on the byline seem inconsequential. Divide the Mess took a nosedive out of the good zone. The Answer stripped off its mask, snarling with a nasty grin: *Gotcha*.

Conquer the Foes. Yeah, right. It was no longer me against a foe fourteen hundred miles away; it was (the ol' one-fell-swoop) little David against the AP's Goliath. Another of Grandma-Eden's Bible stories dredged from murky memories. No way could five smooth stones take my giant down.

Just like little Zeke had done, big Zeke sucked in his breath in reminiscence of an ominous giant and one little boy with his slingshot.

Thoughts tumbled, raced and roamed. I imagined John and Maggie refusing to take my calls. Even worse: booting me out of their lives. Who'd blame them? Not me.

I imagined myself in a courtroom. I envisioned my lawyer walking out in disgust while even the jury gasped.

In my very real-and-present life, Sage left the room. "I think I'm going to be sick." I knew I should follow her to offer comfort, to reassure her everything would be fine. But my legs refused to work. Besides, was it prudent to add blatant lying to my burgeoning list of offenses?

Nauseating fears of a Court withholding justice dimmed in imagined bright lights of late-night talk shows where I would verbally flail at the badgering host's accusations. Thankfully this, also, faded . . . only to be replaced with visions of needing to masquerade as Everyday-Joe just to leave home and return, unmolested, with a jug of milk.

A non-Biblical Grandma Eden quotation emerged from my worries' sludge: *It's an ill wind that blows no good.* I don't credit her for first uttering such wise words. Long ago I researched that arcane detail before abridging it into a book title. The originator was John Heywood who lived in the 1500s (trivia, again; sorry) long before copyright was a problem. So I named a book ILL WINDS without concern over lawsuits.

But today I would have argued with ol' Heywood. The ill wind coming off my sixteenth book seemed incapable of blowing anything remotely good into my life.

It was a writer's worst nightmare: something I created had come to life or, more accurately, to *death.* I want people to read my books, not replicate them. I write the plots and call it fiction. Now, if a pejorative article and TV newscast were to believed, some unscrupulous cad truly had played it out in real life and walked away clean as a whistle.

Clean as a whistle . . . knock it off, Zeke! I refused to be like Nero making music while Rome burns; I needed to aim the largest hose right at the inferno threatening my chosen vocation, not sitting idly by analyzing pithy sayings. See what I mean? Even my self-rebuke isn't without detours.

Merely thinking about what inevitably lay ahead made me tired. More tired than I could ever remember being, even after digging fencepost holes beneath Utah's blistering high-altitude sun. But it was beyond tired. I recognized the churning in my gut as panic: a condition I have described countless times when my characters run amuck with bad guys on their tails.

Sage returned, looking a little green around the gills. *Idiom: undefined, but generally understood to mean feeling ill.* This time I didn't even reprimand myself for mental meanderings. Instead, I pulled her into my arms and we swayed, rocking ourselves into a place of shallow, wordless comfort.

Beyond her shoulder, I saw motion; a shadow darted past the window. I slow-danced Sage into a position that let us watch a raven swoop down to feast. *Soon vultures will be circling me.* I knew it, having observed it happen to other writers, but I never dreamed *I* would be a journalistic buzzard's lunch.

"Could you get us some iced tea?" I asked. Sage nodded mutely and slipped from my arms.

Once again, Leif Schwartz, the dogged reporter credited for reporting much of the decade-long furor that lay behind OFF TRACK's storyline, was in top form. Scooping the story . . . that's what journalists call it, right? Guess who was flopping around in the shovel's scoop this time?

What a waste of time, talking to the photographer. I should have left Greene Phillips alone and nabbed Leif the moment I saw his byline beneath Phillips' damning photo that had spawned this whole new media frenzy.

Finger-pointing left three digits aimed back at me: the too-clever-for-his-own-good author with his oh-so-witty character-naming notions. I had chortled when I came up with what "alert readers" had sleuthed out: Betty Ullallee Daugherty *was* named that goofy combination of names because it *did* bring Rochester's Bulldog to mind.

There was no denying it: My 'Howler' nickname *was* based on Honey Odessa Woolden-Landis' initials. I had scoffed at Rochester for not seeing the potential when they latched on to The Bulldog for her moniker, instead. Now it all felt like junior-high humor—mere drivel; beneath me.

And to think such nonsense as a character's name would bring me down. Numbly I accepted a glass of iced tea from Sage.

11

I respected Leif Schwartz's research abilities; it would not be long before he found the real guy hiding behind my pseudonym. Few have expended any effort, but Leif was now motivated. I could be the Big Story of his career. A buzzard's lunch.

The current news assured that both of my names would soon be irrevocably linked to the crime. "This can't be good," I repeated dourly.

Sage didn't even ask *"What?"*

Over the past months, Milford had grown on me with its plucky pride, numerable curiosities, and laudable ability to emerge fighting after repeated economic upsets. But now my adopted hometown would . . . What *would* they do?

A movie played in my mind, starring:

Fable Hursh . . . Laynie and Waylen . . . and feisty, freckled Uly with an adorable gap between his two front teeth.

Jacey Belk . . . and Abbott—*Did sharing his story on our trip buy loyalty to me?* I doubted it would, when push came to shove. If Shakespeare wrote the tragedy my life may soon become, his counsel would be: *Two loads of gravel do not a friendship make.*

Mathia Meland . . . Dale and Darcia, Kash and Kasey—*Double the flavor, double the fun?* That was a chewing-gum commercial's catch-phrase, but for a guy with a dual identity it was more like *Double the trouble, and no fun at all.*

Cale Ulseth . . . and his cute-as-a-button sister Suvie; their hard-working mom Valarie . . . oh, and let's not forget Rosco—The Law—and his furry partner, the crime-sniffing Nimrod.

Would a prosecutor pull the teens' names from OFF TRACK's Acknowledgements to gain witnesses against me? I groaned several times, unable to speak. Misinterpreting my moans, Sage reread the article as if hoping its message would change.

Even with intricate plots invented for sixteen mystery-thrillers, I could not conceive of the horrors a small mining-and-railroad town could inflict to make an award-winning author's life miserable. It made no difference that Sage ranked high in residents' esteem.

No, I'd be scum, especially since I had involved four wonderful kids in my alleged (oh, yeah; I use only the right terminology) transgressions.

Earnest faces scrolled like an inescapable mental slide show: Cale; Fable; Mathia; Jacey. Poor kids; they hadn't signed on for a witch hunt when they took my class. Even if I did everything I could to keep them out of the spotlight, I was helpless to prevent their education in things beyond their understanding. My knee bumped the drawer still stuffed with copies of their papers. The assignments showed creative thinking, good ideas, significantly improved writing . . . and murder in the making.

I didn't assume the kids' razzle-dazzle memories of our Rochester trip with its in-studio interview and booksigning exhilaration would outweigh the shock and intensity of their Myster-E on trial.

I shuddered, pulling back from bleak musings long enough to wonder if I had ever shuddered before. My characters often shuddered. "Oh, you are pathetic, to thinking about your made-up world in the midst of such a real-world mess," I scolded myself. *Speaking of mess . . .*

Wetting a towel in the bathroom sink, I mopped up the forgotten spilled coffee, dumped soggy papers into the trash, and succumbed again to feelings of impending doom. For the first time since we moved to Utah, I was glad there wasn't a Milford newspaper.

Maybe Salt Lake City media would ignore the Associated Press story. *Yeah, right.*

Maybe Mom hadn't given every neighbor on her block a copy of my book. *Dream on.*

Maybe she hadn't called the leaders of a dozen book clubs in Olmsted County and convinced them all to put OFF TRACK next on their reading lists. *Who do you think you're kidding?*

Maybe major booksellers' shipments would be delayed. Surely books were already flying off the shelves, leaving gaping holes where Kiel Nede had once filled space. After all, nothing sells books like a scandal. *Is that how you want to get more money?*

With any luck, maybe it was the lowest-of-low stats for Leno and Letterman the nights they interviewed me after OFF TRACK's release. *Oh, there's a new definition of Claim to Fame, eh?*

Maybe the sun wouldn't come up tomorrow. *Give it up, Zeke; you're batting zero here.*

Maybe . . . *Enough with the maybes; they won't save me.*

Talk about brilliant title choices. The one Cale innocently devised, claimed the prize: OFF TRACK. My life was skidding so far off track I might not ever hear a train's whistle again.

I uncapped a highlighter to mark key points in the article, just like I had done with Mom's clippings. Highlighting made subsequent searches much easier, though it seemed highly unlikely that I would forget a single word this time.

Key points leaped off the page like children's taunts in a game of tag: *"Ha-ha; you're it!"* They ran so fast, I couldn't catch them. I was doomed to being *IT* for a very long time if the article's opening paragraphs were any indication:

> As readers of true-crime accounts know, a crime scene yields vast amounts of clues to the trained eye. Now, in a strange merger of fact with fiction, the authorities working on the Honey Odessa

Woolden-Landis case are following leads submitted by avid readers of bestselling author Kiel Nede's mystery/thrillers.

Fans say Nede's latest book, OFF TRACK bears an eerie resemblance to the real-life mystery unfolding in Rochester. A local woman, whom local pundits dubbed The Bulldog nearly a decade ago, has been missing long enough for her absence to be considered suspect.

Raven Crowley, the hero in multiple Kiel Nede thrillers, in OFF TRACK, finds the body of a missing woman (nicknamed The Howler: a thinly disguised match to Woolden-Landis' initials) in a setting remarkably similar to the caves in Rochester's Quarry Hill Park. Yesterday, officials roped off an area near the previously barricaded caves as their investigation continues . . .

"Idiots!" I exploded after my third rereading. "With only one brief visit, even four Utah teenagers know there's *no way* a body can be in those caves!" Seething, I resumed reading:

The search continues for the man in the photo of Ms Honey Odessa Woolden-Landis at the Rochester International Airport early on June 29. Anyone with information regarding the man's identity

is requested to notify the Olmsted County
Sheriff's Department. Tipsters calling the
Hot Line remain anonymous . . .

There was more, but I stopped reading. If the
pulsing in my ears was any indication, my blood
pressure was already off the charts.

I pounded the desk, sending pens and paperclips
flying. "Oh, sure; let's involve my family in this
whole sordid mess!"

In even more elaborate, damning detail than the
TV reports, Leif Schwartz' article spelled out several
corresponding points between the paper's depiction
of The Bulldog and my recreation of her character as
The Howler. Schwartz also enumerated key factors
he deemed *"direct tie-ins"* to *"the obvious and
ominous link between* OFF TRACK *and the story rising
off the streets of our hometown like a foul odor."*

I wouldn't argue with him about the stench; I felt
nauseous just reading about it. I was as dead as The
Bulldog was suspected to be. We could both be
presumed dead: The Bulldog without a trace (though
how long would *that* last?) and Kiel Nede/Zeke Eden
without a prayer.

Maybe I could adopt a new pseudonym, or pursue
a new type of story. How would I do with bodice-
ripper romances? No shudder, but I did feel bile rise
in my throat: a symptom I now also shared with my
characters.

Okay; no romances from Kiel Nede.

Maybe travel books? Heaven knows, I've seen enough of God's green earth to hold my own with that genre. But I'd need a new slant; something like Best Getaways for One-Footed Guys. That, also, didn't do it for me. I felt no adrenalin rush, although look where *that* had gotten me?

The vulture outside my office window rose with a furry bone dangling from his beak; I cringed.

Sage usurped my desk chair and began clicking through related stories from other sources. The printer whirred to life every few minutes, spitting out pages.

How did this happen? I needed to retrace my steps, even beyond my bulleted list of nonexistent tie-ins because, according to the news, someone would be calling with questions real soon. The downward spiral was inevitable: my life, my career and—*Please, God, no*—possibly even my marriage?

A chill snaked along my spine. I turned slowly and looked at Sage. Long before she became Mrs Ezekiel Eden, the beautiful, talented, and totally amazing Sage November Crowley was a Milfordian (Milfordite? There's a bit of unexplored trivia). Her loyalties to this plucky town run fierce and deep.

Am I a fool to hope, to believe her loyalty to me is fiercer and deeper?

Her last meeting with the Big-Wigs had been a rough one, but we had barely discussed it. That's how selfish I had become—so trapped in the hell of my own making I hadn't even inquired about what weighed heavily on the woman I adored. I need no help from the media; I disgust myself enough.

The results of my theoretical offense could make or break Sage's career if Milford decided they'd had enough of me and my outlaw ways. What are the odds of that? Another example of one fell swoop: one scandal; two unemployed Edens.

Maybe they'd settle for keeping Sage around as long as I was never to be seen again. A sentence to life in prison for me would certainly guarantee *that*.

"Let's go find a new place to explore," I told Sage a frustratingly grim quarter-hour later. "As long as we're near a computer, it's too tempting to keep clicking keys. The news won't change for the better until they get their heads out of the sand and start looking for the actual criminal. Let's drive 'til dusk, come home, grill steaks, and watch fireworks. Whadda say?"

With evident relief, she turned off the computer. "I say, 'Race you to the truck'!"

We reached the Pass Road turnoff and were rounding the curve that would get us to Highway 21 heading east to the Beaver Mountain range when my cell phone rang. Since I was in no mood to talk to anyone, I tossed the phone to Sage without even checking to see who was calling. If it was Mom (it could be; we hadn't returned her call) Sage would handle her better than I could at the moment.

12

The caller didn't discern the difference between my masculine growl and Sage's feminine "Hello?"

I heard Fable's inimitable voice clearly: "Fire by your house, Myster-E! We're on our way to help!"

"Fire?" I slammed on the brakes and jerked my head around. *Yes, fire!* Flames leaped in dramatic swirls, definitely in the region of our home.

Sage met my eyes in a split-second silent scream.

A Y-turn put us going in the opposite direction and I gunned it. Off to our left, two ATVs hurtled across the bumpy terrain toward our property.

Cale gripped the wheel of one machine with grim determination. Fable clung to his shoulders. Jacey, still wearing her Sunshine Market smock, bounced behind Mathia on the second ATV. Both girls' hair blew wildly as they chased after Cale and Fable.

Propelled by desperation, we covered the distance in record-breaking time. Billowing smoke, flying soot, and crackling embers shot skyward ahead of us. Leaping off the ATVs, which they parked a safe distance away, the kids joined us in a race around the house to where our backyard gave way to desert.

The fire was not on our property yet, but getting frighteningly close. The potential to get closer real soon was evident and paralyzing.

"Thanks for calling us, Fable." Panic strangled my voice; Sage squinted at me, her gaze asking, *"You okay?"*

My nod was a lie.

Watching flames ravage the landscape, we heard a power pole snap just beyond our fence line. It tilted; we all gasped. Nature was up-close and much too real. This was no big-screen conflagration.

Instantly, we were all in motion.

The kids scattered in search of the garden hoses I kept attached to faucets at strategic points around the property. Dragging hoses in a sprawling pattern to cover the most territory, they worked with amazing speed and concentration.

"Get your crutches, Myster-E! You might need them!" Jacey yelled over her shoulder, pulling a hose into position to aim at the north wall of the house. In seconds, Mathia had cranked open another spigot so Fable could spray the garage roof.

"Yeah, put everything important in your truck and drive it far away from the house," Cale called out. Like father, like son. The kid was clearly in charge.

Sage didn't argue. "I'm on it!" she yelled. The front door banged behind her.

My adrenalin rush slowed enough for me to think clearly. *Did anyone call in the fire?* Rather than waste time asking, I had the *9* of 9-1-1 punched on my cell phone when sounds of an engine running at full-throttle filled the air.

Looking to the west, I shaded my eyes. Within moments, Rosco leaped from his pickup. Close behind, a fire engine rumbled onto the property.

"We're staying, Dad," Cale called from the roof before Rosco said a word. His tone didn't invite argument. Using a ladder from the garage, he had hoisted himself over the gutters and now held a gushing hose. "We'll help, not get in the way," he added unnecessarily, drenching shingles closest to the fire.

And they did, hosing every inch of our house. I heard a yelp as Sage raced around inside to close windows.

While volunteer fire crews and their equipment arrived, the kids aimed garden hoses at the pergola, well house, garden shed, woodpiles, and workshop. Water sprayed off rooftops like a shower, giving the nearby sections of the rocky driveway a sheen before the parched ground sucked up the puddles.

Professional hoses snaked from tanks in readiness. Shovels and rakes, canisters of chemical sprays, and other paraphernalia came off fire trucks as members of the various teams donned their apparel, collected appropriate supplies, and assumed their duties. Little was said beyond essentials. They knew their stuff.

The air grew pungent with smoke, ash and scents I couldn't identify which, I assumed, were the odors of burnt desert undergrowth. Word came, via garbled voices, that crews and equipment currently doing a controlled burn between Beaver and Minersville were reassigned to help fight this wildfire now threatening to climb the mountain range. But despite additional human resources, nature seemed to be winning the battle.

Volunteer firefighters from Milford, Minersville, and Beaver dug a semi-circular fire wall to the east of our various structures. This preventive measure marked the path along which a leaping fire could do the most damage to personal property.

Helicopters clattered overhead on reconnaissance trips. Some returned to dump buckets of water lifted from the nearby water reclamation pond in feeble efforts to squelch the flames. Others skimmed low enough to gather on-line reports on the devastation and capture photographs for newspapers and TV.

Messages crackling from radios in trucks or hooked to hips made face-to-face communications nearly impossible. Crisp fire codes mingled with muffled radio codes, leaving the blaring and blurred data comprehensible only to the initiated.

Meanwhile, Sage packed the Volvo and pickup, determined to save everything possible. My dusty, trusty truck looked like a gypsy wagon with tubs stacked high, bags tucked low, and bags and boxes crammed into the seats. With this completed, Sage drove each vehicle away from the house, while Mathia jogged over to help her strap a tarp over the pickup's bed to protect against airborne sparks.

Rosco's fellow deputies arrived, called into duty by the situation's urgency as the fire increased in size and intensity. It consumed acres of nature's combustibles, pausing only to burp black smoke.

An exhausted firefighter pushed his helmet high enough to allow a swipe across his forehead. He looked toward the white-hot smoldering mountains and said somberly, "I've seen plenty of fires, but this one's *huge*. We're not making enough headway."

Empty of all but charred landscape, the stretches of burning land had been fenced long ago to mark otherwise indiscernible boundary lines. Now, those demarcations blocked easy access to all eastern points, whether privately owned or property under the Bureau of Land Management.

It was a logistical nightmare for those in charge. The turn-around area by our garage became Grand Central. It was soon the gathering place for all the officials who must determine how best to reach the fire zone.

The burn ate up vegetation at a furious and steady pace, chomping first north, and then south, chewing at the ten-mile line of power poles. One-by-one, the massive poles caught fire and toppled as if chopped off at the base by overly zealous beavers.

Winds changed, often dropping a piece of smoking debris at our feet. Just when the fire could have consumed our property in a heart-stopping westward resurgence, the wind shifted. As if fueled by a spark consuming a gas-soaked cord, the face of the nearby Yellow Banks rise changed to charcoal-grey while we watched, stunned.

My heartbeat surged, much like the blaze. Sage cried, "Oh, God!" It was prayer, not profanity.

I pulled her close, unable to speak. To come so close to losing things preciously deemed important, and then to discover everything I need was in my arms? Well, it was a life-changing moment. Let Leif and Greene do their worst; I had Sage. She was, is, and forever will be all I need.

Beet-faced firefighters needed refreshment, but had firm instructions: "Only Gatorade, on-duty."

We set out cold drinks for those without such restrictions, but that didn't address hunger. Carrot sticks, sliced apples, an easily replenished supply of my homemade bread topped with cheeses from Beaver's local dairy and the rest of our picnic ham, and a pan of quickly thawed brownies did so.

Six o'clock had come and gone. Several grimy, dog-tired, yellow-garbed firefighters were sprawled on lawn furniture on the pergola for a brief respite. That's when we all heard, "Wow! You really know how to get famous!"

Gull?

"Famous?" I spun to face the voice: *Yup; Gull.*

"Yeah! I was in Vegas, right?"

Compared to the rest of us, Gull looked fresh and crisp, like GQ Meets Huck Finn.

"So, I'm watching the casino's TV, and what do I see? My brother's house! A voice-over says it's Utah's biggest fire in history and it started here! Wow, huh? But they're saying the 'Milford Flat Fire,' Zeke. Didn't you tell me locals call it 'The Bench'? Lucky for me, I recognized your house, so a misnomer didn't keep me from hitting the road."

Hit the road? In what? He flew to Vegas.

Gull smoothly slid into his usual modus operandi: joking with the kids, telling Rosco he "may need to beg a favor if the Highway Patrol catch me!" and asking firefighters their names (especially the gals) under the guise of saying, "Let me help . . .'

Right. I couldn't quite see Gull dragging hoses around in the dirt or with shovel in-hand. Not looking as he did: male model waiting to face the bright lights of fame and stardom. But I didn't call him on his little charade. Live and let live, right?

Instead, I left him to his shenanigans and sought-out Rosco for an answer to a delayed query: "Who reported the fire?"

"A woman driving in from north of the airport saw lightning strike. Soon afterwards, a guy at the copper mine called about a downed power pole."

A dust swirl shifted our attention to the rough road that paralleled the long line of power poles connecting the geothermal plant with its distant clients. Speculation ran wild on the pergola as to the fate of the plant—the first of its kind outside of

California—and how the firefighters assigned to the plant's protection were coping.

As if eavesdroppers heard them, an incoming call bleated the Chief's signal. Hanging up, he requested volunteers to relieve those fighting flames at the power plant. One truck and two men left. It almost seemed quiet, but that was an illusion. We still hosted a fire truck and crew, an occasional drop-by deputy, unidentified Big Wigs with clipboards and cameras, and were the focus of perpetual fly-overs.

Sage sent the teens home before it got completely dark. "Your parents will think we kidnapped you!"

"Dad's not even home!" Jacey shot back. "He had a couple days off, so he's gambling in Vegas."

"Are you home alone?" Sage asked, concerned.

"She's at my house for a sleep-over!" Mathia said.

"Good; I'd hate to think you were alone. Have fun!" Sage gave Jacey a quick hug.

We thanked them profusely and off they went, ATVs roaring, four hands waving. Fable's trilled "See ya, Myster-E!" rose above all other sounds.

After the kids' exodus, Gull also decided to leave.

"It's late!" Sage protested. "Stay here, and leave in the morning."

"You have enough going on here. I'll sleep better at the motel where there's not so much commotion."

"Call to be sure they have a room," I suggested.

That slowed him for a second. "Nah, they will."

We walked Gull to his vehicle, which was a trophy of glitz, ritz, and bling. In all my trips, I've not seen such a rental car. Vegas must not settle for anything less than spectacular, even in car rentals.

Sage stared. "Wow, Gull; quite a switch from your Jeep!"

"Yeah," he drawled, giving me an exaggerated wink, "It being a holiday, I took what was left." When he turned the key, the engine sang such a rich, smooth chorus it impressed even non-mechanical Sage. "Got an early flight t'morrow, so won't see you. Glad you're okay."

With that, the rental car (better suited for uppity-ups than n'er-do-well brothers) glided away in muted puff of dust.

"Well-well-*well*, that's different," Sage said dryly on our return to the backyard. "Gull driving *that* and staying at a motel."

"True to form, he's unpredictable," I agreed.

With all the excitement, we soon forgot about Gull. Each time the official radios crackled, it was more bad news. Flames now endangered the popular Cove Fort, forcing evacuation because the historic wooden buildings didn't stand a chance.

By nightfall, the burn stretching across The Bench had demolished a wide swath up the Mineral Mountains. Even before the fire leaped and closed I-15, it extended beyond the collaborating local and county fire departments' territories. The Bureau of

Land Management took over, but the other forces didn't give up their fight to stand and protect.

Throughout the afternoon, we had heard stories of camping, hunting, rock-climbing, picnicking, or just hanging out in the areas we watched first catch fire, then mar, and quickly disintegrate. It was a tragedy with long-lasting, far-reaching consequences.

Two firefighters remained, assigned to guard our property until receiving the "All Clear" signal. I dragged cushioned chaise loungers out to where the sagebrush began and our lawn ended. The women settled in for a long night. "Go to bed; we'll wake you, if needed," they insisted as the moon drifted through soot-stained clouds.

Feeling guilty to leave two exhausted volunteers with such responsibility—both had put in nearly full work days at their jobs before the siren sounded—I didn't argue, but went inside to have the first decent conversation with Sage since Fable's call.

But my gal was asleep. Still dressed, she had flung herself crosswise on the bed. I knew the feeling. After I nudged her enough to accommodate a companion, I plunged into sleep's depths with singed odors still in my nostrils.

13

Relentless pounding on the front door jolted us awake the next morning. We rose up on our elbows and squinted to see the time: *Nine o'clock!* Visitors rarely noticed our doorbell but, when they did, its Big Ben chimes deafened them and us. Repeated hammering ended our semi-comatose state, followed immediately by the less-than-subtle Big Ben racket. Okay: they had found the bell.

"Good grief, what're they doing? Ringing with one hand and beating the door with the other?" Sage fumed, tying her bathrobe's belt. "Sheesh!"

My crutches were who-knows-where—just not where they belonged next to the bed; blame it on the previous day's craziness. So I quickly strapped on my fake foot, pulled on socks, grabbed a robe, and raced to catch up with Sage.

Hurrying past a window, I saw only empty chairs. *Did we sleep through the racket of a departing fire truck?* Glancing out the next window, I saw Rosco's official vehicle in our driveway. Panic surged: *Has the fire reversed itself? Do we need to evacuate?*

Sage stood in the doorway facing Rosco and a uniformed woman who looked ready to bite heads off. If she didn't, the surly Rottweiler standing at attention beside her was next in line for the privilege.

Beyond them, Nimrod yowled in protest at being caged while his fellow canine roamed free. Given a signal, Rosco's partner could break through glass, but the dog drooling on our front porch had me more worried. I didn't doubt that, at the woman's mere signal and one false move on my part, I could be missing another foot. *Chomp.* My nerves twitched.

"Hello." Dry-mouthed, I hazarded a guess: *This is one mad BLM gal. She can't think we set the fire. Or does she?* It was the only logical reason my befuddled brain could supply for such a glare, but I calmed a bit, confident that a righteous dude like me could handle such a ridiculous accusation.

"Zeke and Sage Eden, this is," he checked his notepad, "Gabriella Knicker," an unsmiling, clearly nervous Rosco said. "She's, uh, an investigator . . . and she, uh, flew into Cedar City from Rochester, Minnesota, late last night."

Huh? Why's Minnesota interested in a Utah fire? I glanced past them. Parked beyond Rosco's vehicle was a nondescript car more similar to a rental car than Gull's had been.

"I told you: I go by Gabby," the woman corrected Rosco firmly before whipping back to face us, "and I've heard 'Don't get-your knickers in knots' too often to be amused, so don't go there. This is Killer," she added, dropping her gaze briefly.

Nothing like naming a dog Killer to keep jokes to a minimum. My smile-attempt failed. Everything about Ms Knicker was unfeminine, brown, and ominous: chopped hair, wide-brimmed hat, steel-toed boots, weapons and gadgets hooked to handy hunks of dull-brown uniform. Whoever nicknamed this Sherman tank *Gabby* possessed a form of bravery I could neither match nor fathom.

My mouth matched the parched Sahara's terrain. "Hey, Killer!" My joviality was forced.

"Don't try to cozy up to him; he's working," Gabby snapped.

Whoa. Someone's way overdue for her refresher course in human relations! Cozying up to any critter with incisors the size of my thumbs was the farthest thing from my mind. I'd give Killer full access to my freezer. Anything he wanted was his if it diverted his unwavering attention from making me his next meal.

Rosco cleared his throat. "Gabri—I mean, Gabby cleared it with the Beaver County Sheriff's office to be in the area for a few days, uh, investigating—"

She interrupted, her voice like a cleaver whacking off a hen's head: "I have questions for you, Mister Eden. May we come in?"

It wasn't really a question. *"No"* obviously was not an acceptable answer, and Killer was her entrance ticket if I gave the wrong reply.

I was about to respond, *"Here on the deck will be fine"* when Sage intervened with, "Surely," and ushered the threesome in with as much courtesy as if they were the Beaver County Welcome Wagon and we weren't still dressed in our nightwear.

Killer planted himself at Gabby's feet and stared at me with soulless disdain, unblinking suspicion, and no hint he had ever been a cuddly puppy. His attitude left no doubt as to his message: *If we're here, you're in one heap of trouble, Buster.*

If Gabby was the "official" whom the TV reporter had intimated was investigating my connection to The Bulldog, I was doomed unless I marshalled my wits. I was a physical mess and would flunk any lie detector test Gabby pulled from her bag of tricks.

Like a compass needle, Gabby's opening question indicated the direction of her intended grilling. "Mister Eden . . . *or* should I say 'Mister Nede'?" The living room spun, taking me with it.

She pulled out a pocket-size tape recorder, clicked it on, and droned the date, time and names of those present into the record.

My record.

Sage reached for my hand, turning the motion into a knee-pat when I didn't reach back. I signaled her with my eyes: *Show no weakness or we're toast!*

"In my opinion, you're a suspect," Gabby said, "but I won't take you into custody for questioning yet. To prevent future problems, I must inform you that you have the right to remain silent . . ."

We could have chanted Miranda Rights in unison. I have rattled off those words via my characters' voices more often than I've been required to recite my Social Security number in real life.

Sitting in my living room, I trembled.

She droned on, ". . . you have the right to consult with an attorney . . ."

"Excuse me?" I interrupted coldly. "While I *do* appreciate your *concern*," the words dripped with scorn, "about my constitutional rights, you're missing a crucial detail. What gives you the right to be here? I have yet to hear evidence regarding what makes me a suspect. And for what crime?"

Startled either by my tone or my boldness, she got down to the business at hand: "I have come here" (the derision coating *"here"* indicated she believed she had landed on Mars; Utah had not soothed her soul) "to pursue tips rendering you responsible, either by commission of the act or by aiding and abetting the actual perpetrator, for the abduction and murder of Honey Odessa Woolden-Landis. When I complete my investigation, I will have sufficient proof to require your arrest."

Just like that, my life turned a corner I had never encountered firsthand. I no longer just wrote about crimes; I was now a completely and professionally Mirandized suspect in one.

I swallowed a lump the size of Killer's paw. "I'm sure you're highly qualified, Ms Knicker, but I am equally sure your confidence is misplaced. I am as innocent as Killer is."

Killer didn't like me saying his name. His upper body tilted forward; his limbs quivered, ready to pounce. My palms instantly become two sweat-producing factories.

Looking official and miserable, in equal measure, Rosco stared at a place above my head. I wondered what had been said when this intimidating two- and four-legged Minnesota entourage showed up in Beaver. Obviously, Gabby had given Rosco his instructions: *"When we get there, I do the talking."*

I coughed. "May I suggest something?"

Silence.

"Of course," Rosco said when it was obvious Gabby had interest only in a confession of guilt.

I leaned forward; Killer wasn't the only one who knew how to use body language to show control. "A preliminary phone call could've saved you a flight and Minnesota taxpayers a heap of money, Gabby. To come to Utah on a whim—that's what this is, not hard evidence—seems premature and rash."

To communicate *Look how relaxed the innocent are,* I rested against the chair, crossing my slipper-shod fake foot over my natural ankle. "Interesting," I mused, milking the moment, "because you sure don't strike me as a woman given to impulsivity."

Her lips tightened; she blinked, but quickly turned steely eyes on me.

My sarcastic *"interesting"* either found or created a minute crack in her façade. While I didn't know much, one thing I knew with certainty was who, in this fiasco, was *not* guilty.

"Gabby, give me the name and contact details for the supervisor who authorized your trip. I want to have a talk with him or her." I sounded intrepid, but my heart pounded so rapidly I expected it to erupt from my chest and land at Killer's feet. No need to ponder what he would do with it.

Had I not stared, I might have missed Gabby's nervous inhalation. Her Adam's apple leaped twice. "I'm on personal leave," she said stiffly, "but I have permission to conduct an official investigation."

"Name and contact info," I repeated resolutely. Sage's eyebrows shot so high they appeared to be trying to escape her face. "I have to wonder why someone would use vacation without cause. A call to your superior should clear that up."

Gabby understood body language, too. With her feet flat on the floor, she matched Killer's attack stance. Muscles rippled in his haunches. Gabby's mud-brown eyes narrowed to slits. As if he were a marionette in her control, so did Killer's. *Spooky.*

"I intend to see justice done, having promised my brother, Howard Woolden, on his deathbed that I'd watch out for his wife. I failed in my mission and now she's gone. I will not fail again." Gabby pounded a fist on her knee. "I will find her abductor and murderer and see that he faces the stiffest, ultimate punishment allowed by law."

I wanted to wail like coyotes who cry in the night outside our windows. *Her brother!* Ms Knicker might be a thoroughly modern enforcer of the law, but she sought Old Testament justice for wrongs against kinfolk. Had I suddenly dropped into a scene from Grandma Eden's tales straight out of A CHILD'S BIG BOOK OF BIBLE STORIES?

"Or she," I boldly corrected. "You said 'he,' but Honey's alleged," my emphatic tone and pause were rebuke enough to make Gabby flinch, "abductor or murderer could be a woman. Try not to let your preconceived ideas warp the investigation, okay?"

Sage looked increasingly alarmed as I brazenly burned bridges with each antagonizing word. Hey, I wrote lines like this for Raven and they worked well, so why not for the fake-footed, slick-shaven middle-aged *wuss* fighting for his very livelihood . . . and doing so while wearing a bathrobe?

Despite stupidity disguised as bravery, I have the sense to know when to shut up. So I did.

Gabby whipped open her notebook, bit the cap off her pen with her teeth and spit it into her hand. Back in control, she employed a more chilling tone: "How ironic, for you to claim innocence when the character you killed in your book so closely parallels Honey. That, alone, makes you a suspect in *my* book. Further facts, unreleased to the public, will make it difficult, if not impossible, for you to prove your novel is fiction."

The contemptuous emphasis she put on "*novel*" showed where she viewed OFF TRACK. For Gabby Knicker, my latest book was on the same level as pornography.

Sage flopped back against her chair.

Rosco inhaled sharply.

Killer licked his lips.

As for me? I longed for Raven Crowley to burst through our front door.

I needed vindication, and only someone with Raven's skills and single-minded pursuit of truth and justice could ensure that. He may be a merely a figment of my imagination who scared the bejeebies out of bad dudes, but I needed Raven to be *real* and right-*here*, right-*now*, and on my side.

14

The pungent scent of dog, acrid odors of human fear, and a dimple (possibly imagined) on the couch where the self-appointed judge-and-jury had sat were all that remained of Gabby and Killer in our living room. Not much . . . but too much.

Sage and I were alone—well, not exactly *alone*. All the wild accusations, blunt derision, and nasty insinuations with which Gabby had pelted me remained like shards of a bad dream. Even an hour after locking the door behind our uninvited guests, we felt bruised and jittery.

We wandered aimlessly from window-to-window, room-to-room. Between the raging wildfire and the Gabby-Killer visit, we were numb from exhaustion and dulled by shock. Whenever our paths crossed, we paused for hugs, but seemed incapable of finding the language that could express our despair and fears rising from Gabby's vendetta against me.

Finally, I poured Diet Cokes over ice, brought them to the library, and we collapsed on our chairs. "Next time you decide to lollygag through a weekend," I drawled in a half-hearted attempt to relieve the tension, "give me a five-minute warning so I can vacate the premises and be long-gone when the doorbell rings, okay?"

Her smile was wan. "No way; if you go, I go. But there's no more lollygagging around here if this is what results." She waved limply, encompassing our living room and the world in general.

Rolling my head back on my shoulders, I groaned. "All these years, I assumed that when the curtains lifted on the Zeke Eden–Kiel Nede dual identity, it'd be almost festive. Maybe an avid fan would trail me to my motel room and hang around, trying to snap photos. Or, bribe the desk clerk to see my room before it was cleaned—hoping to discover something I'd left behind."

"I was so quick to *pooh-pooh* the idea there could be any nefarious connection between Rochester and Milford," Sage said glumly. "You were right to be suspicious, Zeke."

"Nah; that blue-haired snoop behind me in the Post Office can't have friends in Minnesota," I argued. "There haven't been any hints of trouble since I suspected her of blabbing. It must be what Gabby implied: OFF TRACK readers added two-plus-two. Except they came up with five, not four."

"You *did* take the kids and Abbott back there. Maybe one of them blew it. Not on purpose, but just talked where ears perked up. Maybe Gabby came to your booksigning and got them talking? Or, Leif has spies who found Haze and broke her down."

I shook my head. "I would never forget Gabby's face, so nix that idea. And, if one of the kids spilled the beans, the others would tell me. As for Leif? I don't know; could be."

The clock struck a quarter hour while we brooded. Finally Sage set her glass down forcefully and completely ignored the resulting splatter. "You need to go back to Rochester and clear your name."

"What?" My yelp startled a bird in the arboretum.

"Think about it, Zeke: How can you possibly clear yourself from fourteen-hundred miles away?"

I stared at her, barely blinking, speechless . . .

We watched fluttering leaves settle into stillness after the bird flew out of the arboretum . . .

Sage went to the bathroom and returned . . .

We finished our drinks; remaining ice cubes clinked softly as they melted in each glass . . .

The clock chimed the half-hour . . .

Finally I spoke: "You're right, but here's a poser: Who goes back: Zeke or Kiel?"

"Good question." Sage parked her elbow on the chair's arm and positioned her chin on her upturned palm. Her jaw worked several times, but no words emerged. Finally, she said, "Given our post–Nine-Eleven world, Zeke *flies* since Kiel has no photo ID. But *Kiel* is on-site to clear his name: *he* contacts Rochester police. And that leaves *Zeke* undetected in any connection to the dreadful stuff."

I nodded slowly. "So, when does this happen?"

"Now! Strike while the iron is hot, whatever that means." She raised a cautionary hand. "Don't tell me; it was a rhetorical question. Gabby's in Milford, so it's your chance to resolve the whole mess before she returns to Rochester with false leads, assuming she manages to find even *them*."

"Makes sense. Do I tell anyone I'm going?"

"Why would you? I'll call your folks later today. If they're not home, you know where a key's hidden. You're a free man, regardless of Gabby's Miranda-talk and accusations. We still live by 'innocent until proven guilty' in this country."

"Somebody needs to remind Gabby," I groused, "but I'd better tell Rosco so I don't look like a man-on-the-run."

She sniffed. "If anything, you're leaping into the lion's den, Gabby being the fiercest of the herd."

I rolled my eyes. "I can see my work on earth is not yet done. It's a *pride* of lions, my dear CEO!"

"That one wasn't on your September list." Her impish grin left me feeling we could lick this. "I'll log-on to book your flight. Want to fly out of Vegas or Salt Lake City?"

"Las Vegas; it's the place to be, right?" I said sardonically.

While I packed for both of my now-dueling identities, Sage played travel agent. She soon called to me from my office, "How fast can you get there?"

"Really fast," I shouted back from the bedroom where I was matching shirts to slacks. "Especially if you can do a Saint George connecting flight."

Minutes later, she responded, "If you can be in Saint George in two hours, you'll easily make the four o'clock flight out of Vegas, so get cracking."

Sage joined me in the bedroom, bringing the cell-phone charger from the office and the laptop case she'd packed during the fire. "If, as Gabby claimed, she *is* Howard Woolden-Landis' sister, and her last name is neither Woolden nor Landis, do you suppose there was a Mister Knicker who was brave enough to marry such sandpaper-ish woman?"

"Either that, or she and Howie had different fathers. But I betcha there was a befuddled Mister Knicker who said 'I do,' in a weak moment. And then Killer ate him!" We shared a wicked grin, and neither of us felt guilty.

I pulled Sage into a hug. "What will my gal do while her guy is gone?"

"Hold my head high, look people squarely in the eye, and work-work-work. That, and do everything I can to promote the belief that Gabby *does* have her knickers in knots over absolutely nothing that can be substantiated. Plus, I expect to be talking to you on a regular basis. Got that?"

"Yes, Ma'am." I saluted smartly.

I arrived in Saint George with twenty-two minutes to spare and no wailing sirens behind me. I waited until I landed in Vegas to call Rosco at home. Cale answered. I identified myself and, before I could ask to speak with his father, he burst out with, "You'll never guess what I found on the Internet, Myster-E! I was surfing for news about the fire, and there's a picture of your house with all the burned places and smoke and mountains in the background. It's a great shot! There must've been a photographer up in a copter taking pictures."

"Maybe so; Gull said something about seeing a photograph. Could you e-mail it to me?"

He agreed before letting Rosco know I'd called.

"Can this be an off-the-record conversation?" I asked Rosco after minimal small-talk.

"You bet; what's up?"

"Everything Gabby said, except for the bombshell about how I'm Kiel Nede, is a figment of her warped imagination. OFF TRACK is fiction even if I based the premise on a current Minnesota scandal, which is perfectly legal to do."

"Got no argument with that," Rosco said.

"Even if a demented reader turned my storyline into his or her outline for murder, it doesn't make me a collaborator. Here's the off-the-record part: I'm at the Vegas airport with a ticket to Rochester. My goal is to up-end Gabby's outrageous claims and do so on her turf. While I'm gone, I'd appreciate it if you could keep an eye on her, which I'm sure you'd anyway. Understand what I'm saying?"

"Loud and clear. I told her she's entitled to talk to folks, ask 'em questions or whatever she thinks she's gotta do, but she is *not* the law here. Speaking of her turf, I can't believe she's endeared herself to many colleagues, so you may find them willing to help take Gabby down a peg or two. Good luck, Zeke."

"Thanks. One more thing: Can you—*will* you—keep mum or just vague, about where I've gone?"

"Can, and will; you're entitled to roam. Way I see it, Gabby's got nothing that sticks, even after that show-off business of Mirandizing you. I'll keep an eye on Sage and your place, too."

"You're a fine man and good friend, Rosco." His unsolicited promise made me feel better than I had since Big Ben's chimes had roused me not all that many hours earlier.

Flying cross-country, there was little to do besides think. I do my best cogitating at the computer, so I pulled out my laptop and made notes. First on the list: Remind Sage to lock the house and my desk until I returned.

With the house empty all day, I didn't want to tempt anyone with the idea that undeterred access meant freedom of information. Gabby struck me as someone who'd flirt with that idea. Hopefully, she knew that, even in our remote corner of Utah, breaking-and-entering without jumping through legal hoops was a career-ender.

I compiled a list of questions I expected, and spelled out my answers. I created an agenda for my time in Rochester: who to see, and how to counter each accusation with truth.

It felt a lot like writing a storyline for a new book, but didn't give me the same thrill.

Since my departure from home had been abrupt, I would need to use Mom's printer to make a copy of the Proof of Innocence document I had e-mailed to John. While at it, I'd also print this latest document.

Was Haze happy to see me? Oh, yeah. Once she finished exuding motherly love, she grasped the sober message I had come to deliver: Kiel Nede was in town to preserve his reputation, not kiss babies and shake hands.

It was eerily quiet while I explained the bleak situation. I didn't mince words or shade the truth. I saw no point in keeping Mom and Dad from knowing that, if Gabby had her way, their famous-writer son would be trading his blue jeans and T-shirts for a prisoner's orange jumpsuit.

After a few rounds of "How dare she!" huffing-and-puffing, Mom solemnly agreed to let me handle things. "I won't even let the neighbors know you're here. Drats; it won't work b'cuz they'll see you. Oh! How 'bout if I develop a productive cough? I'll make it sound so bad, no one'll get near me!"

A little more melodrama than necessary, but I had to give Haze a little slack to keep her happy. If fake sneezing and hacking did the trick, so be it.

The next morning after Mom's breakfast feast, I (decked out as Kiel Nede) crutch-walked into the Rochester Government Center and approached the desk attendant guarding the entrance to the law enforcement wing. He stared at my footless leg.

"Hello; I'm Kiel Nede. May I speak to Gabby Knicker's supervisor, please? I don't know his rank, but his name is Bill Brandt."

Maybe it was my name, maybe it was mentioning Gabby. Whatever, interest flickered and he nodded. He eyed my crutches and took in my shaggy hair without blinking, though he did concede, "Cool hat," while punching a code on the phone.

The building's automatic doors *whooshed* open and closed again. A disembodied voice called out, "Before five o'clock." The desk attendant coughed, covering the receiver with the fingers of the hand holding it. I shifted my weight.

He seemed on the verge of saying something to me, but then spoke into the phone: "Bill? Kiel Nede is here to see Gabby's boss." He hung up. "He'll be right out. Have a seat." I selected a chair offering the best view of a long hallway.

Within ten minutes, a crisply attired beanpole with an *Only-interested-in-the-facts* aura appeared. I rose, zeroing in on his gaze as he held out a hand. "Kiel Nede?" He had a smoker's gravelly voice.

Nodding, I confirmed his identify via the nametag clipped to his uniform. "I appreciate you seeing me without an appointment."

"Come down to my office." He hugged the wall as we headed down the hall, leaving more space than

I needed for one foot and two crutches. It's a common reaction from those unaccustomed to interacting with the disabled.

Arriving there, he pulled a straight-back chair away from a small table, turned it toward the desk, motioned that it was for me, and then walked to his padded desk chair. Lack of steam from a mug of coffee hinted that he'd poured it before he knew I was on-site. When he offered me a beverage of my choice and I declined, he moved his cup to one side.

Formalities aside, I stared at the desk. No clutter, no cigarette pack, no evidence of interests beyond the office, no photos of dignitaries shaking Bill Brandt's hand. Just the ceramic no-logo mug, a phone resting on a phonebook, a hibernating laptop, and a pen beside a single sheet of paper ripped from a notebook. The paper was either blank or flipped to prevent snoops like me from reading its secrets.

"What can I do for you, Mister Nede?" Bill asked, ending my silent perusal of his seemingly sterile life.

"I'm sure you knew—and *why*—I recently had a visit from one of your colleagues: Gabby Knicker. A phone call could've saved her a trip to Utah."

"Gabby likes to get past the fluff, to leap right into the heart of a matter."

If paired as combatants, Sage and Bill would emerge tied in say-nothing tournaments.

"As Ms Woolden-Landis' sister-in-law, don't you think Gabby is a *smidgeon*," I paused for sarcasm to sink in, "too personally involved for the assignment to be appropriate?"

"She is," Bill allowed. "Due to death of a relative, she was granted personal leave. Gabby chaffs under rules, so it really wasn't a request, as such. She called from Utah to say she was quote, 'pursuing a line of solid clues,' unquote, she believed would solve the crime."

"If she bucks authority like that, I have to wonder, why do you keep her around?"

"She's very good at what she does."

"I know; she told me," I said dryly.

A slight flicker of amusement may have crossed his face, but he remained silent. He picked up his pen. Holding it like a cigarette, he tapped it against the paper, leaving inky dots like ashes on the surface. Finally he spoke, surprising me with his choice of questions: "Was Killer with her?"

"Oh, yeah. *That* was a nice touch."

He shook his head ruefully, falling quiet again.

"May I explain why I'm here? It likely strikes you that I'm like Gabby, coming without warning, but I have tough evidence whereas she has only thin-skinned suspicions, not solid clues." Opening my briefcase, I handed him a copy of my twelve-page comparison of fact and fiction. "I assembled this for another purpose, but it shows what I can prove."

He scanned it quickly; his eyes widened several times; once he frowned.

"I don't expect you to read it now, and maybe you'll only skim it later, but I'm here to preserve my reputation. To paraphrase Shakespeare, 'He who takes my purse steals trash, but he who filches my name, makes me poor indeed.' Gabby seems intent on destroying both my livelihood and reputation."

"What's that from, that quote?"

"Othello."

He clicked the pen and made a single notation in neat block letters on the paper: OTHELLO.

"I write fictional mystery/thrillers, not true crime. Writing is my passion, my vocation *and* avocation. I will not allow someone like Gabby to rob me of my life, Bill." I purposely avoided titles and surnames; I wanted to remind him I wasn't someone in the back of his squad car, heading off to be the next resident in the slammer.

"Go on," he said, unblinking despite my uninvited familiarity.

"OFF TRACK is my sixteenth mystery. Every one centers on a murder. Each time, I spell out how it happened and precisely how it got resolved. This is the first time an actual crime has been linked to a Kiel Nede novel."

"I read OFF TRACK, Mister Nede." No surprise that a guy who kept a swept-clean desk didn't make first-name friends in ten minutes; also no surprise that he didn't gush about my book. "It's good, but many in Rochester wonder . . . Well, if you follow our news, you can imagine the scuttlebutt. It seems you know too much to be ignored."

"It's research, not guilt." I let that percolate for a moment before unveiling my ultimate request: "Will you accompany me in my effort to prove I'm innocent? I won't disrupt the ongoing investigation, but I'll demonstrate how unrealistic the assumptions are that I had any role in Honey's undisputed disappearance or her alleged death. Will you help?"

Bill stared into his coffee cup as if expecting to find answers in the dregs. He sipped distractedly. Half a cup later, just when I thought he would shake that head with its no-nonsense military haircut, he surprised me again, this time with a brusque non sequitur: "How'd you lose your foot?"

I inhaled sharply. *This'll be the first time I tell a stranger the whole truth.* "My wife and I were chopping kindling for our wood-burning stove and she lost her grip on the axe."

He chewed his lip. "You're still married to her?"

"Absolutely."

He drummed his fingers on the desktop in rhythm with my heartbeat. *Da-dum-da-dum-da-dum.*

"Any more questions?" I finally asked.

He rolled his chair back and, to my utter surprise, swung his feet up on the desk and stared at me.

Maybe that's why he keeps it clear—less chance of messes from spilled coffee; I should take a lesson.

"Why not pick Los Angeles or Chicago for OFF TRACK's setting? One more book based either place wouldn't make any difference, and you could've bypassed meeting Gabby." He may have winked.

I reciprocated with my first smile. "My folks and brother live here. For years, Mom has mailed me clippings about Rochester's railroad mess. I decided to honor her pride in me all this time by using one of her ideas in a book. Never again."

"No Nede entries in the phonebook," he tapped it, and glanced at his laptop, "or on-line."

He was checking up on me; now I understand the reason behind my ten-minute wait in the lobby.

"No, but there's an *Eden* listing. Rudy's my dad." *Man, when truth breaks loose in me, it flies like cinders in the wind.* I still held back one detail, though: my first name.

"Nede equals Eden; a well-guarded pseudonym." He nodded, seemingly impressed.

"Yet, somehow, Gabby dug it out."

"Yeah; but she kept your real name under wraps." Just as quickly as they had come up, his feet returned to the floor in an arcing move. Planting his forearms on the desk, he studied me. I didn't flinch.

"Huh. So, you're Rudy Eden's son. How 'bout that. I've played pool with him occasionally over at the Brothers' Bar and Grill. He's a good man, your dad."

"Yes, he is."

"Why use a pseudonym? Guys who are just outta jail, unrehabilitated and eager to kick it up a notch, first thing they do is get phony IDs and hit the streets with new looks and new names. The old A-K-A— the *also-known-as* you see on WANTED posters. Not saying that's behind your reason, but you see why it comes to mind, right?"

"It's a privacy issue. My wife and I prefer quiet lives; a penname allows that. So does a disguise." I lifted my beret with one hand and wiggled my mop of Sixties' hair with the other while extending my footless leg into his line of vision. "You've only met Kiel Nede. His counterpart—the sleek-headed, two-footed Zeke Eden—was fitted with a state-of-the-art lower-extremity prosthesis right here at Mayo Clinic. The eyeglasses came from a Walmart rack."

Bill Brandt was the embodiment of self-control, revealing no facial tic or arched eyebrow. I must have passed some unspecified test because his only response was, "How long you figure you'll require my services?"

The reprieve his present-tense question offered me was as rejuvenating as any blood transfusion. "One, maybe two days."

"Okay; let's get moving." He pushed back his chair. As we left his office, he asked, "Did you know the railroad posted a hefty reward for Honey's abductor and/or murderer? Started at twenty-five thousand, but likely to rise higher real soon."

I whistled long and low. Not only was I a suspect, but there was a bounty on my head. *Fame is sweet, but bounty-producing infamy? Not so much.*

❖

Bill drove his official squad car. Our first stop was Quarry Hill Park. He checked off points on his copy of the printout as I walked us through the progression of how Raven Crowley deduced not only where the body was, but who had killed The Howler.

Despite crutches, I kept up with Bill as he climbed the gently sloping hill that brought us above the cave. Together, we investigated the airshaft through which Raven had speculated The Howler's body was dropped into the blocked cave.

"As police have discovered since clearing the opening, there's no way a body can be lowered into an opening this size. I made that up: it's fiction."

Nodding, he made a few notes on the margins of the pertinent page. "I see what you mean."

"Look, even if the real killer in the actual case dismembered the body, the wire mesh below the opening is undisturbed. Honey's body can't be here. This mess and disruption of people's enjoyment of the park," I motioned toward the police tape and the nearby picnic areas, "serves no valid purpose."

"Yeah; we've gotten calls from the disgruntled."

"If only someone had contacted me first and let me describe what you're seeing here today, it could have averted delays, heartache and expense. Gabby intimated there are facts incriminating me. Any such came from news reports—and I'm not the only one aware of them. Don't view similarities as evidence. I used details from the news to give OFF TRACK's plot believability, not to incriminate myself. I employed a common writer's technique."

Bill sighed deeply. "I hear ya."

"Meanwhile," I concluded, "the real criminal, the actual guilty party, is walking around undetected."

"I see what you mean," he said dourly.

"Interesting," I mused abruptly as my eye drifted toward the leafy canopy above the airshaft.

"What?"

"Look." I pointed out a distinct choppy pattern in one tree. A branch dangled; twigs and leaves were mangled as if something had been ripped down.

"Last week's storm downed trees around town."

"That's not from a storm; it's further evidence somebody's messing with us. Do you remember the fishing net in OFF TRACK, Bill?"

"Yeah; the killer used fishing net to hide a corpse in a tree until the park emptied out for the day . . . Hmm." His eyes narrowed, then slowly widened as he stared upwards again. Tilting back on his heels, he deliberated for a few moments. "You're right. It's not storm damage, and I don't remember seeing anything about it in the investigative report."

"The killer put considerable effort into recreating the scene leading up to the disposal of the body as if there *were* a body here, then ripped down the net. Pretty remarkable attention to detail—but worthless effort, except to further delay his or her arrest. Worthless, given the physical evidence, since it's impossible for a corpse to be in the cave."

Bill climbed the tree with amazing ease, took vegetation samples, and bagged a few of what could well be fishing-net fibers. Back on the ground, he collected telltale litter and photographed the tree from several angles. "In case anyone planted phony clues after we did this the first time, I'd rather be safe than sorry now."

"Take my fingerprints before I leave town—to eliminate me as a suspect, not for proof of guilt," I said, half-joking, as we left the park. "That's why I tried not to touch anything today at the park."

We followed the service road behind businesses whose properties abutted the railroad tracks. Several had built attractive barricades to block sight, sound, and access. We turned around near the edge of town where Bill bought two coffees at a gas station's convenience store, refusing my offer of payment.

"Thanks." I took cautious sips of the steaming brew before resuming my spiel. "In OFF TRACK, Raven deduced that the killer was a business owner who was negatively affected by the railroad."

"Clever and logical, but do you figure it could be true in the real situation?" Bill relaxed in his seat, obviously ready to talk, not drive yet.

I shrugged. "You and your investigative team can prove or disprove that. I used the idea because, as we saw, wherever tracks come close to property lines, each business is of such a type that noise and diesel fumes really aren't an issue."

"Right. The services their businesses provide also produce noise and pollution, whether we're talking about a body shop, or that small-engine repair place, or even the recyclers' warehouse."

"The landscaping company can't complain, either. Don't they conduct most of their business off-site?"

"Yeah. We get complaints about the railroad, but mostly from people who get stopped at crossings, or homeowners mad about the noise in their backyards. Not much we can do about it."

Drinking coffee, we watched traffic in silence for a few minutes.

Then Bill shifted in his seat. "Raven used fishing net to prove the abductor and killer were one person. Your Howler's rejected lover owned a sportsman tour-guide business. There's nothing like that along the stretch of tracks we covered." He drummed his fingers on the steering wheel.

"Why should there be? OFF TRACK is—"

"I know: fiction," Bill finished. He tilted his head for a last swallow; I still had half a cup, having only reached that level by blowing repeatedly across the rim. I decided, *Bill has an asbestos-lined mouth!* "Want another?" His hand was on the door release.

"No, I'm good." *And plenty wired!*

He went back inside for a refill. The set of his jaw as he strode back to the car revealed he'd made a decision. "I'm gonna make a call; you listen." After punching a pre-set code on the phone, he activated speaker mode, and placed it in the console's holder.

A curt "Yes?" interrupted the second ring. *Well-well-well; it's Ms Dropout-from-Human-Relations.*

"Gabby? Bill Brandt, here. Your leave is over, effective immediately. I know you want to solve the crime, but the actual killer is getting away with kidnapping and murder here—not in Utah—while you're chasing the goofy idea that Kiel Nede—"

"Use his real name: Ezekiel Eden. Enough with the phony-name business." Gabby's snarl gave me the heebie-jeebies, even across fourteen-hundred miles.

Bill continued without confronting her insolence: "Call him what you want. No matter if he's Ezekiel, Zeke, or Kiel, he's one hundred percent innocent."

She snapped, "I've made progress, Bill."

"Report in to me by shift's end tomorrow—in person. I'll be watching for you."

"I'm going over your head on this one. I'll report in, but I'm calling the Chief."

Unshaken by her bluster, Bill said, "Do what you wish on that score," and disconnected.

I knew better than to say anything, but every cell in my body was clapping, stomping, and whistling.

No need for the return portion of my plane ticket—I could have flown home on the wings of glee.

Back at the Government Center's parking lot, we made arrangements to meet at his office the next day and review my twelve-page document together. I wanted no unanswered questions, no unaddressed concerns, no *anything* to deter Bill Brandt from going forward with verifiable facts.

By noon the next day, we had finished. From the copious notes he had scrawled on my report, Bill had obviously worked late. He asked good questions and gave my responses the respect that truth deserves.

I treated him to lunch at the Nelson Cheese Factory where we ordered thick Town of Nelson sandwiches on caraway rye, each loaded with turkey, ham, Monterey Jack and Swiss cheeses, and "all the fixings." We ate them perched on bar stools and watched a flurry of to-go orders be prepared and get picked up. It was a popular place.

Back at the parking lot, we shook hands much more congenially than our first handshake had been. I harbored no misconceptions about Bill adding me to his holiday greeting-card list, but I did believe he had my best interests at heart.

15

Before heading back to my parents' house for one more night, I spent several hours investigating on my own. I retraced the trail by the railroad tracks that Bill and I had traversed, carefully making notes of business names in their exact order.

I veered off-course just once to follow a short spur we hadn't pursued in great detail. My detour was strictly personal because it was along this two-block section of track that Gull had bought a building which he had converted into a four-unit strip mall, expecting to flourish as a landlord.

According to Mom, when funds ran low Gull rented his personal suite to endeavors ranging from a secondhand bookstore to artists' studios to a quilting club. For each vision of grandeur (for Gull) or hope (for his renters), signs went up . . . and came down.

The last remaining sign, this one electrical—Windows & Walls: We Wash It Well!—wasn't lit. All tenants had vanished, leaving Gull with empty space to match empty dreams. Based on Mom's mention of lawsuits, I inferred my brother was no one's idea of an ideal landlord.

No surprise, Gull's own storefront was vacant and bleak. No sign indicated which optimistic business no longer existed; no posted hours, no "Call for

Info" number given. No evidence of any last-living-cell-in-a-dead-body activity. An uneasy feeling came over me. *Hmm; does this mean Gulliver Swift Eden has closed shop permanently?*

Several years ago during a personal economic slump (which he refused to discuss), Gull lived in the back of this store, citing his purported need for an "on-site guard" as his legal right to be there.

I gave up arguing that most guards showed up at dark with flashlights, coffee, and thick novels with plots capable of keeping them awake—and left at dawn. He needed a place to live, so he accommodated himself with rationalizations. *Typical Gull.*

For five months, he had subsisted on meals fixed on a hot-plate and by stretching Mom's doggy-bags. These, he accepted every Sunday (cringing at Dad's "He mooching off us, again, Haze?") after a much-needed shower (sponge baths can only do so much), a real-deal homemade meal, and laundry privileges.

With cupped hands around my eyes, I peered through smudged glass on the locked door. The large carpeted area gave no indication the premises were occupied. Not even a jacket left on a wall-hook, or a folding chair tilted against a wall.

Following a hunch, I walked behind the building on the off-chance the back door might be unlocked. It wasn't, but something even more final than empty space was in evidence.

Inside a dumpster I saw a cluster of metal signs that should hang above a door. Each showed a different failed business name:

WOOFERS! (canine companions for troubled kids)

PERK UP! (a roast-your-own coffee beans place)

WING IT! (a bird-banding supply center)

WE'LL MOVE YOU! ("local-only transport")

The bottom lines on all signs mockingly declared: GULL EDEN, PROPRIETOR.

Discovering the signage, even more than seeing four unoccupied suites, punctured any optimism I could rouse that Gull believed he had one more shot at success and, thus, had saved the signs. *Perhaps to resurrect a former business, or repaint for another venture?* No; now even *Hope* had lost its will to live and was awaiting a garbage truck to come by and give it a decent burial.

Glumly reflecting on how different brothers could be (at least, the two Eden boys) I returned to the parking lot where I had left the rental car. I waited to turn the key until I had verified what I suspected would be true: Gull still wasn't taking my calls.

Predictably, Mom had "a little something to tide us over until supper" ready upon my return. What was unusual was that Dad joined us in the kitchen.

Thumbing crumbs from a third snickerdoodle to my waiting mouth, I said, "Mom and Dad, it'll come out in the news soon and I don't want you to feel foolish, so tell anyone you wish that I'm Kiel Nede."

They stared at me with as much confusion and dismay as if I had confessed to having the inside scoop on who killed JFK. After casting furtive and uneasy glances at each other, they turned to me.

"*Okaaay*," Mom said slowly, but two heartbeats later she squinted at me. "Really, Zeke? I can tell people who you are . . . I mean, who Kiel Nede is?"

"Really. Go for it."

Dad frowned. "If it's alright with you, I'll keep things the way they've been. My buddies and me, we don't say much. We fish, or play pool, maybe get a beer or two, but just shoot the breeze, if we do talk."

"Whatever you wish. The stringent restraints of the past thirty years are lifted. It's not my choice and not my doing, but I'm powerless to stop it."

Mom patted my hand, vacillating between her concern for me and eagerness to get crackin' on this new freedom.

Dad selected a ball cap from the coat rack—an obvious sign he was retreating to the garage; if he left the premises, it would be the fedora.

I called Sage from the relative privacy of the back porch and said with forced joviality, "So, Doctor Eden, how goes it in Milford?"

"It's interesting." I intuited an eye-roll in her tone. "Gabby's buttonholing people and pressuring them to recall if they ever saw you engaged in disreputable activities. Remember your seatmate in the van on our Getting-to-Know Milford tour?

"Farming-Barney, of the one-word answers?"

"Bingo. Well, he dropped by my office to inform me that Gabby asked if he knew whether you own a gun. He wanted me to think he was being a good guy by alerting me to her line of questioning, but I think he wanted to know, too."

Despite no mirror handy, I knew my eyebrows formed two inverted v's. "Wonder if that means the inside scoop is that The Bulldog was shot?"

"Could be, or maybe Gabby wonders if you'll take aim at anyone whose pointed inquiries are too close for comfort."

"There is that," I conceded nervously.

"Oh, and get this: She's asking everybody about which days they saw you between the middle of June and the first week of July. Not sure *I* could answer that without my electronic calendar handy!"

"Nor could I, and I rarely need a calendar!"

She ignored my interruption. "I mean, what days was I away on trips? Did I meet you for lunch on a Tuesday, or was it a Wednesday? Did I really know where you were when I was gone? Or where you are when I'm holed up at work every day, for that matter? To any and all of that, my answer is 'No'."

"Thanks for the vote of confidence," I sniffed, but without rancor. "I get the drift. Remember the survey I used when I was writing CLOUDY VISION? Most people have no frame of reference for a given time period unless an earth-shattering event occurs—like

September Eleven, or maybe Katrina, or winning the lottery. Did I wash the truck last Thursday? Beats me, and why should I care? Ditto for what driver pumped gas next to me at KB's two weeks ago."

"That's what Gabby is discovering. People clam up, or duck into stores to avoid her, or zip across the street, or spew sheer drivel in response to her prying. Word is, she's getting frustrated and it shows."

"Shows how?"

"One example: I saw her exit the chiropractor's office this morning. When she got in her car, she slammed the door so hard, people stopped and stared. Must admit, though, she looks like she knows secrets no one else is privy to."

"The Gabby-in-Utah Show has ended. I was there when Bill told her to get back to Rochester PDQ."

Sage whistled. "Hey, I'm liking this Bill Brandt!"

"Yeah; his arctic chill has thawed. I'll be home tomorrow. By the way, have you heard from Gull?"

"No Gull-sightings out this-a-way. Why?"

"No one has seen him since I arrived, despite leaving multiple messages, so I wondered if he'd shown up in Utah. You say 'no,' which begs the question: If Milford is Gull-free, where he is?"

"No idea, but I'm thrilled about living Gabby-free. That woman has riled up more people than a swarm of angry bees. The clerk at the grocery store was in such a rush to get me out of there last evening she could barely count change into my hand."

"I'm so sorry this is affecting you, Sage; the mess is my fault. We'll rebuild any and all bridges Gabby burned, I promise."

At supper, Mom asked, "Did you see Gull today?"

"No." I omitted all details surrounding my visit to his defunct business and unanswered calls. "I'll call to see if he can come over and play cards tonight."

Dad snorted. "He's keeping to himself. Try, but I doubt you'll reach him. What's that thing called that he does, Haze?"

"Screens calls." With inflated patience, she added testily, "He sees a number on that little screen and, if he doesn't want to talk to someone, he doesn't answer. And he won't talk to us," she ended sadly.

"He may answer if he sees my number and thinks I'm in Utah," I suggested. For the third time—*or is it the fourth?*—I punched the number and listened to a string of unanswered ringtones.

Either what Mom and Dad suspected was true, or Gull was beyond the range of cell coverage. Both options were unsettling. I reminded myself, *Just because Gull lives close to Mom and Dad, I can't assume he's interested in or capable of being their support system.* Sure, he was entitled to leave town, but not to let our parents know how to reach him? That was inexcusable, irresponsible behavior.

We played a distracted, unusually quiet game of three-handed pinochle, interrupted by spurts of attempted dialogue. Finally we gave up pretending to have fun and retreated to more comfortable chairs in the living room to watch the ten o'clock news. The lead story was a shock:

"A break in the on-going Honey Odessa Woolden-Landis case has local officials scurrying to pull together previously discounted facts. A report on tomorrow's noon broadcast will unveil startling developments in this imbroglio . . ."

"What's that mean?" Mom asked nervously. "The part about 'a break,' and that word he used."

"The definition of imbroglio is 'a mess,' which I think certainly applies."

Mom sniffed. "Well, why didn't he just say so? All that high-falluting language! And what's the deal with— What'd he call it? 'A break in the case'?"

"It may indicate a provable tip," I responded with purposeful (and faux) calm. "Maybe I'm cleared or maybe they discovered something to the contrary."

Dad tossed me the remote and growled something unintelligible as he stomped off to bed.

Mom scurried to the kitchen, calling over her shoulder, "I'll make cocoa. Want a cup?"

"No thanks; I'm gonna turn in, too. It's been a long day." I turned off the television and listened for a moment to Mom opening cupboard doors, pouring milk into a saucepan, stirring. Her cocoa was never out of a single-serve package from a box of ten.

I wandered into the kitchen and leaned against the counter. "Mom, do you ever wish your two sons had normal occupations? Like if we were cabdrivers, or teachers, a plumber or electrician . . . maybe one of us, a barber who'd give you and Dad free haircuts."

She raised the wooden spoon for a taste, added another drop of vanilla, and stirred a bit more before answering. "I'd *never* let a barber near my head! Why, he'd shave me bald and it'd grow back weird! Besides, why would I want my boys to work at anything as boring as those jobs sound?" She gnawed her lower lip, not looking at me.

Yup; we're thinking the same thing: Better to have Gull bored than always in trouble . . .

Moving the pan off the heat, she patted my cheek. Her hand warmed my skin. "Sure you don't want a cup? It'll help you sleep."

I shook my head and kissed her, leaving the room only after she had filled her mug and settled in at the kitchen table with a sharpened pencil and her crossword puzzle book.

Letting the shower pummel my body into a state of pseudo-relaxation, I debated who submitted the evidence worthy of the newscaster's pronouncement: *Gabby Knicker? Bill Brandt? Did Gabby's false clues outweigh my facts in Bill's mind?*

The answers made all the difference in the world between continued imbroglio and confirmed innocence.

16

We were a solemn threesome at the breakfast table. Dad turned on KTTC's eight-o-clock news while Mom stacked blueberry pancakes on a platter. "Look!" Dad pointed to the author photo from my recent book jacket that accompanied the announcer's opening:

> "Kiel Nede, author of OFF TRACK, is no longer the primary suspect in either the disappearance or alleged murder of Ms Honey Odessa Woolden-Landis. Mister Nede first came under surveillance when tipsters pointed out unsettling similarities between his latest mystery and a case that has puzzled local investigators . . ."

Pancakes slid down Mom's body and landed on the floor, while the plate spun like a top.

> ". . . while clues no longer incriminate Kiel Nede, those details remain under serious consideration as legal officials reshuffle the case in their search for the perpetrator who imitated the book's plot and thus far has avoided discovery . . ."

Mom sobbed and laughed simultaneously. Dad's fist rose in a silent, jubilant cheer. Even though the innuendo beneath ". . . *no longer the primary suspect . . ."* merely shifted my name farther down a list, relief surged through me.

The focus shifted to the next story as I punched our home phone number on my cell. "G'morning, Love," Sage said sleepily.

My gal usually needed my high-octane coffee to rev her engine enough to propel her through a day, but this could do the trick. "I'm cleared!" I yelled.

"Wahoo! Come on home, Stud!"

"I'm flying out ASAP, so be ready for a *real good time,* if you catch my intent." As I returned Sage's air-kisses, I caught Mom's raised eyebrows. "We're married, Mom; it's okay!"

"Don't think I'm too old to know what *that* was about!" Mom wagged a finger before enveloping me in a hug. She smelled like pancakes, coffee . . . and Mom. It's a scent someone should bottle and sell.

She buried her face in my shoulder. "Oh, Zeke! I've been so worried. Before anyone heard I was pretend-sick, I felt *real* sick. Well, not *contagious-*sick, but *heart*-sick."

I hugged her tightly. "I'm sorry about everything you've been through, but it will get better. I might even sell more books. How 'bout if I treat to a cruise? Wouldn't you like to see Hawaii—"

She shoved me away. "I couldn't enjoy a single minute of a cruise if nasty rumors paid for it."

She had a point. I left her to her chosen release—making joyous phone calls—and joined Dad in the garage for an hour during which the most serious topic we discussed was the merits of paint versus varnish. "You and Mom should come see us."

"Haze doesn't like to fly, and I don't want to drive all over God's creation." *All over* didn't even require crossing State lines, according to Dad's definition. He was the one who hated to travel.

"She might surprise you. Sage and I have a great place and we want you to see it. We could shoot varmints," I added, feeling no guilt at dangling such an enticing gambit. "Coyotes, rabbits galore . . ."

"Yeah, well, Gull did say it's pretty nice out there," Dad admitted reluctantly.

"He ought to know," I laughed. "He's been to Utah enough times since we moved there!"

Dad's jaw tightened. *Why did we have to mention Gull?* After several unsuccessful attempts to regain our camaraderie, I returned to the house.

With phonebook open, Mom checked off names on a tablet and muttered numbers as she launched a one-woman campaign to spread the word about who the newly cleared Kiel Nede really was. I stood by, amazed as I watched Haze Eden enter *"Stand Back and No One Will Get Hurt"* land.

"No, I'm not kidding!" she burbled. "Yes! It's just been murder— Oh my goodness, can't believe I said that! Anyway, it's been *hard* not to be able to tell you, but Zeke insisted on secrecy and—" Seeing me, she waggled her fingers in an excited wave and continued talking, even while thumbing the phonebook in preparation for her next call. Grinning, I went off to pack in preparation for my flight home.

As I moved toward my assigned seat on the plane, thankfulness beyond measure surged inside me. I was returning home with a lighter load than I had hauled to Rochester.

Relief is a featherweight; Worry weighs a ton.

When I landed, I called Mom to see what the noon report had revealed. She was miffed. "Not one new thing! They just rehashed the same old stuff. No one I've talked to can believe it!"

"It was probably premature to suggest they would have more, but it will come," I assured her.

When I arrived home that evening, Sage wasn't dressed for company . . . if you get my drift. We skipped supper altogether.

One fact remained unchanged, taking the form of a niggling thought as dawn broke. I was no longer a suspect, but someone had stolen from me when they tampered with my ideas and turned them into crime. Ol' Willie-The-Bard Shakespeare sure was on-target about filching.

Just like OFF TRACK's fictional Howler, Honey Odessa Woolden-Landis was missing. According to reports, the police had as-yet-unrevealed evidence leading them to believe she was dead.

Law officials didn't rescind statements regarding clues matching OFF TRACK, even after Bill Brandt hauled Gabby Knicker back to Rochester in that classic *"Do Not Pass Go. Do Not Collect Two-Hundred Dollars"* edict that gave me unprecedented hope for a brighter future. For me, at least.

Were my efforts really finished? Could I let this go? Or should I let the professionals do their work without further amateur-level help?

Fussing over Book #17. I gave concentration the old college-try all morning. By noon, I knew it was futile.

I tried to tempt Sage with lunch in Beaver, but she had a crucial six-party conference call, followed by interviews with Salt Lake City media. *I've lost out to the phone? Well, now there's a new low-blow.*

Resigned to an afternoon of solitude, my voice narrowly missed sounding whiny when I said, "I need physical activity. I might dig up the junk we suspect is buried in that mound north of the workshop. Get it out of here and off to the dump."

"Isn't that a little ambitious for one guy?"

"If I don't do something *now* besides stare at a computer screen, I'll be worthless in an hour, Sage!"

"Put up a sign or two in town—that's the way Milford operates." She sounded distracted. *She's probably planning her conference call.* "I predict you'll have lots of help in no time," she assured me. "Meanwhile, hook up the trailer for a dump-run."

Contaminating strangers with my antsy, grumpy germs was unwise, but sometimes a one-footed guy doesn't have many choices. I couldn't concentrate enough to write, and cleaning the property seemed more mature than fussing and fuming. *But for me to do so requires help,* I admitted.

I printed four copies of a sign and cut little rip-off stubs along the bottom, each tab listing my cell and our home phone numbers. "Nice," I lauded myself. "If I lose my day job, I can make help-wanted posters. If things go well, I'll branch out to rummage sales and paint SIGNS BY ZEKE on the pickup's doors. This family is not without options!"

Good grief; I'm talking to myself? Bad scene.

I drove to town and hung my snazzy posters at the grocery store, Dolly's Country Floral & Gifts, and both gas stations. Stopping by the Post Office, I caught averted glances from people who normally would greet me. Like Sage had reported, I felt ill-at-ease and wanted to get home. Apparently news of my innocence hadn't crossed the Rockies yet.

Or did Gabby win converts?

One thing was certain: I should *not* involve any more kids in my fiascos until my name was cleared. I called the school and talked to my-pal-the-principal who didn't argue about delaying the next Honors Writing Course until after Christmas. Creating a whole new dimension to the concept of *ill-tempered*, I grumbled, "He could've tried to change my mind!"

I paced until I created a heat source beneath my feet that felt hot enough to ignite. "Hey, *you* called *him*."

Great; now I'm arguing with myself?

In three days, I received only one response to my ad. In my naïveté, I had assumed the phone would ring incessantly and I would schedule interviews, select the best, and let the losers down graciously with vague promises of "Maybe another time."

Each night, Sage listened good-naturedly to my frustration over no calls. "Poor Zeke," she teased the first evening, running her hands over my bald pate. "Won't anyone play with you?"

The second day it was, "Still no playmates?"

When the one-and-only call came, ten o'clock the third day, I struggled to sound nonchalant when a well-modulated voice responded to my greeting with, "Hello; this is Hank Bedlow. I saw a poster that says you need help digging. Tell me more."

Even with so little said, I caught vocal nuances indicating a level of confidence I hadn't expected from anyone applying for manual labor. *Bedlow; Hank Bedlow . . . I have no clue!* "Thanks for calling, Hank. This is Zeke Eden; I didn't put my name on the ad for various and sundry reasons."

"Zeke Eden? Yes: our local author!" Even his chuckle carried inflections that resonated with . . . *what?* It eluded me. "This appeals to me," he continued. "What can I tell you to ensure I'm the one you hire?" Gently rolling laughter followed.

"Are you game for a hot, sweaty job with all the cold water you want, if I provide the shovel? We'll be digging a deep hole to retrieve buried junk, and carting it all to the dump—that's the job. I've done some preliminary work, but I'm not able to finish it alone. I'm offering ten bucks an hour, a hefty lunch, and calorie-laden breaks. Did I scare you off yet?"

"Hardly."

"Good, because you're my only respondent."

"Glad I called! If there's digging to do, let's dig. When do you want to start? Today?"

"Sure, if you're available. I live east of town—"

He cut me off smoothly. "I know the place. See you within half an hour."

I had time to call Sage with the news her husband was finally going to climb out of the emotional slough he had wallowed in for the past few days.

"Hank Bedlow?" she blurted with all the disbelief two words can hold. "I'm surprised he's still around, but even more flabbergasted you'd hire him."

"You know him?" I asked, ready to be amused by hearing of yet another small-town phenomenon—maybe Heather had dated Hank, or Sage had babysat his kids or she remembered him as a plump and pimply classmate who spewed spit when he talked.

"Of *course* I know him; so should you. Didn't you recognize his name?"

"Obviously not. What's the deal?"

"*Reverend* Hank Bedlow? Conducted Mom and Dad's funerals? Ringin' any bells yet, Sweet-ums?"

A blow to the solar plexus. *A minister.* I had just hired a minister to help me dig up junk? Buying myself time to recover from shock, I took a swig of coffee so hot it scalded my mouth and left a burned trail through my esophagus.

"You still there, Zeke?"

"Yeah." I groaned long and loud. "Good Lord! What have I gotten myself into?"

She laughed. "You'll be fine; just edit the 'good Lord' remarks! Don't worry; he was inoffensive then, so a complete personality change is unlikely. After all, it's not as if you've hired him for the rest of time immortal. Dig the hole, dump the junk, and bid The Reverend farewell."

"Yeah, I suppose. If nothing else, spending time with a minister will give us plenty to talk about in the evening. I can treat the encounter as research."

"That's my guy, always looking on the bright side," Sage quipped. "Don't let him change a single thing about you. I love you just the way you are."

17

When Hank stepped out of his car, I recognized him immediately—even if his appearance was now *un*ministerial. Jeans replaced the funereal black suit; the traditional white shirt and dignified tie were swapped for a T-shirt with a pocket; no more wingtips—I was looking at work boots that had survived more than a few challenges.

Most important: No Bible in evidence, but his hip pocket sported a bulge shaped like a billfold likely loaded with all the detritus guys can't relinquish.

Without Sage's heads-up on Hank's identity, it may have taken a while to remember how I knew him. His major visible changes since the latter of the two Crowley funerals created an even stronger resemblance to Kiel Nede than Sage had noticed in our whispered exchange during Lefty's funeral luncheon.

Still sporting cheerfully ruddy cheeks, a slightly enhanced pot-belly, and longer white hair than I recalled, his current appearance said, *The Sixties live, man!* Put him and Kiel on a street corner, give 'em guitars with Kiel's beret placed at their feet, and *Groove-on, man!* They'd bring in some serious coinage, strumming and singing, *"The answer, my friend, is blowing in the wind . . ."*

Seeing as how my companion for the day was a pastor, I decided honesty was the best policy. I dove in with, "After we talked, I called my wife to let her know I'd gotten a response. Sage is a Crowley, and she reminded me that we met you at her parents' funerals. Sorry I didn't recognize your name."

He glanced at the house. "Yes, I enjoyed your in-laws. Wow, that June sure could cook!" Without concern for segue, he rambled on, "As I recall, I made you a bit nervous then, what with all the God-talk that naturally surrounds funerals conducted in a church setting. But, rest assured: I neither bite nor chase, so you're safe!"

I managed a weak smile in return for his honest and no-holds-barred grin.

"However, if you change your mind about hiring me, I understand. I hope you don't; I need exercise," he patted his stomach, "and besides appreciating the money, I'll enjoy the intellectual stimulation of talking with you. But it's your call; no hard feelings if you're uncomfortable."

"Stick around! Sorry your lingering impression of me has been less than complimentary. It's just that I . . . well, Sage and I aren't faithful church attendees so during my adult years, I've had few contacts with ministers."

"Make that retired pastor, in my case. I haven't prepared a sermon for several years. You are the only big-time writer I've met, so that makes us even, hmm?" He pulled work gloves from a back pocket, which I took it as a signal he was ready for action. Somehow, I had an odd feeling I was no longer in complete control of the day.

"Where'd you spend the Sixties?" I asked, also donning gloves.

"Haight Ashbury. How 'bout you?"

Bring on the guitars! "Nothing so quixotic. I was at the University of Minnesota, Duluth."

"Brave man! I spent what seemed like a *week* one October *day* on Lake Superior," he said with a wry smile. "The wind coming off that water is cruel! California didn't even have to whistle—I went back as fast as the trains could get me there. Those days, my mode of transportation was riding the rails. No fares, no fuss, and all the fresh air a guy could want; more, sometimes!"

Suddenly I no longer dreaded working with Hank. As we walked to the pitiful mound of dirt I'd created on my own, I flirted with danger by asking the one question that seemed important as a filter for every conversation we were likely to conduct, "So, you no longer pastor a church, Reverend Bedlow?"

"Not anymore, and please call me Hank. My wife and I came to Milford thirty-one years ago. Four years ago, I decided to bow out so the church could pursue younger leadership than I can offer."

Hurray for small favors, I cheered, adding *wife* to my shallow list of safe topics. "You're married?"

"Widowed. Vivien robbed, molested, and then killed by a vagrant early in our second year here."

My heart lurched. As I tried to picture nearly three decades without Sage, tears fogged my vision. "Oh, I'm sorry; I can't imagine—" I released an audible, jagged breath.

"Nor could I before it happened. It took many months before I could even say Vivien's name without falling apart. It was a hard time, but June—your mother-in-law—ministered to my physical and emotional needs without words. Her casseroles, desserts, and kindhearted generosity all worked wonders toward feeding and healing me. I didn't get to know Lefty as well as I did June, but I enjoyed my encounters with him. Both Crowley funerals were difficult ones for me."

I couldn't speak around the lump in my throat. I had to wonder, *Did Vivien share Hank's life and adventures during the Sixties?*

Hank kicked at a half-buried tire and whistled a three-note slide. "Whew, I see why you need help! It sure isn't a one-man project. From the dimensions of the heap, I'd say things are buried deep."

"Blame it on wind. If wind hadn't blown that tire halfway clear, I may never have wondered what was beneath this rise." I waved at a wash-like mound midst the sagebrush. "I'm interested and leery to see what all is buried here, but I don't have the wherewithal to tackle it alone."

With my unprecedented revelation to Bill Brandt having paved the way to honesty, it seemed silly to be vague with Hank Bedlow. "I'm missing a foot." I extended my left leg toward him. "This is strictly bogus from the ankle down."

He thrust his shovel in a mound. "I'm equipped with two original feet, manufactured and installed by my Maker, and functioning quite well except for an occasional arthritic twinge. Your prosthesis could hold out longer than my original parts!"

We worked together in companionable silence for a few moments and then he started a fresh topic. "Based on a disquieting talk with Gabby Knicker last week, I gather you're going through a rough time. I'm a loyal Kiel Nede reader, so I bet Gabby didn't consider me her most cooperative interviewee!"

Hank's smooth maneuvers from funerals to murdered wife to fake feet to the infamous Gabby Knicker to his own Kiel-Need fan-status floored me. "You've read my books?"

If I had been surprised teenagers enjoyed what I wrote, thinking about ministers flipping those same pages was downright unsettling. Thankfully, I had pegged Raven Crowley from the get-go as a strong, silent type. The alternative could easily have been a foul-mouthed, spittin'-and-chewin' reprobate, the likes of which so many authors favor. That sort of uncouth fellow would *not* have gained enthusiasts among Men-of-the-Cloth.

"Read? More like consumed!" Hank hooted. "A guard up at Utah State Prison in Draper loaned me a copy of STICK-UP and I was hooked. I negotiated a deal with the Milford librarian that if I donated half, the library would purchase the rest."

"Why were you talking to prison guards?" I was completely perplexed, but now knew why Milford's library owned my complete body of work.

Leaning on his shovel, Hank said, "After Vivien died, the anger and hatred I felt grew like a cancer. I had to find a cure, or it would consume me. A wise friend suggested I visit her murderer in prison. I thought, *Yes! I'll dump all my fury on him, then piously kneel, bow my head, and loudly call down God's wrath, making that low-life rue the day he set foot in Milford.*"

Shaking his head over such an attitude, he interrupted himself while I stared, astonished.

"Wouldja look at this, Zeke! If we collected all the rabbit bones scattered here, we could reconstruct a critter just like a kid's science project!" He eased the tip of his shovel under a sun-bleached and fragile spinal cord; a tiny intact skull lay nearby.

Rabbits—dead or alive—were low on my list of interests. "So you went?" I prompted.

"I went, bitter and ready to make Wally's life as miserable as he'd made mine. Ironically, that first visit I didn't see a felon. I saw a kid who started doing drugs, then ventured into armed robbery.

Once he hit that slippery slope, he plunged right into murder. I saw terror in his eyes when he recognized me from the trial. It struck me, we had loneliness in common. He was lonely and afraid; I was lonely and angry. We barely spoke that first day but I kept going back."

"You do realize that what you're telling me defies reason?" I challenged. "It must go along with your career, I mean, turning the other cheek, all that—" I quickly edited "*malarkey*" to "uh, that sort of thing."

"Nothing I've done in my life is harder. Being a pastor means I know more about what I *should* do and think than goes with a clear conscience. Others often express your sentiments, and I've told myself the same frequently. It was, and is a crazy idea—a gamble, some say. I prefer to think of it as a God-thing. Whatever, it worked. I exchanged anger for peace; Wally exchanged fear for friendship."

I heaved a shovelful. "Not many could do what you did."

"What I *do*. I still see Wally; he's serving a life sentence. He's fifty-one, so has a ways to go until he meets the Eternal Judge. His earlier transgressions complicate the appeals. You're welcome to go with me sometime. Consider it research for future books. Draper's an interesting place."

I shook my head in disbelief, not rebuttal. "Forget Draper; you're what's interesting, Hank."

"Enough about me," he said. "According to the news, you're cleared. That must feel terrific."

"It does, but someone out there did do the deed—and used OFF TRACK as their Bible."

Hank lifted his cap to wipe his brow. "Prickly mess, isn't it? What'll you do?"

"Not sure. I can't concentrate enough to write, so I decided to tackle this clean-up project. It seemed like a mission with visible results."

"Nothing like physical exhaustion to help clear the brain," he agreed. "In the first few years after Vivian died, I changed our carport into a garage, and put a fence around our yard—not using a power post-hole digger, martyr that I am! And I hiked at least ten peaks around here. Oh, and I took out a wall in my house. You'll have to come see it."

I couldn't explain why I liked this fellow, but I did, even though his life's work normally would put me on full alert.

"I read an interesting article in the Smithsonian's magazine about the difference between puzzles and mysteries. The author said puzzles can be solved—there *is* an answer; but mysteries have to be framed. Get all the pieces together and a puzzle is done, but you can't collect all the pieces needed to formulate, or solve, a walloping-good mystery."

"Right." *Where is this verbal detour headed?*

"You likely already unconsciously apply those principles to your writing, but have you considered doing the same with the mystery facing you now? Perhaps you could tighten the frame around what you know—disarm the ambiguities. Don't treat it like a puzzle. I'll loan you the magazine if you'd like to read the article."

Hand me a ballot; I was ready to nominate Hank Bedlow as Most Intriguing Person I had ever met. "I would; thanks."

Our efforts that first day produced five bald tires, three ripped screen windows in warped frames, two dented garbage cans which we filled with tin cans and plastic bottles, an oil barrel so full of bullets it rattled like a pair of maracas, and at least a dozen damaged tar buckets. By day's end, all that remained in the pit was a dismantled swamp cooler, and miscellaneous car parts in varying conditions—including half a windshield—and more trash.

Exhausted, Hank and I stared into the deep hole. "We should probably hook a chain to your truck to help us get the really big stuff out so we don't hurt our backs," he said. "What's that thing over there? Part of a wringer washing machine?"

"Could be; I vote we save it for another day."

We had collected more than enough refuse to merit a trip to the dump, so we loaded the trailer. Matching the menagerie of junk, our conversation proved equally broad, ranging from scattered pieces of our life stories to discovering we both loved Bob

Dylan. He hooted at my fantasy of Hank, Kiel and the guitars. "Say when; I'm game!"

Hank worked like a trooper, no complaints and no slacking off. We broke for lunch on the pergola, practically inhaling chips and BLTs with turkey and cheese added to fill the sourdough buns. Other than that, our only pauses were to wipe our foreheads, or to devour leftovers of Sage's fabulous peanut-butter brownies.

After his first taste, Hank scoffed, "Hard to believe you have leftovers of these!" Combined with crisp, juicy apples it was a worthy snack, which we enjoyed beneath a scrawny tree's shade where we washed it all down with guzzled well-water that Hank dubbed "the nectar those Greek gods lauded!"

With the trailer loaded, we replenished our water bottles and climbed into the pickup. Reviving a topic from our far-ranging conversation, Hank said, "I don't mean to tell you what to do, you understand—even if it sounds like that's exactly what I'm doing!—but you should let Raven tackle your conundrum."

"Don't I wish? Love to, except for one significant problem: Raven only knows as much as I do."

"Maybe you know more than you give yourself credit for. Raven could be your answer-man. You said your first thought after Gabby dug her claws into you was that only Raven could help. So let him.

Bring Raven to the scene." He poured water on a bandana and wiped his face.

"Easier said than done," I hedged. "I'm thrilled to be cleared of suspicion, but I've sworn off messing with Gabby or her friends."

He nodded, and we talked of other things.

Unloading at the Beaver County Landfill required much less effort and time than filling the trailer. As we approached Sunny Acres where Hank's car was parked, we followed a familiar vehicle along the last mile.

"That cloud of dust ahead of us is Sage," I said. "My wife, I mean, not the plant!"

He grinned. "I hear she really knows her stuff."

"Indeed, and what stuff it is. Way over my head."

"I'll stay long enough to greet her at arm's length; I need a shower! What time tomorrow?" Hank asked, as I turned the final corner into our driveway.

"Eight's good," I said, tapping the horn in our long-standing three-note signal of *I love you!* to my waiting gal.

Sage stood beside her car, one hand shading her eyes, as we pulled up. "Thought I saw someone in the truck with you, Zeke!" She approached Hank with a ready smile and an extended hand. "Hello, Reverend Bedlow. It is so nice to see you again."

Hank wiped his hand on his jeans before reaching out. "Hello, Sage; I retired the title along with my career, so please call me Hank. I spent an enjoyable day with Zeke, even though he made me work harder than I have in weeks!"

"In that case, you have my sincere apologies! To make amends, may I invite you to stay for supper?" Sage asked, casting me an *Agree?* glance.

"The menu is taco salad," I responded promptly, "and the meat's already seasoned and cooked, so minimal assembly is required. We'll eat out on the pergola so we won't offend the lady even if we do smell like bums!"

"I accept," Hank said simply.

"Oh!" Sage halted on the steps. "If you need to call home, please invite whoever's there to join us. When Zeke makes taco salad, it feeds a crowd!"

See what I mean? Hands-down, Sage is a pro at not saying the wrong thing.

"Just me, but I love taco salad. I promise to eat so much you'll swear you fed a crowd! First, I'll stick my head under that spigot over yonder and emerge slightly more presentable before I join you on the pergola. Or, can I help with anything, Zeke?"

"He needs no help, and you deserve more than a spigot!" Sage scoffed before I could reply. "You may use Zeke's office bathroom, then meet me outside." She leaned in for my kiss. "Glad you're home, Zeke; evenings alone are D-U-L-L–dull!"

I got Hank set up before joining Sage in our bedroom. "Good idea to invite Hank; he lives alone," I said, stripping of my filthy clothing.

"Glad you agreed. I gather your day went well? No proselytizing of wayward souls by hired help?"

"He 'doesn't bite and doesn't chase'—direct quote and true. It was one of the most interesting afternoons of my recent life, which says a lot. He not only lives alone, he's a widower." That synopsis of Hank would have to suffice; there was no time now, even for an abridged version, and I wanted to tell Sage the whole story.

The process of doffing work-blouse, donning at-home shirt muffled Sage's voice. "Most interesting? If you say so," she allowed, while ducking into the closet to retrieve sandals. "Pssst!" Her stage whisper slowed my exit to the kitchen. "Ask Hank to say Grace or he'll think we're heathens!"

By the time I had dishes, beverages and food ready on one of the pergola's spool tables, Hank and Sage were well on the way to becoming friends. Her at-ease demeanor and spontaneous laughter at our guest's droll remarks showed me she agreed: Hank Bedlow wasn't a dangerous guy to get to know.

As for that pre-meal prayer? Before I could ask, Hank offered. "Would you mind if I gush a little to the Lord before we dig into this fabulous food?"

And so he did, over our taco salad and hastily assembled strawberry shortcake—and all without a single *Thee-Thy-Thou*. Not one red flag unfurled in my suspicious little mind.

18

The next day Hank brought the promised magazine; the following day, we analyzed the Smithsonian's article in depth. In all, we made three more trips to the landfill, and completed our ultimate task of clearing much of the buried junk. Along the way, we became friends despite a most bizarre and definite contrast of life philosophies and experiences.

It occurred to me as Hank drove away the final day that if anyone had told me, a year earlier, that my five best friends in Milford would be four teenagers and a minister, I would have scoffed, "Never!" But that's how I felt. Life's weird, huh?

I approached my office on my first post-Hank day with a clear head, a renewed spirit and refreshed body. For three days, no disparaging words appeared in the media about OFF TRACK—only up-beat reviews from around the globe. That was good because Maggie was doing her agent-thing, hustling dates for live Kiel Nede appearances. The next few weeks would be a whirlwind of frequent-flier miles accumulating like plastic grocery bags caught on barbed wire fences.

Maggie's e-mailed schedule included all pertinent details, with her usual few nonessentials added. (*In Denver, there's a new restaurant you might like . . .*)

I noted names of old friends still managing favorite bookstores, and newbies I hoped were up to the frenzy of a Kiel Nede event.

Sage reviewed the tour that evening and decided to join me for two Bay Area events. "Cable cars, Chinatown, chilly winds off Alcatraz, chocolates from Ghirardelli Square? Will I tag along? But, of course, my dear! Table for two, please!" she trilled, flagging an invisible concierge.

Two weeks, twelve cities, thousands of signatures, ten different beds and only travel time during which Zeke was anonymous. That was my fate. Twice (once in Duluth, Minnesota, where I expected it, and in New York where I was surprised anyone cared) I heard comments about Kiel Nede's links to real-life murder. *Did I make more of the Rochester mess than it warranted?* I asked myself, embarrassed.

Back in Milford, the uneasiness and suspicions Gabby had left in her wake gradually faded; Zeke Eden was no longer a pariah. Once again, I whistled while I worked. Life was good.

My second day home, Hank invited me to his house for coffee in exchange for travel stories. I followed a brick walkway to a well-maintained one-story house and paused before I rang the bell to admire lush red geraniums. They overflowed flower boxes below bay windows flanking the front door.

Hank appeared immediately. Over his shoulder, I saw a recliner and end table. A lamp cast a circle of

light over a tottering stack of books. *My kinda guy!*
"Come in!" He had a paperback in-hand.

Questions about what he was reading (a career-based instinct) all evaporated when I crossed the threshold. Opposite the easy chair, a two-foot-wide floor-to-ceiling aquarium that replaced a wall was aglow from recessed lighting. A tidy bedroom was vaguely visible through the shimmering water.

My mouth opened and closed, as if mocking the creatures swiftly swimming between gleaming glass walls. A dozen or more rainbow-hued fish of varied sizes, shapes and distinctive markings, dipped and dove, ducked and dodged in their aquatic heaven.

Watching me, Hank chuckled. "You like?"

"Sure do! It's hard to absorb." Awed, I walked the length of the barrier between the two rooms.

"This was the post-Vivien project that gives me continual pleasure. We'll have coffee in here so you can soak it up—visually, at least!" He grinned.

I couldn't take my eyes off the movie-like display. Hank left the room, returning with cups, coffee, and cookies. "I don't have your kitchen skills, Zeke, but a highly reputable corporation's advertising assures me these are 'just like homemade' treats!"

When I left two hours later, I brazenly invited myself back for a return visit—but, with Sage. "She has to see this—" I grinned. "Calling it a fish tank or even an aquarium is inadequate! It's artistry, and I don't intend to give Sage any warning!"

❖

Flying between Saint Louis and Detroit, I had picked a title for the Milford mystery: LOST GROUND. Sage cheered when I called with the news that I was developing characters who would lend themselves nicely to the plot I had devised during countless hours in airports and airplane seats.

Except for missing Sage, I felt so productive that I suggested facetiously in one late-night phone conversation, "Maybe I should travel more."

"I don't know if Zeke or Kiel had that idea, but both of you get back to home base immediately!"

One thing I no longer wasted brain cells on was solving the mystery of who killed Honey Odessa Woolden-Landis. Gabby Knicker slid into never-never land, like how a bad dream after eating too many County-Fair hotdogs fades in morning light.

Sage worked, and kept the Powers That Be happy.

I wrote, and did house-husband things.

Mom called, and sent articles on the dangers of too much sun.

It was disconcerting to realize Mom's focus was no longer on future mysteries, just concern over me getting skin cancer out on the high mountain desert. Odd, how getting what a person wants—in my case, longing for less maternal interference—leaves a gap.

Dad sent greetings, but didn't mention my open-ended invitation to visit.

Gull resurfaced via calls scattered several days apart, and hinted how I should pursue a co-investor business opportunity that "matched" my interests.

I neither committed nor encouraged. One thing I've learned: Investing in Gull's ventures gives real meaning to the phrase "Life's too short."

"Get the phone?" I called to Sage on my third Sunday home from tour. I was making a recipe that made me wonder why I ever thought I could cook. It featured a hunk of such beautiful boneless beef that Sage insisted *I* be the weekend chef. "The recipe has more levels of complexity than my stories!" I fussed. Waving me into silence, she answered the phone with her usual pleasant greeting.

Within seconds, she was turning on the TV news. "Zeke, take a look—or at least listen." Her tone aborted my concentrated grating of fresh nutmeg for a tricky sauce. "You mom just caught a teaser and says we need to watch national news."

"This is the Six O'clock Evening Report from your network news leader in Salt Lake City," a disembodied voice announced from the kitchen TV.

Upbeat music, zoom-and-fade logos preceded the split-second head-shots of each of the four young-and-beautiful newscasters who were busily arranging their last-minute notes. Introductory splashes of the sounds, colorful scrolling words, and dizzy action, which apparently are deemed necessary to precede each broadcast, regardless of the station chosen.

A nicely coiffed woman met the camera's eye:

"Preliminary reports indicate that discovery of a body near railroad tracks may provide a much-needed break in a case which has captured the nation's attention. Minnesota investigators have released few details, but it appears likely the deceased is Honey Odessa Woolden-Landis.

"Ms Woolden-Landis is owner of the railroad involved in an ongoing dispute with Rochester's citizens and many businesses over rights-of-passage for potentially dozens of daily trains. As of this report, no additional information has been released, pending positive identification of the body."

While the camera shifted between faces for the next story, Sage and I released simultaneous breaths.

I found my voice first: "Questions abound, but this lets me off the hook since it's now proven her body wasn't in the Quarry Hill Park cave."

"Zeke! Don't get all analytical on me; this is a big relief! Huge!" Sage flung herself into my arms. Feeling dampness on my neck, I pulled away to see her face. *Whoa! My cool, calm, always-collected gal is crying?*

Detected, she gave way to full-fledged gulping sobs, shaking shoulders: the whole nine yards.

"Sage! Sweetheart, it's okay!" Running my hands along her arms provided only negligible comfort to her and heated my palms to the tingle-point, so I ceased that and resumed hugging her.

"I'm just so happy and thankful," she bawled. "I never realized how good reprieve could feel!" She handed me the kitchen phone. "Call Haze; she was frantic." While I dialed, Sage blew her nose loudly and continued to spurt tears.

For the next three minutes, my contributions were limited to ineffectual blurtings of "Mom—" and "Yes, it's—" and "I'm—" while I listened to her extol my virtues and expound on how she *always . . .* she just *knew . . .* she *never doubted . . .* and—before she ran out of steam—how *very proud* she was of me and how *deeply* she loved me.

Wanna bet that if I walked into her kitchen in the next half-hour, Haze wouldn't whip up little Ezekiel Daniel Eden's favorite meal of macaroni and cheese with hotdogs cut into buttons? Meanwhile, back to my own menu that involved no wieners, sliced or whole. It was a plate-licking meal, if I do say so, and looked just like the picture.

Someone should do a study on my newly formulated theory that folks who have had a cloud hanging over their heads and suddenly emerge from beneath its ominous shadow become more creative, more productive, and more alive than at any previous time in their history. It happened for me.

Even more than the intense physical exercise with Hank, the knowledge no one would be pounding on our door, pointing fingers or looking sideways at me made the drug-induced highs of the Sixties seem like child's play. I was stoked! My brain burped good stuff faster than my fingers could type.

I worked through the night, almost nonstop. The next day, was a blur: "Hope your day goes well, Sage." *Did I eat lunch?* "Welcome home, Sage." *Did I see the sun today?* "Is ice cream for dessert okay?" *No clean pajamas? Didn't I do laundry?* "G'night, Sage."

I crashed from exhaustion, sleeping until noon. But I awoke still reeling with creative ideas, the best of which was to call Cale and ask him to find a time for the Honors Writing Course students to hold a reunion. I promised to furnish sweet treats.

"Can you come today at two? We'll be at the park b'cuz we're still writing, you know," he said.

I hadn't known, but it pleased me. "I'll be there."

When I arrived, Mathia had already cleaned a blue table in the picnic shelter. "I chose blue, because it matches my eyes!" she chirped as the others skidded in on the gravel and parked their bikes outside the shelter. We were all in capricious moods.

We talked about their writing; they asked about mine. When I told them the title of the new book, Cale frowned and shook his head soberly. "Oh-oh, I don't know, Myster-E." He smirked. "Just jokin'!

LOST GROUND is a super title for a mining mystery. Besides, the next book I name will be my own."

I cheered; he rose and bowed so low his nose touched blue paint; the girls rolled their eyes.

When we all settled down, I told them Honey's body had likely been found. They, being typical kids, had not listened to the news, so knew nothing about it. Given the dearth of information available, my account was necessarily brief.

Jacey's brow furrowed. "This means you're clear, right, Myster-E? Because she's not in the cave."

"Precisely. Someone stole and modified my idea, but I'll let the officials chase him or her. I'm content to be off-focus for anything controversial."

"The librarian said you were on Oprah. Missed it." Fable snapped her fingers in a *Drats!* gesture. "Bet that was fun, huh?"

"Always. It keeps me on my toes because just when I think I've heard everything an interviewer could ask, out pops a new question."

"What was it this time?" Mathia asked.

"Oh, Oprah practically begged for details about my four collaborators."

Four voices yelled, "No!" but their lilting tones belied any true protests.

I laughed. "You're right; I did mention you on my own but don't worry: I didn't give your names. I just dangled a mysterious clue about four teens who are credited in OFF TRACK. People can look it up!"

"Oh, man!" Cale moaned. "If ya wanna mention me on national TV, go right ahead!"

"Only if I had your parents' permission," I said sanctimoniously, masking a grin.

"Do it! Next time, say our names!" Jacey begged.

"You'll let us know what's happening, like where they find The Bulldog—if that's who the body turns out to be, won't you?" Mathia asked.

"You bet," I promised.

They promptly reverted to adolescent goofiness about decomposed bodies, being the ones to discover the corpse, what they'd do with the reward (vowing, like every lottery winner, "twenty-five thousand dollars wouldn't change me at all"). We finally tossed their bikes in my truck's bed, they crowded in, and I provided taxi service.

What a grand hour! I couldn't have been happier if I had won the railroad's twenty-five thousand dollar bounty.

I had gotten lazy about keeping tabs on Rochester news since returning from tour, but there's nothing like an unofficial acquittal to pique interest. Back home from the park, I turned on the radio in hopes of catching any-and-all updates while I multi-tasked— also impatiently surfing the Internet.

The case lurked in the shadows like a tight-lipped suspicious Auntie, revealing little new, but inching suspicions higher simply by its continued and looming presence:

Teasing us with confirmation that the corpse was Honey Odessa Woolden-Landis, but holding tightly to other facts the public longed to know . . .

Taunting by saying nothing about who discovered the body except that the reward would be held until the deceased's identity was public knowledge . . .

Testing our patience with vague inferences about the location where the corpse had spent a silent repose . . .

Tempting listeners with rampant theories that old facts were not entirely useless . . .

Tormenting all with innuendoes that officials were closing in on Persons of Interest to either confirm or disprove their statements . . .

Half-listening, half-working, I diddled with Book #17's first chapter and dubbed it "one of my best," even knowing spurts of concentration interspersed with multiple flights-of-fancy meant serious editing or outright revisions ahead.

Sage had kept a dandy surprise from me and abruptly arrived home with Mom and Dad in tow. When I recovered from my shock—which included discovering that Sage had not been at work all day, but had been driving to the Salt Lake City airport to retrieve them—we all settled down for a late supper.

Inevitably, our conversation circled around to The Bulldog. "Will they ever catch her killer?" Dad asked, helping himself to his fifth barbecued chicken drumstick. Nothing like Utah air to whet an appetite.

"It'll take time, but yeah. With modern forensics and TV programs like America's Most Wanted, it's hard to get away with murder these days," I said.

Mom sniffed. "They better find the s-o-pardon-my-French-b who dragged *my son* through the mud." The message in her rare departure from ladylike language? *Don't mess with Mama Bear's cub.*

"That's probably dropped pretty low on their list, Mom, now that they've found Honey's body. I'm willing to let it go. Onward-and-upward, right?"

We disrupted our card game until after the evening newscasts' top stories, with Dad negotiating to keep listening until after the weather. Our bantering halted when Mom cried out, "Look! It's The Bulldog!" The screen showed an unflattering photo of a tearful Honey, mascara running down her cheeks, her mouth twisted by sobs. The suited-and-necktied newscaster intoned:

> "As occasionally happens, it is not the efforts of highly trained and motivated investigators that unveils clues, but random luck. This time, it was a citizen doing his daily job who discovered the corpse believed to be the victim of a sensational, high-profile crime that has baffled officials.
>
> "The coroner's initial report reveals only that the deceased was a woman. Investigators continue to pursue the

perpetrator behind the alleged abduction and murder of Honey Odessa Woolden-Landis, owner of the railroad at the center of the debate over railroad expansion in Rochester, Minnesota."

"But where did they find her? Why do they need to be so secretive?" Mom protested.

"It's standard procedure, Mom. Revealing too much, too soon gives criminals time to cover their tracks. Officials always withhold pertinent details that only the bad guys would know, hoping to trap them. More will come out, I guarantee it," I said.

In an attempt to ease Mom's frustrations, Sage suggested, "That's why we hear the expression 'stay tuned for further developments' so often."

We packed a lot into the folks' week-long visit. We hosted a repeat picnic for the teens' families (although it required sweaters this time around, and I grilled chicken breasts) so the parents could meet the unusual Senior Citizens who had bedazzled their usually-blasé-about-adults children. Abbott and Dad enjoyed their reunion, and everyone loved Haze.

Hank Bedlow came for dinner the next evening. It was a rowdy affair during which we discovered that, like Mom, Hank could recite Edgar Allan Poe's narrative poem "The Raven" in its entirety.

Bemused, Dad, Sage and I listened to all eighteen six-lined stanzas of the poem, with hardly a missed word, although Mom and Hank prompted each other several times. At the end, Dad cracked us up when he intoned, "Nevermore!" and steepled his hands in supplication.

All-too-soon, Mom and Dad flew out and life in Utah resumed its normal pace. Sage worked, I wrote, and Gull called with another report on his new scheme. It sounded almost feasible, so I was able to be a bit more positive than usual. Amazingly enough, my brother had hatched the idea to open a studio for writers—a quiet place where ideas could flow uninterrupted

Hanging up, I told Sage, "Gull may really have a winner, this time. Whodda-thunk *that* phenomenon could happen?"

When Hank had joined us for supper during Mom and Dad's visit, he and I had set a chess date for later that week; Sage tacked on a supper invitation. But when he rang the doorbell on our scheduled evening, I was stirring mushrooms in a sauté pan—distracted, again, by the day's news, leaving Sage to welcome our guest.

"Sage says you know more details?" he queried.

I nodded toward the counter. "There's the article, printed off the Rochester Post Bulletin's website. Hour-old news; feel free to read it aloud, Hank."

He pulled reading glasses from a pocket, propped them on his nose, and began:

> "Reputable sources revealed today that
> the body discovered in Utah . . ."

"Utah?" Frowning, he peered at us over the cheaters' rims. "Utah!" he repeated incredulously.

"Keep reading," Sage said dryly.

". . . is Honey Odessa Woolden-Landis, the flamboyant owner of the railroad who has been heavily engaged in the ongoing local railroad disputes.

"As investigations continue into what sequence of events placed a Minnesota woman in Utah, there will certainly be many questions to answer—even beyond who her killer was.

"Over the weeks since Ms Woolden-Landis' disappearance, alert readers of Kiel Nede's latest mystery, OFF TRACK, have flooded the Crime-Tip phone-line and website with suggestions that this case closely follows the plot of that story. Positive identification of the body will now send readers back to the book, searching for more parallel clues."

Hank met my gaze as he shoved his glasses up to rest on his brow. "Oh, Zeke, this is distressing!"

I glanced at the clock and lowered the heat beneath two pans. "Let's try to catch TV news."

We had missed the beginning of the segment. With incongruously beautiful scenery as a backdrop to the report, we listened intently to the sophisticated woman continuing her report:

". . . outside Green River in Utah . . ."

Honey's dressed-for-success photo filled the screen before it diminished to a thumbnail image by the reporter's shoulder. We stared at Utah's rocks and ridges in what Sage long-ago dubbed "fifty-nine shades of brown" beneath an intensely blue sky.

> ". . . as new details emerge, we continue our report of the chilling story that leaps State borders. Residents in the Green River, Utah, area are justifiably concerned about a ruthless killer. Few feel safe . . ."

The scene switched to a tattooed bicyclist wearing sunglasses and a backpack, then a mother holding a thumb-sucking toddler, and finally a construction worker heading home with his lunchbox. All soberly reiterated: "Yeah, I'm, well, nervous . . ." or "Everyone's so scared . . ." or "It's bad, real bad . . ." before the camera returned to the interviewer:

> "This is Kathy Limens, reporting live from eastern Utah. Back to you in the studio, Warren."
>
> "Thanks, Kathy. In Boston today . . ."

Scenes of a multi-vehicle pile-up replaced Utah's breathtaking scenery and the numbing discovery that jerked me out of self-induced disengagement.

We muddled through our delayed dinner. Murder took the fourth chair, an uninvited but impossible-to-reject-or-ignore guest at the table.

We ate, or so I presume since I cleared empty plates with food stains spattered on them.

We talked, pondered and debated, never thinking to leave the table, even as moonrise preceded sunset.

"What's your biggest worry, Zeke?" Hank asked as we set up the chess board in the living room and Sage settled in on the couch opposite us with her cross-stitching.

"I don't know; I can't shake my original feeling of uneasiness that someone is going to a lot of trouble to frame me. He's not done; moving the mess to Utah shows he obviously knows I live here. It's like he didn't reel me in when everything was happening in Rochester, so he's shifted it closer to home."

"Do you think you need protection?"

Sage clamped her lips to muffle a gasp.

"No, no; surely not," I protested, but I felt dizzy.

"Remember what I told you when we drove to the dump that day? Even more important now: It's time to apply Raven-like thinking. You can do it."

"That's precisely what I told him ages ago!" Sage exclaimed. "Zeke, *now* are you ready to listen to reason? Put Raven on the case; this is all getting too close to home."

The catch in her voice pierced and deflated my protests. I had never desired to meet Raven face-to-face and I knew Milford wouldn't want him around. *But now*, I figured, *if ever a reason existed to separate conjoined twins in hopes of giving one a better chance at life, Raven and Zeke should be at the top of the waiting list.*

Trouble was, despite medical experts' best efforts in such emergencies, the feebler twin often didn't survive. And it didn't take a rocket scientist, brain surgeon, or Whiz-Kid to spout the correct answer to the burning question: *Who's the weaker one was in this case: Raven or Zeke?*

19

Two days later, Sage needed to attend what the promotional brochure labeled "An Interactive Seminar for Today's Innovative Healthcare CEOs" in Vegas. Well, *innovative* described her to a T and, since the latest news had jarred me enough to make writing difficult, I offered to drive, suggesting that we could connect with Heather. Change of scenery would motivate me either to work on LOST GROUND, or—as Sage hoped—start me thinking like Raven.

On the road, we took turns fiddling with the radio; when one station faded, we searched for the next clear signal. "The Saga of the Dead Bulldog," as one lead-in so crassly described it, was no longer the top story, but eventually we learned:

> "Slowly unraveling details indicate that foul play is suspected in the death of Honey Odessa Woolden-Landis. The investigation is ongoing to discover the circumstances that brought the controversial railroad owner to Utah.
>
> Suicide has been ruled out. Pending additional information, this case has been booked as murder."

"Ya *think*?" Sage mocked. "Duh! Of course it's murder! Who're the buffoons who write this stuff?"

The report's vague and repetitive nature hinted that the investigation was blocked. Wasting costly revenue seconds on scant news indicated either too many clues, or too few solid ones.

Heather fit us into her off-beat and crazy life the first evening and treated us to a stunning dinner, using her employee discount despite our protests. She had heard about a body discovered in Utah, but hadn't connected the story to us.

"Get a big, nasty dog ASAP, and stock up on guns and ammo *now*," she ordered.

"We can't live like fugitives in our own house," Sage protested. "Zeke's working on it; it'll pan out."

"Sage! Are you daft? Sure, we love Zeke dearly, but he's a *writer*, not a professional detective or *whatever*. Aren't you the least bit worried about having him in charge of your protection?"

"Hey! I'm sitting right here, hearing everything! I have feelings, you know!" I protested.

Heather narrowed her eyes. "Listen, *Bub*, if Sage gets hurt, not only are you off my Christmas-party list, but I know some mighty scary bouncers. Trust me, I'll sic 'em on you without any hesitation. You wouldn't stand a chance."

I didn't recall receiving any holiday invitations in all the years Heather had been my sister-in-law, so that portion of her threat didn't hold much water, but I didn't discount her scary-guys warning. Casinos don't hire bouncers for their wit and good looks.

"Maybe you could sic them on the actual *killer* instead of your frightened sister and her worthless hubby." My pathetic attempt at humor fell flat.

"Glad to know at least *one* of you is scared." Her gaze matched her tone: Both were ominous.

Sage gave me a *Let it go!* kick under the table. Since my mind was occupied by the unnerving idea of a bouncer trouncing me, I gladly let the sisters handle the conversation from then on.

The next day after Sage left for her seminar, I fired up the laptop, opened a blank document, and named it "Important Questions." It didn't take long to encapsulate the key issues:

- Why Utah?
- Was Honey dead before arriving, or was she killed in Utah?
- What was the manner of death?
- Who was the last person to see Honey alive? Where was this?
- Who stands to benefit the most from her death/disappearance?
- What OFF TRACK reader hates Kiel Nede so desperately that he/she wants him (that'd be me) to remain the prime suspect?

I leaned back in my chair and stared at the six bullets on the screen. "Gee-whizcles, what good questions! Have at 'em, Raven," I added with roiling sarcasm.

Apparently Raven had left the building.

I pretty much spun my wheels until Sage returned in late afternoon. "I am one pooped puppy," she announced, flinging herself on the bed. "All day long other CEOs told horror stories about tightwad, grumpy, merciless, ignorant, egotistical Boards and Committees." With great effort, she headed off to brush her teeth. "I'm *so* lucky to be in Milford."

"Ah." I hope that sounded adequate, caring, and astute enough to pass muster. "Do you prefer room service or painting the town red this evening?"

She leaned around the barrier; foaming toothpaste lent a rabid-dog look to her face. "Unless you're tired of these four walls, I vote for room service. Order *anything* calorie-laden. I'll be in the shower."

I ordered with no thought of expense or dietary restraints. A much-refreshed and soggy-haired Sage cuddled up next to me to listen to the early-evening news while we waited for our feast to arrive. A familiar face shared the screen with Honey's photo.

"Good evening, I'm Kathy Limens. Our top story comes from Jim Harrison— the railroad construction worker who was replacing Union Pacific tracks outside of Green River, Utah, when anyone's worse nightmare occurred.

"Jim, you told authorities you were moving gravel with your front-loader when you made the gruesome discovery, is that right?"

The camera panned across dusty machinery that hovered near a towering rock pile. "Wha—?" Sage exclaimed, jerking out of her repose. Kathy held a microphone close to the construction worker. He nodded nervously throughout his disjointed account:

"Yeah; moving gravel." A tic creased Jim's face.

"What was your first reaction, Jim?" Kathy prodded.

"Well, first, don'cha know, I thought it was a joke, don'cha know, like maybe a buddy of mine had, like, buried one of them mannequin-things, don'cha know, but then sumpthin' like an arm with dried blood . . ."

Kathy skillfully interrupted what was sure to become a potentially grisly account unsuitable for delicate ears during prime-time broadcasts:

"So, Jim, at that point, did you call the officials?"

"Not right away, on account of it was pretty spooky, don'cha know, and I was shakin' awful bad, I ain't afraid to admit. First thing, I jumped off the loader to go see, but . . . well, she wasn't naked or nothing; can't 'member what she was wearin'."

"But, by then, you realized it was a human, not a mannequin, right?"

> "Yeah, right. See, she was awful dirty, don'cha know, and messed up, with lotsa bruises and all . . ."

Turning to the camera, Ms Limens executed another smooth suspension of sordid details:

> "It has been an experience Jim Harrison will never forget, and a disturbing chapter of the story we are following as facts unfold. I'm Kathy Limens, reporting live, outside Green River, Utah. Back to you in the studio, Warren."

"This is getting too weird!" Sage exclaimed, wrapping the towel like a turban around her head.

Echoing the understandably rattled Jim Harrison, I said, "Yeah, don'cha know." If we were home, I'd be rifling my files and frantically checking the Haze Eden collection of articles for hints.

I was relatively quiet for the rest of the evening, but Sage neither noticed nor commented. Her day had been hectic, and she needed to unwind.

One thing was clear: It was time to get Raven on the case because, while opportunity, motive, and means would solve The Bulldog's mystery, I feared no one else was looking for the villain who was out to get *me*.

Added details of Utah and a railroad construction worker did not make the job easier—if anything, the complications grew. For Honey Odessa Woolden-Landis' death to involve a railroad? That smacked of revenge to my way of thinking. The next reports would inevitably focus on that ominous angle; then, just watch: Speculations would really run wild.

While Sage relaxed with a magazine, I donned my fake foot for a jaunt around the motel. As I climbed stairs at the end of our wing, I passed two children—whose parents had likely banished them with the instructions to *"Go let off steam somewhere else!"* Thus, they were playing a game in the stairwell.

The boy slid down the banister, giving me an off-hand "Hey!" as he whizzed by my shock-still body at an alarming speed.

His sister, who was taking the steps two-at-a-time in the opposite direction, ignored me and demanded of her sibling: "How'd you get past me? Where'd you come from?"

How . . . ? Where . . . ?

Combined with Sage's indignation about the "buffoons" writing the news clips, my opportune observation of two siblings' game of chase cleared my foggy brain like a refreshing rain.

I raced back to our room and brought up the earlier document on my laptop, and added two more bullets to my list of important questions to cover *how* and *where*:

- How did Honey get from MN to a pile of gravel by railroad tracks in UT?
- Where was she immediately before she was buried in the rocks?

The little girl in the stairwell had pulled off the blinders blocking my vision. The questions bubbling in my head demanded prompt attention. Grabbing my cell, I scrolled to the directory's B-section.

"Am I allowed to ask what you're doing?" Sage asked as I thumbed my way to the first BR entry.

"Listen and learn; then we'll talk, I prom—" Hearing a click, I held up a cautionary finger. "Hello, Bill? Zeke Eden, here. You're working late! Figured I'd have to leave a message."

"That's life, some days," he said neutrally.

"Is this a bad time, or do you have a minute?"

"I do. What's up, Zeke? Hopefully nothing to do with Gabby Knicker."

"No, just a question I hope you can answer, or will consider looking into for me. I just caught a TV report saying authorities believe a body discovered in Utah is Honey Odessa Woolden-Landis."

"Go on . . ." Despite warming to me by the end of our face-to-face encounter, Bill still played his cards close to his chest. Hence, he didn't confirm, he didn't deny—but I noticed he also did not qualify what I said with ". . . *allegedly*."

"I'll leave the investigating to you professionals, but my brain keeps processing facts. So, here's the question: Has anyone looked into where the load of gravel that purportedly buried Honey originated? Trains collect cars at various locations, with changes possible at each station."

"Um-hmm." An evasive reply, but I sensed Bill's interest in my mental gyrations. "Continue . . ."

"Normally, I'd know zilch about this, but a while back I talked to a fellow who drives a gravel truck. The gravel his employer produces goes all over the country. Maybe I inferred too much from our discussion, but it sounded like supplying gravel is a competitive business. Part B of my question asks, Is there a company in or near Rochester that recently won a bid to send gravel anywhere west?"

"Worth looking into. If that turns out to be true, your point would be . . . what, exactly?"

"Isn't the likelihood of Honey being dumped out *with* the gravel greater than a load of gravel being dumped exactly *on* her discarded body?"

"Go on . . ."

"Regardless of whether she was dead or alive at the time, it seems more credible she was already *in* whatever hauled the gravel to that spot—and the assumption being, a railroad car—than that someone transporting her, dead or alive, sees a heap of gravel, and thinks *'Ah-ha!'* The risk of detection while burying her in an existing pile seems high, to me."

Bill followed his thoughtful pause with what sounded so wary, my heart sank: "Interesting idea." Before I could formulate a new approach to my plea, he must have had a quick change of heart, because he added, "I'll share your theory with those who can find out. Anything else?"

Hope revived. "That's it; I appreciate anything you can do, Bill. I won't even ask if you'd let a plain old citizen like me know what you learn!"

He chuckled. "Yeah, right; the 'plain old citizen' who plots some of the most convoluted thrillers in print! Let's just leave it at 'Stay tuned,' okay?"

"Fine with me. Thanks."

"You're welcome, Zeke. Call any time."

I disconnected with a sense of having found respite from a storm. I hadn't solved anything, but I'd taken action and it felt good.

"Bill Brandt?" Sage asked; then, her puzzled look quickly changed to recognition. "Oh! Gabby's not-to-be-envied supervisor, right?"

"One and the same."

"My-oh-my, I do believe Raven is on-board!" she crowed and blew me a kiss.

"While you were battling other demons, I devoted my day to trying to think like Raven. I came up with six big questions; what I just asked Bill were two late additions." I gave her a summation of the overheard stairwell chatter between two hyperactive children that produced the new *how-where* questions.

"Keep talking," Sage urged; her eyes glowed.

"It bothers me that a train is involved. Makes it seem like retribution, given how I fictionalized the actual Railroad-Medicine situation. *But*, it may help narrow the search for her killer. On the other hand, a clever criminal might have a different bone to pick with Honey. Let's say, for instance, a colleague with a grievance, or a disgruntled neighbor, or an angry family member. And he, or *she*, latched on to the railroad angle as a diversion. But why gravel? What a mess!"

"Raven will figure it out," Sage said confidently. "What else is on your list?" She marked her place in the magazine; I hopped to my computer, and brought the document out of sleep-mode.

Sage nodded pensively throughout my recitation of the initial six bulleted questions. She hugged her pillow, resting her chin on it. "Speculate on Bill's answer to your new questions."

"I don't care how many loads of rock were dumped at the site, or if every single car came from different places. I just want *one car* to have spent enough time on a track in or near Rochester to accomplish the dirty deed of getting Honey into that railroad specific car, along with the gravel."

"Ah-*ha*, because that would mean, whoever failed to frame you with OFF TRACK tie-ins didn't know Honey would be discovered in Utah—he just wanted her out of Rochester. Forget Watson—it's *you* who is brilliant, my dear Sherlock!"

We were so pleased with ourselves we didn't even listen to the late news. We had better things to do.

20

Bill Brandt sure was the right go-to guy. He called the morning after we returned from Vegas. "Zeke, your '*Where?*' question was a good one. It led to even more crucial information: the '*When?*' Tracking with me, so far? Sorry; really bad pun."

"Yeah, and I'm chuggin' right along with you!"

I heard a smile in his voice: "In railroad lingo, the train that dumped the gravel near Green River, Utah, was called the BMUDR-5 train. It stands for Ballast-Murdock-Denver. Initials indicate departing and end stations, followed by the origin date—in this case, the fifth of July. It'd be a *five* no matter what month because the number refers to the day."

"Hold on; *east*-bound? As in, headed to Denver?"

"Right. The trains are made up of side-dump hoppers and average about fifty cars."

I was so involved in figuring out how a corpse from Minnesota showed up in gravel dumped by an east-bound train that I was slow in reiterating, "A 'side-dump hopper'? What's that?"

"A car loaded on the top, dumped from the side."

"Oh; didn't know the name, but I've seen 'em."

"The original crew departed Murdock on the fifth of July, with a crew change in Provo, Utah. So, now it's a Provo crew taking the train to Grand Junction,

Colorado, where a final crew change occurred before Denver. Still with me?"

"Hope I can read my writing later on, but yeah— I'm with you, and taking notes at a furious pace."

"Two important things are on the Conductor's Delay Report. At some point before the train reached Green River, an electronic wayside detector showed a hot journal-bearing on one of the BMUDR-5 cars' wheels. The conductor uncoupled that car and left it on a passing track, two-and-three-quarter miles west of Green River. Probably a tough call, because other crews would grouse about *'Get that blankety-blank car off the passing track!'* but, I imagine, in much plainer English."

"Count on it!" Having spent time within earshot of railroaders at Penny's Diner, I knew how salty their speech could be.

"The BMUDR-5 conductor had little choice. He had a car in trouble, and was close to where it could be set out, so it was a no-brainer. The hot-journal problem could've been detected nowhere near where the load was headed, and then the gripes would have been, *'Hey! How we supposed to fix tracks without rocks?'* from another disgruntled crew."

"When did this happen?" I interjected. "Leaving the defective car on the passing track, I mean?"

"Give me a second to scan my notes. Here it is: Ballast-Murdock to Provo, about ten hours; Provo to Green River, roughly ten-to-twelve hours. We're looking at—give-or-take—twenty-one hours. So, with the seven-five origin date, that puts our car at the passing track late in the day on the sixth of July."

I scribbled furiously; my mind whirled. "As I recall, the first report from a newscaster at the site was on a Monday. Let me check a calendar . . . Yeah; had to be the ninth." I released a cascading whistle. "Three days later?"

"Right. They put out something known as a 'slow order' to all trains until after the weekend. Monday, the crew was scheduled to fill a soft spot next to the passing track. That's when the report hit the news."

"I saw the pile of gravel on TV, but there was no railroad car shown. Was it already fixed by then?"

"Yeah; there were enough complaints from dispatchers that repair crews got it fixed by Sunday. Well, at least the car was moved by then."

"Hmm." I emitted squeaky sounds through tight lips. Bill was silent, likely also lost in thought. "So, the car in-question sat on the siding from Friday evening until sometime Sunday. Same timeframe for the heap of gravel beside the track? Or was it in the car until Sunday, and then dumped?"

"That, I didn't learn. My source mentioned a manifest train; unfortunately I didn't make notes on what that is."

"At this point, I'm not sure it matters, Bill. But can you follow-up on where that defective car went after Green River?"

"I'm sure someone can, but I sure hope the same fellow answers the phone so I don't have to repeat myself. My questions really tested his nerves."

"Thanks for persevering. What still concerns me is how the timing leaves a wide-open opportunity for an undetected suspect to get close to that heap of gravel."

"True," Bill said slowly. I knew his syncopated pen taps signaled deep thoughts.

"Anything else? Not that I don't appreciate all you've done, Bill, because I'm truly impressed."

"Let me check my list; I've been marking things off as we've talked. Oh, you'll find this interesting, and I see I skipped past it: Do you know where this Murdock-place is?"

"No. My Utah trivia base is regrettably thin, but I'll hazard a guess. Is it somewhere in the northern part of the State?"

"Nope; it's the first station east of Milford, which means a Milford crew was involved in the BMUDR-5 run. That's in your neighborhood, isn't it?"

Bam! The attack on my gut was like being eight and getting hit by a fast-pitch ball.

After distracted remarks on my part and a casual farewell on Bill's end, we concluded our call. My chin dropped to my chest; I clutched my stomach as if I were eight-years-old again. Only this time, no teacher raced across the playground to reassure me *"Everything would be alright, Zeke."*

If I didn't have such confidence in the myriad of products I had purchased to avert cyber-disasters, I could have feared that a hacker had broadcast my list of questions to the news media. I felt besieged.

Over the next few days, I either gained or deduced answers to several of my bulleted questions regarding Honey in Utah:

- Was she dead before arriving in Utah, or was she killed there?
- What was the manner of death?

A newspaper article from the Salt Lake City *Tribune* addressed the question of how Honey had died:

> Responding to questions during a press conference, a representative of the Emery County coroner's office stated, "Honey Odessa Woolden-Landis' body was discovered on Monday, July 9 near Green River, Utah. Ms Woolden-Landis was the victim of criminal homicide, which is a violent crime by definition."
>
> Based on post-mortem conditions which the coroner observed and confirmed, the time of death is estimated to have been several days prior to the recovery of the body, possibly as early as July 3. Based on details regarding train schedules and other details not yet made public, no one disputes that the body was buried in gravel sometime before July 7.

Predictably, the article requested help in "bringing the person(s) responsible to justice." Maybe just to fill space, but it went on to inform readers that Green River is partially in Emery County, with 868 of its 973 citizens ("according to the 2000 census") residing there, and 105 in Grand County—details so far off my curiosity scale they hardly registered.

Or, perhaps the point behind that odd elucidation was political: to explain why one county's coroner had been involved rather than the other official. I doubted either office was fighting to get handed a case destined for intensive nitpicking investigation and time-consuming interviews, as well as endless court appearances. If anything, it was probably more a situation of one county telling the other, *"No,* you *take this one—I insist!"*

Two questions nagged me: How did gravel fit in? And, was it a fluke that the corpse of such a vocal party in the whole Rochester railroad debacle was buried near railroad tracks?

With a heap of rocks involved, my working theory was thus: a man's upper-body strength was a must, given the heavy-lifting necessary to haul a body high enough to deposit it in the railroad car.

And, if the apparent current assumption that Honey had been buried in an existing heap beside the tracks proved to be true, even burying a body in that manner required strength and endurance.

Either way, I decided, *the killer was male.*

Clutching the newspaper, I leaned against the high back of my chair and forced myself to relax. The paper slid from my grip as I plotted Version I of Kiel Nede's imagine storyline: *Honey, at a table with her killer, enjoying a meal. Beneath the table, her companion plunges a needle into Honey's thigh. Hmm.* I scanned the article quickly. No mention of a needle-stick, no named drug. Was she diabetic? If so, did he know, and mess with her insulin?

Version II of Kiel Nede's take: *Honey is asleep when someone creeps up to do the evil deed.* I sat up straighter. Suffocation? Strangulation? Would she be in her own home? At a motel? Held against her will at the killer's house? Was location important?

A puzzle hovered over either scenario: How did the killer transport an unconscious body? Honey was neither overweight nor anorexic, if photographs did her justice. I judged her to be about five-foot-five, weighing about one-ten. Seemingly fit, no visible flab; certainly capable of self-defense.

Back to off-the-cuff plotting: The assassin creates opportunities to test his capacity to lift Honey. He stages an event where it seems natural to grasp Honey's waist and lift her off the ground, whirling in celebration of . . . what? A touchdown for the home team? News of a promotion? Or even something as innocuous as *"Hurray, it's Friday!"* Whatever; he would think as he spun Honey around, *Good deal: I can do this, she's not too heavy.*

As murderers discover at inconvenient times, it is far more difficult to move a dead body—unwieldy flopping arms, dangling legs, droopy head—than it is to heft a jubilant lift-*ee* who aids the process by wrapping her legs and arms around the lift-*er*. The term *dead-weight* is solidly based on fact.

Even if a dragged corpse leaves a trail, any originally resulting marks around the gravel pile in Green River would be long gone by now. Too many people had trampled the ground around possible clues—plus, wind, or soot and debris from passing trains would further mar the scene.

I shook my head. *The investigators have a tough job ahead if they're seeking evidence of how the killer transported Honey to her final resting place.*

"Well, Zeke," I said aloud, "it's time to get to back to work on what *is* your job."

I had spent several fruitful hours fine-tuning my list of character names and descriptions for LOST GROUND, and felt so proud of my accomplishments that I rewarded myself with a break over the noon hour to catch the latest news.

Thanks to a pertinent detail tacked on to the newscast (into which, I readily admit, I projected my suspicions, based entirely on Raven's sixteen successfully solved crimes) I checked off another bullet on my list. The introduction of the official spokesperson being interviewed inadvertently revealed where Honey had died. The reporter said,

"I am talking with Mister Randall Glass who, for nine years, has worked with the Utah Department of Investigations . . ."

Even if Mister Glass' comments added little else to my small cache of facts, the revelation of his professional connection told me the current theory: Honey's murder had occurred within his jurisdiction: in Utah.

Not Minnesota: Utah. That detail meant Honey was alive when she left Rochester. But it did not tell me if it was a very-much live or an utterly dead Honey who had connected with the heap of gravel.

Turning off the TV, I sank back against the couch cushions. Thank goodness for professionals who are willing to plug away at . . . what did the Smithsonian article call it? Something like: *identifying critical factors with the goal of evaluating their interactions.* Our landline phone rang, offering a respite from my fruitless attempts to define ambiguities.

"Myster-E? This is Jacey. Could you come to town? We're all here and *really* need to talk to you."

"Where will I find you?"

"R&R Diner. Uh, can you hurry?"

My eyebrows took a hike. "On my way."

The somber quartet awaiting me sat two-to-a-side at a table in the hamburger joint. They had pulled up an extra chair and scooted close to the wall so I could get my knees beneath the open end. The counter in the adjoining room was lined with laughing kids. My group didn't seem inclined for humorous repartee, so I merely asked, "What's up?"

"What's happening on The Bulldog case?" Mathia asked.

I got the feeling their active brains had sketched out this scene in rough detail, assigning Mathia the opening remarks, and me a walk-on role. *Okay, I'll go along with the drama and then, maybe, they'll let me know where the plot is headed.*

"You likely know most of it," I began. "A track repairman found a body buried in gravel near Green River, Utah. The Emery County coroner's office positively identified the corpse as Honey Odessa Woolden-Landis. Now, they've learned she likely died around the Fourth of July. That's pretty much all the news they've seen fit to print—or say."

Since the detail about The Bulldog dying in Utah was something I'd deduced—not something directly stated—I didn't add it to my truncated report.

The expected clamor of voices didn't follow my summation. Glancing around the table, I observed nervous gestures: gnawing a fingernail, twisting a lock of hair, scratching a pimple, contorting lips left-and-right. "What's up?" I repeated.

Cale stopped itching. "We, uh, have to tell you something, and hope you won't get mad. You know how you told us not to let anybody read the chapters of OFF TRACK you printed out for us?" His gaze dropped. "Our parents read them. Well, Jacey's mom didn't read her stuff; just her dad did." This blathering was very *un*-Cale-like behavior.

Mathia cut in, "We feel real guilty, not telling you sooner. My folks wanted to read my assignments because I was excited about them, and what I wrote didn't make sense unless they saw your chapters first. I'm sorry," she ended in a tearful whisper.

Fable blurted out, "My parents didn't tell anyone about what they read. They didn't see it until right before the trip; they wanted to see what the buzz was about. They really like your book. Mom asked me to check out a couple more from the library for her because she usually doesn't get off work in time to go in herself."

Cale said, "Dad wanted to see stuff we'd done in class after Gabby came to town. I don't know if Mom actually read stuff in my notebook, but I heard her and Dad talking about it, so she must've."

They were so tense I expected sweat to run down their overwrought faces. I knew they anticipated a severe reprimand from me, but for what purpose? To make them feel worse than they did?

"Thanks for telling me. Perhaps my instructions could've been more specific, or less stringent. I don't know; I've never taught before. I'm not upset with you so don't worry, okay? At this point, I doubt there will be any repercussions."

"Uh, Myster-E?" Jacey released the twisted lock of hair; it sprang loose from her finger in a tight coil.

I sensed we were leaving Act I, Scene I, via a rough segue.

"Remember the first thing we wrote for class?"

"Of course, Jacey: a one-page *Where* assignment on Murder in Milford. You wrote what you knew."

"Yeah," she said with a rueful grimace. "Dad works at The GASP, so that's what I wrote about."

It took every ounce of maturity and control I could muster to hold in a groan. *Gravel pit.* My eerie silence troubled the quartet of my white-faced students . . . no, we were *friends*. "Right; you did." Four glances shot around the table, none of which included me. "Anything else?" I asked quietly.

Four jerky nods. Still, no one looked at me.

Act I, Scene II, was stalled. "Can you tell me?" I prompted, managing to retain a neutral tone.

Cale jerked in his chair and mouthed *"What?"* at Mathia. She responded with a silent *"Say it!"* which confirmed my suspicion she had kicked Cale.

"We don't know what to do about it," Cale blurted out, "but Jacey's dad is pretty mad at her . . . and you," he added slowly.

His words jolted like a cattle prod. *"What?* Why is Abbott upset with both of us?"

Cale's quick nod at Jacey pulled the plug on her silence. "Last night Dad got a phone call from a cop in Rochester. Remember at the radio station when Stacey asked Dad if he collaborated with you and he said he drove a gravel truck? Stuff in the news about gravel made her remember what Dad said, and she let the police listen to the program tape. Last night, that cop asked Dad a gazillion questions. Now he's mad or scared or . . ."

Her agonized gaze sliced me to the quick.

Abbott—devoted father, my trusting friend, the rehabilitated ex-con. And now, the target of an investigation that would never have transpired had I not written the murderer's guidebook. This was worse than when I was the bulls-eye.

"Would your Dad talk to me?" I asked softly.

Apprehension vied with anguish on Jacey's face. "I don't know. He was pretty, uh, upset when he got off the phone."

I sensed *"upset"* was G-rated language applied to R-rated emotions.

"I'd like to try. What time does he get home?"

"He's home now; he called in sick. Neither of us got much sleep last night. He just sat, and I paced. He finally fell asleep on the couch this morning."

"When we're done here, I'll go see him."

"O-*kaaay*," Jacey said nervously.

"Anything else?" I did a slow visual stroll around the table, making eye contact with each one.

Cale nodded grimly. "Uh, Myster-E . . ." A tic twitched his cheek. "Mister Belk talked to Dad after he got that cop's call. Then, Dad asked me a bunch of questions, and said I'm to stay clear of you for a while." He looked pale enough to faint.

"Jacey's dad," Mathia said, "called my dad, too, and my folks told me I couldn't uh, you know . . . I hate this!" She pounded the table with one fist.

"Is it ditto for you, Fable, about not talking to me?" Blood pounded like a tribal drum inside my skull when she nodded miserably. "So, you all violated your parents' orders by calling me down here today." I stated the facts without condemnation.

Cale answered for the group: "We needed . . . uh, *wanted* to see you again, you know . . . to explain. It isn't fair to dump you and not say why."

Mathia added, "We all like you a lot, Myster-E, but we're real scared. I mean, what if Jacey's dad gets in trouble with the law and—?" She bit her lip.

I didn't know how much Jacey's friends knew about her family situation, but it wasn't my place to fill in Mathia's blank. I offered weak assurance: "I'll sleuth-out who called your dad, Jacey, and try to run interference. We'll get this mess worked out so there won't be a gap in our friendships."

No gap? Who do you think you are, Zeke? Raven, the "nothing-gets-in-my-way" guy? It's not like your friendship with Abbott is so solid he'll see your face and abandon all fears because, "Thank God, my buddy Zeke is here! He'll fix everything!"

Mathia said morosely, "Stuff we wrote is awfully close to what's in the news. My victim was a girl everybody hated; Cale used a train in his story; Fable had a kidnapping in hers; and Jacey, well . . ." The unspoken hung heavily: *Jacey's had The* GASP.

Fable slurped her Diet Pepsi. "Myster-E, before you got here, we decided we should destroy those first assignments. We think you should get rid of your copies, too. It could look real bad if someone got a subpoena and you had to let them see your files."

Leave it to Fable to inject even more drama into my off-the-cuff first writing assignment.

"Exactly!" Mathia said. "Get rid of the evidence. I mean, what if Crabby-Gabby comes back and finds a folder at your house with the four papers in it and thinks it looks like we all know too much?"

I masked my amusement over her apt moniker for my archenemy. "You're missing something crucial: What you wrote for class covered method or means. But what are the other ingredients necessary for murder?"

"Motive," Cale chanted promptly.

"And opportunity," Fable added a second later.

"Right, and both are quite a stretch for anyone, even Crabby-Gabby," I allowed a smile "to point fingers at you. You didn't even know The Bulldog, so where's the motive? As for opportunity, you live hundreds of miles from her and your modes of transportation are either bikes or ATVs. Kind of a long trip back to Minnesota on those wheels, huh?"

Four weak smiles.

"But they found her body in Utah," Cale said. "Right there, that's a suspicious detail, isn't it?"

"Hey-hey-*hey*, listen to me! When was the last time any of you were in Green River?" I tossed back. "I think you're pretty safe." Silently I added, *And, it's up to me to reassure Abbott he is, too.* "It's entirely your call, but I don't think you need to destroy your assignments. They'd only be evidence if you were suspects. You're not. Got it?"

Four uncertain nods.

"Jacey, take your time getting home to give me a chance to swing by your house. I need to tell your dad that we've talked or he'll wonder how I know what I know. But I'll smooth the way for you to come home and, hopefully, not be grounded for disobeying. Do the rest of you need me to do the same for you? I don't want anyone in trouble."

Three headshakes, followed by Cale's response: "We already agreed to tell our folks we saw you so you don't get in trouble."

Blinking fast, I could only manage a weak, but sincere "Thanks."

21

I sat outside the Belk house, letting the truck idle. I had been here once before, returning the Thermos Abbott had left behind after his second gravel delivery. That visit, we sat on his porch and talked a while—usual guy-talk: trucks . . . hunting . . . sports. He had been as relaxed as I'd ever seen him, and the mood continued when Jacey joined us.

Hating to end what was a pleasant encounter, I had related a humorous story on myself about trying to uproot sagebrush that threatened to take over the narrow dirt road around our property. "I wired some boards on a section of chain link fence to anchor it, and hooked the whole thing to the pickup's rear bumper, and drove around the fence line with my contraption bouncing along behind."

"Did it work?" Jacey asked, her eyes shining.

"Not too well," I admitted. "At least I didn't end up with gobs of uprooted sagebrush to get rid of!"

Abbott smiled, then laughed outright—at which point Jacey looked at her Dad as if he were someone she hardly recognized. He slapped the arm of his chair, threw back his head, and howled. It was contagious, infecting Jacey first, and then me. We three had laughed so loud and long that a neighbor stuck his head out to check on the ruckus.

"Sammy looks like a bird coming out of a cuckoo clock!" Jacey giggled. That set us off again, especially when she mimicked Sammy, substituting a porch pillar for the neighbor's door.

That day, I left dad-and-daughter Belk chuckling when I drove away. I was certain that would be the case today.

If inanimate objects can assume a foreboding persona, the white clapboard one-story structure did. Window shades were down. A bush beside the front door seemed to have given up on trying to perk-up the place. A rug draped to dry over a porch railing had been there so long it required another washing. The chairs Abbott and I had occupied mocked me.

I leaped backwards when the doorbell sparked as I pressed it. *Fitting, but hopefully not predictive of what's ahead,* I mused nervously. No response, but rather than risk electrocution with a second attempt, I pounded on the door. After a worrisome length of time, Abbott slowly opened the door.

I aimed for pleasant, not jovial: "Hello, Abbott. Sorry about not calling ahead to see if it's a good time, but may I come in?"

His yawn swallowed the glare I expected and prolonged any reaction, giving me time to imagine several potential answers. He lifted his T-shirt and scratched his belly. "S'pose so, since ya saved me from havin' to make a trip out to your place," he said stiffly.

Wow; Abbott coming to see me sure wasn't on my mental list of what to expect. Would he come ready to punch . . . or worse? I may have gulped.

Apparently expecting me to follow without an actual invitation, he led the way into the shadowy living room. A dented sofa pillow and rumpled afghan indicated an interrupted nap. However long he had been asleep, it wasn't long enough to erase exhaustion or ease tension.

He didn't exude hospitality, but then neither had I when Gabby Knicker descended on me—an eerily similar situation. I dove into chilly waters with, "Jacey and the other students in the Honors Writing Course asked me to meet them at R&R Diner. At the time, I didn't know they were going against their parents' instructions, or I wouldn't have gone. That's neither here nor there now, but I appreciate knowing why they'll be making themselves scarce, at least until serious issues are resolved."

Abbott stared at me, unblinking and mute. *He isn't making this easy, but why should he?* I cleared my throat. "They said you got a blunt phone call yesterday from Rochester; that must have been unnerving."

"Whadda you know about unnerving? You don't have a rap sheet, do ya?" he snapped.

"No, but I've been under scrutiny," I said evenly. "I've fought to prove my innocence and know how it feels to be falsely accused, even by innuendo."

"So you say, but that blasted radio b—uh, broad," (the quick edit still bared its teeth like his intended *bitch*) "put the cops on my tail. The guy calls, an' he already done his research. It's a kick in the butt after years of me keepin' a clean record for him to start out yammerin' all 'bout how he hopes I cooperate so he don't hafta involve my probation officer."

I hoped *that* encounter had begun with more finesse, but I also knew that what a distraught mind (namely: Abbott's) retains is often at odds with the complete picture. Given Belk's history, any call from or face-to-face meeting with The Law would raise his hackles.

"Do you remember the fellow's name who called you, Abbott?"

"Wrote it down somewhere." He waved vaguely toward an end table. My eyes followed his gesture to a mess of papers around a copy of OFF TRACK. A flattened cigarette pack served as a bookmark.

The book was likely Jacey's copy and, since I knew she'd finished reading it (and hopefully hadn't started smoking) I figured the marker meant Abbott was the most-recent reader. Considering the current situation, this didn't please me the way discovering people read my mystery-thrillers usually did.

Abbott's monotone pulled me back to the gloomy room. "Since that call, all I can think about was how come Jacey did her assignment that way? She knows I served time but, now, does she think I'm a killer, too?" His eyes pleaded for my rebuttal, despite his tone.

"No; the kids followed my instructions to write about murder in Milford, focusing on *Where* it could happen, not worrying about *Who*, *What*, *When*, or *Why*. Writing about *Where* was their first assignment only because describing scenery and places is easier than dialogue or character development."

Abbott stared blankly, as if I'd switched from speaking English to Swahili. I brought us back to common ground. "The place—the *Where?* part of the assignment—that Jacey knows best is your workplace. She wrote about The GASP, not about *you*. She's proud of you."

"Don't tell me what my girl thinks! You didn't see how she was actin' last night. She can't figure out how or why I would-a killed some lady from Minnesota. See, Jacey was listenin' on the extension when that cop called me a 'Person of Interest.' Dang it, that makes me mad!" Her first question when I hung up was, 'Why are they interested in you, Dad?' It dang-near broke my heart."

He leaned forward, rested his elbows on his knees and pressed the palms of his hands against his eyes. When he straightened up, his sockets were two navy-hued circles, like the middle stage in the progression of a black eye from angry purple to bruised orange.

"Do ya know how it makes a dad feel, Zeke?" he demanded hoarsely.

"No," I said quietly, "but Jacey will come around; she's sorting out things in her mind." I paused and tried again: "If you can remember the fellow's name who called, I'll try to make things right for you."

He shook his head slowly for several minutes while I waited, confident that my silence was better than any platitudes. "I dunno; some guy named Will, or sumpthin' like that."

"Was it maybe Bill Brandt?"

"Maybe." He walked to the end table, flipped a couple pages on a tablet, and said dully. "Here it is; yeah: Bill Brandt."

Relief surged within me. "If there's any good news, it's that I know and like Bill Brandt. He's a no-nonsense guy, so I see how he would come across as uncaring, especially when you're not face-to-face. But he's fair; he listens. I worked with him when I was in Rochester trying to prove my innocence. How]bout if I give him a call on your behalf?"

Abbott's shoulders drooped. He stared at his feet and wiggled his toes inside his socks. Catching a glimpse of a bare heel, I realized our lives were poles apart. *Wearing holey socks is just one sacrifice Abbott makes for his daughter. He's right: I have no business telling him anything about being a dad.*

"You can try, but it won't be easy. See, I kinda blew it. I shoulda kept my big mouth shut, but all I could think about when he kept askin' all-a them pointed-like questions, was what I'd read in Jacey's homework, and what she'd told me was in the other kids' papers, too."

Okay; *now* I was seriously troubled. Maybe even approaching panicked. Digging deep, I mustered an unemotional tone for the question that screamed in my head: "You told Bill Brandt about how the four kids wrote about murder in Milford?"

The epitome of dejection, he nodded. "I started to tell him, 'Just b'cuz what they wrote matches stuff on the news—' Right then, he perked up like a lit firecracker went up his butt an' interrupted me with 'I wanna see them papers.' I tried to 'splain it was nuttin' but he said to fax him copies. *Sheesh!* I said, 'I ain't got all the papers, and Milford ain't got fax machines on every corner.' But he wouldn't quit."

"I will definitely call him. Meanwhile, don't send him or anyone *anything*. Not by fax, not by mail. You don't even need to talk to him again—hang up!"

His nod was a series of jerks. "Do I need to get a lawyer, Zeke?" Despair rode each word. "I can't risk losing Jacey . . . she's all I've got, anymore." The sass and vinegar were gone; he was a beaten-down father, clawing his way up a wall of hopelessness.

"Try not to worry; Jacey picks up your vibes. Bill was doing two things: First, doing his job by following up on Stacey's call. Second, fishing for information in case you *were* hiding something. It's standard operating procedure. Let me see what I can do. You're not guilty. Hear me? I'm very sorry—"

"Not nearly as sorry as I am," he blurted with a resurgence of animosity. "*Sorry* I went on that trip; *sorry* I blabbed 'bout gravel on the radio; mostly *sorry* I . . ." his voice trailed off. He shifted uneasily, dropping his gaze to the floor.

"Mostly sorry that you ever met Zeke Eden?" I asked softly. It was more fact than question.

He nodded, but didn't look up. "I figured we had some good times, me an' you. Even thought maybe we'd be buddies. I guess a guy with a past like mine is a fool to expect that with a rich and famous, educated guy like you, huh?"

"Some friendships get stronger after surviving a rough stretch like this, Abbott. I'm not willing to let ours roll over and play dead quite yet. May I tell Bill Brandt how the kids' writing assignment came to be, and vouch for your innocence?"

"I guess." His tone showed lack of confidence in me. "Sure hope ya have a miracle up your sleeve."

A miracle? As I drove away from Abbott and Jacey's house, I heard Grandma Eden's faltering voice singing (when she thought no one heard):

"It took a miracle to put the stars in place,
. . . to hang the world in space . . ."

I turned the opposite direction of home. My mind spouted the definition of miracle: *wonder, marvel, sensation, phenomenon* . . . I had no make-it-go-away miracles for Abbott or anyone up my sleeve, but I knew someone who was on a first-name basis with Someone who didn't need to use trickery to hang the moon and stars.

Although rattled to the core by my mental and emotional turmoil, I made the right turns and soon braked sharply in front of Hank's house. I stared at nothing. *Wait for a miracle, or get off my butt and make something happen?*

A solitary tumbleweed blew across the pavement and caught on a picket fence where it waved like a prickly flag. A cat meandered a parked car's roof. Somewhere, beyond sight, tires screeched and a car's horn honked. A wordless yelp, then an irate "Watch where you're going, kid!"

"H'lo, Zeke! Thought I heard an engine idling." Unnoticed by me, Hank had approached and was peering through the open passenger window. "Are you doing Neighborhood Watch duty for this block, or waiting for me to fall off the roof so you can save my life?" he joked.

I glanced at his house. A ladder leaned against the siding with a thirty-gallon garbage can between it and the house.

"You stopped by to help me clean gutters, right?" His kidding ceased when he noticed my mood-meter was stuck on SOUR. He rocked back on his heels. "Got time for iced tea? I'm ready for a break."

"No; I was thinking about miracles, and ended up at your house. Thanks for the offer, but I've ruined enough people's lives for one day." *And it's time to do something to help Abbott, not dump my problems on Hank.*

I left a puzzled (and maybe a bit worried) Hank Bedlow standing curbside as I drove away. I passed the car where the cat was still on its roof. The wary feline arched her back and hissed at me.

"Same to you, crazy feline. *Sheesh*" I muttered, thinking darkly, *Even the animal world has my number.*

With Hank's suggestion of tea lingering in my mind, when I got back home I took a tall glass of sun-tea out to the pergola. After returning to the house to collect laptop, cords, phone charger, brimmed hat, and sunglasses, I was ready. "Forget about—or at least quit waiting for miracles," I told myself firmly, "and call Bill. The Chinese got it right: "A journey of a thousand miles begins with a single step,' not waiting for someone to offer a ride."

I had to leave a message requesting a return call. Waiting, I employed a technique that helps navigate rough waters when I plot Raven's strategies. I plugged the laptop into the pergola's outlet, opened a new document and typed furiously without concern for proper sentence structure or logical progression of ideas. I bulleted the thoughts that churned like rapids on the Colorado River:

- The GASP?
- Kids' story ideas = fiction, written long before mess began

- Murderer = OFF TRACK reader; too many parallel clues to be random
- Don't blame A.B. for being afraid—he could end up back in prison, even if trumped-up charges
- Body in Utah; was Honey's killer shocked? How will he/she handle that?
- A.B. = in Vegas over 4th; reading OFF TRACK; knows gravel; read Jacey's 1st assignments (knows about the others)
- Access to drugs/needles? (Do Honey and/or A.B. have medical conditions?)
- Is A.B. in contact with cellmate(s)? Probation officer = talk w/ Bill?

My phone rang; I snatched it up without glancing at the tiny screen, relieved that Bill wasn't out of the office. "Hi, Bill; thanks for calling back."

"Sorry, but this is merely your loving wife!"

"Hey, loving wife. I'd left a message for Bill and wrongly assumed this call would be him. You won't believe the day I've had, but I'll wait until you get home to drag you into my mess."

"I saw Darcia at the Chevron; she said Abbott called them, so I have a clue. We'll discuss that later; I wanted you to know I've been moved from stand-by to valid ticket-holder for that small-hospital economics conference in Vegas I registered for months ago. I said 'Yes.' After talking to Darcia, I know it's not good timing, but I should attend. The next one's in Philly, so this one's locale is easier."

"Go for it. You know me; I'm funk-prone, but I recover. It'd be a shame for you to have to go back on the waiting list, and Utah to Philadelphia would be a dreadful trip. Will you fly or drive to Vegas?"

"Fly, if I get a cheap flight from Saint George." I heard her relief. "Much as I love the Virgin River Gorge, it's losing the thrill. Those two-hundred-twenty-five miles and the three-and-a-half hours are *booooorr*-ing!" she trilled.

I grinned. "How 'bout if I'm your chauffeur at least as far as Saint George? I could hit Costco—"

She interrupted: "That'd mean driving to Saint George two days in a row. Not fun. I only called to let you know my plans, not to get a sympathy vote. I'll close up shop here and see you soon."

Soon after we disconnected, Bill called. I said my piece about Abbott and the kids' writing assignment; he listened respectfully, if reservedly. When I asked about new developments, his tone was so devoid of emotion his words sounded like a recording: "One thing: My superiors put a gag order on our talks. The body showing up in Utah puts a different slant on things, as I'm sure you understand."

My lips formed a silent O. What I understood blared between the lines of Bill's spoken words: Kiel Nede had joined Abbott Belk in the role of Person of Interest.

I had become precisely like one of my own nasty characters. For instance, Dustin Thorson: my fictional Ku Klux Klan member in CROSSED OVER. His persistent help had enabled Raven to pull a figurative (and literal) hood off his head, revealing Dustin for who he was: a guy who knew too much to be innocent.

For the first time in our marriage, I was glad Sage would be gone. What I faced required uninterrupted time to think and sort through all the unsettling aspects of everything Bill hadn't voiced.

Abbott was right; I needed a miracle. ASAP.

22

When I kissed Sage goodbye the next morning, the mountaintops were shrugging off their pre-dawn violet-gray cloaks. We had talked, in excruciating detail, late into the evening so I knew she worried about my disgruntled state of mind with both the world in general, and specifically the gag rule.

Despite her desire to avoid a boring trip, she had abandoned flying in favor of saving the exorbitant rates that purchasing a last-minute ticket entailed. "I'll think about you every minute of those dull three-and-a-half hours, and every one of the dreary two-hundred-twenty-five miles," she vowed, tossing her briefcase into the back seat. "Invite Hank for a meal, and tack on chess so he can't refuse!"

Double-checking the lock on her suitcase, I nodded, but still hedged: "Might do that." I closed the driver's door firmly before leaning through her window to savor a lingering kiss.

Off she went. I was watching the Volvo's taillights fade in the distance and musing about love when what Sage had said poked my brain like a determined woodpecker: *Two-hundred-twenty-five-miles . . . three-and-a-half hours.*

Funny how a person knows something, yet it takes a combination of events to have it stand out from the zillion details sweeping across our daily existence. One such detail poked its nose out of the rubble as I stood on the deck, clutching the chilly iron railing on our front porch. A fact mired too long in my brain's morass wiggled to the top of the heap, spitting muck as it shouted, *How'd Gull make it from Las Vegas to Milford in record time—and with holiday traffic?*

The question taunted me, demanding an answer.

Even if he caught the first newscasts about the Milford Flat Fire, Gull still had to pack, check out of the motel, rent a car, and drive the two-hundred-and-twenty-five boring miles. *How could he arrive in Milford less than three hours after the fire started without the Highway Patrol on his tail?*

Best way for the curious to get answers is to ask questions, right? Why did the only logical response give me a stomachache?

Fear oozed from my pores as I punched Gull's number, I opted to present the query on a neutrally-hued palate of a reasonably accurate explanation—though it was fabrication from the first brush-stroke. I omitted the vital detail that I knew the precise distance between Vegas and Milford, and assigned a *just-between-us-guys* mood to my opening:

"Hey, there! I was sitting around, trying to stay awake, so thought touching base with you is a good way to stave off a nap. I'm batchin' it since Sage is off to a conference in Las Vegas, as we speak."

"Fun!" Gull enthused.

"Not fun: work," I corrected. "Anyhoo, she claims it's a three-and-a-half hour drive, so we hauled out of bed at the ungodly pre-dawn hour of four, as in only us and the moon were up. Hence my desire for a nap! I told her, 'Gull got here from Vegas in under three hours, so, even if we slept another hour, you could make the nine o'clock session, right?' But no dice; she insisted, 'It's two-hundred and twenty-five miles.' I tell ya, it's hard to win against her."

Pausing, I yawned audibly. *Nice touch, Zeke!*

"Well, I did put the pedal to the metal and listened for sirens. That's why I told Rosco I'd need his help if the highway patrol caught up with me!" Chuckles preceded his smooth segue: "Hey, have I mentioned the nifty decorator I hired, back home?"

He launched into an explanation of rag-painting techniques and I stuck in an occasional "Wow!" and "No kidding?" while he rambled on.

Under ordinary circumstances, I'd find his latest business proposal interesting. Gull's new venture— The Writer's Cubby—would rent booths to authors, independent researchers, and students—each tenant in search a quiet place on our noisy planet.

I agreed that a subdued decorating scheme would not distract, and could even inspire. Beyond that, I wasn't willing to weigh-in on the benefits of paint versus wallpaper.

Hanging up, I couldn't shake the impression that lies lurked beneath Gull's Las Vegas story. Sure, I'd just fibbed-by-omission, but what was *his* purpose? Why lie about speeding, especially after offering a confession to a deputy?

I replayed the whole conversation that had occurred upon Gull's arrival. Why had he come to Milford? He saw a photo on TV of our house. Luckily, I had saved Cale's forwarded picture.

I waited impatiently for my laptop to unlock its secrets so I could check details. The computer age made fact-searching much easier if one knew where and how to look. Checking the photo's properties, I frowned: *Taken at 4:37 PM, July 4, 2007.* There's absolutely no way Gull could have seen that picture. How could he? By the time it was put on the Web, he was already enroute to Milford.

The only reasonable answer was that Gull saw a different and earlier photo than what Cale sent me. *Must be.* Time to stop seeing purple elephants where there were no elephants of any color.

Unless Gull wasn't in Las Vegas when the fire started. Oh, how I hated that inner voice.

Maybe, after hearing we weren't doing much, he decided to come to Milford, checked out of the hotel, rented a car, and hit the road. But, why fabricate the whole spiel about the casino? If he wasn't there, how did he see the picture of our house?

Okay; maybe he stopped at a bar before leaving Nevada, guzzled a few drinks, hit the road. *That* I could see lying about. It's one thing to confess to speeding; quite another to admit buzzed driving to a deputy.

Did I smell liquor on his breath when he arrived? Surely not; I'd have taken him aside to warn, *"Careful, Gull; law enforcement on the premises!"* No, our greetings had been casual—mine, because I was startled to see him and in a stupor over the fire. Had Gull held back because he knew he had boozy breath? Not much made sense. Something was certainly suspicious.

It was time to find out what that fishy-*something* was. How convenient to have a Las Vegas sister-in-law! Heather kept such dreadful hours, I knew no time was best to call. I punched her one-digit code on my cell and waited.

When Heather answered, I heard a cacophony of voices and electronic sounds surrounding her—the measure of a casino's success. "Hey, Zeke; good news: Just talked Sage into staying with me instead of some uninspiring hotel!"

Talk about perfect lead-ins. "Good work, Heather! She'll love spending time with you—but be ready to share your soap and shampoo since she was counting on the hotel's predictable amenities so didn't pack any. Speaking of boring hotels, do you recall where Gull stayed over the Fourth?"

"Sure wasn't with me. After dinner and drinks, I saw him laughing and talking with some guy, even after he dropped hints during dinner that his plans involved a woman. Hey, are these questions a sneaky way to find out if Gull and I are having an affair?"

"Nope; he and I are engaged in a brotherly *who's-right, who's-wrong* competition. Gull insists he left something at our house on his last visit, but *I* say he left it in Vegas. So I hoped you could help me win our friendly bet," I lied glibly.

"What'd Gull lose that's so important?"

"Huh?" Grandma Eden's voice trumpeted: *"Oh, what a tangled web we weave, when first we practice to deceive."*

"What's lost?" she repeated impatiently.

"Sorry; had to swallow some coffee." *Liar!* "Uh, his prescription sunglasses." *Good recovery, but sure hope she doesn't know or remember he doesn't need prescription eyewear.* "Come on! Give your favorite brother-in-law a break, Heather: Where'd Gull stay?"

"The Majestic. Oops, my table's filling up; gotta go help people lose their money," Heather chirped. She would, too—and so fast they didn't know what hit them. I no longer play cards with her if anything beyond retaining my self-esteem is involved.

Before guilt could make me talk myself out of further digging, I tapped keys to get a phone number for The Majestic—the hotel which, most assuredly, had nothing belonging to Gulliver Swift Eden in their Lost and Found department.

"Thanks for calling the Las Vegas Majestic Hotel where we treat you like royalty!" a sweet young thing purred. "This is Misty; how may I help?"

"Hello, Misty, I'm Gulliver Eden." *What is this, my third lie in six minutes?* "I was a guest at your hotel at the beginning of July and left prescription sunglasses in the nightstand in my room. By any chance, did someone turn them in?"

"I'll connect you with Housekeeping, but first, to make their job easier since we always date any found items, let me verify when you were our guest."

"My check-out date was the Fourth of July."

"Fireworks-Fourth, hmm? No; nothing. Maybe if I work from your check-in date. When was that?"

"Sunday, uh, possibly Saturday. I do so much traveling it's hard to keep track. *Heh-heh-heh.*" My face burned, fueled by that lame cock-and-bull story and faux chuckle. *Good thing Misty can't see me.*

I listened; she hummed, clicking computer keys. Any other time, I'd have been amused by (and likely commented on) her choice of songs: *Misty.* But deceit made me too nervous for small-talk.

"I see you and your guest checked in on Sunday, the first, with a projected check-out of Tuesday, the third. Not a bad guess, Mister Eden; only one day off. You checked out on Tuesday, not Wednesday."

My guest and I? The words trumpeted so loudly in my head I barely heard Misty's declaration that she would transfer my call, and would I please hold?

No, I would not; I hung up. There was no reason to make The Majestic's housekeeping staff search for nonexistent sunglasses. I had made the call, hoping to trap Gull, but ended up snaring him in a nameless something even more disconcerting.

Crystal clear in my memory was how I had asked Gull in his early-morning phone call if he was in Las Vegas alone. His answer was equally clear: "Yes."

So, did this unidentified guest suggest a different hotel for Tuesday?

Did they have a disagreement and part company altogether?

I couldn't determine the reason, but I was now convinced Gull had lied about where he was when he heard about the Milford Flat Fire. To my shame, the past fifteen minutes had exposed how easily lies came to me.

To give Gull the same amnesty I desired, I had to acknowledge that maybe he, too, was caught in a tangled web after years of practicing to deceive.

I had one more shot-in-the-dark idea; it required another phone call and repeated lies. It garnered the same response: Gull Eden hadn't left prescription sunglasses at Milford's Oak Tree Inn. No sunglasses were turned in "either day of his stay."

I now knew Gulliver Eden slept in Milford July third and fourth. My pulse thrummed in my temples. Since I was posing as Gull, I couldn't think of a believable way to inquire whether one guest or two had spent those nights at the Oak Tree Inn. A liar's life clearly required more skills than I possessed.

As I thanked the Oak Tree Inn gal for so patiently answering my questions, it occurred to me that the wrong Eden boy wrote fiction for a career.

Alexander Pope was right so long ago: A little learning *is* a dangerous thing; I felt hazardous. I thumbed pages of BARTLETT'S FAMILIAR QUOTATIONS to prevent the incomplete quote from festering for hours. Finding it, I mouthed what followed:

> ". . . *drink deep, or taste not the Pierian spring: there shallow draughts intoxicate the brain, and drinking largely sobers us again.*"

If I believed Pope, I had to let Raven move beyond all those loose facts' intoxicating draughts and gulp deeply of sobering truth.

With Sage gone, I was tempted to follow her urging and challenge Hank to a chess game, but doing so would only be a delay tactic. The data and suspicions warring in my head demanded action, not postponement.

Bill Brandt's cautionary implications were more accurate than he realized: I *did* know too much; however, that did not make me a suspect—only an accessory if I failed do the right thing. But I didn't have all the specifics yet.

My morning's calls revealed disjointed elements that, if combined and examined as a whole, could solve the mystery of Honey Odessa Woolden-Landis' murder. Despite what I had told Abbott Belk, fingers still pointed to him . . . and Kiel Nede.

I had not yet framed the entire mystery. I didn't know the full details of *How?* but I knew more than the professionals working the case. We were all still in the dark over *Why?* While very disturbing, the *Where?* was becoming clearer, and the *When?* was all over the news. But I held the winning card: I quite possibly knew the *Who?* And the answer to *Who?* scared what Grandma Eden called the "ever-lovin' daylights" out of me.

The path ahead for me was steep, slick, potholed, and riddled by land mines. Robert Frost may have seen two diverging roads, but I knew there was only one rough path through my woods. However, I shared the poet's realization that zillions of miles loomed between me and any sense of peace.

What would Raven Crowley do? Undoubtedly something more productive and responsible than what I did: I threw caution to the winds and invited Hank Bedlow for lunch and chess. Gull isn't Haze and Rudy Eden's only son who lives on the edge. Gull sought thrills; I needed a miracle.

23

Dismayed, Sage listened to my grim account. Her hands shook as she refilled our coffee cups, a second and third time. Moving from the table to the counter to brew another pot of decaf, she finally spoke: "It makes me nauseous. Run it all by me, again. We're bright people, so if we concentrate on finding where your thinking went kerflooey, we can—"

"Won't happen, Sage," I said morosely. I had become personally familiar with nausea. Every system in my body—nervous, digestive, circulatory, and others I couldn't name off the top of my head—had been in upheaval since I lied to Misty about sunglasses.

The coffee's aroma seemed mockingly festive. Outside, dusk hummed with the music a desert croons at day's end. We had done little but talk since Sage dropped her suitcase inside the front door.

I had debated waiting until morning to dump facts and heap fear on her, but she was sure to question my restiveness. I was done with lying and vowed my pathetic skills at subterfuge would never see the light of day, or—like now—the dark of night, again.

"Make another list," Sage ordered when I finished my repeated tale of woe. "It's how you work best.

A list will give you something to refer to so you don't miss a point when you talk to Bill Brandt."

"He's not talking to me, Sage. I may have to go the anonymous tipster route."

"Oh, he'll talk if your first words are, 'I know who killed Honey Odessa Woolden-Landis.' He'd be digging his own professional grave if he hung up on you—especially if-and-when word got out how you offered evidence and he shut you down."

I tucked crutches under my armpits and swung over to pour decaf into the pump-pot so I could make the high-octane version that would fuel courage. Neither Sage nor I would sleep well anyway, so excess caffeine would give us something to blame.

"I'll play scribe; you talk." Sage pulled my laptop across the table and brought up a blank document. "Open your mouth and let the words fly. In fact, talk to *Bill*, not me."

I closed my eyes and put myself back in Bill's stark office. I needed an auspicious beginning or he would have every reason to cut me off.

"Bill, I know you're under strict—"

"No; start with something tantalizing."

"I know who killed The Bulldog. Can we talk?"

"Much better, but don't give him a chance to say 'No,' so don't use a question. And say her name, not the nickname."

"How's this? 'Bill, I know who murdered Honey Odessa Woolden-Landis. Give me five minutes, and you'll have enough information to issue a warrant for the killer's arrest.' Is that better?"

"Much better." Keys clicked; she mouthed: ". . . *five minutes . . . issue a warrant . . .*" Finishing, she said, "I like it; keep going."

"We know Honey was killed in Utah—"

She waved one hand, finishing a word with the other. "Uh-uh: don't waste your five minutes. Hit him with something he doesn't know, or dangle something to make him sit up straighter."

"He already sits like his spine is steel!"

"Think like Raven. He never uses ten words when two will do the job."

"Actually, Raven rarely even uses *two* words— but I doubt making Bill listen to dead air will accomplish much!"

"Go in strong, like: Whoever killed Ms Woolden-Landis pulled ideas from two sources: OFF TRACK and the one-page assignments written by the students in the Honors Writing Course I teach in Milford. I can prove Milford is where the murder took place.' That should grab his attention. Whatcha think?"

Amused and impressed, I said wryly, "That the wrong person in this household writes mysteries?"

"Maybe kindergarten taught Robert Fulghum what he needs to know, but I learned *my* stuff by reading Kiel Nede's thrillers. Okay; if you like it, go from there."

"I like what you said, so write it down before we both forget."

She clicked away. "I won't use 'I can show.' Instead, 'That's where the murder took place.' No, not 'took place,' I'll put 'occurred.' Like it?"

I nodded in grudging approval—no, make that *in awe*—and scooted over to read on-screen along with Sage. We tweaked some more before agreeing on what we read in unison off the screen: "Ms Wooden-Landis' murderer pulled the method from OFF TRACK and four Milford high-school students' writing assignments. That's where Honey died: Milford."

She beamed. "It'll make Bill listen. Okay; next?"

"The killer had access to The GASP and understood enough about how it operates to know a holiday meant no one on-site to witness disposing of a body. Oh, he also knew the side-dump hopper would deposit its load of gravel—and proof of his involvement in the crime—far away from Milford."

"You need to explain The GASP, and tell how you know she was dead before she was dumped."

"I'd rather say, 'Greene Phillip's photo of Honey at the Rochester airport showed the beginning of the end of her life. She had a connecting flight from Chicago to Vegas, where she stayed at The Majestic on Sunday and Monday nights. Tuesday night, as in either the night of or preceding her death, she spent in Milford.' That's as specific as I want to be."

"And your proof?"

I shrugged. "She was here, whether already dead or about to die, so I think 'spent' is the safest word."

Sage shivered. "I hate this."

I resumed dictating: "Honey's killer enticed her to The GASP. Maybe the lure was a chance to see an interesting railroad operation, or the promise of a romantic interlude. Or, how about a better view of fireworks from the platform above the tracks?"

"Mentioning fireworks brings in the date," Sage agreed, typing steadily. "Even with Honey's railroad connections, I don't think the railroad-buff angle works, so skip it. But won't Bill wonder how the killer met Honey?"

"Yeah; they probably had little in common, unless the killer was someone she knew and trusted. However it happened, when the murderer got Honey up there, he pushed her off the viewing platform into the car below the shoot."

"This suddenly seems too real." Sage sucked air through her teeth and shook herself as if dislodging evil's grasp. "Do you need to explain how hoppers pass under the loading mechanism?"

"If he's interested, he'll ask."

She flexed her fingers. "Sure. Okay; go on."

"The only alternative I can come up with as to how Honey got to The GASP is if she arrived already dead. That could be less messy, or certainly made it easier to explain how she got to Milford. Maybe the killer injected Honey earlier—" I gulped, nearly choking. "Oh, no!"

"What?" Sage's tone echoed my panic.

"C'mon; I'll need your help." I swung toward my office, with Sage close behind, and dragged the plastic tub out from beneath the daybed where I had relegated it after my last OFF TRACK rewrite. Sage carried the tub back to the kitchen without comment.

I thumbed through stacks of flagged pages until I found the one I sought. "Read this," I said; my voice cracked as I extended a single sheet to Sage.

She did so; when she finished, she raised fearful eyes. "Oh, Zeke! I'd forgotten this; can't be good, huh? Since your edits happened after the name change, the murderer saw first drafts. So, who saw what used to be ON TRACK?"

I rolled my eyes. "Oh, only four teenagers and maybe their parents, and, of course, John, Maggie and—like Lobo sang—'me and you and a dog named Boo'." Neither of us felt inclined to break into crooning the '70s hit.

"But John had you change the death-by-injection idea, so it only appears in this early draft, not the published edition of OFF TRACK, right? Which means the killer thought he was framing you, but actually trapped himself by using your old stuff. Ho-boy; this just keeps getting worse."

"My thoughts, exactly. Remember the four kids' stories? Mathia's victim was a girl nobody liked who was killed by lethal injection; Jacey wrote about The GASP, thus gravel figured in; Cale incorporated dumping a body onto a train into his story . . ."

". . . and Fable's story had a kidnapping," Sage completed my bleak saga. "Honey's killer is pulling stuff from five places, all with connections to you!" She looked very scared.

"I wish Bill wasn't under a gag order. I'd ask if one unpublished detail is that the method was death by injection of a deadly substance. If so, it could account for all sorts of puzzling things, like how the killer got Honey up to the platform, even how he got her across the State line from Las Vegas to Milford. It's a crucial and missing detail."

"It indicates a different mindset and months of pre-planning. When you used death-by-injection in PENALTY BOX, your perpetrator was a quiet woman, posing as a man without English-speaking skills, who cleaned the locker room. She patiently waited for the perfect moment to catch that hotshot, bribe-taking hockey star until he was drying off after his shower in an empty locker room."

"Yikes. Is Honey's murderer scouring my books, including PENALTY BOX, and collecting ideas from my other plots, too?" Bilious gurgling rumbled in my stomach.

"Could be, but we suspect he had access to four one-page assignments *and* your outdated manuscript. I guess it wouldn't hurt to ask Bill 'Was it death-by-injection?' The worst he can do is brush you off, or be vague, which could indicate your guesses are getting warmer."

"Or, that I'm not merely guessing—that I know too much to be considered innocent. Which is why there's a gag order. I could be hanging myself."

Cringing at the inferences, Sage said, "Let's keep working, but not dismiss the injection idea."

I closed my eyes and brought Bill back to mind: "The murderer may have dragged Honey's body up steep steps to the platform. Anyone driving by could possibly see them, but while two people *walking* up the steps could be considered unusual on a day when the pit was closed, it wouldn't be as suspicious."

"Give Bill both options; he can sort the sordid details. We're almost done; don't quit," Sage urged.

"I'll end with, 'The killer tried to frame me, not realizing he was using a defunct idea which few had seen from OFF TRACK's original plot. The murderer assumed, when plausible ideas pointed to me, it was a done-deal. I live in Milford, I wrote the book; with all eyes on me, the actual murderer could escape detection. A vendetta against me was at the heart of the plan, but there was benefit to be gained in killing Honey—something too great to ignore. *What* it was remains to be determined. The timing for OFF TRACK's release meshed with his agenda.' The end."

"Yes, except for telling Bill who to pursue. And that's when life as we know it falls apart."

"Yeah, we moved to Utah and I felt like I had gained friends. Once I tell Bill Brandt the killer's name, that prospect is as dead as Honey Odessa Woolden-Landis. Even so, print the script; I want to give it a final review before e-mailing it to Bill."

"Will you call Bill today?" were Sage's first words as she swatted the alarm into silence the next morning.

No need to ask, *"Call who?"* so I didn't. Sighing, I flung my forearm over my eyes. "I may run it past Hank Bedlow before I talk to Bill. Hank's not only a good listener, but sharp as a tack and he packs his words with solid wisdom. By the time I hit the high points, he'll get some dialogue going that will help me think through my dilemma."

"Also, he's likely heard confessions, none of which he revealed to anyone. To me, that shows a history of confidentiality or he wouldn't have lasted as a minister all those years."

"The concept of a confessional isn't a Protestant tradition, but, if I asked, I know Hank would honor my confidences."

"Huh? Oh, right—he's Protestant. Well, go for it anyway; nothing to lose, right? We're too deeply involved to think straight, at this point. Can't hurt to have Divine intervention."

I called Hank earlier than either Emily Post or Haze Eden would approve, hoping to catch him before he had his day planned. My timing was perfect. "Am I calling too late to invite you for breakfast? I'm making omelets."

He laughed. "My still milk-less bowl of boring cornflakes offers no competition whatsoever for such a genuine breakfast option as that! Count me in."

He came; I cooked. I brought my laptop out to the kitchen table in readiness for where I knew I hoped our conversation would land. While we ate, I talked.

When I ended with the killer's name, he placed his fork on the plate and met my eyes. "Your fears must seem as vast and treacherous as the Grand Canyon, am I right?"

"Like nothing I ever felt before. The ramifications are—" I couldn't find a satisfactory word as I fought against a flood of tears.

He nodded, although the motion soon eased into a slow headshake. "This probably seems like an off-the-wall question, but who do you credit as being the spiritual influence in your life?"

I blinked in confusion over the abrupt subject-shift. "You're right; it's 'off-the-wall,' but easy-to-answer. It's my Grandma Eden. Why?"

"From the very first Kiel Nede book I ever read, I see Raven Crowley as a uniquely spiritual character. When the Midwest's railroad scandal earned national interest, I suggested that you put Raven to work. You solved sixteen tough mysteries by setting Raven loose. In creating him, I sensed that you revealed a spiritual dimension hidden inside yourself. Did you ever think about that?"

"Can't say I have; but, it's an intriguing idea. If Raven *has* a spiritual dimension, his off-putting—no, make that, his intimidating physical, emotional, and social characteristics—sure do run interference!"

Hank grinned. "Indeed! From the little I know about character development, I've been curious as to where Raven's spiritual elements began in your original plans before you began writing about him. Grandma Eden, hmm? Let's talk about her."

What a happy-sad invitation. *Happy*, because my memories of that wonderful woman were so good. *Sad*, in that I truly miss her. "Grandma Eden adored Gull and me equally, but Gull eventually pushed her away, while I begged for bedtime stories long after I should have outgrown them, simply because it was such a special time between us. Even though I have loving parents, she defined love to me."

I dumped a veritable truckload of Grandma-Eden remembrances on Hank through the dishwasher's entire cycle. "Grandma Eden lived with us from after Grandpa died, when I was a baby until her peaceful death when I was eleven . . ."

When I finished, he said quietly, "Wouldn't such a fine woman be thrilled to know her legacy lives on in the character of Raven Crowley? Not in scariness, but in perseverance and devotion to doing the right thing. You shaped the values she instilled in you through bedtime stories into Raven's character. Are you familiar with the Old Testament's Micah?"

"No, sorry; I'm pretty much Biblically illiterate."

"The eighth verse in the sixth chapter of Micah has rolled through my mind as we've talked. It says, referring to our Creator, 'He has showed you, O man, what is good. And what does the Lord require of you? To act justly and to love mercy and to walk humbly with your God.' That was Grandma Eden's desire for you, too, Zeke—to *become* that verse— even when living it out hurts."

I nodded, unable to speak around the lump of memories in my throat. Finally I managed, "You and Sage both said, 'What would Raven do?' or 'Get Raven on this case!' It's deeper than Raven, isn't it? It's about doing the right thing, about seeing justice done even when it will destroy people."

"Yes; justice heals the innocent and brings the unrepentant to a point where they can no longer flaunt their self-righteousness. If Honey's killer confessed, it could be a time of restoration—even from a prison cell. Think about Wally; he's serving a life sentence, but found *life* in a dimension he never dreamed possible before prison."

We sat in silence for an extended, albeit not uncomfortable, time. I broke in with, "I'll call Bill tomorrow. I'd make the call now, but I want to talk to Sage about what you and I discussed. Thanks,

Hank. May I ask a favor I bet you never dreamed you'd hear from me?"

"Sounds interesting. Go for it."

"Will you pray for me, and for everyone bound to be hurt by what I'm about to do?"

He smiled—pensively, not jubilantly. "Already on it, my friend. And not just scattered petitions to the Almighty; I'll be praying 'til everything's resolved. How 'bout if I start right now in your kitchen?"

I swallowed hard, but said truthfully, "Not at all."

Hank's prayer convinced me he knew Who was listening on a direct line straight through to heaven. I was glad to know such things existed because I needed all the unblocked prayer channels I could get.

The release from worry's tight grip that swept over me with Hank's "Father, we humbly ask these things in Jesus' holy name, Amen," was so great it opened a floodgate inside me. I maintained control (though the bone-crushing grip of my handshake maybe gave a hint of *Not so!*) until Hank was gone.

But as soon as he turned that last corner and was swallowed by his trail of dust, I was crying.

Amazingly, my tears weren't of despair. No, they were of relief that Someone mightier than I—in every aspect—was in charge of His creation. Not only that, but my friend, Hank Bedlow, had His direct number on speed dial.

24

I stared at Sage's e-mailed script for my call to Bill Brandt on my computer screen, but couldn't make myself dial his number. Breakfast was done in Utah; Minnesota was an hour later. Sage was waiting to go to work until she knew how my report was received—and to pick up the pieces if I required reassembly.

Even knowing that Hank was on top of his praying gig, I still waited for Abbott's hoped-for miracle to happen. It played out this way in my busy brain: My phone would ring; it would be Bill Brandt telling me the killer had turned himself in.

That miracle.

The clock chimed eight times; Sage walked into my office where I sat staring into space. She picked up my cell, scrolled to Bill's name, hit CONNECT, handed me the phone, and walked to the daybed where she plopped down against a mound of pillows.

What sat on my face could hardly be called a confident smile, but I tried, knowing we both needed courage. I activated the speaker function so Sage could hear the exchange firsthand: Bill's vocal inflexions, the inevitable pauses. Everything, be it good, bad, or ugly.

"Bill Brandt, here," the familiar voice droned.

I sat up straight. "Hello, Bill. This is Zeke Eden. Do you have a minute or two?"

"Don't wing it—read the script!" Sage hissed, jabbing her finger toward my computer.

I rushed into the prescribed beginning: "I know who murdered Honey Odessa Woolden-Landis. Give me five minutes, Bill, and you'll have enough information to issue a warrant for the killer's arrest."

"I'm listening," he said cautiously.

"I hate to admit it, but the murderer *did* pull his ideas from OFF TRACK, and also incorporated four Milford high-school students' writing assignments as part of the scheme. And that's where Honey died: here, in Milford."

"Milford? Don't you mean Green River?"

"No, Milford. The killer had access to a place the locals call The GASP—that's an acronym for Gravel and Sand Pit. He planned to dispose of the corpse on the Fourth of July because he knew The GASP was closed. He also knew a side-dump hopper would unload both rocks and the body. The place where that happened turned out to be Green River."

"You said, 'the body.' Do you know for a fact— as in: have solid evidence—Honey was dead when she went into the side-dump hopper car?"

"That detail I'll let the medical experts handle, but I have a question for you, which I understand the gag order may prevent you from answering. Did Honey die by lethal injection?"

Several moment of silence ensued, and then he said, "I'm not at liberty to release that information."

I glanced at Sage; she gave me a triumphant thumbs-up before pointing back to my computer.

"The photo Greene Phillip took at the Rochester airport showed the beginning-of-the-end for Honey. You'll be able to verify her connecting flight to Las Vegas. She and her killer stayed at The Majestic in Vegas on Sunday and Monday nights. Tuesday night, which was either the night *of* or the night preceding her death, they spent in Milford."

"Are these dates and places documented?"

"Yes; enough to allow me to call you. You have the authority to open doors, locked to me, for the final evidence."

"What's the name of the Milford motel?" he asked, although I had not committed myself to saying whether Honey was dead or alive on Tuesday night. He was well aware that whichever of the two possible mortal states was in effect then determined if Honey required a motel room in Milford.

"There are two, but, considering Honey's social standing, the Oak Tree Inn seems the more likely choice. On the Fourth, Honey's killer either took her corpse—which ties to my query about an injection—or enticed her out to The GASP, likely presenting it as a great place from which they could see spectacular fireworks later."

"And this gravel pit idea comes from, uh, *where*?"

Sensing skepticism, I answered quickly: "The kids' assignments figure significantly—but, I stress: Without their knowledge or intent, the killer used what he read in them."

"I definitely will need to see those assignments, but go on."

"If an injection was the cause of death, I have another document to show you later. Back to The GASP. Fireworks or not, there was no *later* for Honey. The pit has a platform rising directly above where empty railroad cars halt to collect their loads. I believe the murderer injected Honey with a drug, rendering her unconscious or dead on either the third or fourth of July."

Not surprisingly, Bill made no comment. He was a tight-lipped man and I was technically still a Person of Interest.

"Honey's killer pushed her from The GASP's landing into a car directly below the shoot. The murderer figured—correctly; she wasn't discovered until the following Monday—that days could pass before her body would be found."

"Could she have been alive when she fell into the gravel car?"

"Alive or dead, it's still murder, right?"

He ignored my rhetorical question. A pause on his end, and then: "Is this gravel pit—The GASP—so far off-road that no one would likely see any of this happening?"

"I know you're thinking, *Wouldn't a passerby report seeing someone shove a person off a platform.* Right?"

I waited long enough that he eventually replied, without much conviction, "Uh, yeah."

"Beaver County's total population is six thousand. Two of the five towns don't even have their own Zip codes. In some areas, a person can drive for hours without seeing a single vehicle or house. It's not like places where people don't want to get involved. Here, there are too few residents to cover every square mile. If you checked in the dictionary, 'desolate' should have a sketch of Utah with a star marking Beaver County."

"Hmm. So, if Honey screamed, no one would hear?"

"No one except her killer. The GASP's property sits back from the road. Keep in mind, it was a holiday so fewer folks were around than usual."

"I see several critical, unresolved issues in your theory, Zeke. Why kill her in the first place? Why not do the dirty deed in Rochester? All that zipping around—Chicago, Vegas, Milford, Green River—allows too many possibilities for things to go wrong and for the killer to get caught. There are simpler ways to eliminate someone."

"Yes, but the murderer involved Milford because combining the kids' ideas in the assignment with OFF TRACK's detailed plot gave the killer plausible ways to avoid the investigators' hooks." I opted not to mention ON TRACK–OFF TRACK plot-changes until I knew if an injection figured into the scheme of things.

"How so?"

"I live in Milford; I wrote the book so, with the spotlight on me, the attention is off the killer. The benefit of having Honey gone—something we can discuss later—was too great to ignore. As luck had it, OFF TRACK's release meshed perfectly with the killer's agenda."

Sage hissed, *"Pssst!"* pointing to the wall clock. In my exuberance, I had exceeded my self-imposed five-minute limit by several minutes. I nodded, raising my hand to communicate *It's okay!*

"I've been taking notes." Bill's tone gave nothing away. "I'll present your theories to the others working the case. They'll notify Utah authorities to arrest Abbott Belk without further delay."

"Abbott Belk?" I croaked.

"Isn't he who we're talking about?"

"No! Naming names was my final point, but it sure isn't Abbott!"

"Then, who—"

"Belk's innocent of everything but being snared by the killer's traps! This has been a rough call to make—in fact, I avoided giving the murderer's name because," I fought against choking, "it's Gull. My brother, Gulliver Swift Eden, killed Honey Odessa

Woolden-Landis, and then used Abbott Belk as an unsuspecting pawn to accomplish his crime."

Silence roared in my ear for what seemed an eternity. Then, Bill blurted an incredulous "You're turning in your own brother?"

"I have no choice. It's the only way I can live with my conscience, the only way I can prevent the wrong guy from going to prison and ensure that Gull won't get away with murder, literally. In exchange for this information, I have a favor to ask."

Hearing a faint patter, it was easy for me to visualize Bill's pen rhythmic *Da-dum-da-dum-da-dum* tapping the desk. His slow, shallow breath filled my ear before he finally said, "Go ahead."

"I'll catch a flight and land in Rochester by mid-afternoon. All I ask is that you keep Gull's arrest out of the news until I can talk to my folks, face-to-face. It'll be tough to have both of their sons involved in what is destined to become a sensational case. I'd do almost anything to prevent that from happening. Anything, that is, except *not* do the right thing."

"My supervisors need to talk to you. This case was already a doozy. Now . . ." He sighed. "They may bring Gull in for questioning, but won't proceed further until you substantiate your claims. Bring all pertinent documents, and call me when you arrive."

After I hung up, Sage and I drifted aimlessly on a sea of dismal thoughts, even though I should have been calling about my flight.

Sage came to my office where I eventually landed. "I was in la-la-land to imagine I could work today. I'm calling the Board to let them know I'll be gone for a week. This certainly qualifies as 'family emergency.' We need to be together; I'm going with you. MVCH will survive without me for a while."

I clicked a final key. "Hoped you would. In fact, I just bought your ticket. I was willing to beg, if needs be."

"We'll pack after you answer a question: I know Gull read the kids' papers, but how'd he get access to the ON TRACK version, the *pre*-rewrite one?"

"He stayed in our guest room, AKA: my office. The ON TRACK printout was in a tub under my desk. Plus, I keep copies of the kids' papers in the desk, so he had plenty of opportunities to read, take notes, and even reread." I slumped in my chair.

"Not much effort to find what he wanted—just inappropriate guest behavior. But hey," she mocked, "if a guy's planning a murder, the social gaffe of snooping is no big deal, huh? Still, the *Why?* aspect stumps me. Do you think Honey's the lady-friend Gull wouldn't bring home to meet Haze and Rudy?"

"Probably. When I first suspected Gull, the thing I thought of for motive was that Honey had ridiculed him. I mean, she owned a railroad and he can't keep a business viable long enough for paint to dry."

"What was her attraction to him, if we're correct in assuming such a relationship existed?"

"Gull's a charmer. Women respond to him like bees to honey. He *acts* successful and, even when he fails, he has bounced back so often he has the drill down pat. No failure is ever his fault. It's either the economy is bad, or the competition pulls dirty tricks, or interviewers don't give him enough respect, or the location is— Whoa! That's the connection we've been missing."

"What is?" she asked, pulling blouses off hangers.

"Gull's last business endeavor was The Writer's Cubby. How many phone calls lately have been devoted to him rambling about how research claims that writers' most frequent complaint is about noise? Think about your last conversation with him, Sage."

She halted packing. "Yeah; he invested what I consider huge sums of money in insulation with high absorption he claimed was 'guaranteed to block even high-decibel sounds.' I viewed it as overkill. I mean, really: How noisy can Rochester be?"

"Pretty bad, when a building is near the railroad," I rebutted, letting my words sink in.

A pair of sandals dropped to the floor as Sage gasped, "And Gull's is!"

Feeling numb, I forced myself to keeping packing. "It's off on a spur, but still close. He's under serious pressure from Mom and Dad—Dad, especially—to make this business work. When OFF TRACK proved such a success and the interviews talked about my 'star shining so bright,' he was left even more so in his little brother's shadow."

"So, Gull has an idea that could work—and it is relatively parallel to his brother's success, working with writers—except for one detail. While our little ducks swim merrily along in nice little rows, his are floundering, right? His renters weren't happy, due to the disrupting din of too many trains."

"Trains, every day, and at any hour of the day," I confirmed. "That equals unhappy clients who likely threatened to pull out and leave Gull dangling, once again. Another failure against Gull's account."

"When do you think the reality hit that another venture was doomed before it got off to a start?"

I shook my head slowly; sadness crept into my soul like rain seeking cracks to fill. "Not sure, but there was no sign he was proceeding with plans when I went back to Rochester. His suite was empty and quiet as a tomb." I flinched at the word.

Sage buried her face in a sweater's softness, which muffled her voice. "Gull's thinking was so skewed he didn't see how seducing the owner of the railroad with the intent of killing her could backfire."

"Only a confused and frustrated man would find sweet revenge in wooing Honey, and then disposing of her," I said, adding toiletries to my suitcase.

"Revenge? Not anger, or frustration?"

"No, only revenge comes to mind as I try to deduce why a train was involved in Honey's death."

We made quick work of conducting the standard going-away tasks. We finally locked up and headed down the road. "I'm playing the Devil's advocate, but why do you think revenge was involved in Honey's death?" Sage asked as we left Milford.

"It's the only reason I can conjure for why Gull went to so much trouble. He could've slipped something into her drink—the ol' drug-and-dump method. Granted, trains would still run past his business and notch another failure on his belt, but life—at least, *his* life—would go on. It was revenge against Honey and me: two birds, one stone."

"Life for Honey was over," Sage said somberly, "all because Gull was jealous of you. He thought he'd conceived of a business that'd give him a chance to be in the limelight, but it was not to be. In his mind, Honey's railroad damned him to failure."

"I hate to admit it, but Gull's jealousy is at the core. We've never been close, yet, since we moved to Utah, I felt a bond. Now, I suspect his sudden buddy-buddy act was meant to pump me for what makes writers tick. He's never shown interest in my work like what OFF TRACK produced in him."

"We both commented," Sage agreed, "but we were more pleased, than suspicious. He sucked us in, and we know him; guess it isn't a stretch to see how Honey fell for him. Gull bucked public opinion and 'took up,' like Haze says, with the least popular woman in town—all because, to his convoluted and warped way of thinking, her railroad stood between him and success."

"Mom doesn't help. She's always so proud of me and never hesitant, even in Gull's presence, to brag about me. That's gotta hurt. We know how quiet Gull gets when Mom starts in."

"Do you think Hank's prayers will work? Seems if things are going to turn around, it better happen soon. Like before we see your parents and ruin their lives would be good timing."

"Hank's connection to heaven is solid," I said.

We remained lodged in private ruminations until Sage said, "I always think Gull's too smug for his own good. He's Abbott's opposite, that's for sure."

"Most bad guys are cocky. And that's what it comes down to—like it or not, Gull is one of the bad guys. Abbott has a prison record, which Gull used to *his* advantage."

"Abbott isn't the dark soul Gull assumed an ex-felon would be. Abbott has seen the harsh side of life, and wants no more of it."

"Grandma Eden's bedtime Bible stories featured all sorts of fellows who needed to be taken down a peg or two. They didn't get rescued just in the nick of time—they had to face their fates."

We reached the far edge of Minersville as Sage said, "Too bad Gull wasn't listening, huh?" Then, "Before we lose coverage on the summit, I'll call Hank and tell him where we're headed."

"Good—but hear this: he might pray in your ear."

She was already dialing. "Okay with me. The grade interferes with the connection so I won't put it on speaker; it'd be harder for Hank and me to hear."

Sage rushed through her greetings to get to the purpose of our trip, then, fell silent. When I glanced over, her eyes were closed. I heard faint rumblings and knew exactly what was happening: Sage was on a party-line to heaven.

Soon, she said, "Zeke told me bad guys in the Bible often faced the music; no guaranteed dramatic rescues just because they said, 'Sorry.' Is he right, Hank?" She listened, saying, "Uh-huh" and "Hmm" and finally: "We're cutting out, but thanks. Sure; I'll tell Zeke. G'bye, Hank."

"What?" I demanded when she'd disconnected.

"He says, 'Remind Zeke, many Biblical accounts ended dramatically with lives turned upside-down.' He mentioned Apostle Paul, and said think about Jonah, who he figures was one of Grandma Eden's favorite heroes."

I smiled, remembering. "And he's right."

"Quoting Hank: 'Changes like what those people experienced still happen; consider the situation with Wally up in Draper.' End quote."

I knew the longing in Sage's eyes matched what surged in my heart: *If only such a change had happened to Gull before now.*

Sage drifted off to sleep on the plane, rousing only once to say, wide-eyed, "Do you remember the rental car Gull drove on the Fourth? I bet it had a big trunk. Big enough to hide a—" Tears welled and spilled; she couldn't give words to her fears.

I hugged her. While she drifted back into restless slumber, I added a point to my mental To-Do list: *Have Bill Brandt check with the car rental company about the condition of the returned vehicle's trunk.*

We arrived in Rochester, as promised, by mid-afternoon. I called to let Bill know we had landed, gave him a guesstimate of an hour before my next call, and learned they had not yet brought Gull in for questioning. Why? No one knew where he was.

I didn't, but could have shared our family history of not knowing where Gull was. Even so, I certainly wasn't expecting what we saw when we turned the final corner and had Mom and Dad's house in view.

As we pulled besides the familiar black vehicle, Sage gasped, "He's here!" She leaped out and—as an ardent reader of my plots—knew what to do: She laid her hand on the Jeep's hood. Spinning around, she hissed, "Still hot—hasn't been here long!"

My blood pumped furiously at every pulse point. I'd managed to marshal the courage needed to talk to Mom and Dad, but had not anticipated having Gull as part of our family circle for the discussion.

I pulled out my cell and pressed the preset for Bill. He picked up, first ring. "This is Zeke. Gull's at my folks' house." After mentioning the hot hood and engine pings, I recited the address and vehicle license number, and left it in his hands.

Sage reached for my hand, saying softly, "Hank's praying for us—on his knees, he said—and will do so straight through until we call him after it's over. Let's go inside and see everyone before Hank wears holes in the knees of his pants."

The kitchen curtain shifted. Even before we hit the front porch, Mom opened the door, exclaiming, "Zeke! And Sage, too! Oh, my goodness! This is a wonderful surprise!"

I heard chairs scrapping and Dad appeared in the doorway. But not Gull.

Stepping into the entryway, we four exchanged hugs all around, with me expecting Mom to comment on how my heart was pounding in her ear, which was pressed against my chest. Instead, she fussed, "Where's Gull?" closing the door and leading us inside. It smelled like home.

Empty chairs greeted us. The back door slammed. Within seconds, we heard an engine fire to life and the squeal of tires. Gulliver Swift Eden was gone, vanished too soon for a squad car to have arrived.

Sage jerked toward me, her eyes wide with worry, fright, and questions I couldn't answer because I was asking the same ones.

"If that doesn't beat all," Mom fussed. "He had just gotten started telling us he's going to be gone a while and out of cell-tower range. So, why would he take off when he heard me say you were here?" Shaking her head, she set about getting us coffee, still muttering about her elder son's odd behavior.

Sage and I exchanged frantic glances. I handed her my cell and she went out to the porch's privacy to give Bill with the bad news that Gull was on the move.

Meanwhile, Dad motioned for me to sit down. "What brings you to town without letting us know you were coming?" he asked.

True to her long-standing policy of "always be ready for company," Mom brought out cups, coffee and cream, pretty napkins, and refilled the homemade cookies (three kinds) and bowl of grapes.

Looking at the incongruously cheerful repast she had so effortlessly produced, I took a ragged breath. "Nothing pleasant; I'm working with the Rochester police on something we need to talk about. With Gull racing off now, we need to do so quickly."

Dad's look was a mix of confusion and concern; Mom looked flat-out scared. "What's Gull done?" she demanded, twisting her apron into a knot tight enough to break threads.

Returning, Sage gave me a nod. *Bill's on it.*

"If that boy's in trouble with the law, he's got it coming double from me," Dad said harshly.

Mom shushed him with a wave, and sank into a chair. Now, her voice shook: "Talk to us."

I began with Greene Phillip's photo, and dove into how I suspected Gull had read Book #16's draft before ON TRACK became OFF TRACK.

"I suspected something serious and very wrong was going on with him," Mom whispered.

I quickly moved on to the Las Vegas connection and my suspicions about death-by-injection, segueing into how the gravel pit fit in, and ending one blunt fact: "Mom and Dad, I hate to say it, but I'm convinced that Gull killed Honey."

The three final words ricocheted, puncturing all they touched. Each ounce of pep seeped from Mom, every sparkle of pride died. None of that was surprising, but what she said stunned me: "Don't turn Gull in and ruin our family!"

Sage and I were shocked, but Dad exploded: "Are you crazy, Haze? It's *Gull* you should be pleading with to turn himself in—not asking Zeke go against his conscience!"

Mom aimed a razor-edged gaze at him. "Listen to me, and listen hard, Rudy: Zeke has a good life; Gull struggles. Yes, I brag on Zeke too much, but I keep hoping Gull will be worth bragging about, too, someday. If Zeke turns him in, Gull goes to prison." Her chest shuddered with unreleased sobs.

"Gull's on his way to prison, anyway, Haze," Sage said softly. "Zeke already talked to the police; they'll find and arrest Gull. There's no turning back now—and we couldn't, anyway."

"I'm disappointed in both of you." Mom's eyes flashed fire. "If you'd called me first, I've found a way to save our family's reputation."

I looked to Dad for help. Nothing there; he *had* listened to Mom; all he did was sigh resignedly.

"Gull committed a premeditated murder, Mom. Hard to put a spin on it, and tough to save face."

Sage reached for Mom's hand. "Haze, we're in it together. Sometimes families have hard times, but they survive. We can make it if we keep united."

Mom found a tissue in her pocket and blew her nose. She was cracking, but still unwilling to give in. "It'll be hard to be united if Gull's in prison."

"He's my brother, so this hurts me, too, but Gull needs to deal with many issues, Mom. For him to be part of this family in any real sense, he needs to make some difficult admissions of guilt."

"Does Gull know why you're here?" Mom asked sadly. "Is that why he left so fast?"

"I suspect he realized the trap would spring soon. Criminals can only escape so long. You said he came to tell you he was going away for a while? That shows he knew he needed to get out of town."

Dad muttered, "That reprobate's running like a coward."

"He's our son, Rudy," Mom said sternly, but her steel melted and she whispered, "Zeke, call the police before Gull gets too far away." She buried her face in her hands; her shoulders shook.

I pushed back my chair and knelt beside her, drawing her stiff body into an embrace. "When Sage left the room earlier with my phone, she called."

Eventually Mom melted, trembling, against me. "I've been a terrible mother!"

"No, Gull made bad decisions, and acted on them in ways society doesn't allow. Nothing about this reflects on you," I said firmly. "He's an adult who needs to grow up, and stop blaming you and Dad for every bad thing that happens to him, or expecting any of us to bail him out. That won't fly anymore."

Mom pulled back with a gasp. "Oh, Zeke! OFF TRACK was my idea!" She pressed a fist against her lips. "Why did I interfere with your writing?" She erupted in gulping sobs and pushed me away.

Moving to stand by the sink, she stared out the window. When she finally spoke, it was as if she was speaking to herself, "Today marks the end of a normal life for our family."

"I don't blame you for anything, Mom. Neither should Gull." I glanced at the clock; fifteen minutes had passed since he had fled. I glanced at Sage; she nodded. "I'll call Bill, and go see him," I said softly.

Sage had caught Mom's mood and could only nod. Pressing knuckles against her lips, she waved the other hand at the wall phone. I caught and agreed with her mute message: *No reason Mom and Dad can't hear what is said. It might help healing begin, rather than let false hopes survive.*

With three distraught listeners behind me, I said, "This is Zeke, Bill. I'll be there within the hour. Thanks for your kindness during this chaos."

Sage and I stayed in Rochester for a week during which we all rehashed details until we were sick of talking about the mess that now was our lives.

Gull remained at-large.

News reports twisted every drop of drama from the story. Headlines were the worst. It was hard to ignore the blaring black letters:

A SAD TALE OF TWO SONS

"ABEL" TURNS IN BROTHER "CAIN"

ONE BROTHER WRITES BOOKS, THE OTHER GETS BOOKED

Neighbors came by, some expecting gory details in exchange for cakes or the ubiquitous casserole. Others added their sorrows to our own grief.

Speculations ran high about Gull's whereabouts—purported sightings numbered in the dozens, and all resulted in false leads.

Sage needed to get home, but we both felt the urgency to be there to comfort Mom and Dad but all of us were so equally glum, comfort was an illusion.

Hank called daily—the only light in our dark tunnel—ending each call with a meaningful prayer.

I had it easier than Sage did; I spent several days at the police station, armed with OFF TRACK's first draft, copies of the teens' first creative writing assignment, and my Proof of Innocence document.

I was off the hook: a good place to be. Even so, it felt like I pounded nails in my brother's coffin with each revealed or rehashed detail.

Sage, on the other end of the crisis, stayed with Mom and Dad, running interference with phone and doorbell. She drafted the most sympathetic of Dad's pool-playing buddies to make daily runs for essential groceries and newspapers so she could be on-call.

Bill expressed gratitude that Gull's fingerprints were preserved (no credit to me). These appeared on the pages mentioning injections: the very parts John insisted I edit due to parallels to PENALTY BOX.

I recited my scripted account a dozen times—and, equally often, pointed out similarities between my students' *Where?* assignments and ON TRACK's first draft. At last, I won my last convert.

The officer in charge of the investigation said the magic words, "Mister Eden, we are removing your name from our list of Persons of Interest. Thank you for your assistance." In a break from traditional police verbiage, he added, "Please accept and extend my condolences to the rest of your family for how this devastating situation has played out."

Somehow, I didn't feel the sense of freedom I had imagined would accompany such a pronouncement. In clearing my name, I had destroyed my family.

25

When we arrived back in Utah, Sage let me unpack while she spent the hours until bedtime at her office. I was too restless to face the mundane task of sorting laundry. I needed fresh air, and lots of it. Utah was ready to accommodate me.

Not taking time to doff my prosthesis, I collected sunglasses, a brimmed hat, and bottled water: the essentials for a walk on a high mountain desert. I sucked in pure air, letting it sift through my haggard thoughts to rid them of all pollutants. At the end of the driveway, I turned and followed the fence line to the southwest corner, and then headed north. The afternoon sun felt wonderful.

It may have been wind, but likely distraction kept me from hearing a vehicle career across the rough terrain behind me. As the commotion registered, I spun around, raising a hand to shade my eyes. What I saw was like a scene from a horror movie, not real life.

Sunlight glared off a windshield, blinding me. A Jeep charged directly toward me—*Abbott!* Had Bill Brandt and his cronies not believed me? Had the Utah grapevine warned Abbott they were coming for him? After all I told them, did Minnesota still consider Abbott guilty? Were all my facts against

Gull now used to accuse an innocent man? Did a heart attack feel like the panic thundering inside me?

"No, Abbott, stop! Don't do it!" I yelled, futilely waving my hat like a cautionary flag. "We can work things out!" His response was to rev the engine and keep coming faster, closer.

No time to strategize; rational thought was a mirage. I spun into a heart-pumping run. Sunglasses bounced off and crunched beneath my feet. Wanting nothing to weigh me down, I jettisoned my water bottle. *Was* Abbott my brother's pawn? *Had* I been wrong? *Did* I drag my family through the muck for naught?

Stumbling often, I dodged countless rabbit holes and stinging ants' hills. My left ankle burned. Pain (nothing phantom about it) shot through my partially flesh-and-bone leg.

The prosthesis shifted; with it off-kilter, my agony increased exponentially. I was a fool to think I could outrun a driver intent on murdering me, but still I ran. Preservation was as instinctive as breathing.

My only hope lay ten yards ahead. Sunny Acres' concrete graveyard: my oasis would be an effective obstacle course for my frenzied pursuer *if* I could entice the hunter to follow his prey into the snare.

Adrenalin kicked in. I increased my speed and soon leaped atop the largest of the jagged cement slabs which, much too realistically, reminded me of a tombstone.

No, I edited as I fought to maintain my purchase on my precarious perch, *this is not a graveyard—it's where I stay alive!* My instinct proved right: I was safe; the Jeep was now marooned with its front axle jammed firmly on a slab's sharp-edged pinnacle.

Gasping, certain a heart attack threatened me next, my attention shifted as another mechanical roar assaulted the air. A maximum-size U-Haul truck barreled through our property's line fence, sending uprooted posts flying and dragging broken barbed wire behind it. The vehicle rattled over the sandy washes and skidded recklessly as it created a dust storm of impressive proportion.

Midst the haze, I saw doors bounce open and, disbelieving, watched bodies tumble from the truck. "Myster-E!" Fable screamed as all of my four young friends sprang into action. "Are you okay?"

I waved, but couldn't answer. Everything in me cried with a toxic mess of fear and relief as my eyes sought out Jacey: the girl about to discover her dad enmeshed in a crime far more terrible than grand theft auto. Abbott had come, hell-bent on murder.

Groans erupted from the Jeep as its driver tried futilely to escape the airbag's lifesaving attack. Nearby, the U-Haul's engine loudly protested its recent abuse, and a stretch of broken fence wires sagged, defeated in their efforts to restrain entrance.

Before Abbott could open his door, Cale tossed one end of a vivid orange tow-strap to Jacey, who leaped, caught it and raced around the Jeep. Cale reached for the loose end, quickly inserting it into the clasp and winching it. With Mathia and Fable keeping the strap in position, it tightened at the midpoint of the vehicle like a mockingly festive ribbon around the perimeter.

I was awestruck by what I had witnessed. The kids' quick thinking and flawless execution of this mindboggling idea had effectively trapped a profane and protesting Abbott inside the stranded vehicle, despite his lunges against the door.

Then, I heard an angry voice sputter and yelp, "Hey, let me out of here, you little—"

Gull?

A thousand emotions propelled me to my feet. As facts sank into my rattled brain, I stared more closely at the Jeep—it was not navy blue, but *black*. Not Abbott, but my *brother* was so intent on killing me.

My guttural scream pierced the cloudless sky: "Oh, Gull—*no!*" Sinking down and pounding the concrete slab, I cried to the God of Grandma Eden, Hank Bedlow (yes, also me): "Oh, God, help us!"

I lifted my head to see Mathia reaching through the open rear window behind Gull's seat to release a steady stream of sparkly pink spray paint all over an expensive haircut and even pricier clothes. Grittily determined, she emptied the can.

Meanwhile, Fable wasn't idle. She raced toward the closest outdoor faucet. Sage's garden hose—the only sign of progress toward her dream of a Japanese garden—was attached to the spigot. Fable lifted the handle and ran back to the Jeep, dragging the hose.

Turning the nozzle to full blast, she thrust it through the backseat window's three-inch gap. Gull howled his protests. He tried desperately to reach the knob that would raise the window, but when he fumbled with his seatbelt, Fable's well-aimed stream of water hit him squarely in the ear.

With Fable intent on swamping the Jeep (and blasting Gull each time he moved) the others began letting air out of all four tires. Whooshing sounds attested to their success.

Frantic protests (the kind requiring an R-rating for language) echoed from Gull's Jeep. I deflated like the four tires, overcome by my race against death. Numbly, I took stock of my abused body. I ached in places I didn't know I even *had* places. After so many poundings, throbs, painful shards, my body was a veritable shopping mall of stupidity's symptoms. Why did a one-footed, middle-aged guy figure trying to outrun a killer would work?

The din of Gull's vile protests was met stoically by four kids, three of them armed and ready to lob chunks of concrete, should he decide to act. The fourth vigilante held a garden hose with the goal of turning the Jeep's innards into a swimming pool.

Frantic, Gull looked in all directions, only to have Cale sneer, "Don't even think about crawling out a window. You'd land on a huge stinging-ant hill! It'd be painful, dude b'cuz they love sweaty guys."

"Yeah," Jacey yelled, showing him the fist not holding the hose. "Take your pick: the ants or us!"

Gull withered, jerking away from the leather seat when he obviously remembered *Paint!* He gingerly touched his neck; his hand came away all glittery. He pounded the steering wheel, leaving a hot-pink stain. His fury intensified; his roar exploded.

My prosthesis had performed beyond expectation, despite my infractions of all guidelines about *How to Properly Care for an Assistive Device.* My ankle throbbed at the connecting point. No one was going anywhere anytime soon, so I removed my fake foot, cradling it in belated apology.

"Dad's on duty in Milford today, so where *is* he?" Cale fumed. "You called this in, right, Myster-E?"

Call? Call!

Sheepishly, I yanked my cell off my belt. *What would I've done if these kids hadn't shown up . . . and in a U-Haul?* Before I could wonder how *that* came together, the call connected. "Hey, Rosco," I wheezed. "Zeke Eden. Come out to Sunny Acres ASAP and be prepared to arrest Honey Odessa Woolden-Landis' murderer."

"What! Can you hold him? I don't know what to suggest, but can you restrain him somehow?"

I had to grin. "Oh, he's under the scrutiny of four very motivated captors. He'll be here; you'll see."

I disconnected before asking my rescuers, "How'd you guys know to come, *and* get here so quickly?"

"We saw this jerk," Cale kicked the driver's door, rousing another squall from Gull, "pull two ramps outta the U-Haul, and drive his Jeep out! If it was used in a crime, hiding it is *big trouble*. Fable told us Gull's a fugitive, so we figured he wasn't in town for any good reason."

"Yeah," Fable fumed, "we were worried he'd set fire to your house. We had to do something b'cuz we didn't know if you were home yet."

"He didn't even remember to take the keys out of the U-Haul," Mathia scoffed, "so we put our bikes in the back of it and took off after him!"

What we had here was four teenagers, one of them a deputy's son—not a driver's license among 'em—absconding with a pretty-much trashed U-Haul . . . whipping through Milford . . . tooling across the new railroad overpass . . . wiping out a chunk of our fence . . . desecrating a prized Jeep. I whistled under my breath.

"How'd you happen to have a U-Haul, tow strap, spray paint—all that?" I was flummoxed, distracted by more pressing concerns—such as, my furiously cussing, intent-on-murder sibling still trapped in his increasingly waterlogged Jeep by four gutsy teens.

"This is when we planned to work at the picnic shelter in the park. We brought props that are crucial to the plot in the mystery we're writing together,"

Mathia explained. "Ya know: research! We wanted to see if what we had was realistic."

"Sounds like you have a tried-and-tested plot!" My smile began as rueful, but switched to proud.

"Betcha we're in pretty big trouble, though, aren't we?" Jacey asked, eyeing the U-Haul while still aiming the hose through the window-gap.

"No, you're heroes," I corrected. "But you may not be able to publish your story since everyone will know the ending! Even so, you have the satisfaction of creating a superb plot." I cocked my head.

Wailing sirens and flashing lights announced Rosco's approach. Gull cowered; only the tips of his glittery-pink hair were visible above the dashboard.

Listening to Rosco read Gull his rights, I flashed back on Gabby Knicker doing the same to me. *Oh, how the mighty are fallen*—Was that another Grandma Eden Bible quote? Hank would know.

Of all the indignities facing Gull, hot-pink hair was his greatest frustration. It was one thing to be a cast as a murderer, quite another to have an arrest photo sparking endless and wild guffaws.

Gull's trial was just that: a veritable *trial* for all concerned. As I could have predicted, he maintained his usual defiant attitude through everything except comments about neon hair. At such times, he looked like he wished *he* held a can of spray paint.

Hardly a newscast didn't include a photo of his inglorious moment: in handcuffs, shuffling away from his Jeep, from which water dripped steadily, forming a small pond around four flat tires.

No one remembered to turn off the water after Rosco handcuffed Gull and dragged him to the Beaver County lockup. Water flowed until Sage called from the shower, "Water pressure is lower than usual." By then, the stream seeping from beneath the Jeep's doors had turned the steadily-forming pond into a frog-heaven swampy mess.

Jacey achieved fame (and enough money to pay for her first year of college) when it became known she had snapped the picture of handcuffed Gull for which the media paid big money. Interviewers made an even bigger deal about how the photographer was the daughter of the same man Gulliver Swift Eden had endeavored to frame with the murder of Honey Odessa Woolden-Landis.

Mom and Dad spent the better part of a month in Utah, sometimes with us at the trial, sometimes staying behind in Milford when it all became too much to bear. Sage took a Leave of Absence from MVCH and spent time with me.

Facts unfolded, much like my bulleted list:

As Haze had intuited, Gull had "taken up" with Honey, snaring her attention with his good looks, an unsubstantiated aura of success, and his undeniable charm. As had other women before her, Honey soon saw Gull for the hollow man he was. To her ruin, she went one step further and laughed at Gull, taunting him with stinging words before she stopped taking or returning his calls.

Gull was a lover scorned and spurned. It proved too much for his ego, especially with the railroad's presence (for which he, right or wrong, blamed Honey) that ruined what Gull considered his "best chance" at matching my success. Writer's Cubby renters dropped like flies when they realized the promised quiet was a fraud.

And so the sky fell on Gulliver Swift Eden—our family's perpetual equivalent of Chicken Little.

Honey was alive for her trip to Milford, enticed one last time by a smooth-talking Gull on the pretense of meeting me—the irony of which escaped no one. The glitzy rental car Gull drove to Milford was part of his self-promotion as brother of a famous writer. All eyes had turned to me. Thankfully (if only because it meant one less lawsuit) the rental car's trunk was not Honey's coffin for her transport to The GASP.

An understandably distraught Abbott took the stand to relate Gull's machinations to incriminate him. "Don't know why I hadda go to Las Vegas; I hardly even saw Gull. Lost fifty bucks, an' missed spending a holiday with Jacey—she's my daughter. Guess Gull figured no one'd believe an ex-con, so he made it look like I killed that lady. He acted like me an' him was best-buds. Even used how we both drive Jeeps against me."

The prosecutor said, "Casino cameras show you talking with Ms Woolden-Landis. How did that happen?"

"Gull made a big deal about settin' it up so me an' The Bulldog, I mean *her*, would hang out while he went off to meet some other dame. Like her an' me had a dang thing in common! *Sheesh*! He had no right to use The GASP to do his crime—they never done nuttin' to him. I'm lucky not to get fired."

By the time Abbott left the witness stand, I knew Gull rued the day he got the crazy idea that he had found a pushover in a Milford gravel-truck driver.

As for the injection? Bill Brandt sleuthed out that one of Gull's doomed endeavors was renting space to a group that collected medical supplies for Third World countries: a nonprofit unaware they were missing at least one needle-plunger packet. As for the drugs, Gull had created a deadly cocktail from a variety of sources, few legal and all highly suspect.

The injection occurred at the top of The GASP's platform. The only good thing was, Honey's death was swift and painless. His evil deed accomplished, Gull had returned to the motel.

Realizing he could be spotted driving through town—after telling us he wouldn't see us—he told the Court he was deciding how to explain his presence in Milford when, as luck had it, sitting in his Oak Tree Inn room, he saw a TV photo of our house and marveled. Thanks to a random strike of heat-lightning—Gulliver Swift Eden was, again, the dubious winner in fate's lottery.

Originally, Gull's timing of the whole sordid mess was based on what Abbott unwittingly told two Eden brothers months earlier: The GASP was closed on holidays. The Milford Flat Fire had played right into Gull's hands, ensuring little if any interest from locals beyond what was happened east of town on that hot and lazy holiday.

The jury returned a verdict in six hours. Agreeing with their recommendation, the Judge handed down the stiffest sentence allowed: life imprisonment without option of parole. Gull had committed the crime in Utah, so he would serve his sentence at the Utah State Prison in Draper.

It was a quiet ride back to Milford for the four of us after the sentencing and our awkward farewells with the handcuffed and frantic Gull. I drove. Mom fluctuated between clenched jaw and forlorn sobs. Dad stared out the window, speaking when spoken to, but only giving monosyllabic responses.

Sage, however, kept up a steady patter, pointing out interesting sights, inquiring about everyone's comfort with temperature and airflow. She insisted we stop for dessert at Top's City Café in Delta to break up the trip, hoping to ease us back into normal living. It was a ruggedly uphill climb.

As for me, I kept reliving the moment when Gull had been led away. Turning once, he looked at me with the closest thing to fear I had ever seen on his face. But terror was quickly replaced by his usual cockiness. He was still choosing to appear as *down-but-not-out* before those assembled, despite what lay ahead for the now-infamous Gulliver Swift Eden.

When we passed The GASP as we neared Milford, the abrupt silence in the Volvo resembled a funeral's hush. In many ways, that's what it was.

A few weeks after the trial, Gull used his rare phone privilege to call me. Sage was at work, or I would have handed her my cell. Lacking Sage's adept say-nothing skills, I had nothing to say. Any feelings of brotherly love had gone *Poof!* when Gull added attempted vehicular homicide to a burgeoning list of crimes. It remained too up-close-and-personal to elicit kindly feelings or make me feel comfortable chitchatting with my brother.

But here we were, on opposite ends of a call I would have let go to voice-mail, had I known who was calling. After we got past "How's it going?" questions, there wasn't much left that wouldn't gouge deeper chasms or inflict more deadly wounds.

"Will you come see me, Zeke?" he asked. I heard him swallow, then: "Time goes pretty slow here."

Unbidden, what flashed through my mind was my first conversation with Hank, hearing him say about his wife's killer, *"It struck me, we had loneliness in common: He was lonely and afraid; I was lonely and angry."*

I missed my brother—missed what once had been (before we got wise to each other) and what may have continued into our golden years. "I'm not at that point, Gull," I said hollowly. "Not yet."

"I, uh, understand." His monotone didn't mask his despair. "Just thought I'd ask. I mean, hey, you'd have to arrange ahead of time to be admitted. It's a royal pain, and Draper's quite a trip from Milford."

In more ways than merely miles.

During the uncomfortable silence that followed, I heard background shouts and scuffles. Gull probably only had two or three minutes left of his allotted telephone time.

I imagined him slowly progressing in a winding line until it was his turn, then shifting foot-to-foot as he talked to me on a telephone screwed to a gouged and graffiti-splattered wall. Of all the people he could have called, he chose me: the brother he tried to kill when jealousy, fury, and fear blinded him.

I thought of the mayhem, the quiet and raging grief we all felt. Of lawsuits, the unanswerable questions, the despair that had come to two brothers and our parents, to my wife who didn't deserve the mess that spilled over into her life, too. *Sage—the woman who loves me through everything, for better or worse.*

I stared out the window at the windblown desert—*"A whole lotta nothing,"* I recalled Gull saying on his first visit to Utah. Now, we both had a whole lotta nothing.

At least no prison bars block my view.

Looking at my graffiti-free office walls, I exhaled slowly. "I can't promise anything, Gull, but I know a man who might visit you: Hank Bedlow. He, uh, visits a guy at Draper named Wally."

"Thanks; I appreciate that." *Did I hear tears?*

After hanging up and pacing for fifteen minutes while I waited for my nerves to behave, I resumed the project that Gull's call had interrupted. I lifted four stiff sheets of paper from the printer's tray, holding them carefully to avoid ink smudges.

Standing by the office window giving the best light, I checked each poster I'd made. *No errors, properly spaced, good photo . . . Ready to go.* I cut along dotted lines to separate the eight tabs giving my cell number at the bottom of each sheet. "Yessir, another well-done job from SIGNS BY ZEKE," I said in shallow self-commendation.

I drove Gull's Jeep in to Milford where I hung posters at the standard places: each gas station, Dolly's Country Floral & Gifts, in Sunshine Market and the hardware store. I was hardly expecting immediate results, so was surprised to see a guy rip a tab off the poster as I approached the counter with my grocery cart. I watched him reach for his cell.

Can it be? My phone buzzed on my hip. I flicked it to vibrate, paid my bill and headed outside before answering the last ring before it flipped to messages.

"Hey. Saw your poster at the grocery store about a Jeep for sale. Picture looks good, but what's 'some water damage' mean? Does it involve the engine?"

"No, the engine's fine. It's mostly upholstery."

"Okay." Pause. "Uh, when can I see it?"

"How 'bout now? Come out to the parking lot."

I wasn't looking for personal gain; the money I got for Gull's Jeep would pay for Hank's trips to Draper until I could deal with seeing Gull again.

Meanwhile, I had a proposition for Haze. She needed a diversion from calling me every day, and I needed something to talk with Mom about during the depressing calls that, let's face it, weren't likely to change in content or mood anytime soon.

With the none-too-subtle, all-too-accurately titled OFF TRACK behind me, I had decided to put Book #17 on hold. A title like LOST GROUND invited trouble that I neither wanted nor could handle right then. But that decision left me, also, needing a project.

The way I see it, how hard can it be for two inventive-yet-humble cooks like plucky Haze Eden and her sleek-headed son, Zeke, to write a dandy cookbook? *Beat four eggs until frothy and lemon-colored . . .*

The overpass that bridges the five railroad tracks in Milford, Utah, was completed and opened to the public on July 24, 2007, to much local relief and gratitude.

❖

Here are the facts re: The Milford Flat Fire which, at the time, was the largest fire in Utah's history:

Start Date: July 6, 2007 at 15:45

Location: Started 3 miles north of Milford UT.
    Burned in Black Rock Desert, west of Fillmore,
    and throughout Millard and Beaver counties

Cause: Lightning

Size: 363,052 acres

Estimated Containment Date: July 17, 2007

Fuels: Sage brush, grass, juniper

Structures Threatened: 1 uninhabited summer home
    and 2 outbuildings were burned

Evacuations: None

[Source: www.utahfireinfo.gov]

www.ingramcontent.com/pod-product-compliance
Lightning Source LLC
Chambersburg PA
CBHW030241030726
47493CB00023B/321